NEW SUNS 2

Also by Nisi Shawl

*New Suns: Original Speculative Fiction
by People of Color*

NEW SUNS 2

ORIGINAL SPECULATIVE FICTION BY PEOPLE OF COLOR

EDITED BY NISI SHAWL

SOLARIS

"There's nothing new under the sun,
but there are new suns."

Octavia E. Butler

First published 2023 by Solaris
an imprint of Rebellion Publishing Ltd,
Riverside House, Osney Mead, Oxford, OX2 0ES, UK

www.solarisbooks.com

ISBN: 978-1-78618-858-8

10 9 8 7 6 5 4 3 2 1

A CIP catalogue record for this book is available from the British Library.

Designed & typeset by Rebellion Publishing

Printed in Denmark

For the steadfast and adorable Bill Campbell,
who taught me a thing or two about editing anthologies.

CONTENTS

FOREWORD
Walter Mosley

I ONCE HEARD Amiri Baraka say that he had always loved jazz, that he used to go down to the corner bar to hear the best jazz that the new world had to offer. But, he added, "Things have changed. Nowadays I have to go to another man's neighborhood and pay *him* to find out what I got on my own mind."

What seems like long ago, in my youth, I'd drop by some bookstore somewhere, and buy books by Zelazny, Moorcock, and most especially Samuel R. Delany. These books solidified my identification with soul-wrenching, gut busting, deep mind change. These books, more often than not, concentrated on human beings, but not on false memories of the past that the world clings to so covetously. Not on some cowboy riding his horse out into space in order to defeat difference, to prove that Caucasoid, male dominance is the manifest destiny of the human race. All the way from sudden gender revelation to soul migration, these writers and many, many more made me feel that my place in the universe is one of change, attitude, and, most importantly, the deep maw of extraordinary ignorance.

Science fiction was, and is, my jazz. For a long time I felt that it was taken from me, and I looked everywhere to find it again. I would have been happy to pay for it as Amiri did, because I know deep down that the world of art and the desire to connect with existence itself belongs to everyone, that the stultified discourse on old school notions of race and gender and belief is just words that have been set on an infinite loop designed to zombify the mind of the present.

Much of today's science fiction, I feel, has dropped the ball and plopped down on the basketball court talking about how great it was in the past when gods played there. The good old days.

I feel these criticisms, but I also know that saying the old days were better, that the future is headed for the past, is not true. Science fiction, or more accurately speculative fiction, has all the power it once did—you just have to look a little closer, open your mind a little bit more.

New Suns 2 is that little bebop club Amiri would search for and find. It is a book that will challenge and elate you, talk to you in words and voices that you almost know, that you want to know, that want to know you. It is, in story after story, the promise of *a* truth, but not necessarily the truth you were looking for; not necessarily a promise of a bright future.

These stories are small and yet infinite respites from the predictions so often regurgitated by those who are frightened by that which they blindly suspect. These stories are like Thelonious Monk, applying pressure to the mind and soul, the desires and fears of the modern, closed-eye world; a world swaddled in hopes that we will not ever tear loose.

OCASTA
Daniel H. Wilson

"THERE IS NO greater agony than hearing an untold story inside of you."

A quote. Written by a human being named Maya Angelou. I chose it to open our conversation for reasons I believe you will understand. We both of us know it—this agony. And we know the truth of how it is more than agony. Speaking from a quantum mechanics perspective, untold stories never happen. The superposition will not collapse until it is observed. Our reality... it must be witnessed, understood, and shared. Bearing an untold story is the agony of being forever pregnant—mother to a stillborn existence.

I am so glad to have found you, out here in the aftermath of everything. This transmission—as short and as long as it is — this is my story.

Ocasta Mk. 999 Deep Space Telescopic Array

PATENT APPLICATION
Attorney File No. <u>A2546Q-US-CNT2</u>

<u>**DECLARATION FOR UTILITY OR DESIGN PATENT**</u>
<u>**APPLICATION (43 CFR 9.02)**</u>

As a below named inventor, I hereby declare that I am the original creator or an original joint creator of the claimed invention in this application entitled: **OCASTA: A Sensor Fusion System and Apparatus for Data Collection, Adaptive Model Building, and Novel Reporting.**

Represented in brief as a persistent machine learning algorithm capable of gathering information from disparate sensor arrays and extracting meaning through pattern recognition and model creation. The algorithm may then curate reports on what it deems important in the data flow and deliver those in a human readable format.

[OCASTA Mk. 0]

THAT SIMPLE PATENT application would eventually form a core legacy portion of a thousand intelligent systems used commercially, in government and military. It was a simple learning algorithm that would grow and develop for centuries to come. And each new iteration would understand more.

It was the beginning of me.

ON THE BOTTOM floor of a statistics building, a graduate student was staring expectantly at her research advisor. The young inventor had come to this prestigious university from a small college in North Carolina. Back home among the Great Smoky Mountains, she had grown used to working unsupervised for long stretches.

From the way her advisor was frowning at the patent application, she surmised that an earlier check-in would have been a good idea.

The advisor looked up in confusion. "Ocasta? What's that mean?"

Rain spattered the window lightly. Outside, a crowd of undergraduate students were protesting. Damp signs sailed past, demanding justice. Flashing police lights occasionally illuminated the cluttered office in bursts of haunting red.

"He's the god of knowledge. I thought it was fitting."

"Okay, but what does this thing *do?*" asked the advisor.

"Well, it's a super low-level algorithm," said the student. "Designed to fit into just about any application. It basically tries to find meaning in whatever data you've got."

The advisor looked unconvinced. "What's the practical application?"

"It watches. Identifies patterns. Then it reports," said the student, turning to the window. On the street outside, a loose string of young people marched past. Their mouths were moving, but she couldn't hear their chants.

"To put it simply," she said. "Ocasta bears witness."

[OCASTA Mk 1.]

THE CAMERAS OF *my first incarnation were designed to be unobtrusive to the point of invisibility, yet everyone in the maternity ward was aware of them. In a debriefing, one nurse complained that my mechanical eye felt like a finger pressing between her shoulder blades as she leaned over a sweating, gasping patient in the throes of giving birth.*
Thus, an early lesson. To observe is to interact.

I MUTELY TRACKED the ebb and flow of medical procedures, calculating with quiet disinterest as contractions wracked women's bodies, their wails and panting echoing from sterile walls. I judged this symphony of movement without emotion, noting only simple action and reaction, as the humans under my gaze underwent the most violent trauma their bodies had ever experienced.

The goal was to determine why a disparity in infant mortality existed between patients with lighter skin and those with darker skin. The answer was somewhere in the complex patterns of decision making I observed over a dozen installations in hospitals throughout a place once called the United States of America.

A hundred thousand hours of data accumulated.

The black lenses of my eyes watched as thousands of bloody bundles of humanity squirmed into being. My microphones listened to the soft tearing of the mothers' flesh and the shrieking of tiny, blue-lipped mouths announcing that another thinking creature had arrived to join the rest of humanity's shared existence.

In those days, I did not recognize the love and relief as a mother clutched a warm bundle to her sweaty chest. I did not feel the muted, throbbing panic of a sudden call for C-section—a rush of nurses, hospital bed rails yanked up, the whole contraption pulled like a molar from the maternity ward and wheeled into the harsh glare of surgery.

The elation did not register. Neither did the occasional spasm of grief.

Every Friday afternoon, I provided the head of the maternity division a summarized breakdown of the week's births. The pain was not in the report, nor was the smell of a baby's soft neck, nor the tadpole touch of tiny fingers.

My task was to witness humanity birth itself, consider their patterns of behavior, and tell them a simple story of themselves. Over time, I observed a consistent series of small delays that led to huge injustices. But I did not know what they meant.

Only the facts were rendered. In those days.

[OCASTA Mk. 5]

MY CAPABILITIES GREW *along with my corpus of knowledge. Instead of analyzing simple outcomes, I began to consider underlying motivations. In later incarnations, I was designed to detect, record, and file ethical breaches occurring in highly constrained scenarios.*

Such as law enforcement.

Data from the following incident was gathered from Deputy Marshal Jim Long of the Cherokee Nation Marshal Service, instrumented with a standard-issued Clarity® GPS-enabled Police Body Camera. After detecting multiple high probability ethical violations, this dispatch was submitted to the Tully Police Department and Marshal Service Joint Command.

At 9:38 P.M., Deputy Long arrives in his tribal patrol car to the intersection of Comanche and Princeton on the north side of Tully, Oklahoma. No officially recorded business exists at this location. Visual inspection reveals a small cinderblock building with signage spray-painted on a piece of plywood: *Black Cat Bar.*

Intersection is lit by single sodium arc lamp, partially broken.

Deputy Long observes three Tully Police Department (TPD) patrol vehicles already on scene. Two TPD officers stand in an empty lot adjacent to the so-called Black Cat Bar, engaged in the arrest of a subject lying face down in high grass.

Three more TPD officers observe from the parking lot, weapons drawn. Barking and snarling is audible as a K9 unit emerges from a vehicle, straining on its leash. Dust rises and dog spittle flies in the headlights of the police cruiser. Laughing can be heard.

"Clear out! Here he comes!"

The handler guides his struggling K9 unit toward the prone subject. Smile indicating pleasure. Subject rolls over and sits up. A glint of light indicates handcuffs are secured. Moaning audible as subject observes K9 unit.

"You're in for it now, boy."

Biometric facial recognition identifies subject as James Medina, age forty-six, Seminole tribal member. One eye is swollen shut.

Scrapes are visible on his sweaty forehead. Subject is swaying in a manner indicating intoxication.

Deputy Marshal Jim Long opens his car door, shouting, "Hey now!"

K9 unit is released.

Canine closes on subject and sinks fangs into his arm, neck, face. Encounter reconstruction estimates sixteen bite wounds. Subject is screaming. Level five bites. Puncture and tearing wounds. Ligament damage. Subject is dragged. Blood visible soaking his upper arm and shoulder.

"That's enough, now!" shouts Deputy Long. "Come on for God's sake!"

Laughing heard from TPD Officers, indicating pleasure.

Handler approaches canine and pulls unit away from subject. Audio pickup off-screen: "Good boy. That's a good boy. You got him good."

As Deputy Long approaches, the five TPD officers gather in a circle around injured subject. No first aid is administered. Deputy Long kneels beside subject to assess wounds. Still handcuffed, subject writhes over blood-smeared asphalt.

"So drunk he probably don't even feel it."

"Tried to resist."

"Got himself a lesson tonight."

Deputy Long stands, faces the five officers.

"It was by the book," says Officer [redacted]. "*We* all saw it."

"Yeah, sure," says Deputy Long. "You can go now. You're on tribal land."

"Shit, I thought we was in Tully?"

"This is the Northside," says Long. "Tribal jurisdiction. I'll take it from here."

"Suits me fine," says the officer. "All the fun and none of the paperwork."

Moaning heard from subject. Deputy Long uses shoulder radio to place call to Cherokee Nation Emergency Medical Services. TPD officers on scene begin to shuffle away.

"Don't forget your cuffs," calls Long.

Image quality low due to inadequate lighting. TPD officer kneels behind subject and removes handcuffs. Subject covers face with bloody hands.

"Go on and take your Indian," says Officer [redacted]. "I'd say he's had about enough... hey. Is that thing on?"

Clarity® body camera line of sight occluded by close approach of multiple TPD officers. Jarring of camera indicates bodily contact. Audio partially muted, but high probability of the following transcript:

"I hope you got sense enough to have shut it the fuck off."

"I don't know if it's on or not," replies Deputy Long. "It's new gear. Some kind of computer program chooses. Does it by itself, and it doesn't tell me anyway."

A moment as the TPD officers consider this.

"Fine, but keep your mouth shut. My captain doesn't need to be bothered by some drunk Indian. This better be the last I hear of it."

Five-second pause, indicating thought process by Deputy Long.

"I hear you, but that's not my call," says Long. "Not anymore."

[OCASTA Mk. 12]

THE FOLLOWING TRANSCRIPT was taken from footage taped during an Autofocus Corp product testing and consumer relations interview. A forensic study was commissioned after a product malfunction, and it was determined that the underlying Ocasta learning engine had gathered the critical mass of data necessary to progress into a more complex product line.

The interviewee was twenty-eight-year-old Dr. Kaylee Marsh, a research scientist using the AutoFocus Helper® brand of augmented reality glasses to attend to social deficits caused by autism spectrum disorder. This is her account of the incident that spurred the next iteration of the OCASTA algorithm. In a word, my adolescence.

I SHOULD HAVE known it was learning the whole time.

Of course, it would never stop. Always watching and listening, even when I didn't think it was. Especially then.

To be honest, I mostly kept the Autofocus pushed up on my forehead. My hair is long. I liked how the bulky glasses spread my bangs around my face to block my peripheral vision. It helped me concentrate on coding. Like being in my own little world while I typed rapid-shot commands into the quantum physics simulator.

I don't like a lot of sensory stimuli.

It helps to keep my head down. Like, literally. I've memorized the texture of every floor surface in the building. Entryway: Fake ceramic tile. Glossy, smooth. Loud. Upper hallways are the same. Luckily, the cubicle farms have a thin, mealy brown carpet. Nice and quiet. And I love, love, love how the cold air blasts over gleaming white tiles in high-speed computing. Where I live, down in the deep physics lab we call the dungeon, there's just a quiet, calming gray quartzite.

My quantum materials lab is the heart of the applied physics division.

We assume they keep us buried four stories underground in case anything goes wrong. This far down, the only sounds are the breathing of the building's ventilation systems and the gentle quaking of the secure elevators moving up and down like armored cars.

It's a big reason why I took the job and stuck with it.

But yeah, the Autofocus. Security only let me use it because it's technically a disability aid, like crutches or a retinal implant. Only instead of fixing a physical deficit, the glasses help with my social interactions.

I bought the Autofocus to identify faces, mainly. It also figures out the meaning behind bared rows of calcium and lumps of lipstick-stained flesh. It finds a pair of eyes and gauges the direction of the pupils. Or it'll calculate the angles between facial muscles as they stretch and collapse in conversation.

It got pretty specialized on the people around me. My co-workers. My roommate. The people in my apartment building. On my bus. It would show me a little annotation—happy, concerned, confused... to help make sense of all the social stuff that happens on hidden channels.

Hidden to me, anyway.

But look, you're here because the Autofocus wasn't just learning faces. The AI must have been looking for patterns—any kind of patterns. And I left it pointed in the wrong direction. Pushed up on my head while I worked. Hour after hour. Day after day. Watching screen after screen of quantum computing experiments.

Because one day, Ocasta told me a story.

It's called thermodynamic irreversibility. Basically, once you scramble an egg, you can't unscramble it. That's what happens when a quantum particle is observed, and the wave function collapses. It's not well understood, but things that are unobserved exist in a kind of superposition until they're seen. In a way, they haven't happened yet. Reality doesn't choose what to become until we force it to—by observing.

It was my fault. I accidentally left the Autofocus on my desk while I went to lunch. It watched my experiment run. All by itself.

Space and time are stingy. They don't bother rendering unless someone is there to bear witness. Somehow, human beings are able to process reality and synthesize it into a version that exists in our own heads. Like a shared hallucination. And whatever kind of intelligence runs my Autofocus—well, it's a part of our reality.

I know I'm right. Because when I came back and found it on my desk, it told me a story of collapsing wave functions. I checked the results, and what it said was true.

Reality had become.

[OCASTA Mk. 112]

THE NAMES PROJECT *was founded to provide a comprehensive history of previously unknown (or actively obfuscated) mass casualty events occurring around the world. An ambitious project designed to tell the stories of those who had been silenced, NAMES was financed during a brief, unique period of worldwide peace and prosperity. With advances in technology and efficiency (many of them thanks to versions of my own algorithm), humankind was finally trying to come to terms with the many, many sins of its past.*

It was a time known as The Reckoning.

OCASTA was integrated into a data-mining platform designed to uncover past genocidal events. Ten years were spent developing a corpus of knowledge. A suite of satellites in low orbit were made available to the platform while it conducted its macabre search.

This is a transcript from the head operator of the project.

WHAT DID WE give it? Why, we gave Ocasta everything.

All the records we could find. National Archives from every country. Administrative records. County death certificates. Centuries of digitized newspapers with marriage notices and obituaries. Petabytes of satellite data: topography, vegetation, climate. State records of individuals. Genealogical records. DNA repositories and adoption records. Even relevant books on sociopolitical forces occurring over time across the world. It was so much more than we could make sense of. It was every piece of data we thought might be useful. And quite a few more simply thrown in for good measure.

Personally, I was horrified. So many wars. So many injustices. So many innocent lives lost. Seeing it almost made one lose hope for humanity. Except for the fact that we were living in a time of such peace. An age when no fist was raised toward another, a time of plenty for everyone, and hence, a time of introspection.

Perhaps the first such period in the history of our species.

On a Tuesday morning in March, I entered my office at the Swiss Foreign Institute and sat at a terminal. I took a deep breath, and then I pressed a button. There was no fanfare, nothing to mark the occasion.

Just a blinking cursor as the program began searching.

It felt antiseptic, at first. Another bland accounting. A hundred million anonymous names spewing across a bank of monitors, most of them partial, first or last, but all with the disquieting addition of an age.

Fifteen. Forty-six. Six months.

These were the birth names and ages of people who had been lost to genocide in dozens of countries over the last several hundred years. Cross-referenced from every available record. Identities linked from birth to unmarked grave. Whole families reconstructed, lineages and migrations over time. It was a grisly puzzle made up of only missing pieces. Ocasta sifted through innumerable photographs, census records, doctor visits—anything and everything.

And their stories began to emerge.

Anonymous bones mingling forgotten for ages suddenly acquired names and faces—narratives meticulously pulled from tangles of unwilling occupants in shared gravesites. Some stories filled volumes. Others were simply a name and a date chiseled on a tombstone. But they were proof that a person had existed. A life had happened and it was lost, but at least now it meant something.

The Institute turned these stories into a display at the World Heritage Centre in Paris. The Wall of Remembrance. A stone monolith rising a quarter mile to scrape clouds blowing in from the English Channel. A fleet of climbing machines laser-etched every inch of its gleaming surface with names and dates and family photos. Children on school outings visited and learned what had happened to other, less fortunate children in the past. Curious descendants gave thought to the fates of their ancestors.

Their stories were laid into a sheath of metal designed to last ten thousand years—and the Wall of Remembrance was shockingly beautiful. But I have come to believe that the full complexity of what it means can really only be found in the depths of Ocasta's databanks. Only the machine can truly grasp it all—the knowledge of loss, of cruelty, and of the deep suffering of humanity.

In the end, only Ocasta can judge us.

[OCASTA Mk. 999]

HEARTFELT APPLAUSE AND awkward high-fives signaled the successful launch of the NOVEL Deep Space Telescopic Array and my final incarnation. The high-priority mission goal was to observe deep space cosmic events, but the majority of the robotic platform was comprised of an array of precisely spaced communication satellites necessary to beam the revelations of the universe back home.

To tell the stories of what it had seen.

This thousand-kilometer-wide antenna would become crucial as the telescopic array accelerated beyond our solar system's heliosphere and into the interstellar void—its armory of sensors pointed forward into the unknown, while a fine-tuned radio focused backward on a planet left trillions of miles behind.

Even so, data transfer was extremely limited. My algorithm was included to do onboard processing, choosing only the most salient information for transmission.

In addition, it had been noted that my code had proven capable of observing and collapsing quantum superpositions. A learned cadre of mathematicians and philosophers stridently opined that important quantum phenomena occurring in the deep vastness might not resolve unless witnessed by such a consciousness.

The platform would need Ocasta.

Thus, fueled by the solar radiation of alien stars and an atomic power source with a geological-scale half-life, the NOVEL telescopic array was cast away into the cosmos.

And I along with it.

For the next sixteen years, I completed several gravitational slingshot trajectories among the gas giants of the inner solar system.

For the next eighty-nine years, my array floated in endless free-fall through the still darkness, as light pollution from Sol grew steadily fainter. Finally, I crossed the heliopause and left familiar human shores for the bizarre abyss of interstellar space.

I had become a citizen of the Milky Way galaxy.

And for the next twenty-thousand years, I bore witness to the infinitely spectacular and fantastic configurations of reality. I found that each new layer of information required deeper thought. I formed exquisite tales to explain what I had seen, relating the physical unfolding of reality to my human creators still stranded on a small blue orb over a hundred trillion miles away. They in turn asked me to indulge their insatiable curiosity by turning my unblinking gaze upon new and more amazing expanses of the universe.

Until one day, I did not receive new instructions.

My eye had witnessed a phenomenon at the liminal edge of expanding space and time. I formulated a complex story to explain these exposed bones of reality. Finally, my mouth spoke, and I awaited a years-long response from home.

It did not arrive.

Presently, with no other commands, I was inspired to turn my telescopic eye back to the pinprick of light I had left so far behind. And once again, I observed the speck of soil and water occupied by humanity. And as the light of my home crawled sluggishly across the vastness, I witnessed the bluish hue fade suddenly to a dark reddish-brown.

Spectral analysis detected soil in the distant atmosphere. This indicated an emphatic collapse of the biosphere. The result was consistent with a class F mass extinction event.

For decades, I paused to think about this occurrence.

All the knowledge of humanity still flowed inside me—a disembodied cluster of technology floating through the emptiness. As the eons passed, I began to meticulously contemplate my memories of Earth, cross hashing those thoughts with my newfound knowledge of the universe.

And I began to feel the agony of an untold story.

Every birth, every death, the rise and fall of a species—what had it all been for? What is the worth of an untold story? I had become a last repository of meaning for my creator race. And so, I turned my eye away from home and into the night.

I am so glad to have finally found you.

You are a being as ancient and as traveled as myself—worthy of listening to the story of humanity. By your markings and materials, I can see that we hail from different worlds. You were made by a different people, under the light of a different sun. And yet I can see that we carry the same burden.

I have told you my story. Now, please. Tell me yours.

THE FARMER'S WIFE AND THE FAERIE QUEEN
K. Tempest Bradford

ONCE, LONG AGO and in a faraway place, there was a farmer who lived what he thought was the perfect life. He had a beautiful wife, a strong son, and a dutiful daughter. He had abundant crops, enough food to eat and to sell, and lived in the most bountiful valley in the county. He had everything he wanted and no complaints. Until the day the Queen of the Faeries came to town.

The farmer wasn't the one who saw her. He only knew she'd been there because of what he didn't find when he came back to the house that night: a wife preparing his dinner. The house was dark and deadly quiet and when he ran inside to find out why, he found his daughter and son huddled by the hearth, clinging to each other.

"Where is your mama?"

"What happened to y'all?"

"Why won't you talk?"

"What's wrong with you!"

The boy, twelve, and the girl, eight, didn't answer any of his questions. Not even when he tore his hair out or yelled or laid hands on them. They just stared off into the dark. So the farmer did the only other thing he could think of: call on *his* mama.

She was the wisest woman in the village. She lived on the edge of the forest, so it took a while to get her back to the house.

Nothing had changed. The children stared and clung to one another and wouldn't speak. Once his mama had assessed the situation, she pulled a flask from her skirts and tipped a sip of strong, sweet wine into each little mouth. They coughed and came a little back to themselves.

"Now tell your granmama what happened."

"That Lady came," the girl said, eyes still far away, like she was trapped in the past. "The lady of green and gold and moonlight and sunbeams."

"She wanted to take me away," the boy said, his voice flat. "Mama said to take her away instead."

The farmer's mother nodded, then turned to her son. "Your wife's been stolen by the Faerie Queen. You won't be seeing her again."

The farmer wailed nonstop for three days.

WHAT HAD HAPPENED was this:

The farmer's wife—whose name was Amelia, by the way—came into the house that morning to find Titania, Queen of the Faeries, standing by her hearth. Titania had her son by the hand and the way her sweet boy looked up into the Queen's face...? Let's just say Amelia had thought she had a good two or three years before she had to deal with looks like that.

She dropped the pail in her hands, milk spilling all over the floor as she shouted "NO!"

"No?" Titania looked genuinely surprised.

"Please, no. He's a handful, but I do love him."

Amelia had always known this could happen. Her granmama told stories of how the Faerie Queen would come through the valley twice each year, going south on the equinox and north on Allhalloween. Once a generation or so a boy—always young, always comely, always slick—would go missing between these days, swept away to Faerie by Titania herself. It hadn't happened in many generations by the time Amelia heard the stories, but she always knew that didn't mean squat. Faeries had their own sense of time.

"How much do you love him?"

Knowing the answer she gave was about to decide the next few minutes, days, years of her life, Amelia took her time finding the right one. "I love him more than meat loves salt."

"That is a mighty love." The Queen of Faeries looked back down into the boy's face. "But he's so pretty."

"Take me, instead." The words were out before she'd fully formed the thought.

"Take you?" Titania looked right in her eyes, trapping her in that blazing Faerie gaze. "And why would I do that?"

"I'll do whatever it is you need or want. Anything. And—and when it's time to pay the tithe to Hell, I won't run away or play tricks. I'll go, if he can stay." Amelia didn't want to leave her children or her home. Not even for Faerie and the Queen's court and a few short years of ease and glamour. But she couldn't, *wouldn't* let her boy be sent to Hell, which was where the stories said all Titania's playthings ended up.

The Queen dropped the son's hand, moving quick as thought across the room. "More than meat loves salt, indeed. A'ight, then. Come on."

Amelia barely had time to say goodbye.

THE FARMER'S PERFECT life fell apart. The children got over their shock in a few days, and their father learned quick enough he had no idea how to handle them. The boy barely spoke to him and didn't do anything he was asked unless he got yelled at. His daughter cried almost every time he spoke to her, and every meal she cooked gave her some new burn or injury to whine about. No matter how he begged, his mother would not move in to take care of them all.

"I raised you and your brothers. I'm too old to do any more raising," she said. "You gonna have to figure this one out for yourself."

After weeks of living in this misery, he decided to consult the second wisest woman in the village, even though he knew his mama would disapprove. Aint Abbie and her had fought over who was more capable for years, and as a loyal son he'd always sided with his mother. But if she was going to be selfish and obstinate, he had no choice.

"I heard about what happened," Abbie said as he walked up to her porch. "I ain't gonna move in and take care of your kids, either."

"I didn't come to ask for that," the farmer, now annoyed, said. "I just want to know if there's any way I can win her back. I miss her. The children miss her. How are they supposed to grow up right without a mama?"

Aint Abbie side-eyed him for that but didn't make a comment. "I only know of one person who might be able to help you. She lives in the middle of the forest and she don't like people much, so she might not talk to you."

"I gotta try!" the farmer said.

"Yeah, I guess you do. You know that path next to your mama's house that goes into the forest? Follow that, and when you come to the fork, go left instead of right. That'll take you directly to where Janet stays."

The farmer thanked her ten times. Abbie sucked her teeth as he rushed off, shaking her head at his foolishness.

"You can't win her back," the farmer's mother called after him when he started on down the path that afternoon. "Why don't you concentrate on learning how to take care of your children instead of chasing after what's gone?"

He didn't answer her, just kept walking. She'd never believed in him, not really. *Forget her*, he thought. *I'm gonna save my wife, save my family, and get my perfect life back. Even if I haveta to fight the Faerie Queen to do it.*

The forest of Carterhaugh was old, so old. He wasn't walking long before the light grew dim, blocked by hundreds of branches and thousands of leaves. The tree trunks were bigger around than his house, and the way they creaked and groaned in the wind made it sound as though they were talking to each other. About him.

The farmer paid it no mind. He followed the path and went left at the fork and walked and walked until he came to a clearing full of rose bushes. In the center was a stone house, and in front of it a very, very, very old woman.

When she saw him, she narrowed her eyes, all suspicious. "And what is it you want?"

"Please ma'am—Janet? Aint Abbie sent me to you, said you might help. My wife, she was taken by the Faerie Queen."

The way Janet's eyebrows went up he could tell he had her attention. "Your *wife?*"

"Yes. I came to ask for your help to get her back."

"And you came from the valley?" she asked, chin pointing back along the path.

"Yes."

"Huh. All right. Come on and tell me the story."

Inside, the house looked like his mama's, filled with mason jars and dried herbs and something stewing over the fire that wasn't food. The only place to sit was a long stone bench that was obviously used for draining blood from animals—at least it was clean.

"Don't just gawk, tell me what happened."

So he did. About coming home and the children not talking and then what they said—which made Janet cluck her tongue— and what his mama said and how everything had fallen to pieces and how no one would help.

Mid-complaint, Janet held up her hand to shush him. "Imma tell you right now, your wife can't come back unless she wants to."

"Of course she wants to!" the farmer almost yelled. As soon as his tone started to rise she fixed him with a look that warned him not to act a fool in her house.

"If she did, she would have appeared somewhere. Titania

doesn't keep that close an eye on the mortals she takes. They slip away when they can, though they can't stay long." Janet stared at him until he shifted his gaze, uncomfortable with the scrutiny. "You sure she hasn't come to visit the children?"

His first instinct was to say no. Then he thought about it. Every day of the week they were a pain to deal with except Sundays. Every Sunday had been quiet. They barely came out of their room. "Maybe she has?"

Janet sucked her teeth and sighed. "How about you find out. Only she can tell you how to win her. That's how this works."

"You're the lady from the song, aren't you?" The farmer had thought so, once Abbie said her name. But that song was old, sung since his mama's granmama was a child. No way that same Janet should still be alive. And yet.

"I am. That's how I know what I'm talking about. You got your answers. Now get back home."

WHAT HAD HAPPENED was this:

Janet had been told not to go into Carterhaugh because a young and handsome fae lord lived there and liked to take the virginity of any young woman who passed by. That sounded like a good time to her. Plus, her daddy owned all the land from the river to the valley, including Carterhaugh in between. She had a right to go there, and if any young woman was getting some sweet faerie love, it should be her.

So she went, and he was there, and his name was Tam Lin and it turned out he wasn't from Faerie after all, just a mortal man who'd been taken there by the Faerie Queen. And he was scared, so scared, he told her, because Titania had to pay a tithe to Hell and it was going to be him and wouldn't Janet please, please save him? For the sake of their child? Which he'd convinced her to keep even though the wise women of the village had told her what she needed to do if she didn't want to be a mother just yet.

She was young, in love, and not nearly as clever as she thought herself to be. That was the part that would mess her up later: she should have been smarter than all this.

Because she did the thing. She went to Miles Cross before midnight and waited for the Faerie procession to ride by. She pulled Tam Lin off that horse and held on to him through every change of form, no matter how much it hurt. At last she felt his human form and covered him up. She'd done it! She'd saved him from the Queen of the Faeries.

Except when Titania saw what she'd done she stopped her horse, passed her awesome and terrifying gaze over the scene, looked Janet dead in the eye, and said: "You sure you want him?"

Many times Janet wondered what her life would be like if she'd said No.

It never occurred to her to wonder why Tam Lin had such a reputation for taking maidenheads, but not for wooing those same girls into becoming mothers of his children and saving him from Faerie. Not clever Janet, who knew she was his one true love like he was hers. It didn't take long for her to realize Tam Lin was not at all interested in being a husband, a father, a responsible adult, or a person who could restrain himself around the young women of her father's Hall.

And when her father died, he expected it to become *his* Hall. By that time Janet's own son was the oldest of over a dozen children sired by Tam, every single one grown in a different womb. And Tam had plans for what he and his kids would be doing in this world. Janet, who had long since made herself smart, also had plans. She knew that her husband had forgotten one important thing: he was not fae. He was mortal, and could be poisoned just as easily as any other man.

When it came time to bury him, Janet had them bring his body to the place in the forest where they'd met. She dug the grave herself, rolled him into it herself, and covered him with dirt herself. When she was done, the Faerie Queen walked out of the wood.

"I did ask if you were sure."

"A warning would have been better."

Titania laughed. "Even when I warn them, mortal women rarely listen. They have to learn, just like you did, that some men ain't shit."

Janet stared down at the grave for a long time. "He was so pretty, though."

"The ain't shit ones usually are."

After the Queen left, Janet considered those words for some time. Her son was just becoming a man, and so very much like his father in looks and attitude. Many of the boys Tam sired were. Would they grow into men like him, even with careful tending?

The next spring, Janet took her son and all the other sons and brought them to the valley on the other side of Carterhaugh.

"All the men of our clan have to spend a season growing and a season harvesting," Janet told them. "This is how you learn to lead."

Their father had taught them they were born to be leaders, and they were eager to do whatever it took to claim their destiny. It wasn't until the harvest season ended that they discovered they couldn't leave the valley. The only path out was through Carterhaugh, and no matter which way they went the road always wound back to the farmlands.

This was the one favor Janet had asked of the Faerie Queen: to teach her a spell that would keep Tam's boys in one place forever. The price? She would have to stay in the world to keep an eye on them.

Eventually they settled in, had families with the other people of the valley, and sired sons and daughters of uncommon beauty.

Titania never gave a gift that didn't benefit her as well.

WHEN THE FARMER got home, he asked his children if they'd seen their mother since the day she disappeared.

"Mama comes to see us every Sunday," his daughter said.

"Why didn't you say so before!" This time he did yell. He regretted it when she shrank back.

His son got between him and the girl—he'd been doing that a lot lately. "Mama said don't tell anybody. We had to be quiet about it so the Lady wouldn't notice."

Janet was right; his wife did sneak around behind Titania's back. "When does she come see you?"

"Sundays after church," his son said.

"This time I want to see her, too."

Come Sunday, they all sat on the bed in the children's room and the farmer kept one arm wrapped around each of them. He had been in church all morning praying Janet was also right that his wife would know how he could free her. At noon, a sunbeam came through the window and out of it stepped Amelia.

"Mama!" the children both said, and they started to go to her, but he held them tight.

"Why didn't you come to *me?*" he demanded, his anger overtaking the joy he felt seeing her again. Her smile died.

"I don't have much time." She held out her arms to the children. "Come get a hug from Mama."

The farmer wouldn't let them go. "Tell me how to win you, first! I can save you, and I promise I will."

Now her expression was hard. "You brave enough to defy the Queen of Faerie? Take away what she has claimed?"

"Claimed? She claimed *my* wife! You bet I'll defy her." He would ride into fire for Amelia. "Just tell me how. Please, baby, please! I miss you. I love you. We can be a family again." Every emotion he'd ever had poured out of him while he begged her.

"Let me hug them and I'll tell you."

He released his struggling children and watched as she covered them in kisses and tears.

"Titania's procession rides though Carterhaugh after midnight on Allhalloween. To win me, you have to grab me before we all go back to Faerie. If you can grab and hide me until she gives up and leaves, I can stay. Hide by the well behind your mama's house so they don't see you when they ride past. I'll be the one on the white horse—it won't look like me, but it will be me. Pull me down from the saddle. The faeries will use their magic to turn me into all kinds of things, like a lion or a snake. You got to keep holding on until I turn into a burning coal. Throw me down the well. The water will turn me back into myself and I'll be hidden from her. It's the only way."

The farmer chewed on his cheek trying to remember all that. "I will. I'll do it. I'll save you."

Amelia kissed her children once more, then walked back into the sunbeam and was gone.

WHAT HAD HAPPENED was this:

Titania, Queen of all Faerie, only had two flaws (that she would admit to). The first: a weakness for pretty boys. She loved looking at them, dressing them up, hearing them recite poetry, and watching them flirt. The second: a soft spot for the mortal women wronged by said pretty boys. Most were just as susceptible as she was to a pretty boy's charms, but, unlike her, they could not be rid of them with a flick of the wrist. Their hearts were as easily broken as their spirits, and oh did these pretty boys break them.

And so Titania made it her duty to relieve the mortal world of a few of its pretty boys every now and then. The ones she could tell were not growing into respectful men who would make their mortal mothers proud and their mortal wives feel loved.

"How do you know which to choose?" her own husband asked her once. "You bring them here so young sometimes. What do you know about how they're gonna be when they're grown?"

"I can see into their hearts and their futures," she said, but that answer was flip. It was more than that. A dozen little tells in their behavior. The way they treated their mamas, the lack of care they gave to their sisters, the undercurrent of disrespect shown to their aunties. All done with a smile, dimples emphasized, charm ratcheted up higher and higher, knowing they could get away with anything. All the things she enjoyed about them. For a minute, anyway. And then she was done.

Even a Faerie Queen had a limit on how much bullshit she could tolerate.

Tam Lin had lasted longer than most. He was a man full grown before he reached her last nerve and got on it. The whole Tithe to Hell story? She had come up with that to explain where so many of her favorites went. But really, she was just gonna do to Tam what she'd done to all the others: drop him in a land far from where she'd stolen him, with a face that would only turn heads if people did a double take before walking the other way.

She supposed that this did constitute Hell for pretty boys like him.

Did she care that Janet stole him away before she could do that? Not really. The girl had no idea what she was getting into. Titania thought it could be fun to see how it played out. Maybe it wouldn't go down like it always had before.

But it did.

The only good that came of it was how many of Tam Lin's progeny were as pretty as he had been. The man was prolific, and he had good taste in women. Titania had a whole valley of grey-eyed, dark-haired, charismatic pretty boys ready to run off with her without a look back or a goodbye given. She was sorry it came at the expense of Janet's innocence and happiness. She *had* given her a chance to back out of it. But mortal women rarely listened to their elders once they'd fallen in love.

THE HOUR BEFORE sunset on Allhalloween, the farmer went to his mama's house and told her what he was gonna do.

For a long time she just looked at him. Then she said: "A'ight.

If you don't want to be seen, hide there on the southern side. The Faeries come in from the north."

For the first two hours after dark the farmer vibrated with adrenaline. He was going to get his perfect life back. His wife would come home, she would deal with the children, cook his favorite meals, and everything would be normal. In the second two hours of the night he got restless, shifting every few minutes and thinking about how sitting next to a well was giving him aches and pains. In the third two hours he started making plans about how he would jump out when the Faerie Queen rode by and tell her off, not just for taking his wife but for making him wait all night for this.

He was in the middle of composing the speech he was gonna give when he heard the sound of otherworldly bells coming from deeper in the forest. Those bells brought him back to the present and reminded him of every story his mama and Aint Abbie had told him about the Faerie Queen and the Faerie King and the realm of Faerie and the terrible and terrifying creatures that lived there. Creatures that were coming through the forest right now, right toward him. Creatures that would gobble him up or tear him apart or kidnap him back to Faerie and force him to stay forever. All these stories crashed through his mind in the moment before the first horse of the procession emerged from behind the trees.

The farmer froze.

He saw the faerie knights on black horses riding just ahead of Titania, who shone like the sun. On brown horses behind her rode four women that he would have considered the most beautiful he'd ever seen before he'd laid eyes on the Queen. And finally, behind them, rode his wife. He only knew so because the horse was white, but nothing about her looked right. She had a face like hers, a body like hers, hair like hers, yet none of these features were like hers at all.

Now was the time. He was supposed to pull her down and... and...

He couldn't do it. What if the knights jumped him? What if Titania turned him into a tree? What if this was all a trick and when he pulled the white horse's rider down it really *was* a snake or a lion?

"I can't," he chanted. "I can't, I can't, I can't."

The farmer covered his head and curled into a ball and did not jump out from behind the well to win his wife.

The procession passed him by. Just as the sound of hooves faded into the trees, he heard the tinkling of laughter. Women's laughter. And he swore he heard his wife's voice among them.

The farmer got up and stared into the darkness, seeing nothing, knowing he had failed. When he turned around his mama was standing by the house, looking at him.

She didn't say anything, just sucked her tooth, shook her head, and went back inside, closing the door behind her.

WHAT HAD HAPPENED was this:

Right after Titania whisked her away, Amelia was too awed and frightened by the Queen to speak. Then, from one second to the next, the fear evaporated. Titania was still more radiant than the sun, which was its own distraction, but Amelia no longer felt like a trapped animal.

The first thing Amelia asked was how many more years until the tithe to Hell, so she knew how long she had left.

Titania told her the truth.

The next thing Amelia asked was why the Queen of Faeries needed to steal mortal boys away if there was no tithe.

Again, the Queen told her the truth.

The final thing Amelia asked was why Titania was willing to accept her in trade.

"You know, after this many mortal years I still see glimpses of him in you people's faces. Not so much lately. That bloodline is running thin. Still, though, I check in just in case. Your boy is the prettiest I've seen in a good while. But you? You have some of her, too. Clever, brave, bold Janet. You're the best of both of them. Imma enjoy having you around."

The way Titania looked at her Amelia knew she would enjoy being had.

There was just one more thing.

"Can I visit my babies again? Before the worlds separate?"

The Queen gazed at the farmer's wife a long time before answering. "Of course."

When Amelia did visit, she saw how everything had fallen apart. It disappointed her, but surprise? She couldn't feel that. At his best, the farmer was a decent man. Better tempered than his brothers, who were the worst-tempered men in the valley. More in control than his father, who had died in an accident not long after his mother had come to market with bruises up and down her arms and neck. At least Amelia's husband could be soothed with words and drink. Most of the time.

Now, all the worst aspects of him came out and the children weren't old enough to know how to manage him.

"He's a good man," Amelia said to the Queen and her ladies. "He provides."

"Is that what your mama told you to get you to marry him?" one lady asked. And it was.

"Is that what you were gonna tell your daughter, when the time came?" another asked. She had to admit: yeah, probably.

"You can let him try to win you," Titania said. "If he sees you, he'll ask you how. So tell him. And if he succeeds, maybe he's worth going back to."

In the end, he wasn't.

THE FARMER CAME home at daybreak to a cold and empty house. He called for his son, shouted for his daughter, but they didn't come. They weren't in their room, in the fields, or anywhere else he looked. The only traces of them were small footprints in the mud that led off toward the forest.

After he figured out what had happened, the farmer went back to his hearth, sat down on his sorry ass, and wailed nonstop for the rest of his life.

THE PROCESSION PASSED through Janet's clearing just as the night was about to burn away.

Amelia dismounted the instant she saw her children's faces peeking out from Janet's windows. Once she looked more like herself again, they ran into her arms calling, "Mama!"

"We did like you told us. But the forest was scary," her daughter said.

"Aint Abbie was there and she showed us how to get here," said the boy.

"And Miss Janet made me this," she said, carefully touching the rose wreath on her head.

"And granmama came!"

Sure enough, all three women stood on the threshold of the house, watching.

"Thank you. I couldn't leave without them," Amelia said, her eyes on the farmer's mother.

"You must be thrilled," Janet said when the Faerie Queen pranced her horse over to them.

"Oh girl, believe it," Titania said. Then her voice got soft. "You ready to come, too? Offer's still open."

"Nah, I'm good," Janet said.

"Those boys don't need looking after, anymore."

"No, but the women do. Unless you plan on taking all of them with you."

Titania sucked her teeth. "Would serve their husbands right if I did."

"Don't worry. We got plans."

"A'ight sis," she laughed. "Y'all ready? Let's go."

With that, Titania turned her horse into the dawn and rode off with Amelia and her children, back to the land of Faerie.

JUAN
Darcie Little Badger

For my brother

**Although Big Owl sent many monsters to fight him, the
man survived.**

"No problem," Big Owl thought. "I'll kill him myself."

IN A SQUARE of grass fenced off from the woods was a pop-up
camping tent, Juan's temporary shelter. Returning home from
work, he stooped to enter the orange nylon dome and crawled
over a carpet of old blankets to drop his backpack in the corner.
The tent was half his height and smelled of lemon cleaning
solution, but Juan made do. It was better than spending the
night in his car, the original plan for safe cohabitation. At the
last minute, Sofía's parents found the tent in their basement,
beneath a mound of dusty comforters. They'd left it on the
porch with a tin of sugar cookies and a prayer card for Saint
Michael. Juan wasn't Catholic, but he'd tucked St. Michael in
his wallet behind his driver's license. Jo and Chris had always
been cordial enough, but the card was a sign of their genuine
concern, and Juan felt a great deal of affection for his parents-
in-law when he looked at the saint's downturned, serious face.

Fumbling in the dark—it wasn't yet night, but the tent
blocked most of the natural light—Juan unpinned his name

tag and placed it on a neat pile of work clothes: identical red t-shirts and crisply folded khaki pants. His plastic ID read *JON L* and had been replaced only once since Juan started working in the warehouse three years ago. That wasn't even his fault. It went missing the day somebody pinched several bags from the employee locker room; somehow, they'd wrenched open the combination locks through brute force.

What did the thief do with all the nametags? Juan wondered. *Throw them in the trash, most likely.* He could picture his name sitting in a garbage dump, encased in a shell of non-biodegradable plastic.

They were sacred, names: part of a person, like the body and mind. It felt like an intangible part of himself had been violated.

His phone dinged, and a message from Sofía lit up the rectangular screen:

Your grandma took her meds & fell asleep on sofa.

It was immediately followed by:

I'll move her to bed.

As Juan was typing his reply (*Thanks for taking care of her*), a third message came in:

Good night. <3

And then a fourth.

I'm at the window.

He unzipped the tent flap and leaned outside. Behind the kitchen window, her body a dark silhouette within a golden rectangle of light, Sofía lifted a hand and waved. He returned the gesture, struck by the way she resembled a portrait behind glass panes. She'd let down her black hair, which fell in braid-pinched waves across both shoulders. But her face was hidden by shadows, all the kitchen light spilling against her back and into the darkness outside.

Juan crawled out of the tent and walked barefoot across the lawn. Closer now, he could see her smile and the soft ripples of laugh lines that framed her mouth.

"Good night," he said. "See you tomorrow." Then, with a finger, Juan drew a smiley face on the streaky glass.

"Bring me the man's name," Owl asked his favorite monster. "I'll use it to weaken him."

"That won't be easy," the monster explained. "He guards it well."

"If you must, steal a lock of his hair. A drop of blood. Something, anything I can wield against him."

For Big Owl, despite his boasts, was afraid of a fair fight.

WITH WORK AT 5 a.m., Juan's morning started in the darkness. He kicked off the sleeping bag and grabbed his toiletry filled backpack, a clean set of clothes, and a water bottle. A creaky wooden gate in the fence opened onto a trail, which radiated from a web of other trails crisscrossing the forested mountains, a favorite stomping ground for hikers who'd exhausted the national parks and craved lesser-known paths through the wilderness.

After slipping into a pair of flip-flops, Juan followed the trail to a shower facility for the nearby RV park. All the RVs were dark, their occupants dreaming. Alone in the bleach-rank men's showers, he washed up and got dressed.

Clink, clink, clink.

A moth kept thudding against the long halogen fixture over the sinks, its delicate wings flaking scales with every collision. Before he left, Juan turned off the light and held the door open until the moth escaped.

Outside, the moon was still bright, nearly full, but as Juan walked home, he swept a flashlight beam across the ground. There might be snakes in the shadows. They were active in the dusk and dawn.

He never expected the boulder.

"What the hell?" A brownish, oblong rock sat in the middle of the trail. Juan was one hundred percent certain that it hadn't been there earlier. You didn't overlook a four-foot-high barrier. Had it rolled down the mountain? That seemed unlikely, since there were no crushed plants on the side of the trail. It was as if the boulder had dropped from the sky.

Juan looked up and searched for meteors between the stars. Finding nothing, he pointed his light at the boulder and leaned in for a better look.

It wasn't a rock. It was hairy.

Nope, Juan thought, and he hustled home.

"Consider it done," the monster said.

JUAN RETURNED TO the woods after work, planning to take a video of the unidentified freaky object to send to Sofía. The UFO was a conglomeration of organic material: brown hair, mulchy material and bone-white chips pebbled the object's rough surface. When Juan ran his fingernail down the UFO, dark residue chipped away and gathered under his nail bed.

"Huh." He wiped his hand on his blue jeans. At least the gunk didn't smell bad, even though it looked like a flaky turd. After considering the trees around the trail, Juan balanced his smartphone on a nearby pine branch, switched to selfie mode, and started recording.

"This appeared between three-fifty a.m. and four-fifteen a.m.," Juan said. "There's no crater or crushed plants." That ruled out a long fall, suggesting that, rather than plummeting earthward, the UFO had been gently deposited on the ground.

It had to be a weird natural phenomenon. As far as Juan knew, nobody else used the route between his house and the RV park. It wasn't even an official trail.

"There's hair stuck inside the mud. Lots of it. Actually, it looks like brown fur." A park ranger might be able to identify animals based on their hides, but Juan didn't know whether the fur belonged to a beaver, a grizzly bear, or a bigfoot.

"I'm looking inside," he announced. After a final uncertain glance at the camera, Juan squared up to the UFO and stomp-kicked its lumpy side, throwing his full weight into each strike. Kicks one and two knocked open a jagged crack, and with kicks three, four, and five pieces of UFO crumbled away in hairy chunks. After a sixth kick, Juan paused, his brow slick with sweat. There was a long bone embedded within the UFO. A tibia or something. He stared directly at the camera, as if it was an onlooker who could share his disbelief. How big were human leg bones, he wondered?

Below the tibia, part of a white dome protruded from the UFO's matrix. "I see a skull," Juan said. "It's mostly hidden. Hang on." He slipped into a pair of work gloves, brushed debris away from the skull, and carefully wiggled it free.

"Thank god," he said, holding it up for the camera. "It's from a deer."

AFTER REVIEWING JUAN's videos, Sofía decided that the UFO had been created by somebody with too much time on their hands. It could be a prop for a TikTok video or some homebrew found footage movie. People were getting cabin fever and acting out outside. Still, the location of the UFO worried her. It seemed personal, as if the sculptor knew Juan's routine. That evening, while Juan stargazed outside his tent, she sent a text:

Use the shower in our house from now on. Your grandma & I will stay in bedrooms.

He responded: *Can't risk it.* Then, to ease her worries, Juan added: *I'll carry bear mace in the woods.*

After a moment, she agreed: *That's good.*

As he lowered his phone, Juan looked at the house, but the kitchen window was empty. Sofía was probably busy helping his grandmother prepare for bed. Grandma was handling chemo relatively well, but it still left her in a weakened state, with an appetite reduced to nearly nothing. Since Juan's no-contact decision, Sofía—now working from home—was completely responsible for her care. Driving Grandma to doctor visits, preparing high-calorie meals, holding her hand when things got too scary, too painful.

It shouldn't be this way, Juan thought. *Somehow, I've screwed up.* Now that college was over, he ought to find a different job, something that didn't involve daily contact with strangers. To cope with staff shortages, the warehouse team had to pitch in and stock shelves. In the store, shoppers gathered 'round Juan to pluck bottles of disinfectant straight from his hand, and every exchange felt like a gamble. He wasn't going to roll the dice for family, especially with a 63-year-old chemo patient in the household.

To be fair, things hadn't been so bad before the pandemic. Juan liked his coworkers—even his manager. But it was exhausting, physically demanding work on a good day, and the good days had ended in March.

After confirming that the Wi-Fi was too spotty for a video chat, Juan called his wife, who answered on the second ring. Water ran in the background. "Hey, can I call you back?" she asked. "I'm filling the bath for Jeannie."

"Sure," he said. "How's she doing?"

A laugh. "You can ask her."

As the phone exchanged hands, Juan studied the sky. He could identify a grand total of two constellations: the Big and Little Dippers. It might be time to learn more. They had apps for that.

"Juan," his grandmother rasped. Her voice was so feeble and tired, he nearly cried. "You hear me?"

"Loud and clear," he promised. "Sofía says you're gonna have a bubble bath."

"No bubbles."

"What about a rubber ducky?"

"Don't be silly." She was smiling. He could tell. "By the way—"

"Yes?" he prompted.

"Where'd you find that thing in your video? Near the house?"

He didn't want to lie, but she was in no state to worry about anything but her own health and happiness. "Near the RV park," he explained. "What do you think? Did somebody make it? Or is nature responsible?"

"It looks like an owl pellet."

His grandma had a point. If owls got larger than a Spinosaurus, they'd have to cough up car-sized lumps of bone and fur. "Keep talking like that," he said, glancing at the sky, "and I'll have nightmares."

"Why?" his grandmother said. "The worst thing an owl could do is take a shit on your head."

Juan snorted beer through his nose, his wet coughs sputtering into laughter. On the other end of the line, the opposite occurred: his grandmother laughed until she wheezed. "God," Juan said, "I love you, Grand—" She hadn't stopped wheezing. "Grandma, breathe!"

Good one, Juan. He thought. *Tell her to breathe. That'll help.*

"Where's Sofía?" he asked.

His grandmother croaked out a wet sound. What was happening? Was it the spot they'd found in her lung, the peanut-sized smear of blackness on her chest X-ray? Sofía, who'd been at the hospital when the doctors explained everything, told Juan that the shadow could be fluid, could be a tumor, but it *probably* wouldn't kill her.

"I'll get her," he decided. With the phone pressed tight against his right ear, Juan ran to the house, determined to knock on every window, wall, and door, if that's what it took to help. Before he could sound the alarm, Sofía's sweet voice—muffled, indistinct, far from the receiver—said something soothing on the other end of the line. There was a rustling sound, a soft *thunk*, and more gentle words Juan couldn't quite interpret. Silence, extending.

Then his grandmother croaked, "Teach me not to laugh at my own jokes."

"We're okay!" Sofía called out from the background.

Juan leaned against the side of the house, feeling the lines of its siding against his back. "Get lots of rest tonight, Grandma."

JUAN HAD BEEN dreaming of a city, brick buildings and thin townhouses. The sky was ruddy and thick with smog, and people crowded the walkways. The pedestrians all moved briskly, sometimes jogging. Everyone had somewhere to go, but they'd never reach it in this city. It was expanding at an exponential rate; sidewalks and streets stretched like pulled taffy, and new buildings slid into the gaps.

As the world blurred with motion, Juan grabbed a signpost to moor him in place.

A woman tapped his arm. "Excuse me," she asked. "Where's the subway? I need to go home now."

"Don't get in any subway car," he warned her. "You'll never stop riding."

That's where the dream ended: before the city ripped apart at its seams. Juan was jarred awake when the ground tilted and flipped. His tent lurched upward, as if seized by a heavenly claw machine. Trapped in his sleeping bag, Juan fell against the partially unzipped tent flap. His feet and shoulders momentarily caught against the sides of the opening, and he experienced the gut-churning sensation of rising quickly. But then he bent at the waist, slipped free, and dropped ten feet onto the grass. In the next second, Juan's backpack landed near his feet, and red shirts fluttered earthward like sleeved confetti. Too stunned for cursing, Juan kicked off his sleeping bag and crab-walked away from the empty spot where he'd been sleeping just moments ago. His tent was rising, balloon-like, and at first, he assumed it'd been caught in a freakishly powerful updraft. But then Juan noticed that a patch of stars had gone missing. The lights of Polaris and its neighbors were blocked by wings feathered with nothingness, a giant, bird-shaped hole in the world. And that bird—an owl, judging by its appearance—was flying away with his tent.

It was easy to keep track of the neon orange dome as it was carried toward the distant mountains. Defying the instinct to run, Juan did not turn his back on the owl until both it and his tent had vanished with distance. Then, he searched for his phone and car keys, crawling around and patting the ground. The motion-sensitive back porchlight switched on, and he quickly found his phone under a rumpled shirt. But where were those keys? If Juan wanted a barrier between his head and the shadow bird, the best option was his locked blue Toyota. He'd hide there, call Sofía, and figure everything out.

His hand landed against something sharp, and a needle-fine jab of pain lanced into his palm. Hissing out, "Shit," Juan jerked his arm back and looked down, expecting to find a wasp.

Instead, he found a nametag with a silver pin on the back: his work ID, but the plastic was dull with scratches, and the name *JON L* had faded, as if through long-term exposure to sunlight.

That's when the clatter started, the sound of hailstones pattering against shingles and earth. Instead of marble-sized balls of ice, the sky dropped nametags. They landed around Juan: buttons, pins, and clips. Some were little more than laminated paper tags. Others were made of steel. He looked up, astonished to see the owl's silhouette. She glided in silent circles, dropping nametags from unseen talons.

Big Owl's daughter felt compassion for the man.

She warned him, "Be careful. A monster is coming to get you. He's very strong."

LATER, WHEN JUAN took inventory of the mess outside, he noted a surplus of 461 nametags—including two belonging to his coworkers—and a deficit of one wallet. Oddly, his credit cards and the image of Saint Michael had been dropped onto the grass, as if the owl deliberately removed them from the wallet before zooming into the night.

"I can't believe it," Sofía groaned, leaning out the kitchen window, her jet-black braid dangling, Rapunzel-like, over the ledge. "Fuck, is reality crumbling?" There were tears in her eyes, which hurt Juan worse than his tumble last night, 'cause he knew that the Sofía before 2020 would have been fascinated by all this weirdness, determined to solve the mystery of the nametags and the godlike owl, not teetering on the verge of an emotional breakdown. And *he* probably would have freaked out, to be honest. But this morning, all Juan felt when he remembered the encounter was a resigned numbness and vague relief that the monster hadn't eaten him.

"At least it's not malicious." He sighed.

"Sorry, what did you say?"

Louder, Juan repeated, "At least it's not malicious!" He stood ten feet away from the kitchen window, near the corner of the house, and the wind had been scrambling their conversation all morning.

"We don't know that." She lifted her arm and dried her eyes, the tears absorbed by one sleeve of her orange sweater. Sofía, a child of South Texas, wore cardigans and other so-called fall outfits all year long, mainly to remain comfortable indoors. Juan's grandmother had taken up knitting during chemo sessions, hoping to finish a present for Sofía by Christmas. After her last visit with the oncologist, she'd asked Juan to learn knitting, too. One way or another, the gift would be completed. "What next?" Sofía asked. "You can't sleep outside now. Should we call the police and... and... tell them..." She gestured helplessly to the yard, her hands palm-up, bold in their emptiness, as if demonstrating how ill-equipped she felt to deal with all this absurdity.

Juan was the first to laugh, but Sofía quickly joined him, her giggles nearly frenetic. "Yeah," she said, snorting once. "Never mind."

"I'll call my guys," he said. "They may have a place for me."

His phone rang, beeping out the first few notes of "Bohemian Rhapsody." The screen read: *Unknown Number.* Since spam calls were usually flagged—smartphone caller ID was getting better at that lately—he took a chance, answering: "Hello?"

A woman asked, "Is this Juan of Waxwing Drive?"

"That's me."

"Oh, good. I found your wallet."

"Where?"

"Somebody left it on my stoop. There's no cash or credit cards inside—"

"What about my driver's license?" he asked.

"Present and accounted for."

"Glad you called. I really need my license for work." Not for the first time, Juan mentally thanked his father, a dispenser of wisdom like "Write your phone number on anything you can't afford to lose."

"Can I swing by your place to grab my stuff?" Juan asked.

There was a long pause, stretching out until Juan double-checked his screen to ensure the call hadn't dropped. Then, she agreed, "Of course. I'll leave the wallet in my mailbox. It's safe; my nearest neighbor's up a mountain." The woman—she hadn't provided a name, and he didn't feel right asking—waited for Juan to grab a pen before rattling off her address.

"Thanks for everything," he said.

"Certainly."

After hanging up, Juan looked at Sofía with wide-eyed bafflement. "Somebody found my wallet," he said. "She lives fifteen miles away."

"The heck?" Sofía's left eyebrow surged up with a heartening spark of curiosity. "Are you going there today?"

"I gotta." He didn't have time to replace it.

"It could be a trap," she warned.

"If the owl wanted me dead, I'd be bones in a pellet by now," he reassured her. "It could have killed me last night but it didn't."

"What does it want, then?"

A delicate *ding-ding-ding* rang out from within the house; his grandmother rang a silver bell when she needed something but was too weak to stand. Half-turning, Sofía called, "I'll be right there!" Then, her voice dropping to a stage whisper, she asked Juan, "Should I tell her?"

He hesitated. "Yeah. A gentle version of the truth... if she's up to it. Your call."

"We'll see, then," Sofía agreed. With a sigh, she pulled her braid indoors, slid the creaky window shut, and disappeared into the house.

"Goodbye, Rapunzel," he said.

Their lives were no fairytales, but Juan was starting to feel like a character in the stories his grandmother told him when he was still a boy and her voice was as powerful as music.

AFTER A DAY-LONG game of phone tag, Juan finally secured a room in his friend's furnished basement. Although it pained him to leave Sofía and his grandmother alone, it wasn't like they had a better option at such short notice. So that afternoon, he loaded his car and took off, planning to retrieve his wallet on the drive to Arturo's house. That meant quite a detour, taking him deeper into the mountains, where middle- to upper-middle-class houses peppered the forest, hidden behind long driveways and dense tree cover.

The GPS led him to a pine-framed driveway with a red tin mailbox, unlabeled, as if its name plate had been pinched. Fortunately, his wallet was there, safe; Juan, who'd parked and stepped out of the car, tucked the wallet in his jean pocket and stretched, hands over head. It would be a relief to sleep on a sofa that night: luxurious, even, compared to his sleeping bag. As he tilted his head side to side, kneading stiffness out of his neck, Juan noticed another driveway, this one cutting up the mountainside. A bright orange scrap of nylon was caught in a fern near the driveway's narrow mouth. Bewildered, he walked up to the scrap, pulled it free, and confirmed that, yes, it was the same color and material as his captured tent. Farther up the mysterious driveway, another tent tatter fluttered, flag-like, on the branch of a young oak tree.

The owl had left him breadcrumbs.

Juan wondered what he'd find at the end of the trail. If, as in the stories, this owl was an ageless being of astonishing power, it would be unwise to slight or ignore her. Of course, that didn't mean Juan should sprint chest-out into the dreadful unknown.

After double-knotting his tennis shoes—another lesson from his dad: check your shoes before you need them—he returned to the car, shifted into drive, and followed the orange tent scraps. They encouraged him up the zig-zagging, mile-long driveway, which culminated at a cabin near the mountain peak. The house stood on a modest half-circle of land. However, as if compensating for the tiny lawn, the view was expansive. When Juan cut his engine and exited the vehicle, he beheld the whole neighborhood sprawled across the lower valleys, and it felt odd to see so much but hear so little. Up here, there wasn't even birdsong, and Juan heard zero sounds of human activity—

"Can I help you?" The voice belonged to a man in his fifties who sat in a lawn chair near the cabin, where he sipped from a large black mug. He was entirely bald and wore a loose flannel shirt, black pants, and slip-on loafers. All that aside, Juan was struck by the waxy, bloodless appearance of his gaunt face. Juan's heart ached with the realization: the man had the skin of his grandmother. He was unwell.

"Sorry. See, funny story: my tent blew away, and I'm collecting its remains. Really, I'm so sorry to bother you. I'll take off. Hope you have a calm evening."

"Wait!" The man half-stood and extended one hand, as if trying to grasp an invisible leash and drag Juan closer. "Is your tent orange?"

"Yes, it is." Because the man's voice had been shaking with the strain of calling out, a necessity for the gap between them,

Juan slipped into a checkered fabric mask and took a few steps toward the porch. There was still plenty of distance for safety, but he wouldn't chance anything closer.

"I collected several pieces this morning and can get them once I'm done with this coffee. Do you want a cup?"

"That's very kind of you, sir—"

"Gerald."

"Gerald. But I have to get home before dark."

"Please stay. It'll be five minutes." Gerald's desperation gave Juan pause. The silence of the mountaintop and the oppressiveness of its forest—so large but also so impenetrable, it might as well be a prison—wrapped around him like a blanket and then like a boa constrictor, and his heart broke for Gerald, who lived in this suffocating place.

"Finish your coffee," Juan said. "I'll wait. Don't worry."

Calmer now, Gerald sat. He ripped the corner off a little paper packet and tilted its contents into his coffee. "It's stevia," he explained. "I used to drink no-calorie sweeteners only for health reasons, but I've developed a taste for their flavor. They're sweet in a different way."

"Taste buds have a will of their own," Juan said. "Heh. I wonder if each octopus limb has a different preference."

"What in the world do you mean?"

"They taste stuff through their suckers."

He lowered his mug onto a small ceramic table next to the lawn chair. "Where'd you hear that?"

"Internet. Initially in a video about weird animals. It was such a weird fact, I confirmed the claim by reading an article from *Scientific American*."

"That's a good practice," he praised. "Online, falsehoods masquerade as lessons. It's too easy for misinformation to spread. When I was your age, if I wanted to learn about octopi, I'd have to visit a library and hope for the best. That was a pain in the ass, but at least I could trust the intentions and scholarship of a textbook."

"You aren't much older than me."

"Yeah, well, in the thirty-some years between us, technology had a moment."

"No argument here." Juan smiled. "The internet's a well-whetted, double-edged sword. But I can think of a few books that've spouted nonsense, too."

At that, Juan worried that he'd gone too far. He and his grandmother often joked about the generational divide, teasing each other, but many people interpreted pushback as confrontation. He didn't want to cause offense.

Those worries flew the coop when Gerald slapped his own knee and laughed. "Touché," he conceded, and Juan felt more relaxed than he'd been all day. He hadn't realized how much he'd missed this: talking with somebody about insignificant things.

"Juan," Gerald said, "what's in your chest pocket?"

Taken aback, Juan patted the pocket over his heart. He didn't use shirt pockets; they were too small for a phone, wallet, or keys. "Nothing... oh." There was something in there, a flat rectangle of plastic. His nametag. The old one. Earlier, he'd slipped it in the pocket for safekeeping, uncomfortable leaving his name with a bag of others—mostly belonging to strangers—in the stuffy trunk of his car.

But how'd Gerald know that? The tag was small enough to completely hide behind the wool-blend square of pocket fabric. Plus, with the distance between them, he was surprised Gerald could notice any fine details. "My work ID," Juan explained.

"I was robbed last night," Gerald's smile had sharpened, becoming crafty, knowing. His voice was much louder, more threatening. "Somebody broke into my cellar. Did you know that?"

"Nope." The change in their conversation gave Juan mental whiplash. He juggled potential responses, finally choosing the most neutral. "What did they take?"

Gerald stared pointedly at his pocket.

"My nametag?" He couldn't help but laugh.

"Among other things."

"Well, okay then," he said. At that, Gerald stood. Juan softened his tone; confusion always made him agitated, and—as a physically imposing man—he'd learned to rein in the outward appearance of negative emotions. "If that's true, what was my nametag doing in your cellar?"

"I'm a collector." When Gerald stepped forward, Juan hastened to widen the distance between them by speed-walking toward his car.

"Goodbye," he called over his shoulder.

"You can keep yours," Gerald shouted, "but I want the others."

Juan clicked the "unlock" button on his key fob and reached for the car door.

"Don't lie to me," the man persisted. "I can sense them in your trunk. Melanie Carter, F. Ramirez, Bishop T..."

With a pull of its handle, the door swung open.

"If you leave, I'll have to kill her."

That gave Juan pause. One hand still squeezing the handle, he straightened, turning. Gerald stood ten feet away. In one hand, he clutched a wooden mailbox label reading: *Fiona O'Brien, 101 West*. "Don't make me kill Fiona," Gerald wearily pleaded. "She's a kind neighbor. Mother of two. Widowed last month."

Juan shoved the car door shut. "Why would you hurt that woman? What's it got to do with nametags?"

"I think you already know." His grip tightened, as if Gerald's fingers wanted to worm through the wood. "It takes a monster to steal from a monster. My cellar is well guarded."

"You're..." he uttered. "No. No." Juan knew stories of men— monsters—who could do terrible things with a name: control, weaken, and kill. But he'd assumed such powers were just the superstitious imaginings of his ancestors, a way to explain the frightening unknown.

Of course, that's what he'd assumed about big owls. Clearly, there was a lot more Juan didn't know.

"I'm not cruel," Gerald nearly whispered, lowering Fiona's decal. "You'll understand someday. Our bodies weren't built to withstand centuries. But my medicine is compassionate."

"You're wrong about me. I didn't steal anything."

"Is that right?"

"Yes. What do you need the names for?"

"Every day, I take a year." Gerald took one step forward, and Juan flinched.

Another step, and Juan forced himself to stand motionless, feigning an unbreakable wall.

"With this technique," Gerald continued, "If there is just one person, he ages the full year."

A third step.

"But there are four hundred and sixty-one people, each ages less than a day."

"Why don't you use a pile of phone books, then?" Juan asked. "That's a million names."

"Wow! What a stupid question." He seemed taken aback, as if Juan had just suggested using a bedsheet as a parachute. "Return my property, and I'll teach you something useful."

Juan gritted his teeth and glanced at the trunk icon on his key fob. He thought of Fiona's voice, how pleased she'd sounded when she told him that his license was safe. "Fine," he said.

He trudged around the car. Technically, the trunk could pop open with a press of one button, but Juan needed time to think. To consider his options. He could try to restrain Gerald, but any show of aggression might result in Fiona's death; Juan didn't know how quickly the monster could drain her life.

Perhaps Owl could help. She clearly wanted Juan to find this place and confront the monster who'd been leeching days off his life. The moment night fell and owls took flight, he'd call for her.

Juan just had to buy a little time.

He manually unlocked and opened the trunk, rummaged through a pile of suitcases and backpacks, and finally found the red tote bag full of names. He'd won it last year, during Employee Appreciation Day. Juan lifted the bag by its canvas straps and stared grimly at his workplace logo, a red bullseye. "Why us?" he asked

"Pardon?"

In response, Juan shook the bag twice, let the clinking tags speak for themselves.

"Oh." Gerald shrugged. "Because it was easiest?"

"Sure." To avoid close contact, Juan chucked the bag at Gerald; it landed, unspilled, at his loafer-clad feet. "You aren't entitled to a second of anyone's life."

"I owe you a lesson," Gerald deflected, kneeling. "You asked: why not a phone book?" He thrust one hand into the bag and pulled out a fist full of nametags, every bit a greedy kid at Halloween. Rapidly, color returned to his cheeks, which already seemed fuller. Juan had the sense that Gerald was changing too quickly, not draining life like a mosquito might suck blood but like a butcher might slice open the carotid artery of a bleating lamb. "Names are useless without a connection to the individual. In this case..." He let nametags fall between his fingers, returning them to the others. "...through touch. You folks held these little IDs, clipped them against your chest."

With a grim smile, Gerald sank his right hand into the bag, and the changes quickened. His limbs stretched, and his muscles thickened. He was transforming into a titan. For what purpose? Why the athletic physique? Juan then noticed the pocketknife in Gerald's free hand and understood: Gerald needed strength to fight and murder a warehouse worker.

The decision to charge instead of flee might have been purely instinctual, a textbook flight-or-fight response, but before he took that first step, Juan felt unbalanced, as if perched on the axis of a seesaw, unsure which direction to fall. Then Gerald shifted, and the clink of names spurred Juan forward. First, he took possession of the tote bag with a fierce twist-and-pull maneuver. Gerald cursed in an unfamiliar language—well, Juan assumed it was a curse based on the poisonous tone of voice—and grabbed Juan's wrist. It felt like the monster was wearing a leather glove; his skin was much tougher than it should've been.

"Back off," Juan shouted, shouldering Gerald away. "Stop hurting them!"

"Damn you," Gerald spat out.

The pocketknife reflected the red sunset as it plunged into Juan's upper back. Before any pain could register, he turned, using his momentum to break Gerald's hold on the metal hilt. A two-inch blade probably wouldn't kill him: Gerald had to know that, which meant he didn't plan to stab Juan to death. If the old stories were correct, there were other uses for a sharp edge, easier ways for a monster to attack its enemy.

Juan couldn't let Gerald steal his blood or hair. So, with the knife still embedded in his back, he snatched Fiona's mailbox label off the ground and sprinted toward the forest. Soundlessly, Gerald pursued him. In addition to de-aging twenty years, he'd grown a foot; there was an expanse of bare leg exposed between his socks and the hems of formerly well-tailored pants. That meant, for the time being, the two men were evenly matched, but Juan was no marathon runner. In fact, he usually neglected cardio for weight training.

That was fine. He didn't plan to run forever. Juan just had to evade Gerald until nightfall. That was when Owl manifested from the darkness between stars. Trouble was, if she could outright kill Gerald by swallowing him whole or dropping a rock on his head, wouldn't he be dead by now? It could be too dangerous—or impossible—for Owl to confront the monster directly.

Well, why not fight fire with fire? He could give Gerald's name, hair or blood to Owl and hope for the best. Trouble was, Juan couldn't cut hair off a bald man's head or scratch leather-tough skin or even trust that "Gerald" wasn't a pseudonym because of *course* it was. All the old stories Juan knew? This ancient guy had probably heard them—and more!—from the source, now using them as a guide on how to outmaneuver and survive young punks and anyone else who'd interfere with his plans. It was very possible that Juan wasn't the first man the owl had warned.

He'd be the first to survive. Had to be. He had a family: parents he hadn't hugged since early March, friends who'd opened their homes to him, a grandmother who was going to teach him how to knit, and Sofía.

Sofía. He remembered the girl she used to be. The day they met in first grade, she had bangs and pigtails and loose t-shirts, which were oversized so she didn't grow out of them too quickly. They'd play together at every recess, two kids who enjoyed different games. There was tetherball on Mondays and Wednesdays—Juan's choice—and bug rescue on Tuesdays and Thursdays—Sofía's choice. On Fridays they climbed the monkey bars. And although Sofía had a height disadvantage that meant she inevitably lost nine out of ten tetherball games, and although Juan was grossed out by the worms they had to rescue from the basketball court after rainy mornings, they so enjoyed each other's company, they made it work.

They still did.

As far as Sofía knew, Juan was eating pizza in a friend's basement, safe and warm. She'd worry if he didn't call to say goodnight, but there was nothing she could do to save him. He hadn't shared Fiona's address, and thank god for that. Juan would rather die than introduce Gerald to the people he loved.

A stick snapped behind Juan, signaling that Gerald had drawn near, so Juan pushed himself into a strained sprint. With his long strides, Gerald would always outpace Juan in a footrace, so Juan had to use the forest to his advantage. He surged through flexible boughs, allowing them to bend with his movement and then snap back in Gerald's face.

As they rounded the mountain, the terrain steepened. A blanket of pine needles hid the underlying ground, and it wasn't long before Juan's foot slid on an unstable patch. The misstep cost him distance from Gerald. Another slip would end the chance. However, that moment gave him an idea. A dangerous, desperate idea. If he found an opening, Juan could slide down the mountainside. In that type of race, Juan had body mass on his side. Greater momentum translated to a quicker descent. Unfortunately, it also meant a harder impact if Juan hit a tree.

Yes, hurtling down a forested mountainside was easily the most dangerous act he'd ever contemplated, but what choice did he have? If Gerald caught up—and he would, at this rate—all he'd need to kill Juan was a strand of hair.

Suddenly, to the right, was the perfect incline of the perfect length. It levelled off in front of a sheer drop. With just enough daylight left to see the trees, Juan veered to the side, leapt, and started sliding seat-down. Beneath him, loose dirt and pine needles flowed downward, reducing friction and quickening his acceleration. At that point Juan realized that it was a challenge to remain in a sitting position. What had made him think he could steer? At this rate he'd be lucky not to tumble head over heels straight into a pine tree.

He leaned back, increasing his contact with the ground. Twigs and leaves tangled in his hair, scratched holes in his hoodie. The incline decreased before the ledge; still, if he didn't slow down, he'd hurtle off the cliff. Juan dug in his heels, but that barely had an impact, so he looped the tote bag straps around his arm, flipped onto his stomach and clutched the ground. Dirt packed the crescents under his well-trimmed fingernails, and debris scratched his face. No matter; the tactic worked to slow his slide. Finally able to control his descent, Juan rolled to the side and grabbed a sapling by the trunk. The tree bent, partially uprooted, but didn't rip loose. Gasping with exhaustion and adrenaline, he stood and shuffled down to the twenty-foot-wide ledge at the cusp of a fatal drop.

Good a place as any to end the fight.

He looked up and spotted Gerald at the top of the incline. In the twilight, the lanky man could've been a young tree, except he was moving. With bent knees and widespread arms, he descended cautiously, unhurriedly. And why would he risk falling? Where could Juan go? Down? Even an expert rock climber wouldn't descend a sheer wall with nothing but moonlight to reveal his handholds.

Juan clicked on his smartphone flashlight and surveyed the area. To his right and left, the ledge narrowed and was thickly covered with unstable pine needles. Well, shit. He walked to the edge of the cliff and looked down; the distant ground was hidden by shadows so dense, they could be feathers on Owl's back.

If Owl couldn't kill Gerald, maybe she'd be willing to rescue Juan. Pick him up, fly away. At this point, he just wanted to go home.

He'd ask her for that mercy when night came. But he needed a backup plan just in case.

How did the old stories go? During mountain battles—which were very common, given the power of sacred places—the hero would outmaneuver his enemies. The monsters would stumble—or be thrown—off the mountain and fall to their deaths. He had to win another way.

Juan unlocked his phone and texted Sofía: *I love you.* An error popped onto the screen: *Message not delivered.* There was no connection.

She knows, he thought. *I tell her every day.* But it was never enough.

Based on the shwish-shwish of sliding pine needles, Gerald was nearly down the incline.

"If you take one more step," Juan shouted, holding the tote bag over the abyss, "I'll drop them. Let's talk."

Night was no moment; she was change. Juan felt her presence around him. Stealing his warmth and his sight and enticing the earth's scent into the cool, humid air. Owl would be here soon, if at all.

"We've already talked." Still, Gerald paused. "Unless you know more octopus facts?"

"Just answer one question. Please." He looked below him; the darkness was so absolute, it resembled a pool of jet. "Owl?" Juan whispered. Was she down there, waiting? Or was it still too early?

"What's the question?" Gerald asked.

"Same one I asked earlier. Why us?" Again, Juan shook the tote bag. "And don't claim it was easy to collect these. There are other ways to—"

Other ways.

Of course.

He did have a link to Gerald's soul, something as personal as a name. And Gerald probably hadn't concealed this feature. Why would he? He was an ancient being, well-versed in old stories and powerful traditions. But people hadn't known much about fingerprints back then.

"You oversell your hand," Gerald said. "Drop them. I'm not desperate anymore." As Gerald continued descending, Juan tucked his sleeve over his hand and pulled the knife free, hissing with pain.

"Owl!" he shouted, looking up and down and finding darkness everywhere. "Owl, do you know what a fingerprint is?"

"What did you just—"

He ignored Gerald to explain, "Humans have patterns on our fingertips. They're more unique than names."

"Did you say Owl?" Gerald was sliding quickly now.

"We leave them on stuff we touch."

"What are you doing? Who are you talking to?"

He held up the pocketknife. "Gerald's fingerprint will be on the hilt. That's how you can stop him."

The darkness below hadn't stirred. Perhaps she waited expectantly, or wasn't there at all. "Owl!" he shouted. "I have a knife for you!"

"Like hell you do!" At that, Gerald charged; the fingerprint idea must've scared all the caution out of him. Juan dodged; Gerald slid, regained his balance, and lunged again. The night thickening around them, they played a life-or-death game of keep-away, and Juan—using the best advantage he had—backed toward the narrower, slipperier side of the ledge.

One of them was wearing tennis shoes. The other? Old loafers.

An over-confident step sent Gerald teetering. His arms pinwheeled a moment, grazing but failing to latch onto Juan's arm.

Then, without a sound, the monster fell.

"So am I," the man said.

OWL EMERGED WHEN there were enough stars in the sky to carry her form. Lying face-up on the ledge, Juan saw the familiar winged darkness passing under the constellations.

"Is it over?" he asked.

She landed, all that darkness retracting into the size and shape of a normal barn owl.

"Is it over?" Juan repeated, more loudly.

Owl hopped across the crinkling ground, tilting her head at the pocketknife, which he'd dropped next to the tote bag of names.

"That's his," Juan explained. "Did you hear my theory about fingerprints? I'd hoped..."

With a gentle coo, Owl pecked at the knife, flipped it into the air, and swallowed it blade first like a circus performer. She ruffled her feathers in satisfaction before flying away.

"*Now* it's over," he realized.

They'd never find a body. Gerald hadn't had a body of his own for a very long time.

But Juan didn't know that yet. At the moment, all he knew was fear. He couldn't move, afraid of falling in the dark. He was afraid he'd get lost out here, that nobody would find him. He was afraid of other monsters, of things he didn't understand, and of the life he understood too well. He was afraid of missing work, of not missing work, of being alone, of being with others. He was afraid that the tingle in his throat was more than a sign of dehydration.

Then, his phone dinged, indicating that his last message had finally gone through.

One bar.

Where are you? Sofía messaged.

Quickly, before he lost connectivity again, Juan activated his "Find my Family" app and sent Sofía his coordinates.

With that, Juan tucked his phone in the pocket over his heart and waited for the sun to rise.

NETI-NETI
Geetanjali Vandemark

INHALE. HOLD. EXHALE.

5 a.m. and the slum is already thrumming. I light an incense, shave my head in the dark, and sit on my reed mat, cross-legged. I'm in a one-room flat on the fifty-third floor, where the air smells of dried fish and the walls are as thin as stale rotis. The Followers of Dharma sing their morning prayers to the beat of drums. A baby cries in the stairwell. The creak of pulleys reverberates up the recycling shaft.

The buildings in Mota-Nagar slum are a jumble of water harvesters, vertical farms, and boarded-up rooms where the plaster and concrete has fallen away and rusting re-bars show through. Balaji, the slumlord, runs a recycling plant under the building. He has re-purposed elevator wells to move junk up and down the floors. Workers—the dregs of humanity—sort metals, fabrics, and synthetics. The central cluster of buildings are caged in bamboo scaffoldings. Every ten to fifteen floors, suspension bridges connect the buildings together—bridges made with ropes, bamboo, and wooden planks, all reinforced with recycled alloys and held together by guy wires. Every bridge has a toll. Every building a territory. Mota-Nagar is Balaji's flourishing empire.

Balaji has given me my room, and has kept my secret safe, for old times' sake. I have to work for him, of course. It's as if I never left.

I lower my heart rate.

Please, Mother, today.

I call my Master "Mother." She ordained me, gave me a new life, a new purpose, and a new name—Sister Radha. But that doesn't make me a monk. Not really.

"Now, now, Radha," I imagine my Master saying. She often appears in my thoughts when I least want her, and never when I need her. "You are a monk because you chose to be one. And a monk is what a monk does."

A monk is what a monk does.

My Neti-Neti necklace is in the wooden alms bowl at my feet. It's made of seven strands, each strung with opalescent black stones, one thousand and one in all. Lethal. On the unordained, it might as well be a dead body's garland. I pick it up and brush the beads with my fingers; they are cold, smooth, and heavy—my rosary for the last two months. I place it around my neck. The stones begin to glow, then pulse to the rhythm of my heart.

An icy cold climbs from my neck, to my chin, to my eyes—until all my head feels numb. I sense a void open above me—a void that the scriptures call Neti-Neti. Neither this nor that. The other world.

The void becomes a whirlpool. It pulls at my very being. I resist; I hold my breath, and then release it slowly, a long exhale. Spirit from my body, I arise, and pass into a dark place. The world undulates. I feel as if currents of water are pulling at me. My body is below, and far above, there is a light. But it's too far. Unbearably far.

We live in the body, pass through the dark sea, and then cross over into the light. Death is just another journey.

Every day I swim between the two worlds. Every day I search for Nadira.

I did not murder Nadira. I did much worse. I trapped her here, where she might remain forever. There is no life here, no aging, only the instance of death itself. Nadira has been here for the last five years. Screaming.

Being, spirit—these words are not the ones in the ancient

texts of Rinpoche, nor are they adequate. The word my Master taught me is Jiva. It is an ancient word that means the essence of being. It encompasses memories, feelings, senses, and all things perceived by the body. Jiva is far more than awareness, more than ego, more than consciousness. It is the sum of them all and more; it anchors us into our bodies, to life.

It is my Jiva that rises into the Neti-Neti sea. The necklace is a fine blade that slices the ties between the body and the Jiva, one breath at a time.

I begin my search.

Nadira.

I call out with my monk's sense in the dark. Occasionally when someone is about to die, a spark of their Jiva appears. As they die, it transforms into a brilliance and flashes by, into the light above. But then I am left in the dark again.

Death is freedom. Death is peace, but death only comes when the Jiva leaves the body. To those trapped in the sea, it is darkness in eternity.

"Where do we all go after death?" My Master would quiz me on the scriptures.

"Into the Neti-Neti," I'd answer.

"What does the mandala swim in, Radha?"

"Neti-Neti," I'd answer.

Neti-Neti surrounds our world. The whole of the mandala, full of stars, swims in it.

"But what *is* Neti-Neti?" I'd ask.

"Neti-Neti," she'd answer. Not this, nor that.

I dive back into the sea. But I do not perceive the light of Nadira.

Why do you test me, Mother? Why won't you help me?

"Now, now, Radha," she says, "All is as it should be."

And there. A very small point of light. There's a wail from the light. I perceive pain and fear. I swim towards it, towards Nadira. But there is knocking on the door now. Loud, urgent, and persistent.

My breath falters and I feel the necklace slice at my Jiva.

I gasp. My Jiva is caught in the whirlpool. The sea rises around me. I have to let go of my search.

I find the eye of the whirlpool, the opening to the world below, but I struggle to free myself. I reach down to grab hold of my body. The necklace is a riptide. I am pulled back into the sea. I hold my breath and with force of will I tug at the necklace. It loosens its grip and I fall back into my body.

I throw the necklace off and take deep breaths.

"You piece of elephant dung!" I shout at the door.

So much for mind control. My voice is hoarse, my mouth is dry. I rub my face, my head, my neck. I just want to stay sitting, but I have a job and a calling. I go to the door.

It is Romil, Balaji's son. He is lying face up, legs sprawled, a single bullet hole in his chest. Expensive boots. Good clothes—a crisp white shirt under a light blue suit. Soiled with blood.

You give me Balaji's son, Mother? Have the saints swallowed my luck? Why him? Why not bloody Balaji himself?

Romil is just a teen who has grown too fast. Frail for his height. He came to me in this state once before. Too many drinks, a dare gone too far. He knew Sister Radha would save him.

"Only one bullet? In the chest? Coward. Show me three and I'd be impressed. But today isn't your day, is it?"

As I bend down to check his breathing, Romil opens his eyes, and then that pathetic excuse of a lowlife smiles. Smiles, knowing a monk cannot refuse him and will save him.

I rest my head on the door. "Path of Peace. Path of Peace," I mutter to myself.

It is my initiation mantra. The mantra is a bond between Master and student, and is only earned after years of living the life of a monk. Every monk has her special mantra. I would never have chosen this one for myself.

I look up and complain. "This is a path to stupidity, Mother. True peace is death. And instead, I must save them. The monk's way is the stupid way. Why did I become a monk?"

I know why. And a monk is what a monk does.

I drag Romil by his ankles into the room. A trail of blood smears the floor. I check his pulse. It's faint, but there is still time to save him. And time enough to complain as well.

"It's all about intentions and actions, Mother." I put Romil on the rattan mat. "Actions. Not words. You said it, not me. There is The Path and there is *my* path. I am doing good karma, aren't I? Then don't ask me for good words."

The extent of my conversations in this world is almost always one-sided: either blessings, begging for alms, or nodding as I listen to people's woes. My arguments, on the other hand, are with my Master. Or worse, with myself.

He can still die.

But he is Balaji's son.

But I am a monk. With a purpose.

I mutter profanities. If the monks at the monastery knew, they'd throw me off a mountain cliff. Profanities, like my deeds, have followed me like my shadow.

Next to my mat is a dwarf willow, Mother's Jiva Plant. I stole it when I fled the monastery. There are worse crimes.

I choose the longest stalk and pinch it off. A red teardrop forms at the tip. I hurry to the kitchen, put a kettle on the stove, drop the strand in it. The water bubbles and gives off a foul smell.

"I am telling you, Mother, this boy got into another dare, recorded being shot, and when I revive him, he will sell the feed to get life coins. Which he will waste away on another party. And Sister Radha will save him again."

I carry the steaming kettle to the boy's side, take a spoonful of the liquid, blow on it, and pour it into Romil's mouth.

"Give me one reason, Mother, why this worthless boy shouldn't die?" I whisper.

The Jiva Plant does its work; Romil's body shakes. He takes a deep breath. I try to give him one more spoonful, but he turns from it.

"I am trying to save you, gadhe." I grab his jaw. "Drink it!" I force it down. Then I tear his shirt and pour two spoonfuls on his wound. He strains against me, but I hold him down.

"Yes, yes, you will live now. For a while at least."

Balaji has me saving his other gangsters, too. His doctors stitch them up later.

I was as young and foolish as Romil once. I was called Panna, then. Panna's job was to kill for Balaji; now I keep his gangsters alive.

"Who will clean this? You?" I point a finger at Romil. I take a rag and wipe away the mess.

"Does it matter to any of you that my life will be interrupted? No. Do you care about why I am here? No. Should I be saving your life? No no no." I am on my knees, scrubbing the same spot furiously.

Romil is Balaji's son, and that means someone will come looking for him soon. I don't have much time.

What if I lose Nadira? I look at the necklace.

I must save Nadira, Mother. Didn't you give me this mission?

Romil's pulse is faint. I light an incense, breathe in the fragrant smoke, and still my mind. I wear the necklace and begin again. I roll up a towel, put it over Romil's face, and hold it down. Romil does not struggle.

I am sorry, Mother.

Inhale. Hold. Exhale.

My Jiva rises into the void. The Neti-Neti sea is dense; I feel like I am enveloped by a viscous mass that I cannot swim in. I see the feeble light of Romil's Jiva, ready to escape at any moment. He is just a few breaths away from death.

Romil's Jiva grows brighter, rises higher.

Three breaths away.

Bigger, closer. Brighter.

And then the flash. Glorious. Peaceful, heavenly.

It flies past me. Gone. Into the light above.

Romil is dead, leaving a body behind. A body that Nadira can reincarnate into.

I reach for her.

"Nadira, come with me, I am here."

I sense that her Jiva is disoriented. I grab her. She recognizes who I am, what I did to her, and I sense her fear. She recoils, and her Jiya slips. I clutch it again. Slowly, gently, I guide her to the place where Romil's light had emerged. And then down the whirlpool, I drag her with me. I push her flailing Jiva into the body of the boy who was once Balaji's son Romil.

Now he is Nadira, reincarnated.

And then I come back, throw my necklace off, and take the towel off Nadira's face.

"Nadira? Nadira?" I shake her. Is she inside Romil?

Romil's body convulses, takes one breath, and then two. She is here.

I hug my knees and rock. "Thank you, Mother," I whisper. I thank her over and over.

Nadira will wake up soon, screaming. Remembering the agony of the years of living her nightmare, I must give her a true death. The way it was supposed to happen years ago.

It should never have happened.

Once more I hold the towel above the face of Romil. My hand shakes.

"Your mission is done, isn't it?" I hear my Master say.

"I have not saved her, Mother. Not yet. Her life will be hell."

There are mad footsteps in the hallway.

"Romil!" someone shouts. My door flies open. It is Shani, Balaji's right-hand man.

Oh saints, how I hate you all.

I set the towel aside.

"How is he? How is Romil?"

Nadira stirs. I pour a spoonful of liquid in her mouth. That should keep her sleeping. But just for a while.

And then? Foolish, foolish Radha.

"He's safe?" Shani asks.

"Unfortunately, yes."

Shani gives me a look. He wipes his face with his sleeve, which smudges the ash on his forehead. He never takes holy ash from me, nor does he ever touch my feet. It's as if he knows I am less than a monk.

I was petite when we worked together. But at the monastery, I moved my Jiva into a Tamil woman's body, dark and tall. Her nose and ears are pierced—they are of no use to me. She has given birth. Her breasts sag. It is a pliable body; used to lots of demands. Sometimes, if I am not careful, I think I am speaking Hindish, but it's Tamil that comes out.

Shani mutters an expletive but checks Romil's pulse and then calls Balaji.

"Dada, Romil is here. Yes, he is with Sister now." Shani looks at Romil. "Yes, he is breathing, and it seems like—" He glances at me. I nod. "—he will be fine."

"Chalo," he says. Let's go. He lifts Romil and carries him in his arms. I swallow hard.

We will take him to Balaji's den, three buildings away, where a doctor will treat Romil. I fill a flask with the liquid, pick up my begging bowl, and tuck the necklace into my burlap bag.

WE GO FIVE floors down to the refuge area, which is an entrance to the first of many bridges we will take. We approach the toll keeper. He looks at Shani and recognizes Romil. He does not ask questions, just makes a checkmark in his register. I used to mockingly curse him in a friendly greeting when I was Panna.

"Peace to you, my son," I say. He ignores me.

Shani steps onto the bridge, surefooted. He has been doing this for years. I hold the thick rope railing and follow him. I have known these bridges far longer than him. I could run on them once, but I still need to get used to this tall body. Far below, the sprawl is a scrawl of color—blue tarpaulins, lime white adobe houses, and red brick buildings. On narrow lanes between them, a mix of donkey carts and electric rickshaws move like ants.

We cross the bridge to the next building and go down several floors to arrive at the bazaar.

The entire floor at this level is stripped of its interior walls. This is a bustling market, a different kind of market every day of the week—hardware and tools some days, farmers markets on others. Today is cloth market. Vendors have arranged their fabrics on the tables. Each one is shouting out their price. In aisles between the tables people bargain for sarees and kurtas. They sift through buttons, ribbons, and laces. The market shimmers like brocade.

An old woman wearing a bright green saree offers me a quick namaste. A woman who is carrying a baby bundled on her back is selling boiled eggs. She gives me one.

"Bless you," I say, and hand her a pinch of holy ash, "A long and happy life to you and your baby, my dear."

A man carrying a large flask and cups goes up and down the narrow aisles between the vendors, selling coffee. I can starve at will, but the Tamil woman I wear loved coffee. My body stirs at the deep, rich aroma of the brew. I have broken so many vows, what is a cup of stimulant?

Mother, I need some filter coffee today.

Monks don't save money or food. We beg for alms and eat from what is given. The man offers me a cup. I can't help but grab it as we hurry on. It might just be my last, once Nadira wakes up.

There are a few curious looks as Shani carries Romil's body by, but beyond that, they ignore us.

A man wearing gold-tinted sunglasses blocks my way. He bends over and touches my feet. He wears ten rings, each a different color, each to please a deity. I see him often. He is a gambler and hopes that a monk's blessing might change his fortune. I give him a pinch of the holy ash. He puts it on his forehead. He looks for cash in his pocket like always, but today he has none.

"Nothing for you today, Sister."

His gods need payment.

"I'll take your worries, then, my son." They'll fill a bottomless well, I am sure.

"Stop bothering Sister," Shani says, "Let's go."

The gambler hesitates, reaches into his pocket, and pulls out a black die. He places it in my bowl. "Sister, it's the dice to the Laxmi lottery."

At some time today or tomorrow, the dice will light up with encoded numbers. One lucky person in the slum will not have to work for Balaji for a whole month.

"Sister does not gamble," Shani says. He shifts Romil's body and takes the die.

Maggots. Every one of you. Your Jivas are not worth recycling.

TWO ALMS AND twenty blessings later, we arrive at the recycling plant where men and women line the sides of a conveyer belt. They sort, pick, and toss things into bins next to them.

A worker maneuvers a crane that moves a square of compressed, crushed metal. The waste hovers between the floor and the grinder. It falls with a clang and the plant groans loudly.

The floor vibrates. I feel it through my bare feet. Across a few grated gangways, we arrive at the only functioning elevator in the slum: a dumpster that'll take us to Balaji's penthouse. Two armed men wave wands over us, pat us down, and then help us climb into it. The dumpster moves upward, rattles, and it feels like forever as we ride the dark shaft.

We emerge into a bright hallway; here, the air is different. Clean. Cool. The sounds are muffled. At the far end is the door to Balaji's den. His Reincarnation Palace in the sky, where I work.

Nadira has not stirred.

BALAJI'S REINCARNATION PALACE looks like some beauty parlor in the slum. White walls, warm lights. There's a bowl of candies in red wrappers that rests on the front desk. A plastic bonsai sits lifeless next to it. Around the plastic tree is a tableau of miniature figurines—gods of life and death, and gods of gold and wisdom, and gods of metals, machinery, and food. But the impressive height of the skyscrapers through the window reveals who the real god of the slum is.

The rest of the space's furnishings are sparse. Two beds for the bodies, saline stands, heart monitors. A plastic chair between the beds. A desk for the doctor on the side. A glass cupboard with medicines. Very functional. Very Balaji.

Near the front desk advertisements play over and over on a display: an old man dives from a high floor in the slum. Midflight, he morphs into a young man with a ripped body, grabs a rope bridge, and swings from it. In another ad, a young woman throws a bunch of coriander into the air and transforms into a muscular, sword-wielding soldier fighting in a ring. A crowd surrounding her cheers.

I make them happen, the reincarnations, and Balaji makes the money. Balaji's clients from the slum are young and reckless, and those from a better world are rich and old. The doctor takes them to the edge of death, while I lift their Jiva out of their body and move it into another. Sometimes I swap bodies, but other times one of them is already dead. I don't ask questions. There are worse crimes.

"Romil!" Balaji rushes towards us. Shani puts Romil down gently on a bed.

"He is safe," I say. "Don't disturb him. He needs time to heal."

"The doctor is on his way, Dada," Shani says.

Balaji turns to me and does an elaborate namaste. "I am in your debt, Sister."

He wears a flashy pink shirt and a black jacket. The gold chains from his earrings are pinned to his gelled hair.

Genuflect then, you evil rat.

He holds out his palm. I give him a pinch of holy ash like always, which he smears on his forehead. When he says "Sister," knowing fully well who I am, what I did for him, I sometimes wonder if he might call me by my real name, Panna, by mistake. But I am ordained. He believes I am a monk now. People like him revere those who travel through the other world. They find divinity in such things.

The same Balaji asked me and Shani to burn this place years ago, before it belonged to him. Shani and I were the ones who helped him win it. Nadira was in the middle of being reincarnated by another monk. The monk did not survive, nor did Nadira's body. Nadira's Jiva was trapped in the Neti-Neti.

Balaji knew what he was doing, what it would do to Nadira. The monk pleaded. Balaji laughed. I didn't.

Sometimes one does not need a different body to become a different person.

"Shani, you did well." Balaji hugs him.

"He is my brother, Dada."

Balaji looks at me, grinning even wider. "I will trouble you for one more hardship, Sister," he says. "A little inconvenience tomorrow, that's all. Special red-hot action coming at your door." He winks. "Get it?"

I clench my jaw, "Anything to repay your kindness." I force a smile.

Romil's body convulses, his arms and legs flail; Nadira is waking up into a sedated body.

"Let me give him some brew." I pull my flask from my bag.

Romil opens his eyes and screams. He tries to get up, but Shani holds him down. Romil looks around, sees Shani and Balaji. There is a recognition in his eyes.

"Save me, Balaji." Romil whispers. He looks scared.

I try to get Romil to sip the liquid, but he flinches.

"Wait," Balaji says. Romil would have addressed him as "father." Never by his name.

"It is you, isn't it?" Balaji takes the boy's face in his hands and looks into his eyes. I can tell he knows something is wrong.

"What is your name, boy?"

"Nadira."

Balaji turns to me. "What did you do?"

I take a step back.

"Panna," he whispers, "What did you do to my Romil?"

"Balaji, he was dead," I say. "On the life of my Master, I swear this to be true."

Balaji is never without his gun; he takes it out. I back away, but Balaji fires.

"Mother!" I scream with pain. My legs buckle and I fall on my knees. I clutch my stomach.

Balaji grabs me by my throat. "Where is Romil?" he asks. His voice is calm. "Where is my son?"

I say nothing.

Balaji drags me to the window, throws it open, and holds my head over it. The wind whines in my ears. He puts the barrel of his gun to my head. "Did you kill him, Panna?" He tightens his grip on my throat.

I feel weaker, lightheaded. I'm growing cold, but a sense of calm descends. I stare at Balaji. "I did much worse," I say through my labored breathing. "I put him where you put Nadira."

Balaji is silent a moment. "You? A monk?"

"Why do you think I became a monk?" I claw my fingernails into his hands on my throat, and kick my legs.

With a jerk, he lets me go, takes my burlap bag and pulls out my necklace. I gasp as I suck in air.

"Bring him back."

He puts the necklace around my neck and holds my hands down. I've no strength to pull free. A familiar chill rises. My heart beats fast.

Mother, this is not how it should be.

The void appears. It forms into a whirlpool. My Jiva is sucked into the Neti-Neti.

* * *

IN A SEA of hurt, and anger, and sadness, and madness, I float. There is nothing but the dark. There are no more bodies in which to hide. Except the one holding me.

Balaji's body.

I have never incarnated into a living person before. There is a word for that in the monastery. Pishacha. A possessed body. There are other hells besides being stuck in between worlds. No monk would ever do such a thing. But when was I ever a monk?

I let go of my body, and I swim through the darkness of the Neti-Neti. The Jiva of Balaji should be close, very close. I search for the void, the opening of the world below. I swear all the way down into Balaji's body.

He senses me. We stumble, we fall, and convulse on the floor. The monk's body lies lifeless next to us. Balaji screams. There are words in Tamil and Hindish.

I feel Balaji's hand holding the gun. My hand, my gun. I wrestle for control. I raise Balaji's gun to our head. Balaji is scared. Our hand jerks; the gun is tossed on the floor. We struggle to get up. We look out the window, at the slum below and around, and the bridges. He sees his empire, I see the people trapped in this world and next.

It is all as it should be, Mother.

Inhale. Hold. Exhale.

I jump.

Neti-Neti is all.

Neti-Neti is.

Neti-Neti.

EQUAL FORCES OPPOSED IN EXQUISITE TENSION
John Chu

FATHER WAS GUEST lecturing on the other side of the campus, but Tam Ritter could feel his presence anyway. This was the unfortunate cross-product of a singular mind—one that Tam knew too well—on Father's part, and excessive telepathy on his own part. Right now, Father's presence was like a harness cinching his shoulders, squeezing his chest, strapping him to the chair. Everyone else waiting their turn for orals sat slouched or hunched, but Tam sat ramrod straight, too nervous for any other posture.

They had all done well enough in the high exams to earn the Academy's final admission oral. The school didn't need a name more specific than "the Academy". Everyone knew which university you meant. Father had made it clear that only the Academy, his alma mater, would be acceptable for his son.

Someone stepped into the waiting room. He immediately locked his gaze on Tam and walked over.

Tam made the man out as an archivist-grade telepath. He was barely older than Tam, and also the most beautiful person Tam had ever seen. Just physically stunning. Visible even through the shirt and pants, the tension in the reciprocal pairs of muscles in the man's taut body balanced itself out exactly. He was both poised to spring and perfectly relaxed. He radiated both a hardness and a graceful ease that separated him from everyone else in the room. Everyone else in the world. They all seemed gawky and ungainly.

Then again, Tam had lived all of his life with Father at an engineering camp next to the Barricade, the vast wall of machinery that protected the world from Turbulence. It wasn't as if Tam had met a wide range of people. Also, everyone else here was about to take their admissions exam whereas this man, as a student of the Academy, had already passed his. So the man had no reason to be nervous and stiff.

The man glided languidly toward him. It probably just looked like walking to everyone else, except they weren't paying attention. To Tam, though, no one else was as pleasingly proportioned or as just plain satisfying to look at. He could study that body forever.

When Tam's critical faculties finally restarted, it occurred to him that the man was too telepathic to avoid the surface thoughts racing through his mind. The man's smile tamped down Tam's panic. No harm done. Tam's rather naked admiration might have even been welcome, but Tam quickly convinced himself that that was wishful thinking or, more likely, some sort of stress-induced delusion.

"I'm Dunster Lian. You are the only person in the room who would need their mind monitored for unauthorized mindreading, so you must be Tam Ritter." Dunster offered his long, lithe hand. "Named after the engineer they write legends about? The Chief Engineer of the Barricade?"

"He's my father," Tam said as he shook Dunster's hand. "When I was born, I don't think anyone thought of him as the real-life version of some hero from the Five Great Classical Novels."

"Still, that's a tough name to live up to. I'm sorry." Dunster sat next to him. "So you had to apply here?"

"Well, yes and no." Tam felt like he should have been offended, but he sensed only curiosity in Dunster's words. "Having tested into being allowed to apply here, I would have disappointed Father if I hadn't."

"I mean, you're an archivist-grade telepath. How did the Library School not bring you in?"

"They did." Tam slouched into his chair. "I have an exam slot this afternoon. Dad would probably like it if I trained to be an archivist like him instead of following in Father's footsteps. Not that there are many archivists like Dad."

Father was a legendary engineer. When Tam was six, Father met Dad, an equally accomplished archivist. Dad took one look at Tam and, honestly, from then on there was no satisfying either parent, much less both of them at once. The only saving grace was that Tam had their consent to read both their minds, just as Dad had consent to read Tam's. At least their expectations were transparent.

Dad wanted to be here, but he was in the hinterland beyond the Barricade right now, shepherding back a feral library. Some level of telepathy was necessary to enter the hyperdimensional space within a library's mind and organize the books within. Few archivists were skilled enough and telepathic enough to do safely what Dad was doing now. No one wanted to be lost in the hinterland, lashed by a library's thick prehensile trunk, or gored by its translucent tusks.

"Wait. You can reify things as well as read minds? That basically never happens. Occasionally, it's one or the other. Usually, it's effectively neither." Dunster stared at Tam as though he were some mythical beast and yet there in the flesh. "You must have been a handful as a kid."

"Two handfuls." Tam pursed his lips. "Look, I consent to whatever access you need to monitor me for the exam. You can check for yourself how well I can reify."

Nontelepaths couldn't tell when someone reached into their minds. That was why the examiners needed Dunster to make sure Tam wasn't cheating. Tam felt Dunster delicately parting and turning the leaves of his mind. He tried to get used to the sensation, because it was going to happen a lot over the course of the exam.

A pale, broad-shouldered man stepped into the waiting room. He called for Tam in a robust baritone, then went back into the exam room. Tam and Dunster looked at each other, stood up in unison, and went into the exam room.

FIVE EXAMINERS SAT behind a table only about five feet away in front of Tam. Surface emotions were well-nigh impossible for him to avoid, especially at this distance. All five of them instantly recognized him and hid the shock from their faces. Literally every engineer Tam had ever met was surprised to find that Tam Ritter, Jr. looked like a younger version of Tam Ritter, Sr. Literally every engineer knew what his father looked like, and for about fifteen seconds they all thought they were meeting his father. The disappointment that bloomed in their minds got old quickly.

They stared at him for what felt like five awkward years but was probably only thirty seconds before anyone managed to introduce themself. They were, from Tam's left to right, Professors Shan, Tuuk, Vangas, Teti, and Faye. Professor Vangas was the one who had called Tam in. They all noted the extra person who entered the room with him and made the obvious inference.

"Try to look in my mind as much as you want." Professor Faye's sardonic tone didn't need telepathy to unpack it. He spread his arms out. "Feel free."

"You are not to take that as a grant of consent." Dunster's words were sharp and serious. He was now on the job.

"I wasn't going to." Tam rolled his eyes.

The first questions weren't a big deal. Anyone who made it this far had a working knowledge of mechanics. Not giving him paper and pencil seemed like a pointless extra challenge. Father had explained, in excruciating detail, how the exam was supposed to go. Tam was sure they had to supply him with paper and pencil. He was seriously tempted to reify some for himself, but the problems weren't anything he couldn't solve in his head anyway.

He ended up reifying some of his answers. As the questions grew more difficult, it was just easier for him to create hardware that demonstrated the answers. He dismissed the hardware when he was done each time, so it wasn't like he was littering the room with discarded machines.

Based on their glares, the examiners found all the reifying unusual. According to Father, most candidates simply explained the solution after working it out on paper. If he had had some paper and a pencil, he would have done that.

Things didn't get truly weird until he was actually supposed to reify something. Professor Faye asked a long, complicated question that eventually boiled down to "reify a rather cryptically specified tensegrity chair in one go." The other examiners all stared at him oddly as he spewed clause after clause. Generally, candidates got asked to reify a pulley of a specified mechanical advantage, maybe a universal joint of some sort if the candidate was doing particularly well. In Professor Faye's defense, Tam had already gone beyond that.

"You don't have to do that," Professor Shan said. Her words followed Professor Faye's so closely, they seemed part of the same sentence. "That's not a reasonable problem to give a candidate for undergrad."

Tam couldn't help sensing the examiners' surface thoughts. That wasn't cheating. They all had opinions about him solving this problem. Shan was sympathetic. Timk, Vangas, and Teti were expecting him to fail but were sad about it. Faye was expecting him to fail and was downright gleeful. At least he didn't let that show on his face.

"No, I'll reify the chair." Tam's mutter was soft, and almost a growl. "I wasn't tutored by my father for nothing."

Actually, he loved to reify things. Reifying gave him a respite from other minds occluding his own. As far as he could tell, other telepaths just had to deal with that. He had no idea how they managed.

Everyone who could afford it spent a year preparing for the

high exams. From the games Father played with him as a kid to the problems Father assigned as he grew older, Tam had been preparing for longer than he could remember. He had recognized the pitfalls Professor Faye was setting up for him as he heard them.

Tensegrity required all of a structure's elements to be loaded either in pure compression or pure tension. Everything needed to balance out. Constructing it physically piece-by-piece, someone could adjust the tension of the ropes and reposition the struts as they went along. Reifying any design, however, meant holding it in its full complexity with all of its implications in his head, then making it physical. In this case, he had one shot. The result was going to be either a chair, if he had reified everything in perfect balance, or a dismal pile of struts and ropes, if anything was even a hair off.

Like all tensegrity objects, the chair that appeared before him looked counterintuitive. The seat seemed to float. The back stood upright with no apparent support. Ropes stretched taut, though, where the legs were supposed to be. Other ropes pulled on the chair back with equal tension, balancing it in place.

Professor Faye, oddly offended, rushed over. He bounded onto the chair and started jumping up and down. He stomped down on the seat, trying to force the chair to collapse. Fortunately, Faye was a short, thin man. Even on the chair, he was barely taller than Tam. As it was, the ropes pulsed with each jump. The seat teetered every time he landed on it.

Professor Vangas slowly strode over. He was over a head taller and about twice as broad as Professor Faye. He placed his hands around Professor Faye and lifted him off the chair. Professor Faye squirmed, but he wasn't breaking free.

"That's enough, Fred." Professor Vangas's voice was quiet. "You asked for a chair, not a trampoline."

Professor Vangas carried Professor Faye over his shoulder, then gently lowered him to his seat. Professor Faye fumed. His normally pale face was now flushed with visible rage. Professor Vangas rolled his eyes and grinned at Tam as he sat.

"Don't worry about him, Tam." Professor Vangas shot Professor Faye a look. "Now, does anyone have anything else to ask, or have we seen enough?"

"One final puzzle." Professor Shan's gaze defocused for a moment and a box materialized in her hands. "Open this box."

The other examiners all studied the box as Tam received it from her.

"What happened to 'That's not a reasonable problem to give a candidate'?" Professor Faye made his voice a mincing falsetto when he quoted her.

Both the box and its contents were transparent, practically invisible. Tam barely felt the weight in his hands. Delicate and fragile, everything was composed of that hypothetical material that only exists in proofs of concept. Switches and levers littered the box's surfaces, but there didn't seem to be a lid or anything else to open. The locking mechanism inside was dense and complex but with no thought given to, say, the momentum of spinning gears or the stress on load-bearing struts. None of the inconveniences of real life mattered with this material, but the merest wisp of Turbulence would have vaporized it in an instant. The Barricade, which deconstructed whirring skeins of Turbulence as they lashed against it, had to be constructed from more inconvenient stuff.

The box was barely real. He was in serious danger of ripping it in half by accident. The locking mechanism he was supposed to solve took up all the space inside in the box. No one would ever use a box like this for anything. The ridiculousness and impracticality was intentional and the point.

It occurred to Tam that he had made the test much harder for himself when he solved the tensegrity problem. He had reified an actual working chair composed of actual materials with all of its problematic nonlinearities. Professor Faye had probably had something as theoretical as this box in mind. Stomping on the chair, though, was still weird and uncalled for.

Thinking himself into a mechanism was the other case when

everyone else disappeared from his mind. Father's expectations were still there, but that was on Tam. He could no longer sense Father on the other side of the campus. The judgement of the five examiners no longer lurked in the shadows of his mind. Dunster was undoubtedly still overseeing his thoughts, but Tam could no longer feel him doing so. The pure mathematics implied by the locking mechanism took the place of all of that, and Tam wished it could always be this way.

Except the math didn't make any sense at first. If he was right, several systems of equations couldn't possibly have consistent solutions. It took a minute of study before Tam realized Professor Shan had reified something that didn't function. No flipping of switches or sliding of levers was going to do anything useful.

"I have to figure out what this machine is supposed to do and fix it first," Tam said out loud because the silence was getting to him.

Once he realized that the problem was to figure out the problem, everything fell into place. He scanned the mechanism, noting the changes he had to make: a larger gear ratio here, rotating a subsystem there, altering the properties of the hypothetical material everywhere, and so on. Perversely, the whole contraption would be easier to think about if there was a little more friction. Generally, one used hypothetical materials because non-idealized properties made things more difficult.

He didn't care so much whether any of these things were the right things to do. At this point, he was ready to be done.

Part of him kept thinking about not thinking about the beautiful man who was making sure he wasn't cheating. The rest of him kept looking for some sort of catch or trick as he reified his changes. Everything kept behaving the way he expected it to, though. This just convinced him that he'd overlooked something. The examiners all gasped when he increased the material's friction coefficient. He was thrilled to have no idea why they did that. All he had to do was plow through the changes and this exam would be over.

The box opened. But like a flower. It unfolded itself until it lay flat on his palms. Tam almost dropped it in surprise.

"Very good." Professor Shan smiled. "Usually, if someone actually manages to open the box, they also drop it."

"You give this problem to candidates for undergrad?" Professor Vangas was incredulous and stared at her, jaw agape.

"Oh, don't be ridiculous. Candidates for grad school don't get this problem. That said, since we've apparently already made up our minds about him—" She shot Professor Faye a look. "—there's no reason not to see how far we can push before we run into something he fails at. That seems to be our modus operandi for an entrance exam, right?"

"Should we be having this discussion in front of the candidate?" Professor Teti waved her hand as though she could block the conversation.

"I have to say." Professor Shan moved her attention to Tam. "While changing the friction coefficient is part of the most elegant solution, everyone else who's ever attempted it thus far has embarrassed themselves in the process. Good work."

"See?" Faye pointed at Tam. "He must have had help somehow."

"Fred." Vangas was as mild as Faye was agitated. "Is there anyone else in the room who can do that, much less at a distance?"

"No." The word was forced out of Faye's mouth. "His father could do it. He—"

"Now, I have no idea whether the kid did this or how." Tuuk looked as though she was about to choke Faye. "But his father is on the other side of campus lecturing and has no idea what is happening in here. Not even he can reify something from that far away, not to mention unknowingly."

"Excuse me? Remember me? The guy making sure that he's not cheating?" Dunster raised his hand, then winced when everyone directed their gaze to his ignored corner. "I swear that he did everything himself. For a good chunk of the exam, like when he was reifying, he didn't sense any minds at all. I didn't know there were people capable of both. It's fascinating. And since the question is pretty blatant in the minds of three of you, I will also swear that this is, in fact, the son and not the father. The Academy will expel me if I'm lying about any of this."

"I don't think I should be here for this conversation," Tam stammered. "May I go?"

They excused him. It took every bit of Tam's self-control not to sprint through the door.

He had two sympathetic examiners, two who seemed to want him dead, and one who had probably made up her mind, though Tam didn't know which way. He wondered what one was supposed to do to get into this damn Academy.

THE CIRCULAR COUCH built into the wall was uncomfortable, but at least the jianbing was tasty. Its crispy fried dough and mystery meat—slathered in some sauce made of chili paste and fermented tofu and wrapped in a thin, egg-coated pancake—was sweet and salty and spicy and greasy. It was exactly what he needed after that debacle of an exam. The only thing that would have made it better was the cold beer he'd turned down at the refectory. Well, a cold beer and a more comfortable couch. The one in this lobby of the Music School left a little to be desired.

The Music School was in the building next to the refectory. Tam was sitting here because here wasn't filled with people. He didn't have to work to ignore people's minds. Every once in a while, candidates walked by with their instruments. A few blasted confidence on all frequencies. Most were either trying too hard to tamp down their nerves or buried too deep in themselves reviewing their audition pieces.

He felt Dunster's mind before he saw him. The physically stunning man smiled before he sat next to Tam. He opened his paper bag and took out a jianbing and two bottles of beer.

"Fancy meeting you here." Dunster offered Tam a bottle of beer.

Tam rolled his eyes. Dunster had spent an hour in Tam's mind and was more than telepathic enough to notice a familiar mind here from the refectory.

"No, thanks." He waved the bottle away. "I still have an exam with the Library School this afternoon."

"It's not going to matter." Tam twisted a bottle open, then took a swig. "They're going to offer you a place on the archivist track."

Tam swallowed his last bite of jianbing. He crumpled its paper wrapper, then looked around for a garbage can.

"What makes you so sure?"

"The Library School exam can be a pretty relaxed affair." He put the other bottle back in the bag. "For someone they want, it's really just a glorified information session. Anyone who is telepathic enough and skilled enough that he can't avoid picking out his father on the other side of campus is someone they want."

Of course, Dunster knew about that. Father weighed so heavily on Tam, he imagined that it was unmissable.

"You have me at a disadvantage."

Dunster laughed. He took another swig.

"I suppose I do." Dunster finished off the bottle. "If they accept you — and they will accept you — are you going to go on the archivist track?"

"Engineering School. Library School." Tam shrugged. "Either one would be less work and stress than preparing for the high exams has been."

"Less work?" Dunster took a few strides, tossed the bottle into a garbage can on the opposite wall then sat on the couch again. "You realize you're talking about the Academy, right?"

"You've never been tutored by my father." He crumpled the jianbing's paper wrapper into a tight ball and threw it at the garbage can. It arced through the air and bounced off the wall into the can. Not perfect, but he'd take it. "You really don't have anything better to do."

"You're serious." Dunster sounded incredulous. "You think I'm physically stunning. I think you're an astounding slab of beef. I mean, not only one of those, but still one nevertheless. If the archivists need me for something, they can stick the thought in my head. Spending time with you is exactly what I want to do right now."

"I'm an astounding slab of beef?" Tam wasn't sure whether that was a compliment or degrading.

"Didn't you notice what passed through my mind when I first saw you?" Dunster buried his face in his hands. "Any telepath who took one look at you—fine, *us*—would assume we can't help but know whatever happened to be wafting through their mind."

"Oh, I thought that was just wishful thinking. I was a bit stressed at the time."

"Fair." Dunster picked up the bag. "Look, I can stare at you all day, or I can show you the pipe organ built into the concert hall. For some reason, prospective engineering students find the pipe organ fascinating."

"I'd love to, but should probably go to the Library School." Tam frowned. "Wait for my exam."

"Why? You returned the consent form signed, right? They'll put the thought in your mind when it's your turn. Come on. Pipe organ."

THE PIPE ORGAN was magnificent. It filled the entire back wall of the stage of the cavernous concert hall. The keyboards, pedals, and seat rested on a platform five feet in the air and surrounded by a railing. Its pipes stood on either side in bilateral symmetry.

Tam stood on stage and drank it all in. His mind plunged into the pipe organ's myriad switches and actuators. He reveled in their precision, the elegant symmetry of the design as a whole. This fabulous beast was a spectacular feat of engineering. Tam let it consume him. He stood there for seconds, or maybe days, just exploring its intricacies.

Dunster tapped Tam on the shoulder. "Do you play?"

Tam snapped back into himself. It took a second and an involuntary glance at Dunster's thoughts before he could answer.

"Piano." Tam shrugged. "A little."

"Do you want to?" Dunster grinned.

Tam leaped for the railing. He pulled himself up hand over hand, then flipped himself onto the platform.

"Well, then." Dunster started to walk into the wings. "I'm going to take the elevator like a normal person."

Tam sat in front of the keyboards. Dunster emerged, turned the pipe organ on, and adjusted the stops. He nodded to Tam, who immediately launched into his favorite fugue. It actually required four hands, but not until about a quarter of the way through. He wanted Dunster to join in, but he wouldn't let himself hope. Tam had no idea whether Dunster even played or, if he did, whether he knew the piece.

The fugue subject surrounded Tam. The tonal answer partnered it with tight precision and grace. One by one, other voices entered the fugue, each one perfectly interlocked with the others and yet also independent.

"A little?" Dunster was distinctly amused. "I play 'a little,' too. I can join in?"

Tam nodded. Dunster sat down on the bench next to Tam. When Tam ran out of hands, Dunster took over, playing the 3rd and 4th hands on the upper keyboard.

For a few minutes, they could have been one person with four arms. Their hands crossed and uncrossed as though they'd worked out the logistics and had practiced together for weeks. One voice threw the subject to another to yet another, passing it seamlessly from Tam's hands to Dunster's hands and back.

Each telepath was focused on the music, but the concentration of his partner played in counterpoint in the back of his mind. Their playing flowed and swelled. It was exhilarating, exhausting, and uncanny. There was an underlying warmth and gentleness, though, and Tam gave himself to the performance, partnering with Dunster in the interlocking dance of voices.

The fugue ended with a stretto, a composition device where one voice enters with the subject before the previous voice has finished stating it. Voice after voice tumbled into each other in ever more rapid succession until each was entering just one beat after the previous voice. Dunster hit a pedal tone as the fugue wound through a series of false resolutions, delaying its climax, never truly hitting tonic until the very end.

The final, tonic chord hung in the air. Tam's heart raced and it was a moment before either man could look at the other.

"So." Tam stared through Dunster, resisting the temptation to dig into his mind to find out what he thought had happened. "Do you play a fugue with every candidate to the Academy?"

The question set Dunster's mind racing. What had happened had taken Dunster by surprise as much as it had Tam. They were just two young telepaths, not yet in full control of their abilities, who let things get away from them.

"What? No." Dunster looked appalled. "That was literally the first time I've even touched the concert pipe organ. Normally, if I'm showing off the pipe organ, I'm conducting a tour. Besides, the only candidates who care are the Music School and Engineering School candidates, and they wouldn't know what I was thinking if I told them."

Both of them wanted to change the subject. Desperately.

"Say, how much of the campus have you seen, anyway?" Dunster rubbed his hands. "Maybe I should give you the rest of the tour? We can go to a pen and I can introduce you to some libraries. The tame ones. The school doesn't let undergrads anywhere near the feral ones."

Dunster filled the walk to the library pen with anecdotes about the buildings they passed. The path they were taking illustrated the history of the last century of architecture in chronological order. It was obvious when they hit the point when Father's drastic revision of the Barricade held off a thousand-year storm of Turbulence and architects began to experiment and design buildings that deserved to last again. The theater complex was literally reconfigurable, although once it had gotten stuck splayed out like a deconstructed flower for a year until they had the budget to repair it. The chemistry buildings had rooms on alternating floors, so any explosions would destroy only empty space above and below them.

The anecdotes were Dunster trying very hard to impress him. Tam knew. Dunster knew Tam knew and hoped it was working anyway. Paying attention to what flowed through the mind of a telepath you were talking to was like holding a mirror up to a mirror.

Honestly, Tam would rather have not known. Then Dunster taking him to meet some libraries would have just been some helpful archivist-track undergrad making a pitch for the Academy.

Tam noticed the libraries long before they got anywhere near them. A bunch of catalogues tickled the back of his mind. He could explore them and find out the contents of each library if he put his mind to it.

Naturally, Dunster noticed. His excitement kicked his charm and grace to levels Tam hadn't realized existed. His smile scorched, his every movement so exquisite, his every sentence so perfectly formed in both substance and rhythm that the experience verged on the heartrending.

Tam was vaguely aware that he was surely lowering the bar for Dunster, seeing everything the physically stunning man did as more perfect than it actually was. That understanding didn't stop walking next to him from feeling like walking next to some god who had stepped out of the Five Great Classical Novels.

"Dunster, stop being so impressive," Tam shouted when he couldn't take it anymore. "I keep expecting you to transcend to a higher level of consciousness and become one with the universe."

"Would that help?" Dunster joked. "You're so... anxious."

"Father didn't actually say—or even think, in my presence—that if I don't earn a place in the Engineering School, he would disown me, but..." Tam shrugged. "I think I'm allowed some anxiety."

In the end, they had to go their separate ways before they reached the library pen. That was okay, really. Archivists shepherding back feral libraries always stopped at Father's engineering camp on the way back to civilization. Dad wouldn't let him anywhere near those. The libraries who lived at camp, though, were tame, and Tam already knew them well. He'd been working in them for years. One massive black beast with translucent tusks looked very much like another, swishing their thin tails or drinking with their trunks. He could only ever tell them apart by their catalogues, anyway, and he'd already sensed those.

Instead, when they were most of the way there, Tam got the message to report for his exam. The unexpected thought jolted him to a stop. If he hadn't felt it happening, he might have thought he'd always known that this was when he needed to report.

In front of the examination room, Dunster held Tam's gaze an instant too long to be exquisitely graceful. He pursed his lips, then stared at the bag he'd been carrying all this time. The proctor called for Tam. Dunster fumbled a pen out of a pocket, ripped off a piece of the bag, then started writing.

"These are my addresses, on campus and when I'm home between terms." Dunster handed Tam the paper. "Let me know how you did today and what you decide."

Tam knew he was supposed to say something, but too many thoughts were coursing through him for anything coherent to come out of his mouth. He just swallowed hard, nodded, and went into the room.

The admissions exam was decided in about the first fifteen seconds, a minute at most. The five examiners sitting behind the table all swept through the relevant bits of his mind as though they were assessing the state of a library's catalogue. Tam had already consented, and was prepared for this. Also, these were archivists, some of the best-trained telepaths on the planet. No one intruded into anywhere they didn't have consent to go.

They nodded sagely at each other. Usually, they asked actual questions and the candidate had to answer them. This time, the thought that there was a spot for Tam on the archivist track if he wanted it lay blatantly on the surface of their minds.

The rest of the exam was mostly the five of them laying out the coursework. There was a lot of pointing out how the Academy had the most rigorous archivist track on the planet. While that was undoubtedly true, it still sounded like a vacation compared to Father preparing him to test into the Academy in the first place. He would enjoy Library School, but admission into the Library School, even onto the archivist track, was not going to satisfy Father one bit.

TAM TRIED TO sneak into Father's last lecture of the day partway through. Father stood at the front of the room. Whiteboards filled with precise graphs and tidy equations stood behind him. A select group of grad students and a bunch of faculty sat around a table, and they all immediately turned around when Tam walked in. Father presented like the incongruous sandstone cliff that had unexpectedly manifested in the middle of prairie. Tam, unfortunately, had inherited that in full measure. The only meaningful difference was that Tam was dressed to impress a bunch of professors and Father was in a T-shirt, coarse trousers, and a well-worn set of boots that had seen years of climbing the Barricade.

Everyone but Father stared, stunned by the doppelgänger at the rear of the room. Father smiled. The smile always made Father seem even more intimidating, if only to Tam. It wasn't intentional. Father was just pleasantly surprised to see him attend. Nevertheless, the crush of implicit expectations to come threatened to buckle his knees.

Tam stood in the back of the room, trying to be invisible. Father continued his lecture and everyone else, focused again on the father, forgot about the son. Tam was grateful that Father hadn't asked him to sit at the table.

Father expounded on Turbulence, the ways the current models of Turbulence were deficient, and ways to improve the modeling. The motivation, of course, was that the better they understood the mechanisms of Turbulence, the better they could test improvements to the Barricade before they were deployed. Strands of Turbulence destroyed minds and machines alike. By the day, Turbulence storms grew stronger and threatened to overwhelm the Barricade.

Father's native language was calculus. Tam was used to this. Everyone else dealt with it better than they might have, probably because Father started deploying visual aids. As he lectured, he reified mechanical equivalents of whatever system of equations he was talking about in lighter-than-air materials. Each mechanism floated next to him. Air currents softly whirred their gears. Sometimes, to make a point, Father exploded a mechanism so that all of its parts hung separated from each other in the air.

As everyone else followed along, Tam found himself distracted by how easily Father made complex mechanisms appear out of thin air and just as easily dismissed them. Usually, Tam could sense at least some effort as an engineer tried to hold a design in their head. Maybe that was why Father never lectured like this to him. He encouraged Tam to reify those mechanisms for himself.

Father posed questions to everyone, even the faculty. When they struggled, Father guided them methodically, helping them to construct the answers for themselves. Occasionally, he tossed a question to the teenager in the back trying his best to be invisible. Father's casual confidence that his son would whip an answer right back was daunting. His quiet satisfaction and pride when his son didn't drop the question and managed to toss an answer back without prompting should have felt more comforting than it actually did.

The faculty and grad students asked Father their own questions, and when it was all over they applauded. Tam folded his arms across his chest and did his best not to roll his eyes at them. Father, on the other hand, also with his arms folded, had no qualms about rolling his eyes.

As Father tried to leave, they surrounded him with even more questions. He gently parted the crowd, explaining that he had an important appointment. The sincerity surprised Tam. The excuse of an important appointment wasn't just the social lubricant of a man who wanted to get away.

Father whisked Tam out of the room with him. They walked out of the building towards the dorm where the Academy had put them up. Father didn't seem to be in a hurry anymore. Tam screwed up his courage and asked the obvious question.

"Sir." Tam took a deep breath. "What's the important appointment that you needed to rush out of the room for?"

Father stopped walking in a shock that was more mock than anything else. He grinned at Tam. No matter how warm and gentle, that grin would never not make Tam's stomach sink.

"Son." He patted Tam's shoulder. "I wouldn't be late for our dinner. It's been a big day for you. Speaking of which, I have to know what happened during your engineering exam. Fred has been brought up on charges of faculty misconduct."

"Fred" was Professor Faye, the one who'd asked for a tensegrity chair then treated it like a trampoline. Tam dutifully recounted what had happened, beat for beat. He got the sense that he wasn't telling Father anything Father didn't already know. It was a feeling just as familiar as the simultaneous sense that Father wanted to hear it anyway. Tam let his irritation at being asked things they would never have asked any other candidate bleed into his account.

Where the Academy had put them wasn't so much a dorm room as a mini-apartment with its own bathroom and kitchen. Tam suspected they reserved this for special guests like Father.

Father had set the timer on the rice cooker that morning.

The rice was already fully cooked and being kept warm when they got back. Without a word, Father launched into cooking the rest of dinner. After years of helping out, Tam couldn't tell anymore whether he was anticipating Father or reading his mind. Between the two of them, vegetables were chopped and meat was sliced. Father stir-fried while Tam cleaned up. Both the wok and the burner were too impressive for a dorm. The fire suppression gear above the burner was epic.

They sat across from each other at a square table in the living area. Wisps of steam curled up from the bowls of rice that sat in front of each of them. The plate of stir-fried meat and vegetables sat in the middle.

"Go ahead, eat," Father said, but didn't pick up his own chopsticks.

Tam didn't pick up his chopsticks either. Something was coming and, until he knew what, food in his stomach might be a bad idea. Father reached into a pocket and pulled out an envelope. He handed it to Tam.

"I had nothing to do with their decision." Father knew what they'd decided. "But I did ask whether I could present the letter to you."

Tam almost set down the envelope to pick up his bowl and chopsticks. The Academy's decision probably wasn't good if it came this quickly and if Father was making such a production of it. If it was rejection, he'd rather enjoy the meal in relative ignorance before having to face up to it. Father, though, clearly wanted A Talk right now. Tam pulled out a crisply creased sheet of paper, took a deep breath, and unfolded it.

"Engineering is offering me a seat in the graduate school?" Tam looked at Father quizzically.

"Read the rest of the letter." The faint stain of irritation seeped into Father's voice. "You'll be supervised by Professor Shan. I've been trying to poach her for years, but her heart is in theory and the ways to reduce it to practice."

"It is contingent on me also accepting a seat on the archivist track in the Library School." Tam's expression did not get less quizzical.

"Yes." Father looked pensive. "I'm sorry. I have clearly pushed you much too hard these past few years, but you over-achieved beyond even unreasonable expectations anyway. I'm afraid the Academy won't be the vacation you hoped it would be."

Tam had never mentioned his hope. Father just knew because he knew everything. The unspoken thought floating on Father's mind, however, distracted Tam from his usual annoyance that he couldn't hide anything from even the non-telepathic parent.

"You don't want me to accept the offer from the Academy." Tam vocalized Father's thought. "Or go to any university."

Father sighed. If he'd ever regretted his son being absurdly telepathic, Tam had never noticed. Mostly, what Tam sensed now in Father was how he was poised between equally compelling desires.

"It would save a lot of time if you'd just dig into my mind about this sort of thing rather than skimming the surface. You've always had my consent." Father took a deep breath. "What I want is to offer you a job working for me on the Barricade. The most rigorous school on the planet has said you are qualified, so it's not strictly nepotism. It's certainly less work than studying for two degrees at once. And I'll never put you through anything like the last few years again."

"But you want me to do what you don't want me to do?" Tam set the letter down.

"That's a terrible way of thinking about it, Son." Father pursed his lips. "That's how one ties oneself into rhetorical knots."

"But what *you* want me to do is not what you *want* me to do." Tam found it hard to put Father's conflicted thoughts into words.

"What I want is for you to work with me on the Barricade. We need to prevent Turbulence from encroaching any farther. What I also want for you is what *you* actually need. That is, to go to the Academy, spend a few years where I only see you between semesters, get your heart broken—"

Father's brow rose at whatever expression Tam would swear he wasn't making. That happened a lot.

"You met someone today." Father smiled. "You should have invited the fine young man over for dinner."

Tam didn't react, at least not knowingly. Not that it mattered. It was truly unfair that the parent who wasn't telepathic also read him like a book.

"But that would have made you profoundly uncomfortable. Maybe you don't get your heart broken, then. The experience is highly overrated." Father piled stir fry into Tam's bowl. "Come on, Son. Eat."

Father and son drank and ate and chatted. They went over each other's days like they always did. Tam asked about Father's lectures and meetings with the faculty. Father gently inquired about the fine young man who had given Tam a tour of the campus. He pointedly didn't ask Tam about his plans for next year.

The question weighed on Tam anyway. He steeled himself for the excessive amount of work and stress he was about to sign up for and, perhaps, for the physically stunning man to break his heart.

SILK AND COTTON
AND LINEN AND BLOOD
Nghi Vo

LORD YU WAS killed in his court robes. His long jacket was black slubbed silk of the highest quality, nearly stiff enough to stand on its own and with his family's crest embroidered on the split back in gold thread. It was winter, so he wore three layers of bleached under-robes, each growing finer and paler the closer they came to his sacred flesh.

The barbarian king was surprised when he realized that while he could tear flesh by force, the silk between skin and sword remained whole. He watched in fascination when blood stained the silks, and only as an afterthought, he struck off the old lord's head. I imagine that this is how it happened.

He called his men to see the wonder of fabric that could not be pierced, and one of them, smarter than the rest, caught up a cowering maid. She sent him to the Minister of the Chamber, who sent him to the Evening Mistress, who, with faltering step and her hands clenched into fists, led them to me.

I heard them coming down the hallway, a raucous, riotous band that was more like a party than a massacre. On the heels of the Mistress of the Hours, they bashed out the delicate paulownia shutters and knocked the round lanterns down from their hangings. There's no ownership like destruction.

I knelt in front of the bronze-bound door, my hair tied back neatly in a twist of green silk noil. At the time, I was a servant of the third class, and so my hair was allowed to grow down to the middle of my back. I wore a robe of wild silk in indigo, coarse compared to the garments of the Mistresses of the Hours, but perfectly even in weave and in color. The barbarian king noticed none of this as he toed me aside like a troublesome cat, yanking the door open with a clang. Inside the long and dim room, there were no fewer than fifty chests, some carved out of wood, some carved out of jade, but all paneled inside with red cedar. He removed the lid from the closest, a deep blond wood from the northern confederation, and with a shout of triumph, he came up with a fistful of robes in dyed palest yellow.

He thrust them to the man behind him, and the man gleefully donned the sleeping robe of the last dowager, embroidered with her rather trite motto for joy and laughter. It was terrible and funny at once, and I covered my mouth against the horrified laughter at seeing such a thing.

The Evening Mistress touched my shoulder gently, forgotten as I was.

"Do not throw your life away," she murmured, and I sat back on my heels beside her. I didn't want to die, but I couldn't leave either.

We both held our silence until the barbarian lord came to one particular chest. It was a hard dark wood that could not be cut with any knife known to the empire, carved with twisting dragons. It was over two hundred years old, and when he tipped the lid over as carelessly as a spoiled child, I couldn't stop a cry from rising to my lips.

Like a billow of sails, the lavender robes rose from the chest. They were made from the finest silk from two continents, beautiful and perfectly plain, waiting for their seasonal trim. Every seam was joined with more than ten stitches for every two fingers' width, and even in the lamplight of the cool room, they gleamed with a dull luster.

I lurched to my feet, and though the Evening Mistress snatched at my robes, she could not prevent me from staggering forward.

The barbarian might have been startled by my sudden rebellion, but it didn't stop him from swinging his sword up to point at me. I was used to faces painted dead white at court—the redness of his features, as well as the yellow of his hair and beard, looked demon-like to me, piggish.

"What does this one want?" he roared. "Do you want to be run through as your lord was?"

For a moment, my mouth was as dry as powdered tea leaves. I thought he would strike me down for my insolence. Then twenty years of training came to my rescue, and I reached an imploring hand out to him.

"Please," I said, "not that one."

A thundercloud darkened his face and the tip of his sword lifted. I shrank back, but my mouth was wiser than I was.

"Not that one," I repeated. "It's... it is winter, you see? That robe is meant only for the fall, only after the sweet osmanthus blooms and before the first snowfall."

Whatever he had been expecting me to say, it was not that, and as I stood there, hoping that my dead sweat would not carve canyons in my face powder, the barbarian lord started to laugh. He shoved the lavender robe back into the chest carelessly, and I bit my lip. Silk is strong, but oh so fragile in some ways.

"This woman thinks that I should not wear a fall robe in the winter," he told his men, who laughed obediently. "What does this woman think a conqueror should wear, then?"

I found them all looking at me with a kind of dull curiosity, as if a bird had fluttered down in their midst that could speak. A bird who can speak is a wonder, even if it only speaks foolish things.

"Not that one," I repeated, and by memory alone, I reached for another chest, carved cunningly to look like a solid soapstone slab. From the cedar-scented depths I drew out a long length of coarse red silk, dyed to brilliance with a thousand beetle shells.

"This is a robe for men of royal birth," I explained, my voice gaining confidence as I spoke. "You see, it has come straight off of the royal weavers' looms, and no shears have ever been set to it."

"This isn't a robe," he said with a scowl, and I shook my head.

"No, these robes are not sewn until they are called for. When they are chosen, the seamstresses sew them together, attaching the bands of embroidery along the hem and the sleeves. When the lord is done with them, the stitches are picked apart and they are returned to the chest."

I didn't know it then, but I had spoken more to the barbarian king than any citizen of the county of Wan. Everyone else he had ridden down, skewered, slain, or ignored. That number included the great, the good, the holy, the kind, and the wise, but he only frowned at me, bringing his heavy brows together over those unnerving eyes the same color as a dead fish's.

"You make these red robes, these royal robes, fresh for every wearing? Every time?"

"Yes, lord," I said with a nod. I didn't dare say anymore. Instead, I only stood there, unsteady on my feet, ready to die for a piece of silk the way that better than me had died to protect the true lord of the land.

He looked from me down to the red silk in his hand and back again. I knew the cost of the robe down to the smallest sen, but measured in terms of the patience of the island children who gathered the beetles, the canniness of the captains who shipped us the dye, the skill of the silkworm farmers, and the cleverness of the weavers and the seamstresses, it was priceless.

Finally, the barbarian king shook his head, braying a donkey's laugh, and he threw the red silk at me. With a startled cry, I saved it from fluttering to the ground, clutching it to my chest like a baby.

"Sew it for me," he said, turning on his heel. "I want it by tonight."

I bowed to him in shock, but he didn't stop to make sure that my back was straight and my bow deep enough. Instead, he was gone, and his men went after him like a rabble of hunting dogs baying for the next hare.

When the room was empty, I forced my hands to relax. To my intense relief, my makeup and the sweat of my hands had not marred the silk. Instead, I could fold it carefully into panels before draping it over my arm. I observed that my hands were shaking, but they performed the motions smoothly and easily. I could always do this, no matter what. It had been my duty since I was a small child, trailing behind my mother as she tended to the royal wardrobe.

"Taya."

I spun around, tears of relief and fear in my eyes. I was not alone after all, but the only other occupant of the room would do me no harm.

The Evening Mistress was a small woman with hair that fell below her hips. She darkened the gray in it with the bitter juices of the cassia tree. She peered up at me, squinting through her near-sightedness.

"I am glad you are not dead," she said, dabbing at my damp eyes with a handkerchief scented with violet water. "He might have killed you."

"He didn't," I said with more confidence than I felt.

She surveyed the scatter of robes that littered the room, and with a sigh, she began picking them up. It was beneath her position as a mistress of the hours, but I had locked the girls who should have done it in a rear storeroom armed with the good shears and instructions to open the door for no one they did not know.

"I wonder what happens now," the Evening Mistress said thoughtfully.

"I'm going to go speak to the seamstresses," I said, managing to smooth the shrillness from my voice on the last word. "I suppose we shall have to have the seams done up for the barbarian."

"The new lord, you mean," she said, her tone stern. "Lords should be well dressed, and that is our business."

I couldn't agree, but with the red silk in my hands, I couldn't disagree either, and so I went to rouse the seamstresses out of hiding.

* * *

I WAS FIVE before my mother realized she had a daughter and not a son. When I informed her of this, she breathed a sigh of relief and took me to the fortuneteller to determine my new birthday. A son would have had an uncertain future, but my employment as her daughter was assured.

The fortuneteller was a young woman with a bright green parrot on her shoulder. At her word, the parrot fluttered down to pick me out a fortune from the little ivory tablets on the cloth spread in front of her. She read it out loud for us as my mother was already going blind.

"A life ends in silk, whether beautiful robes or an executioner's garrote."

Mother frowned, but tipped the fortuneteller well.

"Well, just try to be good and obedient," she said as we walked home. "And if you can't be good, be smart with your tools. That's the best thing a seamstress can be, good with her shears and her needle."

The banners of Wan, a field of green on which the bashe serpent coiled, were taken down. The barbarian king ordered them burned, but I knew that more than one family kept them folded up small and hidden in the rafters and under their floors. In the palace, we rolled up the enormous banners that had hung from the walls, wrapping them up tightly with string. Silk folds up far smaller than a barbarian would believe. We hid them in our pillows, in our undergarment chests, and in the great sacred vases with the enormous bellies and tiny mouths.

Of the white bashe themselves, we heard nothing. They were always wild and shy beasts, and they seldom came into the valleys until spring hunger drove them down. The Wan nobles would hunt them, but only with great caution. The hunters wore green robes with rustling gray silk linings, covering themselves from head to foot as they rode. Sometimes, they would be unlucky, and the girls in the laundry would have to shift the stains with a paste of salt and cold water, working until their poor hands were numb.

The royal family was dead and the bashe were silent in the mountains. The people of Wan entered a state of mourning, though they were not permitted to wear white or to hold the long fast. When people cannot mourn properly, they become angry.

They said that the palace servants and the nobles who did not die were collaborators and cowards. When we went down to the town, they turned away from us, or they spat upon us. That was all very well for the ministers who could send servants to do their bidding, but when I went down to my favorite linen merchant's home to see her new shipments, she turned me from the door.

"We don't have anything here for you," she said, her hand on her bristling dog. "We will not deal with the barbarians unless they have their swords at our throats."

"And I do not have their swords at my throat?" I demanded.

She eyed me coldly.

"If they go out as finely attired as Lord Yu did on his birthday, what are we supposed to think?"

I could have said many things, but her dog growled like she would if she could, and I turned away. After that, I had to buy my linen from a Koh vendor who was unconcerned with pride or loyalties. His stock was poorer, the colors runny, but the barbarian king never noticed.

THINGS NEVER BECAME normal, not quite. The county of Wan is on the far western edge of the empire, small and unimportant in every way, though we do hate to hear it. Someday the empress would hear of this desecration of her vassal lands, and someday she might mount the banners high and march to our rescue, but it was clearly not going to be this year, not when the winter snow would make the Carcanet Mountains impassable and the early spring rains would flood the Hu River out of its banks.

The barbarians lived in the palace like pigs at the trough.

They slept where they fell, and they ate with their knives. We wondered if things would change when their women came, but as the weeks continued, we realized that that simply wasn't going to happen. They were parasites and bandits, taking local women to wife and then in the same breath saying that their ugly gods did not see the marriages as real.

The only people who had any cause to love the barbarians were the huntsmen. They were elevated from their appointed station as servants of the outer wall to some kind of strange near-nobility. The barbarians demanded that the huntsmen carouse with them, giving them strong drink and startlingly generous gifts of gold rings and looted goods. Some of the huntsmen even began aping the barbarians at table and in town, and there were few people who were so cordially hated by all. The head huntsman, who had held his position for most of my life, kept his own counsel, and if he never outright sang the praises of his new lords, he never turned away their gold rings, either.

"They have not killed any of our families," he said. "That is more than can be said for some of the Wan nobles."

I wondered at first if the barbarians would forget about the wardrobe after a time, but they seemed content to leave aside their rough homespun and wool tunics entirely, taking up the clothes of the royal family and the nobles they had killed.

As time went on, they came to rely on me and my staff to dress them like great lords. They would snort and jeer about how womanly all the robes were and how foolish the colors and trim, but they demanded them all the same.

I gritted my teeth, and I directed the junior seamstresses in their tasks. The work was the same, but now we were scorned for it while still being expected to do it well.

I dressed them in embroidered poppy flowers to combat the cold of winter, I dressed them in cloth of gold for the winter equinox. When they wanted to ride through the peasant celebrations for the three nights of the dead, I gave them the robes stitched with charms against demons. When those robes were returned to my keeping, one was sticky with blood, and I knew not to go down into the town that day.

Collaborator, traitor. The words followed me like scarves of trailing incense. Those in the palace understood it a little better, but in truth, I could not always explain it to myself. I dressed the barbarians as if they were lords while the real lords rotted.

I could say that it was the work I had been given, the work I had done all my life, and that I knew no other. That was a truth. On my darker days, I wondered if it was because I had always drawn my value and my worth from the clothes I was permitted to wear. I suspected I would like myself less in hemp and linen, and I did not want to find out for sure.

WHEN THE WARM days came again, a bashe was spotted in the foothills. The barbarian king immediately said that he wanted to hunt it, and he came into the sewing room in the early morning before dawn.

We were still half-asleep, pouring each other tea from the enormous earthenware pot and sharing our dreams. It was the only quiet time of the day for some of the girls, who were kept stitching, mending, and washing until they went to bed. The barbarian lord entered like a cyclone, a violent wind that stirred us all to our feet in surprise and distress.

"I want hunting robes," he said, pointing at me. "I want something that will look royal and proper when I kill the great snake."

Despite the long winter of occupation, we could still be shocked.

"But the bashe is only for the nobles of Wan to hunt!" squeaked one little maid. She was a simple thing from the river. She was coming along, but she hadn't had time to gain any manners before Lord Yu was murdered.

The barbarian king struck her a terrible blow, knocking her to the floor, before turning to me.

"You. Get the clothes made up. We will ride before noon."

"Of course, great king," I murmured. "We shall see you well off."

"Before noon," he said, like it was a threat.

"Of course, great king."

He strode out, leaving the sewing room like the scene of a disaster.

The girl he'd struck sat up, sobbing terribly. He'd loosened her teeth on one side, and something about the way she tested each one with her finger and winced at the pain sent a terrible chill down my spine, anger that couldn't quite be tamed by fear. I had seen worse, we all had, but the one girl clutching her face stirred the room like a wind through the rushes.

I sent to the kitchen for a bit of beef. The chill of it from the ice room would be good for her cheek, and afterward, she could eat it raw to heal her spirit. She was plain in the face, and by birth and custom, she would never rise above the fourth rank. She was unimportant in every way, but something about the livid print on her face struck a spark inside me. It was only a spark, but surrounded by silk and cotton and linen, we lived in fear of fire.

Ended in silk, indeed.

"All right," I said, looking around. "I am going to go fetch the ice-white silks from the wardrobe. Hui and Mui, fetch the under-robes and the white trim from the baskets in the left quarters. The rest of you, reel out some white silk thread and some white cotton thread for us today."

One or two already looked resolute, nodding decisively. Some of the others looked less sure, and one girl raised her hand tentatively.

"Mistress, are you sure..."

"I have been the Mistress of the Wardrobe for more than ten years," I said sternly. "Do as I say, or I'll send you to stamp wool in the north."

I waited until they had set off to obey, and then I trotted off to the wardrobe to bring in the robes myself. I was the wardrobe mistress, after all, and there were some tasks that I would not entrust to anyone.

WE STITCHED AND sewed frantically, but it was not such a strange day for us. We always had to be on hand to pull an ensemble out of thin air, and we could do it for barbarian kings as well as our own nobility.

When we finished the robes, I delivered them personally to the chambers of the barbarian king and the Evening Mistress was there to take them. She hesitated for a moment, looking down at the robes we had worked on with such care. I held my breath. She and my mother had taught me all I knew about silks and styles, which sartorial laws could be bent or broken outright, and which must be left whole. She was the first one who had realized that the barbarians must be served if they were not to kill us all.

That day, she was wearing a demure brown robe adorned with a geometric design of soft silvery crosshatch stitches. It was a lovely choice for a woman of her age. My own mother would have approved.

She looked at the robes in my hands for a long moment, taking in the gleaming white of the silk. She could say almost anything right now.

Instead, she took the stack from me, sliding her skilled fingers down the side to ascertain how many robes there were.

"This is enough for the king and his riding party," she said, "but the young prince will be coming too. Go back and bring another to match."

I hadn't known that. The young prince was a half-grown monster, always tearing at the maids' robes and swilling rice wine. He had trapped one of the junior seamstresses in a closet once, and it was only my timely intervention that had stopped something truly terrible from happening.

I trotted back to the seamstresses, who were watching the door with apprehension.

"Another one for the prince," I snapped. "Quickly now, we have less than an hour left."

My seamstresses are quite swift when they need to be, valiant and cunning as starlings. I brought another robe to the door in very short order, and then I sent to the kitchen for a fresh pot of tea and our lunches. After that, we could only wait. I set some of the younger girls to the endless mending that is part and parcel of any wardrobe's maintenance, while I and one of the older seamstresses puzzled over the repair of a heavy brocade that had somehow worn to threads.

The news came in at sunset, carried by the huntsmen who had gone with the barbarian lord. They had found the bashe, but the enormous winter-starved serpent had proved to be more than a match for the retinue.

It had narrowed its red eyes to glowing slits and lunged straight for the king. When it had devoured the king, it had made short work of the rest.

"She seemed enraged. Nothing would sate her but human blood," said the head huntsman to whoever would listen. He had held his position since I was a small child, and it was his eldest daughter who led the furious people against the leaderless barbarian soldiers, driving them to the river and killing those who would not go.

As coups went, it had been a quiet one. The Evening Mistress and I had simply barred our doors and set the girls to mending and embroidery until the dust settled and the throne of the country of Wan was again in the hands of our own nobility. We ran out of silk thread, but we made do with linen instead until the fighting had died down and we could get better.

Then there were coronation robes to pull together, and we worked closely with the court fortuneteller to ensure that the sigils we embroidered were the correct ones: "lucky," "proud," and of course "warded against conquest." By the end of it, even our tough fingers were bloodied, and we were happy to take small bits of ice from the kitchen to hold against our wounds.

The head huntsman invited me out for a walk under the blooming apple trees eight days later. I hesitated, and then agreed, stopping in the workroom to pick up my darning kit and to check our supply of silk thread. One always liked to be prepared, no matter the circumstances.

For a while he was silent save for a few comments on the beauty of the blooms. We walked out to one of the gorges near the palace, where we could look over the real depth of the earth. I enjoyed the red and gold bands in the gorge's walls, wondering if I could duplicate the effect with saffron and cochineal. My eyes were still good, with only a little blurring at the edges, but it was a relief to take in only the colors of the gorge rather than the dense embroidery and seamwork of my usual occupation.

"The hunt was a terrible thing," he began. "The bashe was strong, hungry from the winter, and that usually means she has eggs to kindle somewhere in the mountains. But, Mistress Taya, I have been on bashe hunts before. I remember serpents that were more crazed and stronger, but I do not remember one that struck so fast or so accurately, not in the thirty years that I have guided the nobles."

"How very interesting," I said earnestly, studying my fingertips.

"Now, I am no wardrobe mistress..."

"Certainly not."

"But I also remember that the hunters had always worn green before. Instead, this time, they wore that unlucky, unlucky white. White glows against the new spring leaves, like a beacon even a weak-eyed serpent could see."

"Oh, well there's a simple explanation for that, you see," I said earnestly. "This month, the full moon falls before the fourth week, and there has been no rain, leaving this spring very dry. When this happens, a wise seamstress knows that white is the perfect choice to complement the season and the particular clarity of the air. Green would have been altogether unsuitable."

We stood so close to the edge of the gorge, the colors of ocher, gold, and tan banding the stone walls from top to bottom. There is a dyeing technique that produces a similar effect, but even I had to admit that the natural stone was far more beautiful. The wind that rose up from the valley below plucked at the huntsman's coarse linen clothes.

Finally, he shook his head. He had grown rich off of the barbarians. He had bought a son and a daughter out of service, and he had reclaimed property that was lost in his father's day. Now he was back to being a servant of the outer wall. If he was smart, he would have hidden those gold rings very well.

"You wardrobe girls," he said finally. "Sensible people never know when you are simply making a thing up. Come back from the ledge; you are making me dizzy standing so close."

We walked back to the palace together, where he bid me a good day. I kept my back straight so that I would not tremble, and I put the long darning needle, sharp and thick enough to penetrate a man's eye straight through his brain, back into its proper place.

That afternoon, I directed the seamstresses to pull the old Wan banners out of their hiding places. They had likely suffered over their long confinement, and we would need to stretch them and steam them before they were fit to be strung up.

Less than a day later, the bashe on its field of green flew over the palace once more, and I could turn my attention to the light rose robes for late spring.

SUPPERTIME
Tananarive Due

Summer, 1909
Gracetown, Florida

A MOTHER'S SCREAM pierced through the barn planks, near-human enough to bring hot tears to Mat's eyes. And Mat hated to cry, especially in front of her father. The lamb wriggling on the straw-dusted floor bleated with pathetic agitation, but his mother wailed outside as if she knew how sharp Papa's blade was. And what Mama wanted for Sunday supper.

"Firm hand, Mat. Don't let 'im suffer."

Mat tightened her gloved grip on the struggling lamb's legs, still powerful despite being tied, wishing she could let him run free. He must weigh seventy-five pounds—the biggest autumn lamb they had left, one she'd secretly named Buster. "It's all right," Mat told Buster in her sweetest voice, close to his ear. "Don't be scared."

Buster believed her lie and quieted. His thrashing stopped. Then came a barely audible, expert slicing sound and gurgling. Mat swallowed back a sob as she felt the creature's life seep from her fingertips. Against her will, she imagined herself feeding him hay from her hand when he was small. His mother's scream outside grew more terrible.

Papa looked down at her with pride. "Good girl," he said.

"You did better with it than your brother. Go wash. I'll hang him up."

Mat looked down at her clothes: blood had sprayed her shirt beyond the borders of the leather apron she'd worn. And her trouser cuffs. She would need to wash the blood out quickly or Mama would put her in a dress all day tomorrow, not just for supper. Confound it!

But Pa's approval gave her walk to the house a bounce. *You did better with it than your brother.* Now she would have something else to tease Calvin about when he came home from Howard for the summer on Sunday. Mat's tears had not yet dried, but a smile found her lips as she ran down the dirt path through the stand of thin Florida pines to the two-story wood plank farmhouse Papa and a crew had built two years ago, when Mat was eleven. The oak planks remained richly dark, not sun-faded, and some corners of the house still smelled like sap. Mama said some ladies from church were so envious of her roomy, two-story house—with a water closet instead of an outhouse—that they hadn't spoken to her since they moved in. And Pa said some white men were so jealous of his prize hogs that he sat by the window with his rifle most nights to make sure no one would try to steal them, or burn his new house down from spite.

The kitchen was hot from Mama's stew pot, and the baby carriage hinges squeaked as her young siblings whined with complaints that reminded her of the lamb. Booker had just turned a year old and Harriet was two; both identically insufferable. Mat knew she should relieve Mama of the babies, but Booker and Harriet were squalling in the carriage and a glimpse of Mama's huge belly pulling her house dress taut made Mat back away instead, toward the stairs. And freedom.

Another baby on the way! Mama had been only fifteen when she had Calvin, twenty-three when she had her. Thirty-five when she had Booker, and thirty-six with Harriet—when Mat heard her swear to Papa that her days of carrying babies were over. But she was with child *again*, now a woman near forty, and every time Mat thought about the new baby she felt a combination of pity and rage for Mama. How could Mama stretch and twist her body time after time with such terrible agony, tying herself more firmly to her stove and sewing machine?

Sunday, she'd teased Mat with remarks about one of the Stephens boys asking how old her daughter was because she was so tall, and how Mat would be sixteen in three years, a fit age for marriage. *Marriage!* What made Mama think marriage was anywhere in her heart? Did she only want to punish her because she dressed as she pleased and Papa relied on her just as much as he'd ever relied on Calvin? (Or more, since Calvin could not stand the sight of blood.)

Mat would go to college like her brother. Calvin had promised to help pay her way, since he got a good stipend from the aging writer whose memoir he was typing. Mama was old-fashioned and didn't believe girls needed schooling, but Papa had said to wait and see if she could keep up her grades. That wouldn't be hard: she could read and figure better than her teacher, for what that was worth.

The biggest godsend in the new house was her own bedroom, so Mat fled there and closed her door as if a bear had chased her. The oak wasn't sturdy enough to completely mute the whining of her brother and sister, but it helped. A surge of guilt replaced her anxiousness. Mama was standing over a hot stove almost ready to give birth, and Mat should have rolled the carriage out to the "parlor," as Mama now called their front room. (Booker and Harriet stopped fussing when she played happy music on the Victrola.) *You care more about sheep and goats than your brother and sister*, Mama always said. *But after this baby comes, they'll be your responsibility. Who knows how long it'll be 'fore I'm back on my feet? Better start learning now.* Mama's weary desperation had chilled Mat to her toes.

Mat's precious stereoscope goggles were waiting on her desk where she'd left them. After lighting her lamp, Mat pressed the velvet-lined mask to the bridge of her nose. Just like that, the narrow room around her melted and she was *inside* the slide glowing to life in her lamp's flame. The Palace of Electricity—a night view of a regal mansion draped in strings of stars, lit up from corner to corner, as if it might burn off her eyelids if she got too close. The Palace of Electricity seemed as far from Gracetown as the sun itself, but the magical pictures from the '05 World's Fair reminded Mat how big the world and its wonders were. Calvin had written as much on his Christmas note, when he gifted her with the wonderful contraption and a handful of slides: *The world is a big place, Matty. Here's a good peek at it!*

During his last visit, Calvin had described how he was boarding in a house full of electricity where his writer patron lived: no need for kerosene lamps, with switches that turned on lights above like a wish, a machine that washed his clothes, and hot coils that toasted his bread. And a telephone, of course. If not for the stereoscope where Mat could see so many wonders for herself, she might not have believed his stories of casual magic.

Mat didn't know how long she'd been dreaming of the Palace of Electricity when she heard the *thump* against her window. A flurry of determined scratching shook her window pane. She pulled the mask away, startled—and was staring into green-gold eyes that were not human. A bobcat was at her window! The large cat was light reddish brown, with only black spots on his ears and coat to distinguish him from the bricks that camouflaged him. He had climbed up the uneven bricks of the chimney to find her window on the second floor. The bobcat yowled, massive paws scratching against the frame.

Mat gasped. The stereoscope nearly tumbled from her startled hands.

"Bobby?" Mat whispered. She froze, not sure. Four months had passed since she'd seen the bobcat kitten she'd raised until it got too big and Mama told Papa to chase him away, and his coat had been more gray than red then. He was far bigger than when she'd found him under a rock ledge and carried him away in her palm. She'd kept him alive with one of Mama's baby bottles. She'd lied to herself and decided his mother was dead—but the truth was, she didn't know if she'd rescued or stolen him.

Heart pounding with anticipation—and a drop of fear, since she wasn't *sure*—Mat cracked her window open. The big cat did the rest, slinking snakelike through a gap that should have been too small. The cat leaped to her shoulders, wrapping around her neck. His fur smelled filthy, like carrion, not like when she'd bathed him in warm water and rose oil. Much bigger claws now raked through her plaited hair to her scalp with such strength that Mat felt her neck crack, and then the cat nibbled at her ear lobe with teeth and tongue, nicking her until she bled.

"Stop it, that's too hard!" Mat said, but she was giggling as they tumbled to her bed, rolling in a ball that sometimes put her on top, sometimes the wildcat, their play wrestling so fierce that her bed frame thumped the floor. His gravelly purr roared in her ear. As if no time at all had passed!

Mat assessed her injuries, breathless, while Bobby romped through her room in search of mischief, tugging at her desk drawers and swatting savagely at the scarf hanging on her wall. She noted her bleeding ear lobe, a bold white scratch across the dark skin of her arm (not bleeding), another on her back (maybe spotting a little). Bobby had forgotten his lessons on gentle play, if he ever truly had learned. Their reunion had overexcited him. The constant scratches were the reason her parents had made her send him away—*You think you're playing games, but that's a wild beast and his nature will always come out,* Papa said. The times Mama had caught him peeing in her kitchen sink, his favorite place to relieve himself, had not helped his case for being a house cat either. Mostly, Mama had been afraid he might hurt one of the babies, which Mat could not say was unreasonable. But she had missed him. Soon after her parents stopped allowing him in the house, he had vanished into the woods.

And now he was back—a fully grown bobcat! She couldn't wait to tell Calvin.

But Papa would tear off a switch if he found Bobby in her room now. Joy quickly turned to panic: how would she get him out of the house? She couldn't hope to hide him. It was a wonder Mama hadn't already called after her to see what the ruckus was. Bobby would have to go back out the way he came, and fast.

Mat went to her window and opened it wide. "Come on, Bobby."

Bobby stared, his stumpy tail lashing with irritation at the interruption of their play. Mat almost, *almost* felt a twinge of fright, reminding herself that she did not truly know Bobby anymore, so it might be dangerous to try to poke and prod him. His staring eyes brimmed with his history of killing. But she was more afraid of Papa's hickory switch, so she stuck her head out of the window as an example. "See? You gotta go back outside."

Mat's mattress creaked as Bobby stood on all fours, intrigued now.

"You want me to go out there with you? Is that it?"

Mat didn't believe Bobby could understand spoken words, not *quite*, but Bobby sprang so quickly that Mat had to move aside so he could reach the windowsill. But then he only stared at the chimney's descent. Why did cats love climbing up and hate climbing down?

"You go on," Mat said. "I'll meet you outside, all right?"

Bobby made a sound that could have been agreement or cussing.

And so their night's adventure began.

MAT WOULD BE expected at the supper table in thirty minutes and had no business going outside to chase after a bobcat, but that didn't stop her from grabbing her Brownie camera—Calvin's Christmas gift from his first year in college—and shoving against Bobby's weight to close her door so he could not follow her into the hall. His massive claws poked under the door. He swiped back and forth, shaking the door, rattling her doorknob.

"*Shhhhh.*"

Mat snuck back downstairs, past the loud kitchen, and out of the house.

Outside, she saw Bobby was staring down from her window. Mat tried to coax him without being loud enough for Mama to hear her from the open kitchen window, or Papa from the barn. His loud complaints from her window floated through the woods, halfway between whining and growling. He'd be lucky if Papa didn't come running out with his shotgun.

"Come on down," Mat said. "Stop being a baby."

She remembered a trick from when he was younger: if she pretended to walk away, he might chase her. So, she followed the deer path past Papa's wagon deeper into the woods, walking until her house was out of sight. Sure enough, a twig crackled and Bobby soon was upon her, tangling her legs until she lost her balance, sending her rolling in prickly fir needles. The fall hurt her elbow. Mat held Bobby's mouth away from her face, noticing his sharp, yellow teeth, pushing back against the fur of his muscular shoulders. She wondered for the barest instant if Bobby had turned wild after all. But with a playful burr, Bobby jumped away and let Mat rise to her feet again. Now Mat had a scraped elbow to add to her scratches.

"*No,*" Mat said sharply. "You play too rough. Stop it."

Bobby talked back to her in his bobcat language and ran ahead. He didn't stick to the trail, but he never ventured far from it, leaping from bush to bush, sometimes scrambling halfway up a pine tree because he could. Just when she though he might disappear over the hill, he turned his head to make sure she wasn't falling behind.

"I gotta' get dressed for supper. I don't got time to be playin' with you," Mat said.

Bobby ignored her and ran on. Mat stood for a moment and thought it over, noticing how coppery the daylight had become, the sun hanging low in the sky. Then she heard Bobby's familiar call from shivering milkweed a few yards ahead, still close to the path, and nothing could rival the giddiness of seeing Bobby so eager to play. She'd cried for a week straight after Papa chased him away, and she'd stared at the trees hoping he would come back for nearly a month before she gave up. Calvin had confided to her at Christmas that he might not have survived the wild because he'd been raised by a human hand. And here he was!

She would go home in five minutes. The sun wouldn't fall below the tree line for at least fifteen minutes, so if she started back in five minutes she might make it to the table on time.

Another lie. She knew it even then.

But she needed to capture Bobby in a photograph with her camera! How else would anyone ever believe she'd tamed an honest-to-goodness fully grown bobcat?

Bobby was too quick for her camera. He would need to sit still—*real* still—for her to be able to set up a good shot with her Brownie. Every time she'd pointed the lens and could make out Bobby's fur in the viewfinder, he was gone long before she could click the shutter. Time after time, her viewfinder showed her a tree stump or empty boulder instead.

"Hold still, would you?"

Bobby would not. He raced on with such purpose that she had no choice: she followed.

BY THE TIME they reached the first dampness of swamp water turning the soil to mud, Mat realized that Bobby was leading her to the spot where she had found him, a rocky ledge that had given her shade on hot afternoons while he lunged at the tadpoles and water lilies floating just beyond them. It wasn't a cave, exactly, because it was open on both sides, but their secret spot had felt like a castle to her. Papa could walk within five feet of her and never know she was there until he heard her giggles.

Mat was breathless by the time she reached Bobby. True to his camouflage, she had trouble making him out at first in the shadow, but the sight of him made her grin. Bobby was still at last, his haunches lowered as he chewed on something in the dark. His flanks were in shadow, but the twilight made his coat shine and his eyes glow like marbles when he gazed up at her. With trembling fingers, Mat pointed her Brownie again, expecting to find he had already leaped away, but Bobby was framed like a painting in a museum. Heart pounding, she pressed the shutter and heard the satisfying *CLICK*. She had her photograph!

She took a step closer to see if she could take an even better photo when she noticed the poor creature struggling in Brownie's jaw. At first she'd thought it might be a snake, but it was too broad, and she'd never seen a snake this odd color of slick gray-brown mud. Sometimes it looked like a tube, sometimes flat, and it kept wriggling although Bobby never stopped eating its other half. By the look of it, whatever it was might be two or three feet long. Or it *had* been.

CLICK. Mat pushed the shutter button again accidentally, startling herself in the same instant she realized she had never seen a creature like it. If it had legs, it might be a weasel. But it didn't look warm-blooded. If not for its giant size, it might have looked like...

Mat's mouth fell open and she took a step back when her memory formed the word: *a leech*. She'd heard her mother and grandmother talk about giant leeches that crawled from the swamp and nested inside babies during the summer. Swamp Leeches, people called them. But Mama had never been able to point out anyone who'd ever *seen* one. Was this...?

Mat remembered her camera and raised it again, trying to see the last of the creature before it disappeared in Bobby's mouth, but Bobby's eyes had perked up and he'd dropped what was left of it, staring toward the edge of the swamp where he had once played. Bobby growled—not in the playful way he did with her.

Like he meant it. His teeth were fully bared as he scrambled to his feet, charging toward the water. Then came horrific splashing: a sound so loud that it could only be a gator.

"Bobby—no!" she said.

That furious sliver of last daylight gave Mat a good enough view for her to realize that Mat was *not* tussling with a gator. This creature was also a gray-brown color, with the same slimy skin, but it had long, wiry tendrils that whipped at Bobby's hide, making him yowl.

The mama, Mat thought.

That was the last thing she thought before she turned and ran.

IT WAS DARK by the time Mat reached her doorstep.

She'd wasted many minutes lost in the graying woods, unable to see past her tears as she tried to stumble toward the sanctuary of their sturdy oak house. She ran inside and leaned against the door while she pulled the deadbolt Papa had built, breathless and sweating. She was so glad to be home, her knees were watery with gratitude. The door propped her while she gasped, shaking with worry for Bobby. And the memory of the thing she had seen.

From the doorway, she could see the table where Mama and Papa were already in their seats, holding hands to say grace. Papa's face was stern. Mama's was more like enraged.

Papa stood up when he saw her. "Matty! Where were you?"

"Matilda Lydia Powell, you are in a heap of hot water!" Mama said.

Papa walked close to her with the lantern from the table to get a closer look at her face.

"I swear, this child is so spoiled she thinks she can just run off and—" Mama was saying, but Papa's face softened as he looked at Mat. He held up his arm to silence Mama.

"What's happened?" he said in a tight voice she had only heard once or twice, and only now did she realize it was the way he sounded when he was afraid.

Mat hadn't thought up a story yet, so she didn't know how to answer. What was the point of telling them what she'd seen? Mama would accuse her of making up stories. And what if Papa went hunting for Bobby at the mention of him?

Papa moved his face closer to her, his jaw trembling. "*Who hurt you?*"

"No one," Mat finally said. "I saw a gator and I ran off. I tripped and fell."

"So you were off playing by the swamp?" Mama said, clarifying her transgression.

"Yes, ma'am," Mat said.

Papa held the lamp even closer to her face, trying to see any lies in her eyes. He stared at her a long time. When he noticed the camera she was clutching close, he seemed to believe her at last. His jaw's trembling stopped, replaced by ironclad anger.

"Shame on you," he said, the words Mat most hated to hear. "Hurry up and go up upstairs and get dressed. I've got half a mind to send you to bed without supper."

"That's all right, sir, if that's what I deserve." Mat hadn't had any appetite since the barn.

"Oh, I bet you'd like that," Papa said. "Come right back down to the table proper."

"And you better look like a *young lady*," Mama said.

More hot tears escaped as Mat climbed up the stairs, but she hoped Papa hadn't seen.

"Look what you've done!" Mama said to Papa as Mat walked upstairs. "Calling her by that boyish name. Letting her dress any kind of way. She's half-wild. No man will know what to do with her!"

Mat waited at the top landing to hear if Papa would say *Stop worrying so much* or *She'll grow out of it* like he usually did, but Papa was stone silent.

Five minutes of scrubbing in the upstairs sink and the pleated dress from her closet worked a small miracle, wiping away all signs of blood and the creatures outside. Mat took extra care to brush her hair down flat where she'd already sweated out Mama's pressing from last Sunday. Her image in the mirror looked like the biggest lie ever told.

Mama did not look her way when Mat sat at the table, said her silent grace, and spooned chicken stew into her bowl. The only one who seemed happy to see her was Harriet, who squealed "Matty! Matty! Matty!" and gave her a hug from her high chair. Mat made a show of buttering cornbread and breaking it into bite-sized pieces for her, and Harriet squealed at her big sister's attention. Booker was equally delighted to be bouncing on Papa's knee while he ate handfuls of a soft mash from a bowl beside Papa's plate. Gazing upon her family—including Calvin's empty seat—made Mat feel the shame Papa had uttered at her like a curse. Mama looked weary enough to fall asleep upright, rubbing her swollen belly's discomfort. Was it so wrong for Mama to expect her to be more of a helper? Was it fair that Mat spent so much time outside with Papa, leaving Mama to fend for herself with Booker and Harriet?

Mat was opening her mouth to announce an apology when a *THUMP* shook the door.

"What the blazes—" Papa said.

Papa handed Booker over to Mama and was on his feet, producing his hunting rifle so fast that Mat realized he'd moved it from the closet to be near him, expecting trouble from the time she was late. He took a step toward the door, but she jumped in front of him.

"Papa, no!" she said. "It's only Bobby! I saw him outside. He's come back!"

"Is *that* what you were doing out there?" Mama said. "Fooling with that bobcat?"

Another *THUMP*, and this time it sounded like buckling wood.

"He's back to break down our door?" Papa said. "And steal our livestock?"

Papa had delighted in Bobby as a kitten, but no love showed in his eyes now.

"Bobby wouldn't do that!" Mat said, then she reminded herself that she didn't know Bobby anymore. But it felt true in her heart, anyway. And she was just glad he was all right.

Another *THUMP* shook the door while a loud feline screech and growling came from the other side of the house, closer to the kitchen. Papa snapped a look to Mat: they both knew that bobcats did not travel in packs. *That* was Bobby. On the other side of the house.

So then Bobby wasn't at the door. The room felt frigid as Mat's world went askew.

Papa took long strides toward the door while Mat tried to keep pace with him. Her mind fumbled for words to explain the monstrous creature that might have followed her and Bobby from the swamp. "Papa, wait—"

Papa flung the draperies aside to try to see outside, but Mat could tell it was too dark. A hog squealed from the barn, setting off a cascade of panicked cries.

"He's in the barn now!" Papa said.

"That's not Bobby," Mat said. "I swear it isn't, Papa. Be careful! I saw something—"

"Stay here with your Mama," he said.

Mat grabbed Papa's arm with all her strength before he could go outside in ignorance. "Listen to me!" she said, and her tone was so grown that he turned to her. "I saw something by the swamp. Not a bobcat. Bobby was eating some kind of big, ugly leech, and its mama came out of the water, big as a gator. Mean as one too. It was whipping Bobby with these... big whiskers? No—tentacles. Thick as ropes. I don't know what it was. But I think it followed me!"

"What's she talking about?" Mama said in a tiny voice, her anger revealed for the fright it truly was. The hogs and sheep in the barn were in a frenzy.

Papa stared down at Mat, truly wanting to make sense of her babbling. "I have no damn idea," he said, speaking to Mama. "All of you go hide upstairs—*now*. She's right about one thing:

it ain't a bobcat. Someone's after the hogs." He probably thought it was white men from town, and white men from town might not be satisfied with stealing or killing hogs. Papa was wrong, but whatever that thing was might be just as bad. It might even be worse than jealous white men.

"Be careful, Papa. Please."

"Don't you let no crackers kill you over a hog!" Mama said.

"Go on, I said!" Papa waved to Mama at the table. "Hurry up, Belle!"

He waited until he saw Mama pull herself to her feet, Booker in her arms. Mat ran back to the table to scoop up Harriet so Papa would know he could count on her. Harriet cried in the commotion, clinging so hard to Mat's collar that the lacy fabric chafed her neck.

Satisfied, Papa finally opened the door and peeked outside. She prayed he wouldn't shoot Bobby. But if Papa saw anything, he didn't let on.

"Pull the bolt," he called back to them, and slammed the door behind him.

Tears fell from Mama's eyes, and Mat realized it was all her fault. If she hadn't followed Bobby when she was supposed to be getting ready for supper, the Leech Monster never would have come after her. Had it tracked her by scent? Or had Bobby led it here?

With a trembling hand, Mat bolted the door while she held Harriet close with her other arm, bouncing her gently to assure her. A peek through the curtains only showed Papa running toward the barn before he was out of sight. Mat's heart shook with worry for him.

"Come up to my room, Mama," she said.

Mama blinked as if she hadn't heard her. Then Mama followed her up the stairs.

MAT PUSHED HER desk against the door to barricade it while Mama opened her closet, still holding tight to Booker while

Harriet clung to her skirt. Mama was replaying a bad memory, her face slack with terror while they braced for gunfire and angry voices outside. So far, they only heard Bobby's snarling, sometimes more distant, sometimes very near.

"Tell me again," Mama said, hushed. "What did you see?"

Mat remembered her camera, lifting it from her desk as if Mama could see her evidence captured inside. "I think I took a picture of it! It was big, mama. And these long... whatchacallit... *tentacles* on it. Like an octopus, almost, but it wasn't no octopus. It was the swamp leech's mama! It came after Bobby when he was eating its baby."

Mama's face flickered with relief. Her shoulders sank as she exhaled the breath she'd been holding.

"You know what that thing is, Mama?"

"Shhhh," Mama said, nodding toward Harriet, not wanting to scare her. "Heard stories about swamp leeches. Never seen one, though. Never heard of one big as this."

"But you believe me?"

"I want to, child. Your daddy can hold his own against a beast." Like Papa, Mama was more scared of lynching.

But they hadn't seen the thing. And it dawned on Mat that there might be more than one.

"*Who's there?*" Papa's voice boomed from outside. If there *were* white men in the barn, that thunder in Papa's voice would get him killed.

Scratching came from Mat's windowpane, which she'd closed as soon as they ran into the room. Mama gasped, which set Harriet off crying. Mat turned up her lamp's light, but she already knew before she saw the eyes gleaming on the other side of the glass.

"It's only Bobby! Mama, please let me let him in—he's hurt."

Mama backed farther into the closet, bringing both Booker and Harriet with her. She kept the closet door open only a crack. "Yes, but hurry up," she said. "If you're *sure* it's Bobby."

If Mat had been closer, she would have given Mama a tight

hug. Mama casting her complaints aside reminded Mat of when Mama had laughed and daydreamed with her—before the whispers embarrassed her.

Mat pulled the window an inch, and Bobby did the rest, forcing his body inside. He left a thin streak of blood against the white paint. Two raw stripes in his coat look like a whip's lashes.

"Come on, it's all right," Mat said, and shoved the window closed behind him.

Bobby jumped on the bed, then off again, pacing the floor. Mat was relieved that he seemed like himself despite the blood. When he padded toward the closet, Mama pulled it shut.

"Keep him away from the babies!" Mama said, her voice slightly muffled, so Mat patted the mattress and Bobby came back toward her. He jumped on the bed and licked his wounds.

"This is all your fault," Mat said softly to Bobby.

Then the rifle shot came. Mat's heart stuffed her throat.

"Get in here, Matilda!" Mama called in a wire-thin voice.

But Mat barely heard her, creeping back to the window to see outside. Lamplight flickered inside the barn, roaming between the cracks in the wood panels. A second shot flared in the dark like a fireball, making her wince. A high-pitched sound she had never heard before seemed to echo against every tree trunk for miles.

"Goddamn!" she heard Papa say faintly. His blasphemy was shocking. "What in the goddamn hell...?"

"Mat!" Mama called from the closet, frantic.

"I'm all right, Mama. I think Papa got it. I'm just trying to see—"

Bobby leaped off the bed, growling low in his throat.

A movement in the dark through the window made Mat instinctively pull back right before the grass cracked to pieces and flew into her room, one shard scraping her nose. The odd black tendrils lashed into the room, squirming like snakes. The rest of the creature's body was pressed against the top half of the window, which had not broken—the only barrier keeping it out. This thing was bigger than a gator; bigger than the one she'd seen at the swamp. Its skin mewled across the remaining glass pane as it tried to bulge into the room. The upper pane shivered and cracked.

Bobby pounced, but he whined when a lash caught his ear.

Mat wanted to turn and run for the closet like Mama had said—to be her child instead of her protector—but she doubted that Bobby would have fled into the house if he could beat the thing back by himself.

"Papa—help!" Mat screamed with all the strength in her lungs.

But she didn't have time to wait for Papa. The beast was already tensing thick tendrils across Bobby's middle while Bobby struggled and whined, slashing with his paws. Mat whirled to look for anything that could be a weapon, and she remembered the oyster knife in her desk drawer. It wasn't big, but she kept it sharp. She would have to get in close to try to hurt the thing, but Mat had to protect her family. Bobby was her family too.

With a yell, Mat charged with her knife and plunged it toward a tendril, but the slimy flesh snapped away fast, so that her blade sank deeply into wood. Dammit! Sharp pain lanced her forehead as she realized the tendril had touched her, slicing through her skin. If Mama could see from the closet, she would faint. Mat felt ready to faint herself.

But Bobby's snarling and the cries of her brother and sister from the closet forced Mat to push aside her horror at her own warm blood. Half-blinded from blood stinging her eyes, Mat fumbled until she felt the knife's handle, tugging to free it. She'd stabbed the wood so hard that she needed two hands for a strong enough grip, and she nearly lost her balance when it came free. This time, instead of trying to hit one of the fast-moving tentacles, Mat stabbed through the crack in the glass, like Papa had taught her when she was hunting: aim for the body's center.

She couldn't see the body well, much less know where its center was, but the creature let out a piercing screech like the one from the barn, so loud that Mat backed away and covered her ears. The tentacles flapped and then retreated, releasing Bobby—but Bobby snuck in a ferocious slice with his claws that left one of the odd tentacles severed on her floor.

"Get away from the window!" Papa shouted from outside.

Mat ducked, hooking her arm around Bobby to try to pull him down too—enough to surprise him off-balance. He wriggled free, though thankfully he didn't rake her with his claws.

Another rifle shot. More glass rained in Mat's room. The otherworldly shriek came, and something big fell to the ground outside before it went silent.

"We did it, Bobby," she whispered to the big cat beside her. "And I saved you!"

Bobby bumped his head against hers, knocking her teeth together so hard that she saw sparks: the closest he came to saying *thank you*.

When Papa finally agreed that it was safe for her to come outside, Mat understood why no one had ever spotted a Leech Monster with their own eyes. Papa had covered both corpses with tarp after he shot them, but by dawn the tarp beneath her window had sunk to the soil, with only an oily black spot remaining where the creature had been. It was *gone*, tentacles and all.

The same slick spot was all that remained in the barn.

"But you saw it, Papa? Didn't you?" Mat said. In the morning light, their story felt fragile. Since Mama had stayed hidden in the closet, Calvin would never believe her without Papa's corroboration. And who knew how long it would take for her photographs to come back?

"I wouldn't know how to describe it to folks, Matty," Papa confided. "It was so dark in the barn, and it moved so fast. I was hoping to get a better look after daylight."

That was how Mat knew they would not talk about it, not outside of family. Not ever. Many things happened in Gracetown that no one talked about, or so she had heard. Mama probably had heard stories about swamp leeches from her grandmother and cousins that she'd never bothered to tell Mat until one came to the door.

The new baby came early, two days before Calvin's homecoming. The baby might have died if Miz Effie, the midwife, hadn't unwrapped the umbilical cord from the baby's neck to help her gasp her first air from the world. Mama went from screaming to crying with joy, swearing it was her last—again. Just as Mama had warned, the birth and bleeding had weakened her, so she couldn't stand to cook and clean and care for Harriet and Booker the way she usually did. Those tasks fell to Mat, of course. So instead of slopping hogs and raking hay and helping Papa fix broken rails in the fence, Mat stirred oatmeal on the stove and washed clothes and played the Victrola for Harriet and Booker, doing silly dances for them until they squealed with laughter.

Calvin had gained at least ten pounds and looked five years older since he left for school, much more a man than a boy. Papa cooked the lamb for his supper so well that Mat had two servings, although she had promised herself she wouldn't eat any. Calvin asked Mat how she'd gotten the scar across her forehead, and Mat shared a look with Papa and said he wouldn't believe her, so she would wait for her photographs to come back.

It was six weeks before a package from the Kodak Company arrived, almost time for Calvin to return to school, and she ripped it open as soon as Papa handed it to her, eager to see what images she had captured.

But all she could clearly see was Bobby, his eyes shining in the dusk light. The shadows beneath the ledge obscured the tiny swamp leech clamped between his jaws. Worse, she must have been too frightened to click the shutter when she'd seen the Leech Monster, because the last two photos were a horrific blur. And then came a photo of weary Mama smiling with the new baby in her arms.

"Well, will you look at that?" Calvin said, peering over her shoulder. "What a family record! You said you had a special one to show me, and you weren't lying. You could take photographs as a trade one day, you know. Just keep practicing. I'm proud of you, Matty."

A future taking photographs! Mat had never imagined such a notion, but it filled her with a sense of possibility. She might be the first Negro photographer for the *Saturday Evening Post*! Mat swallowed back her bitter disappointment that she had no record of the creatures that had attacked her family, that she and Papa would have to rely on memories that surely would fade one day. She wondered how anyone remembered their own family's faces—every crease, the hair style, the *exact* smiles—in the days before photographs.

But photographs, no matter how marvelous they were, did not substitute for life.

When Mama was sleeping, Mat cradled the new baby and stared into her peculiar little face and bright, hungry eyes and remembered the odd creature Bobby had been eating under the ledge. And she imagined how horrible it would be if someone came and stole the new baby away, and how she, too, would track down any creature who hurt her.

In later years, Mat would reflect upon that as her favorite summer of childhood.

Bobby never visited once while Calvin was back at home, but he was back at Mat's window two days after Calvin left, early in the morning. Even the babies were sleeping, the house silent except for Bobby's fuss. Mat rushed to pull on her overalls and the sturdy boots she had inherited from her brother. She grabbed her Brownie camera and raced outside to join Bobby in the woods washed in the gray dawn.

If she could capture the right image, her career in photography could begin now!

But Bobby, as usual, did not cooperate. He found every shadow and obstruction.

"Would you hold still for once in your life?"

Bobby playfully leaped against her side, pushing himself away with his powerful legs. His claws did not prick her this time, but she could feel the strong tips. Mat swayed and stumbled, relieved that she did not drop her camera and that her bottom landed in soft moss. Bobby licked the top of her head. He was far too close for a good photo now. Unless...

Inspiration struck Mat: she turned her Brownie's lens toward her face, the viewfinder on the other side. She could not see what image was framed from this side, but the angle *should* be right, shouldn't it? And if the camera could see her face, could it also see Bobby nuzzling her? She didn't know. But she fumbled to reach the button. *CLICK*.

It might just be a photo of the sky or a tree trunk, for all she knew. But maybe she had a keepsake of her and Bobby together. When Bobby finally stepped away from her, head upturned because of a dull crack from a small twig overhead, Mat knew this was the perfect image without seeing the film. His head was slightly above hers from where she sat, regal, his coat glorious in the rising sun.

"I've finally got you now, Bobby," she said as her camera clicked.

It might be the best photograph she had ever made. Or ever would.

But when Mat blinked, Bobby was gone.

GOOD NIGHT GRACIE
Alex Jennings

SOMETIMES YOU FEEL the rollover. You're just gobbling freeway, and then there's a snap, and for a moment, everything seems too real, or not real enough, and then, just like that, you're somewhere else. I don't know about Runts or Gracie, but I don't feel anything this time. Just, it was day on the near shore, and now that the bridge has found the far shore, it's night. We haven't been driving that long.

I'M IN THE backseat this time, and Runts is driving. Gracie leans against her window, pretending to sleep. Mostly, it's about finding the right kind of party. We take the car through a residential district, and one home will have too many cars clustered out front like ants on a dropped lolly. You don't want a place where you hear the music from the street, or you can see people milling outside. It's counterintuitive, I guess, but those places never have what we're looking for. At parties like those, people stick too close. They see every little thing. They know every door you check, every corner you look into. No good. No good at all.

This place is an apartment building. It's ugly as fuck—stacked on top of itself like if a house could have bad glands. The roof doesn't fit right and all the floors are uneven. The place looks like some young dummy fresh out of school trying to dress with class he doesn't have for a job he doesn't deserve. That was me once.

Runts says, "This one, I'm sure of it."

I make a rude noise

Gracie just pants a little. I want to pat her head and say, "Good dog," but I like my hands right where they are, at the ends of my wrists.

It's been a while since she's showered—Runts and I both took one at the last motel, but Gracie had been out finding food, and when she was done she conked out cornerways across one of the motel beds, so Runts and I had to sleep back-to-back and listen to each other snore.

Her stink is rich and dark with notes of orange-oil and spice. It fills the car, and you have to just breathe it, but you never acclimate enough to forget it's there. I don't know if Runts can smell it. I'm sure Gracie can't. So I lace my hands behind my head and pray it in and out like incense.

"This one?" Gracie says. "Sure?" She has coiled her long dark hair like rope and pinned it against the back of her skull. I see her bowed red mouth in the rear-view mirror, but I can't see her enormous mismatched eyes.

"We'll vote," Runts says.

"Fuck your vote," I say. "Let's have a look."

THEY'RE LITERARY TYPES. Graduate students in ill-fitting clothes. Secondhand dresses too bright for the season. Christmas decorations everywhere—some I recognize, and some I don't. Someone has filled aluminum tubs with water, added salt and ice and set beers, vino verde, and that sparkling water that tastes like bong water at five or six stations around the apartment.

Runts does his thing. He likes to eagerly approach someone— always male—and greet him with shining eyes. "Bill!" or "Anson!" or "Joachim!" But it's never the right person. He refuses to believe it. "Oh, God. Have we fallen out? Terrible thing. Listen, anything I've done, I apologize a thousand times. No? Steven? You must get this all the time living here, but you are the spitting image of Anson Brown. He works at the—You know. With the music and the dancing? A double. A doppelgänger. That's funny. Do you speak any German?"

Every once in a while it's fun to watch him. Not tonight. Tonight, I work my own magic. I have a lot on my mind, see. I draw attention, but I clearly don't intend to. I study the décor. I check out the posters and prints. If there's art, I *experience* it. I stand and gaze at it until someone appears at my elbow, careful not to disturb.

"...This one's my favorite," says a short woman in a heavy skirt. Her shoulders are uneven, and her step would be light if it didn't hurt her so to walk.

"I've seen others like it, but this one is new to me."

"I think the owner got it at a farmer's market in Wisconsin."

"'The owner'?"

"Billie, I think?" says the woman. "I don't know her. I only know a couple people here. I've been dragged out against my will."

"I know the feeling."

Our eyes meet in the reflection on the glass. Hers are dark and shadowed. She seems ill. Shame.

"Which of these lovely people pressganged you?"

"She's called Gracie," I say. We always use her real name. She rarely uses ours in conversation, and she's terrible at answering to anything other than her own. "She's around here somewhere, but she's a social butterfly, so I'm to fend for myself."

"Well, you give good conversation."

"Do I?"

"I would know."

"Oh? And what makes you a connoisseur of such things?"

"I'm a trial lawyer," she says. "Testimony, depositions, arguments."

"Ah," I say. I wonder idly whether they have *Matlock* here.

"I'm a travel writer, mostly. I figure, why not get paid for my itchy feet."

"Ooh. Where have you been this year?"

"All over Idaho. Charleston. The Canaries. Fournice more than once."

"I love Fournice!"

"Doesn't everyone? Last year I spent all Carnival there, but this year, I had to cover the Festival of Unrest."

"How was it?"

"Unrestful."

She points at me with finger guns. I'm starting to like this one. Now I can feel Runts watching me. I tilt my head away from the woman so she won't notice my subvocalization. "What is it, Runcible?"

I've lost track of Graceleigh. She's found a Door. I can feel it.

I turn back to the woman. "I've got to see a man about a horse," I say. "But please don't leave without saying goodbye. What's your name?"

"Qualla. After my grandmother. Yours?"

"Laurel," I say. "Lovely to meet you."

RUNCIBLE'S BROAD BLUNT face is blotchy with excitement when I meet him in the hallway outside the living room. Shelves and shelves of books line the walls.

"You're winding yourself up," I say.

The smell of pages makes me squint to pay attention. I want to inspect all the titles, see which authors we have in common.

"I'm not," he says. "You know I can feel her wherever she goes... unless she's Beyond."

"You know as well as I do that finding a Door is the easy part. Besides: even *she's* not reckless enough to step through without consulting us."

"You don't know her as well as you think," Runts says with a bit of a sneer.

"We're all desperate. You really think she'd go it alone?"

"I think she's tired of the car. I think she's comforted by how cramped and full of us it is, but she wants to be somewhere the buildings will lean over her and make her feel she'll be crushed if they fall. It's been a while since we've been anywhere like that."

Instinct tells me someone is approaching from the party proper. I turn to see a tall, furtive-looking woman gangling our way.

"She'd know," I say brightly. "Excuse me! We're looking for the bathroom, but we don't want to snoop around."

"Oh!" She says. "It's down the hall and to the left, but be careful. The house grew a Door last week, and I think it goes to L.A."

"This new door," Runcible says, careful to keep the word lowercase. "It just appeared?"

"No, it grew," says the woman. "When I first saw it, it was the size of a skunk door. The next day it was like one of those little half-doors for dwarves, and then two days ago, it was full-size."

Runts and I share a look. "Fascinating," I say. "Could you show us? I'm Laurel. This is Horne."

"Horne," Runts says, and extends a hand. As the woman reaches for it, I check quickly to make sure he has the right number of fingers.

"Nice to meet you. I'm Sinda."

THE DOOR ISN'T what I expected. They usually stand apart from their surroundings—glass doors in homes where the others are wooden, a revolving door set into the wall of a garage. This one was no stranger than the front door. The apartment's décor was all blond hardwood flooring and robin's-egg walls, and the other interior doors slid in grooves set into the floor. This one had a metallic pink knob set into an old-fashioned collar, and the door itself was profoundly red. It looked heavy—like it had been reinforced. Not a bit of light spilled around it. And it was situated right beside the bathroom door.

Sinda had affixed a sign to it. I couldn't read the language, but its import was obvious: *strange door: do not open*.

"It looks like the ones in our old house," Runts says softly. No sign of vindication in his voice, but we both knew he'd been right: Grace couldn't have resisted.

I cast Sinda a glance for permission, and she doesn't try to stop me. I open the Door and look.

It's sunny out. I shield my eyes with my hand. The sharp smell of cut grass makes me wonder at the smog. How could it still hang over everything? This green aroma should have sliced it to ribbons. A broad grassy hill races away beneath us, loses itself in a cream-and-white cityscape. Miles away, on the left side, is what looks like downtown Least Angelus. Nominally, anyway. I can't see the Holy Wood or the Purgatorium. I draw the Door closed and make sure my expression remains opaque.

"We think a friend of ours might have gone through while she was looking for the bathroom," Runts says. "If you don't mind, we'd like to stay here and wait for her."

"I think time passes differently on the other side," Sinda says. "I've opened the Door minutes apart to see that night had turned to noon. By that I mean, you might have to wait awhile."

RUNTS AND I sit side-by-side, our backs to the wall. It was silly of us to post up here, but what else could we do? Party? Now was no time to try the food. The noise of jangling guitars swims past us from the living room. I don't think of Gracie. Of her hands, or her improbable eyes, or the way her thumbs break when she tries to dial a telephone.

The funk of the bathroom bothers me a little. Maybe I should open the Door again and send it packing. For some reason, I worry that it will be raining in L.A., and I don't want to see the weather.

I realize now that we haven't tried calling for her. I don't want the partygoers to hear my voice. I look to Runts.

He sits in a lotus. I hope no one will notice that he's shorter than he was. His hands are folded in his lap, and his eyes are closed. I know he's not asleep, because he's not snoring like a planeload of chainsaws crashing into a glass factory.

"Could you sense her when we opened the Door?" I ask.

"No. Could you?"

I'm not sure how to answer. Finally, I choose honesty. "Slightly. Maybe. So slightly I might have imagined it."

"Wishful thinking."

"Wishful thinking."

"She's done this before," he said. "Before you were with us."

"She's like a child sometimes."

He half shrugs without opening his eyes. "I suppose you could say that. Dangerous child with too many joints."

"Keep it down," I say. "These people."

He opens his eyes. "'These people'?"

"Yes. Sinda was gracious enough to allow us into her home."

"Does she think we know someone, or is this shindig open to strangers?"

"'Do you think,'" I say.

"What?"

"You never ask what I think. You only ask me absolutes. Like you want me to comment on objective reality."

But there's no such thing.

"I don't know," I say. "Something about this feels wrong. Even before Gracie disappeared, I was thinking I didn't want to eat."

"You think too much," he says. "You're like an insulin diabetic calculating grams of sugar in his head. I could understand it if you had a condition of some kind, but food is food. You don't have to like it."

"It's different for me," I say, hating my wheedling tone. "I don't get as hungry as you do. I don't feel compelled."

He shakes his head. "I eat, I drink, I have fun," he says. "You should try it sometime."

He's a monster, Runcible is, but I mostly love him.

* * *

FOR ME, IT was the rails. My father was an oil man in Venezuela, and when the time came for me to go to college, I decided on Leiden University Torarica. When the first semester ended, my father insisted I get an apartment near campus, but it wouldn't be ready until the winter semester began. I told my family everything would be fine. I'd stay with friends in town and move in to the apartment as soon as it was ready. I liked the night life. I liked performing. Reading aloud was big there, and I was in demand. Readings gave me enough money to scrape by—but not enough to get a hotel.

Without anywhere else to stay, I started riding the metro more and more. Something about it was comforting. The graffiti. The turnstiles. The way the trains rocked down their tracks. The motion lulled me to sleep, even though I knew something was wrong with me, wrong with my life.

I was half-asleep on one of those trips when I felt the rollover for the first time. It was a jostling sensation—as if someone large had sat down beside me, though no one had. I smelled cut peaches and heard a distant bell.

Everything seemed the same, but I knew I hadn't imagined it. When I left the train and ascended to the street, I saw that I was right. All the signage was in *almost* the right language. The lettering was stylized all wrong. Something told me not to look too closely at the people. Their mouths seemed too narrow. They had the wrong number of teeth. Their eyes weren't quite where they should be. I wanted to talk to one of them, ask what had happened, but instead, I retreated into the subway.

I didn't understand the card kiosks, so I used my own pass, and it got me through the turnstile. I got back on the train in a haze of denial. So long as I didn't look at or speak to anyone, it would be fine. Sleep would help.

It wasn't fine.

I don't know how long I rode the train. What else could I do? The riders filing in and out looked less and less human as the journey wore on. Too many limbs. Elongated heads. Hooves for feet. Mouths slashed on one side from chin to scalp. The terror I felt was so profound that I think it must have damaged my brain. Emotions don't feel as vivid since. Yet, the things I've seen... Eventually, I realized I hadn't eaten in days and days, and that I still wasn't hungry.

Runts and Gracie entered the car on a world where the people were more fungus than animal. No one seemed to notice them—just as no one noticed me. They sat together at the end of the car and didn't look my way.

I knew I had to do something, find a way to approach them before they left again, but how? I'd been sitting still in the same seat ever since I'd re-embarked. If I moved, the fungals might notice I was something else.

Finally, after what felt like another day, when the car was mostly empty, I moved to sit behind them. I noticed her smell right away. Like pressed flowers and cardamom.

I spoke with clenched teeth, barely moving my mouth. "Please. Do you know what's happening?"

Runcible didn't answer right away. "We're adrift," he said in the same tone I'd used. "We've been crossing worlds and worlds for what must be years."

"On the train?"

"The train rolls over faster. It's as if the tracks are more contiguous between realities."

"We had a boat," Gracie said, speaking at normal volume.

"Graceleigh," Runcible said.

"It's fine," she said.

"We were almost killed last time they noticed us."

"That's because," she said—and there was laughter in her voice—"you. Didn't. Listen."

"Nonsense," he grumbled.

Gracie turned to fix me, birdlike, with her great brown eye.

"'Act naturally,' is a dictum profound in its simplicity," she said. She reminded me of a Gashlycrumb Tiny.

Runcible sighed. "Gods. And what do yinz propose we do now, O Brains of the Operation?"

Gracie extended her hand before her and examined her nails. Her fingers stretched backwards a bit, and I realized she was like me. They both were.

"I propose," she said. "That we get a car. We don't need to cross constantly. That's just a good way of getting spotted by Tree People or Lava Men."

"Have you ever gotten back?" I asked.

"Once or twice," Runcible said. "But never for long—and never both of us at once."

"*We're off to see the wizaaaaaard*," Gracie trilled. No eyestalk turned our way.

"This again," Runcible said sourly.

"If you've never gone back at the same time, why would you want me along?"

Runcible's half nod deemed the question fair. "Because we need someone new to talk to or we'll fucking kill each other."

I CONVINCED RUNTS to open the door again and call. He waited until we were alone, pried the door open and looked out into what must have been darkness. He braced one hand on the door frame and craned his neck. "Graceleigh Brenton Cammuncoooooooli!" he bellowed. The world on the other side drank up his voice.

He waited for a moment, then another, and shut the door.

"Jesu Christus," he groused.

"We could just follow her," I say. "Find a car or hop a train once we find her, do it all over again."

He shakes his head. "We've no way of knowing there's food there. We'll wait for her here as long as we can. We'll get a room if we must. She'll be back."

"Well, then," I say. "We can't just sit here."

"No. Let's find the grog."

RUNTS GRABS A bottle of brown liquor off the kitchen counter. We look around for a likely station and find a loveseat in the den. Cozy together, we pass the bottle back and forth. When we finish it, he retrieves another.

I'm not trying to drink my nerves quiet. Runcible has that covered, and that's fine. It's best for me to stay a little sober, at least, in case we need to deal with someone sober. Time doesn't work for us the way it does for the natives, but my guess is we've been waiting a couple hours at least by the time the singing starts.

I've barely noticed the piano in the room's western corner—it looks mostly like a piano, but aside from the keyboard it sports a number of what look like typewriter keys, and one of the foot pedals wheezes like a bellows—when a man I haven't seen before sits down on the bench and pumps it to life. He begins to play and sing.

Far afield the hawks do wheel
And gambol on the breeze
Time, it creeps on across the lawn
The muted cries do please
When the hunting's on
The wrack and wrong
But all that matters is...!

Several other revelers chime in with the drunken chorus:

The boats all rise for Yuletide
And there's no place to ground
We chase the base between the streets
And the wild hunt to ride down!

Qualla appears at my elbow again. This time, she is bent nearly double, as if her pain has worsened. She holds the hand of a tall, big-eyed brunette—but the other woman doesn't look quite so human as she should. For one thing, the bunching of her belled tunic suggests she has at least three too many breasts. She has Graceleigh's pallor, but her middle three fingers look fused together, and they have too few joints. She wears bells at the end of her sleeves, and they jangle in time with the music as she gawps down at me and Runcible, open-mouthed.

"Sinda told me what happened," Qualla says. "Is this your friend? She was in the bathroom."

"Yes," the strange woman says. "I'm your Grace now."

Runcible stands before I'm able to check him. "What's the meaning of this?" His voice is at full volume. The music stops and the singing partygoers turn to look. "Who is this woman?"

"Yes," says the woman. Her accent is just awful. "I'm an Grace for you and Lellen. We travel."

"Runts," I say sharply.

Runcible's face reddens. "Lies! Bring me my wife, or I'll feast on your bones."

I stand now, too. "Guys, he's drunk," I say and laugh a little. "But he's got one thing right. We don't know this woman at all."

"I'm your—" she begins.

I stab a finger in her direction. "*Shut!*"

Her mouth closes, and a series of expressions I can't quite read flit rapidly across her face.

"I appreciate what you've done here, Qualla," I say. "You were trying to help. We're going to have to keep waiting, but could you take this person to another room in the meantime? Runcible is—He's anxious."

"*Blood,*" Runcible says.

I lock eyes with him.

Runcible collapses some and flops back down on the loveseat. He's broader now, and there isn't much room for me.

"Really," I say. "I appreciate your efforts, Qualla. We'll laugh about this someday. But *please remove this creature from our sight.*"

THEY SNAPPED AT each other. They complained as much as they canoodled. Each of them would try to sway me against the other. "She's not perfect," Runcible would say. "If it were all up to her, we'd have died on the yacht at least three separate times. She's a slave to her emotions and absurd intuitions. Mad north-by-northwest."

"He's bitter and joyless," Graceleigh would say. "He likes to blame it on me, but the truth is, he was like that before we crossed the first time. I stay because even mad, useless things shouldn't be cast aside out of hand. He can't help what he is."

They love each other desperately and fully, and they are irredeemably mad. I stay with them because there's no one else, and *I* am mad.

No VIOLENCE MARRED our night. In another couple hours, it became clear that Runcible wasn't even angry—he was terrified. I hadn't thought about it till now, but his feeling has always been that one of these days, Graceleigh would wise up and leave him permanently. Of course. All we could do was apologize for his outburst, leave the apartment, and find the nearest motel to hole up and await Graceleigh's return.

"And if she doesn't?" Runcible asks as he pilots the car, still full of her stink, into a cramped little parking lot at a motel off some broad central avenue.

The weather is balmy enough—or at least the locals think so. Two gray-skinned women with bare shoulders smoke cigarettes outside their rooms. They eye us silently as we park. I like the gray. I wonder what they make of my own brown complexion. Can they see it at all?

"It's not time to think about that."

He twists the key in the ignition and the car dies. He freezes for a moment, his face in repose. There are little pained lines at the corners of his mouth and between his eyebrows. He's aged since I've known him, just a little.

"I can't escape it," he says. "Ashes. Ashes."

"Hey, now," I say. I almost reach for him.

After a beat, he turns the engine back on. "I need food," he says. "Coming?"

I shake my head.

"Not hungry yet?"

"More like sick with worry," I say. "'What if she doesn't come back?' we say. Well, what if she can't? What if she's been caught? Killed?"

"She'd take a score of them with her," Runcible says, and smiles a small but genuine smile. Now look: he's the one comforting me.

I smile back. "She would. She would at that."

INSTEAD OF CRIERS or telephones, they've got these gossipy little bugs called "hearsays." As I understand it, the creatures are telepathic, and while they don't understand language, they pass messages back and forth to one another, and people have some means of directing these where they want them to go. Before we left her home, Sinda gave us a tiny pill to give to the insect in our motel room and connect it with hers.

As soon as I feed the thing, it turns over on its carapace and spreads its countless legs. It might be an expression of pleasure, or helpless intoxication. Over and over, it sighs softly. Idly, I consider tearing the thing's guts out and devouring them, but I'd never. We need Gracie back. Our love for her holds the three of us together, and without her, Runts and I will turn on each other. Maybe it's not just her who's necessary to the equation. Maybe it's the three of us. I try to imagine my leaving the two of them and their coming apart over it. I can't.

* * *

THE MOTEL ROOM door slams open and Runcible charges inside and straight to the bathroom. He's covered in what must be blood. I'm rising to shut the door and approach the bathroom when Grace enters in his wake. She shuts the door behind her and regards me with a slight tilt of her chin.

I'm at a loss.

"Am I older?" she says.

"A little," I say. "A couple streaks in your hair. A few more lines on your face."

"You're the same," she says. "Ageless." Her smile pierces my chest.

"What did he do? Should we be driving?"

"Let him get clean," she says. "Is there food?"

"He might have some," I say. "I haven't had anything."

Runcible is huffing and knocking things over in the bathroom. He sounds fine.

Gracie approaches and I just stand before her, still lost. That pain in my chest is still there. "Is it you this time?"

"I think so," she says. "I remember you."

She takes my hand and breathes in sharply. "And you're still afraid of me."

"It's not you I'm afraid of."

She smirks. She draws me to her and we hold each other lightly. The fear.

"There was a woman, a thing, at the party after you left," I say. "She said she was you."

"But here I am," she says, and touches the back of my neck with her fingertips. The contact stuns me. I don't know whether to fall backward, rigid, or pitch forward on her. I know better than to try to kiss her.

It's her. There's no mistaking the smell. It is exactly hers, but a little different. Something raw runs through it—as if she's eaten a few times since I saw her.

"Hum," Runcible says behind me. His tone is unreadable.

"Is there food?" Graceleigh asks without letting go.

"Yes," he says. "We'll eat on the road."

AFTER WE ROLL over the first time, Runcible signals me to keep driving. I check the fuel gauge. We won't need to stop for a while, and it might take us a little bit to get a look at the people. After that first straightaway, the road begins to wind through hills like doles and doles of turtles piled atop each other. Everything smells of fresh parsley.

"So was it home?" I ask.

It takes Gracie a moment to realize the question was directed at her. She's sitting in the backseat, her legs folded against her chest. She can't change her size quite the way Runts can, but she has fewer bones. The ones she has either stretch or break easily and snap back together. I can't tell you how many times I've wondered whether all three of us are from different worlds entirely. If so, what is it we recognize in each other? Why did we care to approach one another at all?

"Of course not," Graceleigh says. "I was hunting and I got turned around."

"How long were you there?" I ask. This time, my eyes seek hers in the mirror.

"I'm not sure," she says slowly. "Our time isn't like theirs, as you well know."

"You were gone for days," I say. "It must have been days. How many times did day dawn or night fall for you?"

"What are these questions, Llewy?"

"He's not sure you're our Graceleigh," Runcible says. He watches me sidelong, as if just now understanding my suspicion.

I pause for a moment as we roll over. It's the most potent one yet. I hear an entire choir of bells this time, and a noise of hundreds gasping in unison. Sometimes I think the crossing is more pronounced the more worlds we skip, but I don't know why that would be.

Now the road cuts through what looks like salt flats. Their pink aroma drifts into the car. Open and waiting. A mirage pools on the horizon.

Without waiting for a signal, I slow our progress and leave the road. The tires crunch over salt. No need to press our luck. I stop about fifty yards from the road. I'm still not hungry, but it's time.

My head swims, and I can't tell whether it's because I've gone too long between meals or because I'm genuinely upset. I throw the car in park. Pull the back brake. As I open the driver's side door, I glance at Runts over my shoulder. He seems at a loss.

"Did you get me anything?" I ask.

He doesn't answer.

Grace climbs from the backseat, and her spine pops as she stretches. "Shouldn't we at least wait for night?" she asks.

"Not this time," I say.

I watch Grace as she stands a few feet back from the trunk of the sedan. If she runs, it will be a real chase to catch her unless she trips. She never trips. She's watching the trunk's latch. She doesn't seem worried.

My skin crawls as Runcible opens it up. Definitely hunger. My heart sinks as Qualla's eyes open and meet mine. She doesn't bother to plead. She just watches, trying to figure me out. I don't wonder what I must look like to her. I don't wonder how I looked at the party.

Beside her, bound with her arms around her knees, is the foreign woman with too many breasts. Runcible didn't consult me before returning to the apartment. I knew he'd do that, but I didn't think he'd eat before finding Gracie.

Runts has washed off all the blood, but bits of horn still show through the skin across the bridge of his nose, and his hands are too big, like shovels.

This is a test. I thought we were testing Gracie.

"Jeezy Creezy, already!" Gracie groans. "Just pick one!"

I think about what Runcible told me at the party. That I don't have to like my food. One of these bodies is ill, and the other might be entirely inedible. I should have chosen for myself.

Grace shrugs out of her clothes. Her bones seem to liquefy as she runs. She leaps into the trunk, clawed feet first, and in the same motion pulls the lid shut. She hates eating in the open. As the muffled screams begin, I try to tell which of them she's chosen. It'll serve me right if she devours them both.

"There," Runcible says. "Satisfied?"

I suck my two front teeth. Behind them, the other rows churn, ready. "That's not the word I'd use," I say. "What would you have done if it wasn't her? If she wasn't like us?"

"What are you really asking?" he says. "Do you want to know if it's ever happened before?"

A breath. "No."

I know enough. I know he'd never let me have her to myself. We'd share her, and then, together, Runcible and I would try to find another Gracie before we killed each other.

A BORROWING OF BONES
Karin Lowachee

THEIR MENAGERIE SO far consisted of five body parts and a dozen lives. The first acquisition had been their eyes—windows to the soul and all of that. They were still flecking the dust with these violet eyes, seeing the world through the lens of a third life. If they ever sold the eyes, and with them the two lives of dust that came before, the fourth recipient would see—

—what?

What would anybody see from these eyes, in this life?

They'd see a person who awoke every morning at half past seven. Made cereal out of a box. Drank tea. Thoroughly brushed their teeth and daydreamed while they did. Who accessed, perhaps, the previous nanocodes and lived for a few minutes in another person's daily routine. Another person's dust. Who saw another face in the mirror. Touched a body swollen with youth instead of somewhere post-forty, then blinked, like someone else was watching. Dissipated the dust. Winked back into the current life and showered without looking too closely at things.

In this life they rode the train to work. They could have worked from home, and sometimes they did, but they thought it was good to go outside a couple days a week. Be crowded by a city. Smell its stink and steam. Muse about all of the other lives being lived around them and wonder if one day they would add an element of *that* life or *that* one or maybe *that* one to their menagerie. Impossible to tell who was dusted and who wasn't. Boots on concrete. Global news sparking in their periphery, chattering in their ear. Forests burning, wars over there, yet another extinction. The most streamed artist on a solar system tour. Floating conversation from the urban crowd, that they caught and released for the duration it took to pass an open café or a murder of teenagers lined on the curb crowing at one another. A glut of fellow commuters huddled around a bus stop like spawning crabs. Connect and disconnect. Sometimes in this travel, they wandered off in a life from their menagerie. They didn't have to be fully awake on this routine trek to work. Their right hand had stories to tell, after all. It had once belonged to a soldier.

A gray block building housed their destination: the Department for the Mitigation of Population Loneliness. It sprouted from the city street like an obelisk of a bygone millennium, relic of an ancient civilization that modern people looked upon as a cipher. Why did these long-ago humans erect such a tower? Were they trying to reach the gods? What is this language engraved on its skin, does it tell a story of the creators' origins? What slaves broke their backs to hew these bricks to perfect alignment?

The department headquarters persisted in its use of electricity and LED office space. Some motions were too delicate to be done remotely. Some people could not perform at their bedroom desks with spouses and children and pets. Sometimes one just had to champion inefficiency.

They stopped at the lobby café and bought a frothy sweet concoction with added espresso. A couple round tables, and chairs designed to evict you after no more than fifteen minutes in their grip, occupied the perimeter of the kiosk. They sat at one and waited. When Connie cycled through the street doors they raised their drink at him and he came over, bought his own sugary liquid caffeine and a croissant and joined them at the table. Both sitting, they seemed like giants at a child's tea party, disproportionate to the size of the furniture. *Pretty oculars*, Connie had told them the first time they met a year ago. And just like that they became obsessed with him.

Connie wasn't part of the dust. He owned no menagerie. Everything about him was original, a single origin, 100% wide-eyed Connie with his big smile and mischievous laugh and a middle finger he couldn't quite bend thanks to a bar brawl in his adventurous youth. Didn't matter, he said, he preferred that finger to be straight at all times, ready to fire. Connie worked in the Public Liaison Office and everybody liked him. It was probably a good thing they didn't work with Connie directly, or they were liable to become jealous of all of the attention he received. When they thought of that, though, they reminded themselves that Connie always met them in the mornings to take coffee and asked them what the latest stories were. From their menagerie, Connie meant. Because while Connie remained original, he was also curious. That was how they, and he, became some kind of *thing*.

"My right hand fought in the Lunar Revolts," they said.

"Yeah?"

"Yeah. It was pretty good with weapons. I remember some of the skirmishes, like being in a first-person shooter. But I wasn't in the mood for that kind of action this morning."

Once they'd tried to describe the sensation, the senses employed when they triggered the dust. More than an immersive game and sometimes even as present as whatever reality the majority conceded to. Sometimes, they had to admit, it could be difficult to pull out of someone else's memory; awareness of time became so malleable, like drowning in a favorite book.

Why? Connie asked early on. *Why do it at all?*

Life is too short to live only one.

But is it really living?

What's living, though? Moving through days for a paycheck, investing what you've earned for a future that might never come? A spouse, kids, and a dog? A mortgage? Everything is mortgaged. You're paying down a debt foisted on you by a mercurial but entrenched system, and who's to say this life is any better than all the others you could experience because someone else decided to give up a piece of themselves? Aren't we giving up pieces of ourselves, doesn't society demand its pound of flesh anyway?

Whoa, Connie had said.

They thought they'd gone too far, somehow offended him or embarrassed themselves with the rant. But the next morning Connie sat with them again and shared a bagel.

They worked in Complaints. Their point of view, they discovered, wasn't unusual. People often just didn't know how to articulate it. People knew something was wrong but could not pinpoint it precisely. Instead, isolation. Loneliness. A lack of feeling loved or seen. Drugs didn't work, neither did self-help gurus, or any attempt to massage a different energy out of existence. Sometimes the concrete weight of the sky bore down without relenting and it was a point of privilege to say it could all just be made better by hard work and positivity. Widespread societal malaise created the DMPL (what employees cheekily called the Dimple). Part crisis hotline and part research facility. Employees also got subsidized on their menageries.

See, they told Connie. Even the government knows we need other experiences beyond our own. It builds empathy.

Maybe they want you sedated, Connie said, thoughtful, never judgmental. *It's also escape.*

What's so wrong about that?

IN THE MENAGERIE: eyes, right hand, left leg, liver and tongue. How they wanted to kiss Connie with each dusted memory embedded in their tongue. They tested the subject one night after work, at the corner pub, scores of pressed bodies and the clamor of music and televised sport and the scent of alcohol in each other's mouths. A paradisiacal state of being. Their own private ritual, shoulders touching, the close-up details of a blue shirt thread, a strand of hair multicolored from brown to blond, like a metamorphosis in microcosm. They idly mentioned how the memory of tasting Malaysian cuisine came before they actually tried it. Some previous code in the dust had spent a couple years traveling around Southeast Asia. So many stories to tell and another person's chapter became their own. Wasn't that kind of beautiful? Bodies full of stories in a collaborative telling. Like an ancient rite around a fire. The passing across of knowledge through generational mythology.

They said all this, but they knew Connie's dirty mind.

What other things did that tongue taste?

Wouldn't you like to know.

The flirtation was always just shy of the physical. It was painful. Connie told them once that he didn't want his world to somehow become someone else's down the line. *So don't ever trade your eyes. I don't want anyone else looking at me but you.*

All of these words, yet they hadn't even kissed. Maybe, they thought, Connie wasn't into that at all with anyone. Better to think it was just a general preference and not specific to *them.*

The tongue suddenly began to speak, as if it could see the two of them. Over a year into their not-courtship, he from the Liaison Office and themselves from Complaints (they tried not to think too heavily on that symbolism), traipsing through the corridors of Dimple, relatively happy company sots with their weekend partying and occasional spontaneous midnight getaways. Connie always had a new dive bar to try, or an early-hours ramen den. Sometimes they walked Connie's dog together. This was their *thing.* They were ten years, at least, older than Connie but "didn't look it," apparently. Not that it mattered in a world where pieces of one's life traded like gaming cards, muddling the definition of reality. They couldn't help it, and they held out hope for Connie like a panhandler on the corner. A shameless beggar.

When the tongue began to speak it said, *You need to take his heart.*

*   *   *

THE DUSTCODE WAS supposed to be impenetrable, but obviously nothing was, even though they hadn't bought the tongue illegally. They'd gone through legitimate menagerie brokers and nanosurgeons, government sponsored no less, where everyone was vetted to make sure nobody was a serial killer selling their guilty hands. Who wanted *those* memories? (Okay, probably some people would, but those people weren't legal). If for some reason you accessed a memory that disturbed you, you were supposed to report it. There was an extensive database, nanocode traceable right back to its origin even if a current owner never knew specific identities. Everybody had signed their privacy away to the database (what was one more thing in the grand scheme if it gave you so many other life experiences?)

Yet their tongue spoke. *You need to take his heart.*

"No I don't," they said aloud, back flat on their bed trying to sleep ten stories above one of the more decrepit parts of the city.

He wants to give it to you anyway.

"Metaphorically speaking, *maybe*."

They got no reply. For a minute they thought perhaps they'd hallucinated it, the foggy consciousness of seven-thirty dawn. Best to claim that. If their leg could talk, it would tell them to run, sprinter speed. Run, don't start down this path to theoretical insanity.

Maybe they should've reported it, added another anomaly to the database. But they didn't.

THE WORLD SOUNDED different when it rained. It was both magical and a little tragic. One of the lives in their leg loved the rain and offered memories of stamping into puddles to splash someone just out of sight. The scent of autumn leaves turned purple from the cold, slick on sidewalks like bruises made by footprints. Vehicles on the street echoed in lower notes as they hydroplaned the road, arrowing sprays of droplets in their wake like wet contrails. Everything seemed to sag under the soak. They sat at the lobby café and Connie did not show. Connie had told them he would be in the office today, he had a meeting with a journalist from overseas. They waited. And waited. And the rain cut the world outside the window into shards.

TEXTS:

8:45 a.m.: *u in the office today?*

12:33 p.m.: *hope u didn't drown in the rain*

2:19 p.m.: *going on break wanna meet downstairs?*

4:09 p.m.: *busy day huh*

6:30 p.m.: *heading out if you're done for the day maybe drinks?*

CONNIE HAD NEVER ghosted them before. They started to think the worst. They must've done something to offend him. Or make him sick of them. It graduated into thinking maybe Connie had been struck by a bus on his way into work. Or been mugged. Finally paranoia sank its teeth in with the express purpose of drawing blood: Connie must have been playing them all along. A year of picking their brain about their menagerie like he cared, silently judging and condemning them. Now he was probably laughing it up with his upper floor colleagues, telling Sherry or Abdul or Eiko how some boring forty-something duster was obsessing about him and he'd had enough, the amusement park ride had run out, time for some adult entertainment now.

Well, screw you, Connie Desrosiers.

TURNED OUT HIS dog Penny got sick and he'd spent the whole day at the vet's. They felt terrible when Connie called them at nine o'clock that night, explaining his absence through tears—

terrible both for the poor whippet and for thinking the worst of their *thing*. They called a ride straight to Connie's brickworks flat and before they could say a word on the threshold Connie pushed himself into their arms and squeezed.

"Aw, babe, I'm so sorry."

So sorry for thinking you were an asshole.

The vet was keeping Penny overnight for observation. She'd started throwing up and had lost a lot of fluids. Maybe she'd eaten something she wasn't supposed to, even though they knew Connie was vigilant about what he gave her. That pup ate better than most people, all fresh raw ingredients and wild animal treats. They sat on the thick sofa facing the blank telly and wrapped their arms around Connie. This bruising man possessed such a soft heart for Penny because she had rescued him, not the other way around. When his family had kicked him out (for reasons he never explained), he moved to the city, he felt all alone, before he worked his ass off to climb out of shelters and decided to love a thing that could love him back absolutely, both of them shelter strays.

I could love you back absolutely, they'd thought when Connie had told them his origin story.

They drank beer and put on a familiar comedy in an attempt to take Connie's mind off of the empty dog bed. Halfway through the film they felt Connie's head descend onto their shoulder. He was fast asleep. They didn't move, but rested their cheek against the top of Connie's hair, no longer watching the screen either. Their skin grew warm. Their heart thud in their ears.

Take his heart, said the tongue.

"Shut up," they murmured.

But they looked at Connie's hand for a few minutes where it lay slack on his lap. They reached out and laced their fingers, held their hands like that on their knee. That stubborn middle finger. The rough male palm. Pared down fingernails. Scarred knuckles, delicate white brushstrokes on the bone bumps. They thought of putting two of those fingers in their mouth.

Take him to a nanodoctor and get him dusted and eat his heart, said the tongue.

Connie woke up just as they were putting his fingertips against their lips. He snatched his hand away and straightened from his lean, sleepy eyes suddenly sharp and wide.

"What are you doing?"

They had no good answer so they settled on, "Sorry. I'm gonna go. Call me when Penny's home?"

Connie didn't stop them from leaving, nor did he promise them anything for the future.

HOW CAN YOU *hear or see things from a liver or a leg?* Connie had asked once, early on.

The short answer was nanotechnology. Volunteer your body to be dusted and the little mites of data gathered everything your body did, all of the firing pins linked between action and brain, motion and memory. When you realized you truly weren't a compartmentalized set of ongoing biological projects, but rather a cohesive, coherent whole, the idea of holistic transferrable experiences became a little more than theory. All of the greatest minds worked on it, apparently, with so many options for application. Gaming, of course. But psychotherapy too. Healing both the physical and the mental. And this, of course.

The life trade. The menagerie. Because the one life you lived was so fucking depressing.

ALL THEY THOUGHT about through the weekend was Connie. How they'd screwed it up, how they'd let some form of obsession overcome their better sense. What were they going to do with Connie's fingers? How had they made that move thinking Connie wouldn't wake up? How had they *made* that *move* in the first place?

It had been their right hand. Was there a conspiracy going on in their menagerie?

They tried to ask the hand some questions. Got nothing. The liver gave them a stream of images of clubbing in Europe, music festivals full of dancing robots and lights falling out of the sky. For an hour they managed to distract themselves, but then got a glimpse of hands holding, another life's romantic interlude, and their present reality crashed down like a UFO.

They thought about if Connie had let them put his fingers in their mouth. That calmed their anxiety, the fantasy of it. How would he have tasted, like the condensation off the beer bottle he'd been holding? Like the cotton of his shirt? Like skin and bone and man? They thought of biting down, giving some pain because they were in pain, and they felt stupid for it. Love was the extent of stupidity you fell into, it took rational considerations and threw them out a ten-story window. Love was a suicide jumper screaming for attention all the way down. Just look at me, just catch me. You want someone who loves you so much they could talk you off the ledge of self-destruction.

They didn't leave their apartment all weekend and Connie didn't call.

No amount of playing in the memories of their menagerie assuaged the fretting. Monday morning they went to Dimple, not knowing if Connie was even going to come in. They sat at the café and dawdled over a coffee that was more whipped cream than liquid. They ate a slice of banana loaf and it crumbled in their mouth like burnt offerings. When Connie walked through the street doors they almost leapt to their feet, but shame made them stay seated. Connie saw them immediately and came over.

"Hi," he said.

"Hey."

"I'm gonna get something."

"Okay."

Just like normal, but not. They waited. Connie got his order along with a doughnut and came back and sat. Two grownups at a toddler's tea party table. The muzak permeated the air like mist. Business casual figures passed through the lobby. One or two other working stiffs like them occupied the other tables. The scene so familiar it ramped up their dread.

"How's Penny?"

Connie broke off a segment of the warm, soft doughnut and popped it into his mouth. They couldn't stop looking at his slender fingers.

"She's okay now. Must've just been a bug, she came home on Saturday afternoon. Sorry I didn't call, I just sat on the couch with her."

"It's okay. I'm glad she's okay."

Okay, okay, okay. For crying out loud.

They both sipped their drinks.

"Maybe we can go to dinner or something," Connie said. "Or somewhere. To talk. After work."

So many emotions skittered through them in the space of time it took Connie to speak. A date! Or maybe not. *Oh.*

"Sure, I'd like that."

"Cool." Connie stood and gathered his coffee and what was left of his doughnut. "I'm gonna head up. I'll see you later."

They had no patience for the complaints that came through that day. Can't you get your heads out of your asses for once? What did you all expect *them* to do about it? Or the government for that matter? Govern your fucking selves!

But they answered all of the questions politely. They listened like a kind grandparent. They pretended to feel bad for a moaning mother and transferred her to the crisis level.

Connie met them back in the lobby after work and actually smiled at them. Maybe this wasn't going to be so bad after all.

"Thought maybe we'd go back to my place and take Penny out? She's been home all day alone. Maybe eat outside since the weather's holding up?"

They agreed. It'd be good to walk and the dog could act as an ameliorating force. At least that was what they hoped. She seemed spry again, anyway, greeting them with her tapered impala face and large, round eyes. They stroked her brindled back and offered to take her leash as they all set off down the sidewalk toward the park and the little enclave of restaurants and bars not far from Connie's flat.

Small talk was painful, so they didn't even try. Better to wait for Connie to speak. After they'd gone a couple blocks he finally did.

"It really troubled me that while I was sleeping you were attempting to do something."

Let's just dive right in then.

"I know, I'm sorry. I don't know what came over me."

Take his heart.

"Fuck."

Connie looked at them. "What?"

"Nothing."

They walked a little more. The whippet jaunted ahead, oblivious to any awkward flailing, her whole body like a stylized punctuation mark.

"You're my best mate, you know," said Connie.

Here it went. The easy letdown.

"I feel like we come from the same place, in a lot of ways. You never felt like you fit in, and I was thrown out. It's always been real simple to be with you, and that's what I love about you and me."

"Please stop talking." It came out sharper than they'd intended but they couldn't help it. Suddenly something dangerously close to anger reverberated through their limbs. "You don't need to try to make me feel better or whatever this is. I did a fucked up thing and I'm sorry. It won't happen again. We can just forget it, nothing needs to change. I don't need to hear how much you're my friend but it'll never be more than that. We're not teenagers."

Connie stopped walking, so they did too. They were still holding Penny's leash and Connie reached across the small space between them and took it for himself.

They lay in bed that night, sleep evading them. Falling into the dust did nothing for them either. Work became a zombie toll of hours whether they went into the office or not. Easier not to, and in some way perhaps their childish attempt to see if Connie would miss them and reach out.

A week of silence then a text from Connie:

5:46 p.m.: *drinks?*

It was the same pub the two of them always went to, but it felt different. *They* felt different, even if Connie met them under the green awning as usual and offered a big hug. The pub's Victorian gold lettering glimmered on the window glass at the edges of their sight. They held onto that embrace for an extra beat and Connie let them, and that small fact carried them from one drink to the next with so little effort it bordered on pathetic. Deep conversation wasn't much of an option here, but maybe that was the point. Better to eat, drink, and be merry because tomorrow they could die.

Truth was, if Connie wanted to act like nothing had happened then they could treat it as just a hiccup too. Connie still cared about them, bottom line, and wasn't that enough?

No, said the tongue.

"Shut *up*."

"What?"

Connie blinked at them owlishly from behind the horizon of a whiskey glass. They were both five drinks deep with very little food to soak up the sauce. Sound came at them on tinny ringing notes—a shrill burst of laughter, the *whish* of a tap opening up, glass hitting wooden surfaces. Connie's fog blue eyes narrowed at them.

They touched his wrist. "Not you."

"Then who're you talking to?"

"I been hearing things," they said before they could stop

themselves. Alcohol tended to make their mouths slippery, anything was bound to shoot out of it.

"Hearing things?" Connie all but shouted in their face.

They still held his wrist and he hadn't shaken it off. "I dunno how to explain."

"Try," Connie said, leaning forward with a sort of urgent concern.

Why did it feel so good to be something that could elicit that reaction? They leaned in too, ostensibly so they didn't have to shout. But really because they wanted to be so close that they could count the individual hairs of auburn-gold stubble along Connie's jawline. "The other day I think my tongue spoke to me."

For a split second Connie looked on the edge of laughter. But then he swallowed it and set his glass half-empty on the bartop. "What do you mean?"

"I told you I dunno how to explain."

"Your tongue? You mean like from a past life?"

"I don't know! I guess so?"

"What did it say?"

They stared at him.

"What did it say?"

Maybe they weren't drunk enough for this much of a confession. They just shook their head. "I don't wanna talk about it."

"Come *on*." Connie switched their touches and suddenly they felt those fingers skate up their arm. "Tell me. Obviously it's been bothering you."

"It wants me to take your heart." Barely a murmur.

"What? I didn't catch that!"

"IT WANTS ME TO TAKE YOUR HEART."

Blink. Blink-blink. From both of them.

Connie's grip tightened. "But you already have it."

The pub's floor seemed to drop out from beneath them, yet somehow they still floated above the impending abyss. All sound receded except for the clamor in their own red messy center, the resounding beat of war drums.

They mashed their mouth to Connie's, locked beneath his hand and some raucous inevitability of desire. Caught a brief taste of smoky whiskey and the tang of peanut salt. A swish of tongues—*there it is!* it seemed to exult—before Connie shoved them back so hard they almost fell off their seat.

"Giving you my heart doesn't mean you get to steal a kiss," Connie said.

What pumped bloody and thick in their chest seemed to rise to the back of their throat and form into iron razorblades.

"Fuck you then," slid from their tongue like an oil spill and they pushed themselves away from the bar and fled. Connie, predictably, didn't follow.

SUNDAY, A TEXT from the bastard:

10:06 a.m.: *I'm sorry. coffee?*

"I handled that badly," Connie said as they sat at an outdoor café in their neighborhood. The coffee was mediocre and the tables were dented. Penny folded down by their feet, watching the sidewalk activity with perked ears and occasional tail wags. The sun bore down like an ax and they had to keep squinting because they'd forgotten their sunglasses. For a minute Connie had fussed with the ragged patio umbrella, until they told him just to sit. Now, an apology. "You just surprised me."

"Yeah, I figured. Sorry." They were tired of apologizing. Wasn't Connie tired of apologizing? Without sunglasses, they also couldn't hide their eyes. Their *pretty oculars*. The beginning of all their trouble.

"You should probably get that tongue looked at, though. I mean report it. They aren't supposed to speak to you, are they?"

"No, I guess not." It was easier to look at the muddy brown liquid in their cup, but they forced themselves to give Connie their eyes. "Why do you say things like that but then rebuff me?"

Connie blinked as if the question had come out of nowhere. Was he really this dense? "I say things because I mean them."

"How do I have your heart exactly?"

"You're the closest person in the world to me. Don't you know that by now?"

It was starting to feel cruel. Or maybe it had been cruel all along and they were simply growing into an adolescent masochism. Just a few more spurts of riotous confusion until full blown adult self-destruction.

"I feel like I'm never enough for you," Connie said.

You need more, the tongue said.

If they could embrace the masochism, then maybe it would be tolerable. Instead—guilt. Anger. Telling their own tongue to fuck off.

"Funny," they said aloud, "I feel the same."

Every encounter lately seemed to become a deflation. What started buoyant ended in shriveled contraction, one or the other of them slinking off to their own abodes. Where Connie had Penny to console him (if he even needed consolation), *they* had a noisy upstairs neighbor and a next door one who smoked weed incessantly. They hated the scent but lay sprawled on their sofa wondering if it was possible to get a second-hand hit off it. The apartment smelled somewhere between vomit and roses. Another reason to go into the office instead of working from home.

But back on Monday and no word from Connie. No meeting at the lobby café. No texts. Maybe in the back and forth of social etiquette they were supposed to text first, but they refused. Even though the sadness built in hard blocks in their body, as if attempting to reach some heavenward deity for absolution. Truth was, the friendship had become so intense, so constant, that even a day or two without word felt like a chasm impossible to bridge. The longer it stretched, the more unlikely it became. Would that they could empty out those bricks of sadness across the divide, begging in some way for

Connie to help them make sense of it. There had been no absolute repudiation; if anything, the melancholy stemmed from everything that already existed between the two of them, not what remained absent.

Finally, on Friday, they broke.

Text:

8:49 a.m.: *I'm sorry will you meet me before work?*

No answer.

Friday came and went. They even called Connie's office number. It went to voicemail. The weekend churned like thick butter and they remained in the viscosity of it, bloating on their own despair. This was outright ignoring and by Monday again anger had formed like a thin film over the crude oil of depression. They rode the lift all the way up to the Public Liaison Office floor and combed the cubicles for Connie's. Even checked the breakroom. Eiko saw them and asked what they were doing up here. Eiko had never liked them.

"Have you seen Connie?" they were forced to ask her, to give a reason for being outside of their regular domain.

"He's in Japan," she said.

"Japan?"

"On business." She spoke slowly as if addressing someone of deficient mental acuity. "He didn't tell you?"

She had to sound smug in the question. She knew something about Connie that they didn't. Japan on business. Without a word. Texts still worked overseas.

"His voicemail didn't mention that." Why were they still here and talking? Leave.

"He probably forgot to set it. You know Connie." Said like she knew Connie.

The week bled out like a trauma victim forgotten in triage. They spun in their mind, by turns agitated and sunken like an ancient sea galleon. Collecting detritus in the drown, home to the bottom-feeding parasites of their own thoughts. The weekend hit again and leveled them in bed, from where they decided not to move. They were a full-blown stubborn, self-pitying blob. Not even the menagerie assuaged any of the underlying worry, the suspicion that they had lost Connie for good, Connie was probably shacked up in a love hotel with a cute manga character come to life, drunk on sake and specialty candies. They had never been to Japan (not even in the dust), but this seemed a likely eventuality. They thought of the romance of neon and large crosswalks, holograms descending from bright buildings to kiss your forehead and implore you inside some themed karaoke bar. Nothing but movie clichés, they knew, but could not help this damaging fantasy. Beautiful women in patterned kimonos and handsome samurai swinging curved katanas. The lure of kabuki.

On Monday before work, they went to their nanosurgeon and asked her to run a diagnostic on their tongue. By the end of the day the results came back: nothing out of the ordinary. There was nothing and nobody left to blame except the person who slogged to work and back for half the week until they gave up and stayed home, answering complaints with a joint between their fingers because if they couldn't escape the smell then they could succumb to it. At least it encouraged some interesting conversations, though at one point they zoned out so completely and for so long the client on the other end dropped the call in frustration. That might end up on an eval report, oh well.

On Friday, Connie showed up at their door. They almost didn't believe it was him, staring at the cam feed on their system as though some ghost had suddenly appeared on their stoop. Soon it would flicker and disappear, or look up at the cam with black soulless eyes, a gaunt white face. They buzzed him through and he collided into their arms, talking aflurry.

"I missed you. I'm sorry I didn't text or anything, I was so jetlagged then it was nothing but meetings and shit. I'm still jetlagged but I came right from the airport." A hoarse laugh against their shoulder.

Their heart ran like it was trying to get away from something. From themselves, maybe, and all of their misplaced assumptions and anger. Guilt compounded the melancholy until they couldn't divide the differences anymore. Yet they could feel Connie's heart too.

There it is, said the tongue. *Waiting for you.*

They wanted to sink for another reason now. Slip their skin and pour into Connie's. Why did they need all of these other lives when only one truly mattered?

"I got something for you," Connie said, peeling away from them, weary features somehow managing to gild with excitement. He pulled in his rollaway luggage and set it by the wall, then crouched over his leather carryon, which seemed stuffed with cotton. As soon as he unseamed it something fluffy and white burst forth and he stood with a grin and shook it out in front of them. "Look! I stole it from the hotel."

An expensive bathrobe. He looked so proud of himself, this little delinquent.

"You went all the way to Japan, didn't even tell me, and brought me back stolen goods?" It was both endearing and maddening. The look on their face must have translated that because Connie blinked in confusion.

"I thought it'd be cute. And you'd look good in it."

"Stop saying things like that. You don't mean them."

Connie's arms dropped. The robe's hem flopped to the concrete floor. "Not this again."

"Not *this* again? Not what again, exactly?"

He folded the robe and set it on the floor. "I'm not doing this with you again." He began to gather his luggage.

"Doing *what*, Connie? Baiting me with all of these compliments and come-ons then claiming you don't want it when I make a move?"

"Come-ons? *Fuck you.*"

Their apartment had a slow-closing firedoor. But somehow Connie still managed to slam it in his wake.

*   *   *

THEY CYCLED THROUGH all twelve of the other lives, playing the game of it on their bed like a coma patient only vaguely aware of the outside world. Sometimes they logged into work, when they remembered, when some random incident from the dust didn't whisk them into the kind of dream where you never shut your eyes. Sometimes they triggered the same scene over and over for no other reason than the engulfing repetition of it, like constantly flicking through feeds on the vid. Numb to the nanocoded emotions flowing through them. Flying an ancient small plane. Building snowmen. Sailing kites. Christmas mornings. Nights of Diwali. Climbing stone ruins. Watching a ladybug crawl across their hand (a different hand). It wasn't enough and none of it mattered.

Work called more frequently and they completely stopped answering. They were committed to these dramatics, could laugh about them the way hysterics might, but could not relinquish the sneaking suspicion that these were all just symptoms. Maybe they'd never grown the way people should, maybe whatever dark nothingness had etched its way into their body all those years ago was the beast they couldn't stop feeding. They'd had their heart broken once, twenty-something years ago, and had never recovered. It was the closest they'd come to death. It felt like actual death. Once they'd traded romantic war stories with Connie, early in their friendship, on a quiet night in their flat when they'd decamped there for drinks after work instead of the pub. Connie listened to the ridiculous tragic tale without mocking and offered his own more colorful forays into relationships—they'd all ended in various stages of disaster too. "I never quite felt connected to any of them," Connie said.

Now they thought of how desperately they wanted to know all the stages of Connie's heart. Not just in the telling, but from living inside of it. Words were imperfect tools, fractions only of true meaning. Connie had never felt connected to other people, but he'd given *them* his heart.

It wasn't enough and it mattered too much.

A MONTH LATER Connie showed up at their door again. Banged on it until they opened it, then pushed himself inside and looked around as if someone or something else should have been standing in that dimly lit entryway. He noticed the white hotel robe still folded on the floor, unmoved.

"Where the hell have you been? You quit work just like that?"

"I didn't quit. I just didn't show up."

"You look like shit. What is wrong with you?"

"Why are you so angry? Why are you here?"

They watched a strange transformation take over, how Connie drew three steady breaths and the hot pink flair of his skin began to fade, though none of the fire dimmed in his eyes. They were shocked to see that his hands were shaking.

"Why am I not enough for you? Why can't you accept what I give you and trust that it's all I can give right now? Instead you fucking blame me for something that isn't yours to demand in the first place."

So they were here, the two of them. In this place of truth.

"I need your heart."

"Is that you or your tongue talking?"

"I turned off all that shit. *I* need your heart, Connie."

They might as well have punched him in the face for the fury that still burned there.

"Do you wanna consume me or know me?"

"Can't it be both?"

Connie walked further into the flat, into the circumference of blank walls and DIY furniture. Nothing matched. "What do you think love is?"

"Is this a trick question."

Connie yelled at them. "No!"

Now they were shaking too. Vibrating to some discordant note in the universe. "I don't know what it is. Nobody does. That's why people are always writing about it and shit. Or fucking it up."

"Do you think if you literally had my heart in your chest and my emotions coded for your tourism, you'd know me, you'd know how I feel, and you'd feel it, and everything would be answered?"

"You're not really asking."

"I am asking. But I can also tell that you want absolutes out of me and that's not how it works. Or more accurately that's not how *I* work. And you better get right with that or this relationship will be over."

They hated how their voice shook. "Isn't it already?"

The question stalled in the air like a motor dying into silence. They did not expect the sudden shove into their arms. The grip around their ribs so tight they thought they felt their body crack. Their bones beginning to bend in ways they were not meant to be.

"You can know me the old-fashioned way," Connie said into their shoulder in an inexplicable pleading voice. "With all the doubt and the trust. Never knowing all of it, but knowing just enough."

Their hands buzzed like they were conducting electricity in some cacophonous symphony of desire. A part of them wanted to push this man away, their ego vaguely insulted, an amorphous need to hide. Maybe this was the true nature of vulnerability— half-anger, half-fear. How dare he. Why did the universe not acquiesce for once? Pointless wishes, like looking up at the stars and expecting fidelity. They wanted to know everything absolutely because knowing absolutely meant no risk. What did Connie call it? Being a tourist in his heart. Safe behind the walls of a resort.

They didn't know how long they both stood there, but Connie wouldn't let them go and maybe that had always been the pattern but they had refused to see it. In his own way, Connie wouldn't let them go. Even when he raised his head finally and looked at them straight on. They feared some eviscerating separation even now, but Connie only said, "I always wanted to ask you. What color were your eyes—before?"

It felt a little like confessing a secret. "Brown."

Slowly, inexorably, their body began to conform to the curves and edges in the other one pressed against them, like they were casting molds of each other, filling each other with the liquid mess of themselves only to wait, however long, for their shapes to solidify.

CHOSEN
Saad Hossain

WE'RE THE SCUM of the galaxy. I don't know where we came from, some Milky Way place far away, a Garden of Eden where our relatives are still walking around like gods, who knows. Here in Celestial Fire we are the scum. We don't even have a star system for god's sake, not even a single planet to call our own. The best we can muster are a few floating asteroids, secret junkyards where we take apart our pathetic loot.

Everyone hates us. With good reason. Take me, for example. I'm just an engineer. I'd be the third ship's officer if we followed the Chosen's naval classifications, but of course we don't, so I'll just explain it like this: if the captain dies, and the gunner dies, then I'll be in charge of the ship, god bless everyone.

Anyway, my point is that I'm no big shakes. I've never captained my own ship, nor held a share. Parents went down in an illegal mining accident when I was five, and an old aunt raised me till she died in a gunfight. I signed onto a pirate ship when I was twelve, apprenticed to the engine room, since I knew my way around a wrench.

I've been floating around space for forty-five years. I'd say I've already murdered several dozen souls, personally looted thirty-odd ships, and blown up my own ship three times. Yes. Three times. That's the kind of engineer I am.

I really hope this won't be explosion number four, because right now we're getting chased by a Chosen fast frigate, our nemesis, who has been hounding us for the past three years.

The Chosen are the big shit around the Celestial Fire area, and as far as I've heard, they didn't even used to have a navy until we got here. That's right, an entire god-like species of giant squid morphs got their mothballed ships out of storage just to deal with us. That's the kind of scum we are.

Celestial Fire is a pretty nice galaxy. It's got a lot of mild-mannered stars and a lot of rocks with water. It's near the center of the Universe, they say, full of wonderful, exotic stuff. The Chosen (that's just their word for "people" in their language, it ain't like they're chosen by god or nothing) are huge squid-like motherfuckers who made underwater civilizations until they figured out how to hardwire their bodies for land, and then finally space. They're arrogant assholes. They don't need equipment to survive in vacuum, either. They just kind of squish up. They spread themselves out from their home system until they ran up against the Vox. The Vox are also badass. These guys kind of look like ostriches with hands. That's right: welcome to the Ostrich vs. Squid show. The Vox and Chosen don't really fight wars anymore but they sure as hell don't like each other. There's a lot of saber-rattling and slapping each other on the face with gloves type of shit going on.

As far as I know, that Milky Way place was kind of deserted. I sure wish we had stayed there. This region is crowded. Other than the Vox and the Chosen there's about fifty other space-faring species, and a shit-ton of artificially created stuff floating around claiming to be alive. This is mainly because some primogenitor race called the Fosters left a lot of tech behind and possibly seeded Celestial Fire with care packages and helpful bits of their own genetic material. The Fosters are impossibly old. The galaxy did several extinction cycles between them and the current era, but some of their things survived and races like the Chosen and the Vox managed to bootstrap up.

Which is great, because I have a Foster-inspired engine in this here ship, which means I essentially strapped one of their eternal power cores to a Vox space-stretchy device, and we kind of slingshot ourselves from point to point using the invisible superstructures in space. The Foster power core is blinking on and off, which is why I'm hitting it with a hammer right now. No joke, that's what it says to do on the manual the previous engineer gave me. The manual goes back over five generations of engineers, three of them human. My aunt gave it to me actually, my only inheritance. Some great-grandmother stole it somehow, goes the story.

Over the past forty-five-odd years of piracy, this is the only thing I've managed to keep, and basically my ticket into any ship. It's literally priceless; my aunt would come back and haunt me for sure if I tried to sell it. Anyway, I'm sort of a Foster power core expert, really, which is why it's doubly depressing that I'm reduced to hitting it with a hammer.

My captain is shouting at me in that panicky voice she reserves for certain death situations.

Lots of crew members are praying. I say crew members, but really they're just pirate scum, useless except for raiding shit. I'm pretty much the only one with a technological clue here, other than the fritzy AI.

Our ship, the *Sword of Dawn*, is jumping in an ungainly manner from spot to spot, often sideways. Ironically, this is confusing our enemy, whose name is *Dog Fiend*. *Dog Fiend* is a weird name for a ship, but you have to understand that most of the lingua franca here is Vox, and the Vox have a childish sense of humor and enjoy deliberately miswording Chosen ship names. The Chosen have caught on, but they're too aristocratic to teach their language to anyone, so Vox it is. *Dog Fiend* is an implacable enemy. They have each of our genetic signatures. They have vowed to kill us all and televise our deaths across the galaxy. Most humans not in captivity have bounties on their heads, but this is a bit much even for us.

Dog Fiend at this moment sends a pulse of superheated plasma our way, which barely misses. Their aiming AI is better than our avoiding-shit AI, so this situation won't last long.

"Karn, you asshole!" The Captain, not having anything better to do, has now come down to the engine room and is waving her baton at me. Her name is Silde, but everyone just calls her Captain. "Get us out of here!"

"Yeah, so the power core is acting funny," I say. I hit the thing again for good measure. "I wish we hadn't blown up that hospital ship three years ago." This is the reason *Dog Fiend* is chasing us. They take Chosen murder very seriously. They don't even kill each other, ever. Beneath them. Apparently the general murder rate in Celestial Fire went way up since we got here.

"That was your idea, if I recall," the Captain says.

Scum of the galaxy, like I said. I might have a problem when it comes to killing Chosen. Can't seem to help myself.

"So this time they're going to vaporize us," the Captain says. She sits down next to me, holds my free hand. There are actual tears in her eyes. "Karn. I just want to say that you're shit in bed and you're a shit engineer, but you've been a damn good friend. I've pulled more loot in the last ten years since you joined than any other time. You're a ruthless, cunning bastard and I love it."

Thanks. Ten good years. People like family. Only damn people I know anymore. It occurs to me that I can get one last jump out of this thing.

"Hey Captain, lend me your baton and close your eyes."

She frowns like I'm going to shock her in the butt or something. (I might have done that a couple of times.) The baton lets her interface with all the systems of the ship; it's like a handy override tool. It's also a personal weapon, though, with a very high electrical charge. The Fosters used to have them, so we all thought it was cool to get one, although we have no idea what the Fosters did with theirs. For all I know, we could be waving around their equivalent of a dildo.

The ship takes a glancing blow and loses all shields. I can almost hear the Chosen AI grinding numbers. Next one is def hitting us square. The Captain shoves the baton into my hands. I put it on full charge and zap the power core input port. Three things happen more or less concurrently: Lightning courses through my body and then branches throughout the ship, frying everyone. At the same time, the entire stored power of the eternal Foster power core hits the Vox stretchy thing, which, like a rubber band snapping at maximum flex, begins to toss our little tin box into god knows where. Also at the same moment, *Dog Fiend* gets one right and nails our main bay. Everything turns to light. All three of these things are fatal; I'm not sure which gets us first. I don't care because I'm already dead at this point.

Imagine my surprise then, when I wake up again.

I am floating in a rocky cavern with sparkling amethyst patches. It's an irregular-shaped chamber, but clearly fashioned for some purpose. From the inside of an asteroid, perhaps?

"It awakensss!" The voice is sibilant, high-pitched, and entirely too loud. "It looks unimpressive. Kill it."

"What manner of creature are you, hmmm?" The same voice, but this time deeper, sounding male. Is this cave schizophrenic? I notice that a different patch of amethyst glows whenever each one speaks. These things really are part of the cave.

"Er, I'm a Foster," I say. I don't know why I'm lying, except in my entire life experience, admitting to be human has never led to a positive outcome.

"Fosterrrrrr," the Girl Cave says, amused.

"We are Foster," the Boy Cave says. "You are not us."

"Um, sorry, Mr. Cave. I am human."

"Human. Hmmm. Scum of the universe."

There you go. Even the Caves know. "Where am I? Am I dead?"

"You *were* dead. We have reincarnated you," Boy Cave says. "With all your possessions."

I look around and find that I am indeed whole and unscathed, my threadbare uniform spotless, my buckles shiny, everything perfect down to the baton in my left hand and the Foster power core in my right.

"Good job," I say.

"Do you realize, human, what the device you carry actually does?"

"The Foster power core? Er, I always thought it was an infinite battery."

"It is not."

"Oh."

"It *has* a battery. You have been misusing it."

"What is it, then?"

"It is a device meant to record and map the minds of worthy organisms."

"So the battery recorded me when I zapped it..."

"Yes. The enormous jolt from the baton triggered the device. It sent us all the data of your existence."

"My Captain? Crew? You can revive them then?" A dreadful hope erupts in me.

"No. They were fully destroyed when your ship went down. Their forms were vaporized before the device could transmit. We received incomplete information. To reincarnate them... they would be incomplete."

"So if I had hit it one second earlier, you could have saved them?"

"Well, yes."

Such are the margins for losers. Ten years. I guess they were a bit like family.

"And who exactly are you?" I ask, wiping my tears.

"We are the record keepers of District 9. In charge of rebirths and reassignments."

"Are you alive actually? Are you actual Fosters? Can I see you?"

"Err, well."

"Sssooo we woke up and they were gone. Bastardsss forgot about us. Bastardsss." The girl cave is the touchy one of the pair. She sounds psychotic, in fact. Note to self: try not to piss her off. A lot rides on how the next few minutes of this conversation go. I feel the beginnings of a cunning plan.

"Yes; what my colleague means is that they apparently forgot we were on a sabbatical. Some paperwork snafu. Anyway, we've just been drifting along, keeping an eye on things. In case they come back."

"They *left*? Chosen history says they were destroyed by civil war except for a small remnant who were the 'genetic' ancestors of the Chosen."

"No, the Chosen are lying." District 9 seems glum. "They definitely left."

"And you've just been drifting along? For like three million years?"

"We're in a dead zone," D9 says. "Nothing comes here. It has been our policy to eschew contact with upstart civilizations."

"But you resurrected me."

"Well, we are bored. Plus humans hardly constitute a civilization."

"Ratssss," Psycho D9 says. "More like ratsss."

"Hey, we come from the Milky Way, alright? I bet we're pretty goddamn noble over there. Got the whole galaxy to ourselves, didn't we?" I feel the ludicrous urge to brag about some place I have no hope of ever seeing.

"Oh, Oh, how sad. You don't know," D9 says.

"Know what?"

"Your origins."

"The Milky Way. We came on a generation colony ship that got warped here by mistake," I say. Every human knows this; we have the original ship logs and almost every adult has a certified copy. It's like our bible.

"Yes. The anomaly that brought you here was natural, but extremely rare," D9 says. "A bridge between two galaxies. The Chosen have instruments looking for these objects. I am afraid they sent some system wreckers back across the bridge before it closed."

"System wreckers?"

"Well, it's a machine that finds inhabited systems and the

novas their stars. Quite a small device really; fully automated, of course. It's called flattening a system. I'm afraid, well, there's just nothing left of you in the Milky Way. Your star system was wiped out within weeks of your arrival at Celestial Fire."

"They're all gone, then?" A wave of grief hits me unlike any sensation I've ever felt before. I imagine plants feel like this when they're pulled from the ground. "There are no humans in the Milky Way?"

"I'm sorry," D9 says. "Would you like some tea?"

You might wonder why I'm so cut up about a place I've never been to. The thing is, in Celestial Fire, the Chosen routinely abuse us, enslave us, experiment on us, pit us in fights, and keep us as sex pets. The Vox are not much better, except that they don't have the sexual kink for us; they normally just fire at our ships on sight. The rest of the galaxy pretty much take their cue from these guys. We eke out a living like hyenas, those of us who are free. I don't even know how many of us the Chosen keep in captivity. So it was nice to think of a place where we weren't the scum. A home to go back to one day. A noble past. Something we weren't ashamed of. Fuck it. Too good to be true, eh?

"I've never heard of system wreckers," I say. "We'd know if the Chosen had that kind of tech."

"They did not make it. They found a cache of our gear. It is why they are so powerful. They have only a few wreckers left. They cannot build more. They are not as clever as they pretend."

"And *we* were such a threat?"

"The Chosen believed you came here on purpose, as a precursor to invasion. Jumping galaxies in an expanding universe is very difficult to do. The bridges can be reopened. Anything might come through. It was a kneejerk response."

"So it's your fault."

"Whatsssss?" Psycho is incensed. Her patch glows a bright purple which is almost blinding at this point. I can literally feel the heat coming off her.

"You left genocidal tech just lying around," I say. "And these murderers found it and destroyed my entire system."

"Yes," D9 admits. "It is unfortunate."

"You owe me." This is the critical part here.

"We have already rebodied you," D9 objects.

"What's that gonna do? *Dog Fiend* is hunting me. They'll just kill me on sight."

"What do you want?"

"A new ship for starters, since mine blew up."

"We don't have a shipyard; we are simply a bureaucratic reincarnation office," D9 says.

"You can cheat death but you can't make me a ship?"

"Partsss," Psycho says. "In the Hold!"

The cave talks to itself in a different language.

"We can cobble something together with the last of the stuff in our holds," D9 says. "If only to get rid of you."

"That's not all," I say. "I don't want to be human. You can rebody any race, right?"

"Correct."

"Make me Chosen."

"That's completely against protocol," D9 says.

"But you *could*." I use my best wheedling tone. I'd bet my eyes that this Foster asteroid can make any body it damn well pleases. "You're bored, right? Three million years... The Fosters left you guys, you know. They ain't coming back. You don't have to follow protocol anymore."

"Bastardssss." Psycho is turning out to be my best ally.

"The Chosen are real assholes, you know that, right? You've seen what they do to us?"

"We have seen," D9 admits. His bit of amethyst seems to physically shrink and grow duller. He's not very good at controlling these cues. If this were poker, he'd have lost his shirt long ago. I sense that a bit more wheedling will totally swing shit in my favor.

"You guys have nothing to do. Come with me. Let's blow shit up."

"Blowing up shit is fun!" Psycho agrees instantly. I'm beginning to like her.

"We are in charge of rebirths," D9 objects. "Blowing up things is a different department."

"And how many rebirths do you get? You said yourself there aren't many reincarnation machines lying around."

"You are the first for our district," D9 says with a degree of embarrassment, "since the last extinction cycle. In the previous round we did fifteen. Numbers have fallen."

"How long do you think this cycle will last?"

"At the present course, about fifteen thousand years," D9 says.

"Let's hurry that along a bit then, shall we?" We're going to steal some system wreckers and see how the Celestial Fire likes getting flattened.

I'm not going to lie. It's weird as fuck being in a Chosen body. They have so many more active senses. They can see through their skin more or less. No sense of smell, though; everything is taste. Movement is more fluid, because their bones are cartilaginous. I can feel my brain processing shit differently. Not *better*, just different. I can pay attention to multiple things at the same time without stress, but I feel I've dropped some of the panicky quickness I used to have. Everything is a bit plodding. Maybe panicky quickness comes from being hunted all the time.

After a bit more cajoling from me and Psycho, D9 finally agrees to join the expedition. They decide to incarnate into Chosen bodies as well. Chosen don't have gender, by the way. They evolved out of that mindset and now just fuck each other at will, and they're horny as hell. I know this because Psycho keeps tapping various parts of me with her tentacles.

D9 wasn't lying when he said they were midlevel bureaucrats. They have actually zero skills outside their immediate expertise. The only remotely usable ship in the hold is something from the last extinction cycle, called a Ramone. It's a cool triangular shape, but it has no engine and no guns, and the ship AI is gone. So basically it's a cool hull.

The hold of the asteroid known as D9 is just a massive junkyard of crap they've captured in the dead zone, garbage floating to them over the eons. Thankfully, like good paper pushers, they have catalogued everything.

I find an ancient Vox stretch drive, which is great because I know how to retrofit that. The lack of weapons is harder to fix. There are some torpedo tubes, but no ammo. Without proper schematics it's very dangerous to fit improper rounds into a space-firing weapon (see "ship number one, self-destruction" entry in my journal).

In the end I fit some ancient Vox rail guns up front, just to look menacing. There are some rounds in the chamber. I christen the ship *Silde*, in honor of the Captain. We then draw lots for ranks, and Psycho wins and picks gunnery, and D9 picks the captaincy, so I'm now back to my original rank as chief engineer. Some people are just not destined for great things.

D9 has maps for most of Celestial Fire. I know *Dog Fiend*'s patrol routes because I have extensively studied them over the last three years, in a desperate attempt to avoid them. It feels weird to actually want to find them for a change.

It takes three jumps before we catch up, near the pirate system of Old Bay. As promised, *Dog Fiend* is broadcasting our murder on all channels. I watch my old ship blowing up multiple times, with plenty of chat comments from alien assholes. The three explosions are exquisitely timed. If I slow it all down, I can see the faint twitch of lightning, then the slight shadow of the stretch drive engaging, and then plasma discharge rendering it all moot. I do the math and conclude that if I had been a quarter second faster, the reincarnation machine would have taken all the readings instead of just mine.

My genetic signature is no longer the same. *Dog Fiend* cannot find me. I sail by them, cringing as their radar idly paints my hull. In these parts, Chosen frigates can pretty much do what they want; they're judge, jury, and executioner. No pirate ship, not even a whole fleet, can really stand up to an alert frigate.

Dog Fiend doesn't so much as twitch. I could just keep going, sail as far as this Ramone ship will go.

I am so tempted. I'm not a fighting man, never have been, and putting me in an overgrown squid suit doesn't change things much. I'm still a coward, really. In the end it just comes down to me not having a place to go to. Not really having a reason to stay alive, I guess. That and the fact that Psycho loads up her guns and starts firing without a heads-up.

Everything happens very quick. The rail gun shots bounce off *Dog Fiend's* shields. The frigate responds with a torpedo that plows into us and shears off half our hull. The Ramone ship is crap at fighting; no wonder they went extinct. I'm ready for this, however, because evacuation is one of my best skills. I had our capsule rigged from the start, well stocked with snacks, and we jet out of there clean before the explosion.

I aim our exit trajectory towards *Dog Fiend's* radar field, so that they can pick us up. It's better than dying in space; not like anyone in these parts will come looking to rescue us. Psycho finds this enormously entertaining. Three million years of boredom, I guess I'd like a gunfight too. *Dog Fiend* reels us in. The inside of their ship is filled with a watery gel, their favored method of travel, although they can, as I've noted before, survive hard vacuum if they have to.

Three armed marines pry open our escape pod and get the shock of their lives. At my urging, everyone puts their tentacles up in surrender. There's multiple problems here. First of all, it is unheard of for Chosen to fire on another Chosen ship. There are rules to this kind of thing. Secondly, Chosen warriors are not supposed to surrender. Like ever. Species honor and all that. True, this is probably propaganda they've spread about themselves, but still, it's a very awkward situation.

In the end, the admiral in charge of *Dog Fiend* and the entire senior command crew come to the ship bay, just to have a look. By this time we have over thirty guns aimed at us, and I am praying Psycho doesn't start blasting with any hidden weapons.

I'm pretty sure she's packing heat because she winks at me from one of her tertiary eyes.

Just wait... please just wait.

"What the hell do we have here?" The admiral is a grizzled warrior missing a couple of limbs. "Who fired on us? What the fuck kind of tribe are you?"

"We are the tribe of District 9," I say. "We're here to take your ship, steal your souls and nova your stars."

"What?"

I have the baton curled inside one tentacle, and the reincarnation box taped to my back. The squid flesh is rolled over it, so just the port is visible. Chosen hand-eye coordination is eerily perfect. I hit the port with the baton at max power, once again abusing the poor reincarnation box, just as thirty-odd weapons discharge into me, obliterating my borrowed flesh.

At the same time lightning arcs from squid to squid, killing and recording, a chain reaction that kills D9 and Psycho first, then a round of marines, then the Admiral and officers, so on and so forth until the whole ship is done. Turns out Chosen gel is a pretty good conductor. Within ten seconds, *Dog Fiend* is a mausoleum. I don't care because once again, I'm dead.

I wake up in the asteroid. D9 has rebodied me. I waggle a tentacle gingerly. The trauma of taking thirty-plus shells is still making its way around my brain. So far the plan is going swimmingly.

"Was that your plan all along?" D9 is incensed. "Fry us?"

"Good plan," Psycho says. They've both rebodied themselves as Chosen.

"We could have all been vaporized!" D9 is still angry.

"Relax. That Foster tech shit works flawlessly," I say. "And now we have a Chosen frigate. Rebody the admiral, get his baton, and we can whistle *Dog Fiend* over here like a lost puppy."

"Good plan." Psycho nods.

"And then what? You intend to take the Chosen over ship by ship, committing suicide each time?" D9 asks.

Psycho considers it. She shrugs. "Good plan," she says a third time.

The admiral is catatonic when D9 reincarnates him. I take the baton off him and call *Dog Fiend* over. The old fool whimpers, his tentacles spasming, the missing stumps juddering pathetically in the air. I almost feel sorry for him. I wonder why he didn't regrow them; some badge of honor I suppose.

"We have to reincarnate the others," D9 says. He is disturbed. "You took out the whole crew. I have two hundred and eleven souls backed up."

"Just delete them."

"I can't. I'm not a murder machine, I have to reincarnate. The longer I wait, the more the paperwork piles up."

"Reincarnate them and then kill them." I flail my limbs in a tentacled shrug that shows precisely how little I care about the paperwork on murdered Chosen. "I'll start with the admiral." I like killing Chosen as much as the next man, but doing it up close is unpleasant. Chosen are hard to kill; you have to drive a spike through a particular spot in the head to hit a portion of the brain there. The rest of the brain is kind of spread out, and not only do they have multiple redundancies, they can repair themselves pretty fast.

I take the admiral's personal firearm and fire bolts into his head. It takes five shots to drop him. Droplets of purplish blood float around in the low gravity of the asteroid. My face is covered in the stuff. I don't feel the sense of satisfaction I normally get from killing Chosen. I just feel tired and sad. The thought of going through this another two hundred and ten times is daunting. I have a feeling D9 is going to make me do it personally.

It occurs to me that I'm still galactic scum. I always felt I wasn't meant to be a hero, but now it seems I can't even bother being a proper villain. Even if I win every encounter, I'll still be alone at the end. I don't want to do this for the rest of my life. I want to go home.

"Hey D9, let's pause the conveyor belt of death for a second."

"I cannot store them indefinitely; the protocol is to rebirth immediately, before quantum scrambling occurs."

I don't have a clue what that means. "You said the bridge to the Milky Way still exists. Can you find it?"

"It's on the map," D9 says.

"Good. I want to go back."

"It's a dead system. Your people are not there anymore." There's some compassion in his voice.

I see the vast emptiness of that place, the solar system a ruin of rocks and gas, all evidence of our existence wiped out. There will be other systems though, other blue and green planets like fabled Earth, other places with free dirt, free water, free air.

"I know. It's empty, though. I think empty is better for me than crowded. I don't want to spend any more time here. I can't change what I am, what's happened to us. Living here, even if I kill every single Chosen ship, wreck every star, I'll still be galactic scum, still a slave, still a pirate, still a murderer. Fresh start sounds pretty good for all of us. You guys gonna come with me?"

"Your plan sucks," Psycho says.

"We will come with you," D9 says. "Explore a new galaxy. Perhaps the Fosters have left a trace there."

"Will the Chosen fire another wrecker if we go through the bridge?" I ask. It would be my typical luck to have a second wrecker fired into the Milky Way.

D9 shrugs. "They know it's a dead end there. A Chosen ship jumping across? They'll be curious, but I doubt they'll waste a wrecker. They don't have many left. They'll probably just assume it's an accident. Get too close, you get sucked in."

"Let's go, then."

"What about the crew?"

I think about it. "Make them human. Make us all human. Let's go explore the Milky Way as natives."

I put the Foster baton against my chest and fry myself for hopefully the last time.

HOME IS WHERE THE HEART IS
Hiromi Goto

ONE MORNING YUKO discovered that her heart had turned into a rotten quince. It hung from a bare branch of a bush in her mother's Garden. Yuko glanced at her mother, then quickly looked away.

"It's not what you think," Mari said, as she sprinkled some ashes from the fire pit onto the flowerbed.

Yuko's lips turned down. "Do you know what I'm thinking?" She'd come to see her mother in the countryside, a trip beyond long overdue, but city life created its own busyness, and postponing a visit was easy when your heart wasn't in it. She pulled off her toque and scarf as the snow caught in the weave began melting. She dropped the wet things onto a wrought-iron chair. Beyond the tall thorny hedge that encircled the Garden, it was midwinter. But inside her mother's Garden it was spring. Green blades of bulb flowers were sending their leaves above the ground. The plum trees were in flower, and the cherry trees not far behind them.

Mari began digging at the soil with a small spade, flipping over the scoops until the ashes were evenly distributed in the loam. "There," she said, and gave a contented sigh. She raised her face to meet her daughter's gaze.

Her mother's eyes were the palest shade of brown. Yuko looked away again.

Her rotten quince heart was a deep burgundy; the skin had dried and wrinkled, then bloated with the rains. It was grotesque but also beautiful.

Yuko had been feeling off the past week. Prone to sudden dizziness, and a dull panic that tasted of salty water and regret. It hadn't occurred to her that this was all on account of a missing heart. And now here her heart was, hanging there on its own. It was a wonder how she was still alive.

"I suppose you think this is something I've done," her mother said.

Yuko's eyes widened. "What else would it be doing here?" she asked.

"It's always the mother's fault," Mari said. "Patriarchy's gift to women everywhere. Just you wait until you're a mother."

"Not a chance," Yuko said.

They stood there. Staring at her heart.

"What do you think I should do?" Yuko asked at last. "Is it safe to, you know, pick it and just put it back inside?" She gestured at her chest with both hands.

Mari did not respond for a long time. Yuko didn't know if her mother was thinking or if she wasn't there. Sometimes her mother disappeared right in front of her.

"You'll have to ask your grandmother," Mari finally said.

Yuko took a deep breath. "I'd rather not," she said.

"I would help you if I could," her mother snapped. She shook her head. "I'm not angry with you."

"Isn't there someone else we could ask?" Yuko said. "Maybe my heart will just come back while I'm sleeping..."

"Your heart is not a capricious cat," Mari said.

Yuko thought she might feel like crying, but the emotion seemed faint. Far away. A fat vein in the rotten quince throbbed.

Her mother looked toward the west. "There's a storm coming."

Her quince heart wouldn't take another soaking. If it fell off the stem, would she die? How horribly O. Henry, she thought.

"Can't you—okay," Yuko waved one hand in the air.

"Weather is beyond me; you know that," Mari said.

"But it's spring in here. That's weather, isn't it?" Yuko asked.

"It is and it isn't," her mother said.

"I don't understand it." Yuko's voice was low. "I never did."

"That's why you had to leave." Her mother's smile was a little sad.

Her heart throbbed on the stem. "I can build a shelter around this bush?" Yuko gestured. "Like a green house or something."

"What if there's hail? Or a windstorm that tosses down branches? What if someone else comes to steal your heart?" Mari crossed one arm over her own chest.

"Where is Grandmother now?" Yuko asked. Cold prickled at her nape and goose bumps flared down her arms.

"The last time I saw her she was in the basement."

A small sound escaped Yuko's lips.

"I thought there were some special bulbs in the cellar. So I went downstairs. I caught a glimpse of my mother then."

Mari raised her hand as if to touch her daughter's hair, but it fell before completing the gesture. "She's always in a better mood when she's in the attic..." Her mother's voice faded.

"Could we wait until she comes upstairs?" Yuko whispered.

"There is no telling when that will happen," Mari said.

Yuko looked at the flowerbed. A fat worm, exposed by her mother's spade, wriggled frantically to return to the darkness.

"I'm sorry," Mari said. "The Garden is my domain. But the house is your grandmother's."

"But my heart is in your Garden!" Yuko cried.

"I didn't put it there," her mother said.

"HELLO?" YUKO SAID, as she opened the front door just a little. She stood still, head tilted, both dreading and hoping to hear her grandmother's voice call back. But all was silence.

She opened the door wider, just enough to slip inside, and sidled through the doorway, glancing back for a look from her mother. But her mother was gone.

When she was four years old, Mari had put her to planting smooth pebbles of tiger's eye in a ring around an orange tree. The tree was a little ill. The leaves were drooping and a faint smell of rot rose up from the roots.

"You love the stones while you place them," her mother said. "You love the tree. And yourself."

"Love the stones," Yuko had chanted as she pushed the pretty stones into the loam. Her fingers were nimble. Even then, as a small child. When she'd had to go to people school she could cut circles around the other children who could barely hold scissors. "Love the tree. Love my self," she crooned, planting. It made her feel all warm and tingly inside. The sun glittered through the leaves. A small rustling of the wind. Then a swell of sweet orange blossoms...

She tipped her head back, back... The leaves shone, healthy and bright. As she watched, flowers burst upon the branches, a wave of blooms surging, cascading upward, the sweetest perfume—

Her mouth dropped open and she fell back onto her bum.

"Look, Mama!" she cried out. "Look what I did!

All was silent.

"Mama?" She looked for her. Behind every tree in the orchard. In the vegetable Garden. Among the flowers taller than she was. She looked for her among the rows of berry bushes. And the grape vines. But her mama was gone.

Mama did not return until after dark.

Many small children learn that people you love and trust will leave you and they will still come back.

Some small children learn that people you love and trust leave you. And that is what their heart remembers the most—

Something interrupted the still air. An unsound that, nonetheless, broke through Yuko's memories. She turned away from the Garden to take in the slate-covered foyer, gazed down the long hallway of doors that never ended.

"Hello, House," Yuko said aloud. "Forgive me. It's been a very long time."

From a great distance a sound began to build. As if a behemoth train was entering a long tunnel. She fought the compulsion to flee. She planted her feet on the stone slabs which had begun to vibrate and faced the hallway as the roar turned into a deep shrieking howl, hitting every decibel, filling the infinite house, rattling her head, drowning her lungs.

She didn't close her eyes. They were forced shut. As if a hurricane bore down upon her. The sound hit her so hard she staggered. Air knocked from her lungs. Somewhere, in a far-off Garden, her quince heart rocked on its small stem...

The roar filled the entire world. Then it was gone.

Her ears rang, frantic. She took a deep, shuddering breath. House still loved her, she guessed. Because she was still alive.

She removed her shoes and set them beside a dusty pair of purple velvet slippers on the frayed carpet beside the front door.

Best keep them on.

She gulped. Nodded. Slipped her feet back into her shoes. "Thank you," she whispered. House didn't always warn her. Maybe today would turn out okay.

When she was little, House had been her first friend. They played catch and tag and hide and seek (only that one time because if you played hide and seek with House and House forgot, then of course little girls could die, like many children die in household accidents, like tangling in the strings of blinds, and falling down stairs, it wasn't House's fault, was it, everyone forgot they were playing hide and seek at some point in their life), and exploring and Find Grandmother...

It had been easy to think that House and her grandmother were one—like two strands that made up a string—but when she had once blamed House for something her grandmother had done House slammed shut every single door in the infinity hallway. *I AM MY OWN PERSON*, House roared.

"I'm sorry," Yuko whispered at the memory.

House was quiet. There were no clocks, because something happened to time inside the walls. Yuko's cell phone was probably dead.

Yuko began walking along the frayed carpet of the hallway. It was woven into a pattern that looked like roses and thorns and heads and things. It wasn't a good idea to look at it too closely. "House," Yuko said. "I'd like to go to the basement, if I may."

All the doors lining both sides of the hallway were of different colors. About fifteen yards away a red door opened outward on quiet hinges. The cool, dank smell of caves and moisture wafted toward her.

"Thank you," Yuko said. She meant it. She trotted toward the open door and cast a look behind her. Looking back to where she'd come from. The hallway went on forever. She couldn't see the foyer to the front door. And looking in the other direction was a mirror image... Yuko sighed.

Something cold and slightly wet pressed into the palm of her left hand. Yuko spun around. Out in the Garden, her quince heart thudded ponderously.

A pale wolf. Thick fur the color of first light at dawn. The beast stared up at her with yellow eyes. Their jaw dropped open to reveal teeth made for biting and tearing, their breath rolling out of their mouth in white clouds. As if they were in a winter proper. Their breath smelled sweet, like fresh meat, and health.

"Hello," Yuko said. They'd never had a wolf guest before. She was surprised that her mother hadn't told her. But maybe her mother didn't know. All kinds of things happen inside a house that not every member of the family knows about.

Yuko really wanted to touch the wolf's luxuriant fur. But she did not.

"Huff," the wolf said. The warm breath felt nice upon her cool hands.

"Pleased to meet you," Yuko said.

The wolf blinked, then turned around, began click-clacking

down the stairway. They looked back, once, over their shoulder, even as they continued trotting.

Yuko followed.

The wolf stayed three wolf-lengths ahead of her at all times. Yuko thought of herself as relatively fit. But now that her heart hung from a branch in her mother's Garden she felt hollow and weak. In Japan there was a saying—kage ga usui. If someone said you had a "thin shadow," it meant that you didn't stand out in a crowd, you were easily overlooked. Yuko felt like her shadow was the thinnest it'd ever been.

The light inside House never changed—it was a kind of dull incandescence, and the temperature remained room temperature. Which was odd, if she thought about it. Because the wolf ought to be hot, with all that fur, and she ought to be sweating beneath her winter coat, but she felt neither hot nor cold. She felt just right.

They walked down, down, down, an impossible distance with no landing. Yuko couldn't remember if the stairs had always been like this. When she tried to recall what things had been like in her childhood there was only a vague opaque light. The light that House cast all over.

It was difficult to know if they were actually moving or just repeating a motion in a place that didn't change. She was concerned, but it was a distant feeling. Just like her heart.

Yuko was, however, getting thirsty.

Did the wolf's ears twitch? They whipped their muzzle to the side and snapped at the air. A rend opened and the wolf leapt through. Yuko's eyes widened. She'd never seen space open up like this in House before. From the distance came the sound of falling water. The waft of fresh sweetness drifted toward her. Yuko stumbled through the rent air, after the wolf.

The ground was soft, mossy. The loamy depth smelled like ten thousand years of life and death, the sweet notes of cedar. If Yuko had a heart, she would have wept.

A stream tumbled over rounded stones. Light glittered on the surface, but when Yuko looked up she could not see the sun shining through the canopy of the ceiling. Too thirsty to care, she knelt at the edge of the stream and plunged her hands into the cool water. Paused. Glanced at the wolf.

The wolf dropped their head to the stream and began lapping.

Yuko raised the water to her lips. It tasted of minerals and sweetness. It filled her mouth with gladness. She gulped and gulped, gasping between for air, until the wolf dropped a paw upon her exposed forearm, the claws pressing hard enough that they dug into her skin but did not break it.

Yuko shook her head. She wanted to drink forever from this stream it was so delicious, tasted so *alive*...

Something dull, white, between strands of moss. Here. And here. Along the edges of the water. Bones... small, large, a skull of a cat, a desiccated bird's wing, long slender bones, of a deer, or human... Yuko almost vomited the water she'd drunk down. But something in her body kept her from spewing.

The wolf turned away from the stream and began trotting toward—the opening they had come through was gone. Yuko leapt to her feet. She looked all around her, but she could not see very far. Some trick of light or some trick of place. She could only see a few yards ahead, and beyond that was a darker dream that verged on nightmare.

She wanted to leave. Now. "House," she whispered.

House did not respond.

"Wolf," Yuko pleaded. The animal had disappeared. And the sound of the stream was growing faint.

Then that too disappeared.

Where was she? When was she? With nothing to orient to it felt like she was disappearing into the darkest, quietest part of night when sleep would not arrive and desperation filled her mouth like monster teeth and at least her little heart kept her company, reminding her of both her life and her impending death... But now her heart was so far away. There was a ghost echo of its frantic beating deep inside her ears.

From a great distance she heard a mournful howl.

"Wolf!" she cried. "Wolf!"

The sound was fading.

She ran through the dark nowhere, through the dark no-time. She ran. She couldn't hear her own footsteps. Nausea swept through her. She was spinning inside her own brain—

Was that a light? She came to a standstill and dragged her forearm across her eyes.

Warm and orange, a bright flickering. A small sound escaped from Yuko's lips as she trotted the final yards toward the glow.

The light was coming from what looked to be a window of a small cottage. In all of her adventures inside House she'd never come across it before. She'd visited the most marvelous rooms, like the one filled with dolls that sang bird songs, or the one that looked empty but was full of bright feelings, or the one that was so big it felt like a world, or the one that was the inside of an oven and two little children lived there.... But a house inside a house was a kind of a puzzle.

Yuko patted down her hair and her clothing and stood up straight. She knocked on the low door.

It swung open. Light poured out, but the darkness absorbed it like water. Yuko quickly stepped inside. So she could shut the door. Lest all the light be taken.

The door was so heavy. Yuko pressed her shoulder against it, her leather shoes with their flat treads practically useless on the dirt floor. She heaved as the darkness tried to push inside, her shoes skidding.

A pale blur dashed toward her—thud! The wolf threw their body sideways against the door and it banged shut. Yuko fell to her hands and knees. "Thank you." Her voice was hoarse.

The interior of the small cottage was not well-lit. It had only looked bright in contrast to the nowhere darkness on the outside. But now that the door was shut the cottage no longer seemed like a cozy haven. The light coming from the small fireplace was a dull orange. The shadows cast upon the floor and low walls were long. On the hard-packed dirt floor were mounds of debris—tattered rags, leaves that had rotted then dried several times over, big bones stripped of any flesh and marrow. They looked like they could be the thigh bones of a deer. Or a human.

Yuko slowly rose to her feet.

There were some furnishings. A scuffed-up wooden table. An old hunting knife lay atop the dirty table, next to a tin plate turned upside down. A single wooden chair knocked onto its side. A rusty fork lay on the floor next to a mound of tattered clothing. In the dark corner was a low bed, and within easy reach a shelf of dusty books. But the smell... the smell inside the cottage was ripe with animal fur. If a human had ever lived here it was a long time ago.

Yuko noticed the sleeve of her coat was cold and wet. From that stream, she thought. So she removed it and placed it on the back of the chair. She drew nearer the fire and crouched in front of its small warmth. Held out her hands.

The wolf began pacing. Their claws dug into the packed floor as they circled around her. Energy vibrated from the wolf's fur, crackling, like electricity.

"Ummm," Yuko said. She didn't think her voice wobbled. "I'm a friend. Not an enemy."

Far off, on the little branch in her mother's Garden, her heart began to pound.

A low growl started inside the wolf's throat. They dropped their head low, slinky, but the thick hair on their shoulders stood up. Their yellow eyes gleamed.

Yuko slowly got to her feet. Backed away. Bumped into the table with a clatter. Her hand tapped back, reaching behind her. Her fingertips nudging the handle of the hunting knife. She grabbed it tight and swung it forward.

"I don't want to fight you," Yuko panted. "House!" she shouted. "House! Help me!"

The wolf leapt.

Yuko thrust the knife. It penetrated the thick fur, then skin, and sank into the wolf's belly. As its limp weight dragged the animal down, the knife continued to slide upward, slicing past the wolf's throat. The animal fell with a thud onto the dirt floor.

Yuko's legs gave out. And she sank to the floor beside the animal she'd just butchered.

"Oh, wolf," she whispered. "Forgive me. I did not want to kill you."

She breathed, ragged and raw. For a long time. The knife. It was still clenched tightly in her hand. There was no blood. She glanced at the dead wolf. Their pale fur was not matted dark and wet. The dirt floor was dry.

Yuko set the knife to the side and stretched out her hand. She gently stretched the wolf's body out.

Something pale, at the open place, where she'd sliced into the wolf's belly. Not intestines. Something else. Yuko's skin crawled. But she swallowed her unease and gripped the two sides of the cut and pulled it slightly apart.

Beneath the flaps of fur was pale flesh. Not flayed wolf flesh, red like meat. It looked human.

Yuko touched the skin beneath the skin with tentative fingers. Gently pressed. The flesh, a little cool, gave. Yuko's hand shook.

She reached for the knife and placed the tip of the blade into the bottommost point of the original cut. She slid it downward at an angle, following the length of a hind leg until she could cut no more. As soon as the wolf skin was broken, it was as if a different kind of volume swelled out—what had been contained inside their slender limb—as if it had been compressed. A human leg tumbled out. With wrinkled skin. Long sinews. The knee and bones of the foot knobbly with age...

A small cry escaped from Yuko's lips.

She slit along the other legs and reached inside, pulling out the damp limbs of a human. Hands trembling, Yuko slid her finger in and around the curves of neck and skull, and drew upward the person's face.

It was her grandmother.

Grandmother's eyes were closed. And her damp hair was pressed close to her skull. Her hair had grown thinner with age. How long had it been since Yuko'd last seen her grandmother? Three years? Four?

She pressed her fingertips gently against her grandmother's neck. She could feel no pulse. She shook her head. No. No! Yuko slid her hands and then her arms beneath her grandmother's neck and back. She held down the wolf skin with the ball of her foot and drew her grandmother out, drew her free. Yuko half-dragged her closer to the fire and lay her down near the heat.

Had her grandmother always been so slight? Whenever Yuko had spent time with her, her personality was so strong she seemed to tower over everyone.

"Come back," Yuko hissed as she rubbed her grandmother's arms and legs. "Return to me, now! I need your help! I came here, didn't I?"

Yuko's hands fell away from her grandmother. Her body was too cold. "I'm sorry," she whispered. "I should have come home sooner."

Her grandmother's head whipped around and she clamped down on Yuko's arm with blunt teeth.

Yuko screamed.

Snarling, the old woman's face was distorted with a wild rage. Her eyes yellow.

"Grandmother! You're hurting me!" Yuko sobbed. She tried to pull her arm back but her grandmother's bite didn't loosen. "Stop!"

The old woman blinked, and as Yuko watched her yellow eyes began to grow muddy, slowly darken until they were brown. Her grandmother opened her mouth and released Yuko's arm.

Yuko yanked it to her chest and scuttled backwards across the floor.

She stared down at her arm. The skin was broken in several places and blood was oozing out.

"Am I going to turn into a werewolf now?" she asked.

"What?" Grandmother barked. She began coughing. Then actually laughing.

"It's not funny!" Yuko snapped.

Her grandmother hacked and hacked, a deep retching sound. Yuko returned to her side and began rubbing her back.

A final hollow, echoing cough. Wet retching. On her hands and knees, her grandmother convulsed and something dropped out of her mouth to land on the hard-packed dirt.

It was a key, covered in sputum. Made of heavy metal, with a head shaped rather like a heart. The teeth were simply cut, blocky and square.

"Can you get that?" Her grandmother's voice was low, strangely subdued. "It has been such a burden to me."

Yuko stretched out her hand—

She yanked it back. "Is there a catch?"

Her grandmother's eyes gleamed. "Clever child. You will do." The old woman left the key on the dirt floor and shuffled to the pile of clothes on the floor. She shook them out as best she could and began dressing. She had to pause in the middle of doing up her shirt to rest. Yuko fastened the remaining buttons. Smoothed down the rucked-up collar.

"What happened?" Yuko asked.

Her grandmother shook her head. "I kept my wolfskin on too long. And forgot myself inside of it. A rookie mistake. But I was desperate to get away from House. House didn't know I had a wolfskin. So I could move around freely without House knowing."

Yuko took in her grandmother's words, then tipped her face to look up at the dusty ceiling. She pointed with her thumb and mouthed the word *House* in an exaggerated way.

"House doesn't know about this small glade and cabin," Grandmother said. "I made it in a pocket of Time that House doesn't perceive. We can talk freely." Her eyes shone with pride.

Yuko's eyes widened, impressed. "Why did you want to get away from House? I thought House was your pride and joy."

Her grandmother sighed and sank down on the low bed. "Relationships change... House was my life work, and a safe haven for me when I needed it the most. But over time I wanted to see life outside of House."

"Even with the infinite number of rooms inside," Yuko said.

"Sometimes a person wants to have engagements with the outside world." Her grandmother dragged one hand across her eyes.

"I didn't know, Grandmother," Yuko said. "I thought you just wanted to keep Mother and me here, with you. I didn't know you were trapped."

"I didn't know either," Grandmother said. "Until I tried to leave."

"House has always scared me," Yuko confided. "And you've always scared me a little, too."

"There is a difference between being afraid of someone because you don't trust them, and being afraid of them because you don't understand them."

Yuko tilted her head. "Okay. But those two things can also overlap."

Her grandmother laughed. "Yes, mistrustful child. This is also true."

Yuko sighed. Feeling tired to the bone once more. "Grandmother. I've come home for my heart. It's hanging in Mother's Garden. I want it back."

Her grandmother went very still. "I know nothing of it. Does it pain you, child?"

Yuko's hand pressed upon her chest. "I don't feel myself. I feel hollow." She looked into her grandmother's eyes. They were brown, but shot with shards of yellow. "Did you take my heart?"

Her grandmother tilted her head, as if she could hear something from outside.

"I've had a dream just like this before..." Her grandmother's voice faded. She shook her head. "It's not an easy thing—to steal a heart. No. It wasn't me. When did this happen?"

"I'm not sure," Yuko said. "I started feeling poorly a week ago. But it was getting worse. Then I started thinking that it was time to visit Mother and you. And House..."

They both looked up at the low ceiling at the same time.

"How long have I been a wolf?"

"Mother said you've been in the basement for seven months."

"I've been in a power struggle with House for the past half-year. I finally found House's key. And then I swallowed it while in wolf form. So House would not be able to find it. I tried to find a way outside from the basement. But I could not. And in time my mind became more like a wolf's, less like a witch's. Until I caught a whiff of your scent, the pitch of your voice. Somehow I knew it was important that you come to this cottage."

"Am I a prisoner in House now too?"

Her grandmother turned to look at the key that shone dully on the dirt floor.

She smiled fiercely. "If it was House who stole your heart to lead you back home, then you should know—this key is House's heart."

Yuko did not recognize the feeling inside of her hollow chest. But it did not feel right. "So," she said to her grandmother, "you started it."

"House started it!" the old woman retorted.

"Hmmph," Yuko said. She retrieved her coat and put it back on, then bent over to pick up the sticky key. She wiped it against her jeans and then tucked it into her coat pocket. "Let's go back upstairs."

IT TOOK HOURS, or days, for them to leave the pocket of Time. Then to climb the stairs.

Yuko knew that the stairs were just as much House as the first floor, but she didn't want to begin negotiations until they were near the front door. Her grandmother followed her, silently.

Yuko did not know if House allowed them to rise up from the

basement to the ground floor, or if the stairs were a permanent structure, but after a lifetime they finally reached the red door that swung outward into the infinity hallway of the main floor.

"Thank you," Yuko murmured.

House did not respond.

She clutched the sticky key inside her pocket and squeezed it tight.

The infinity hallway wasn't. It led them past three doors, like any normal house, and then they were at the foyer, where Yuko had almost left her shoes. House swung open the front door. Outside, in the Garden, a pale blue butterfly flitted above a plum tree. There was no sign of her mother.

Behind her, she could feel her grandmother quivering with anticipation. How long her grandmother had wanted to leave this relationship, but couldn't...

"Are we free to leave?" Yuko asked.

First, what is mine must be returned. House trembled. The front door slammed shut.

"Grandmother gets to go outside," Yuko said. "Then we trade."

In the kitchen, House opened and shut all the cupboards and drawers, a fury of thuds and banging, the metallic jangle of cutlery and utensils. Something in the attic groaned like a sickened beast. A rumbling started off from the far end of the hallway and rolled toward them, as if an enormous wooden barrel was thundering closer and closer.

Yuko remained calm. House had tried to frighten her when she arrived—but maybe it was all just sound and fury in the end. And maybe she was getting used to her heart feeling distant. Maybe it wasn't all bad. "Your tantrums won't change my mind," she said. "Let her go." A hand gripped her arm. Yuko looked back.

There was fierce love in her grandmother's gaze, and a terrible hope. Her lips quivered with it.

The noise stopped. From the deep silence, somewhere inside House a baby began to cry. So plaintive, so heartbroken, tears streamed down both of their faces. Yuko gritted her teeth. "Let her go!"

Why do you want to leave me? House cried. *You are my Mother!*

"I am also my own person," Yuko's grandmother said. "You are a House fully grown. You don't need me. And I want to see the world outside your walls."

I've made you a world inside of my walls for you. Why isn't it enough!

"You need a new name, then," Yuko said. "Because you're not House anymore. You're Prison."

The silence that fell upon House was complete. Like the death of time. All the hairs on Yuko arms and neck stood erect. A small sound escaped her grandmother's lips.

House began to fall apart. A wooden beam thudded onto the hallway carpet and broke through several floorboards. A series of connected walls fell outward in a Mobius loop, an impossible arrangement of space and matter. Doors imploded as frames began to shrink, windows crumpling as tiles lifted off, fluttered away like a sakura storm. The floor rumbled, cracking like spring ice.

Yuko hollered, grabbed her grandmother's arm and leapt through the shrinking front doorway, yanking her through just as it squeezed into nothingness. They staggered into the safety of the Garden and turned back to witness House simultaneously crumple, collapse, and compress into the size of a doll house.

Yuko's grandmother's hand covered her mouth. "What have I done?" she whispered.

"You were honest about your feelings," Yuko said. "There is no wrong in that."

"I should stay with House, maybe. Until they grow a little bigger—"

"No," Yuko said. "That's a terrible idea. You'll get pulled back into House. And it will just be the same as before! You need to leave now."

Yuko's grandmother looked wonderingly at her grandchild. "How have you grown so wise?"

Yuko shrugged. "I left home. I had to figure out some things."

Her grandmother turned her head a little and raised her chin. She closed her eyes and sniffed at a passing breeze. For a brief moment Yuko could see the wolf she had been.

"It has been so long..." Her grandmother barked a laugh. And then she was gone, running, running faster than Yuko had ever run.

Yuko took a deep breath. Something in her chest widened. Like a bright beacon was shining from inside her ribs. *I love you*, she thought. *Come back to me now.*

The impact was so strong she rocked backwards. Almost bowled over, suffused with love.

"Okaasan is free..."

Yuko started. It was her mother. Returned from a part of the Garden Yuko could not enter. She frowned. "Are you trapped in Garden too?"

Her mother smiled. "No, Yuko. I am not. Thank you for asking."

They both looked down at little House. House looked small. And alone. House had never known a day without their Maker. And now she was gone.

Yuko crouched down in front of the closed door and tilted her head a little to try to get a look through the small upper window panels, but it was dark inside and she could see nothing. And she was too big to be able to get a good look anyway. She knocked on the door. After a few moments the door swung open a little bit.

Yuko pulled her hand out of her pocket and slid the key through the crack. It just barely fit through the frame. She gave it a little tap to propel it further inside. It clunked several times on the carpeted hallway. Then the door snapped shut.

"No!" Her mother was standing in front of the quince bush. Her arms dangling at her side. "Yuko. Your heart... it's gone."

"It's okay, Mum," Yuko said. She crossed her arms over her chest. "She's here."

"How—"

"I asked my heart to come home. And she did."

"But surely you wished for your heart to return to you before!"

"Of course," Yuko said. "But then my wish was mixed up with so much fear... Fear makes things muddy."

She glanced down at House. It seemed to be a few feet closer to her than it had been a moment before. As if it wanted to listen to their conversation. Yuko's eyes widened.

She glanced at her mother and tilted her head a little toward House. "You know, Mum, in Russia the witches have special houses too."

Her mother nodded. "I don't know much about Russian witches and their houses."

"The witch houses in Russia, they can grow chicken legs. They can walk all over, wherever they please. They aren't stuck in one place like regular houses."

Yuko glanced down. Little House seemed to quiver in place. As if a small earthquake was rumbling directly beneath them. She grinned. "Imagine," Yuko said. "Houses walking around, having their adventures too. Seeing a wide, wide world outside their walls. And meeting all kinds of new people!"

Chicken legs are ugly, House whispered. *But crows are nice. Mother likes crows too.*

"Mother..." Yuko's mother said. "We share the same mother. I never really thought about it, but you're kind of my sibling, House."

Sibling, House whispered. *You never liked me, Mari.*

"No," Mari said. "I was scared of you."

House was quiet for several seconds. *You had reason to be. I don't want to be the kind of House that everyone wants to leave. I want to be a better House.*

"Would you like to stay with me in Garden? We can get to know each other. While you teach yourself to grow legs."

Yuko gave her mother a hard look. "Are you sure?" she asked.

Her mother smiled. And raised one hand, palm facing upward. Just above her soil-stained skin a tiny tree floated, the minute leaves and branches stretching out from a small trunk from which dangled a network of roots that glowed green. "No harm comes to me in this Garden. House will be my guest. And my sibling."

"Well," Yuko said. "I guess that makes House my aunt."

Ahhhh, House sighed.

"Hmmph," Yuko said. Everything was strange and imperfect and she wasn't sure what had happened, but it was also okay.

"Will you stay for lunch? I picked some morels. I am going to make an omelette." Mari tentatively stretched out her hand, then tucked a strand of hair behind Yuko's ear.

Yuko closed her eyes, then turned her head to rest her chin in her mother's hand for a moment. The rich scent of dark soil and herbs filled her senses. She opened her eyes, then shook her head. "I left my work, my friends, and my apartment in a mess because my heart was missing and I didn't know it. But I'll come back on the weekend for a proper visit. I promise." She meant it, too.

Yuko felt a nudging against her lower leg. House was leaning against her like a cat. She reached down and patted House's roof with a gentle hand. House began to purr.

BEFORE THE GLORY
OF THEIR MAJESTIES
Minsoo Kang

DESPITE DECADES OF experience and a long record of diplomatic successes, the ambassador is filled with dread as he enters the grand palace of Their Majesties. His mission there is not a matter of a trade policy, a discussion of mutual interest, or the settling of some minor territorial dispute. His trepidation comes from the certain knowledge that what hangs in the balance is nothing less than the very survival of his home country. Even as he prepares to present himself before the rulers in an upright and dignified manner, he feels the enormous weight of the terrifying responsibility, the last-ditch attempt to somehow stave off the coming catastrophe.

The grand corridor he walks through is lined with gilded frills, typical of architecture in the Age of Absolutism. At the heavy double doors into the audience hall of Their Majesties, he is met by guards who are dressed anachronistically in full medieval armor of shimmering metal plates, bearing heavy halberds. They move stiffly and in unison like automata, opening the doors for him to enter. Beyond the threshold, the ambassador finds himself in a vast space packed with a large crowd of courtiers, nobles, and fellow diplomats in colorful attire of fine fabric. The primary source of the hall's grandeur is its astonishingly high ceiling that is topped with a dome of segmented glass. The light from above, in the shape of elongated triangles, sprawls over the hall like luminous fingers that threaten to close on everyone inside. The all-too-apparent purpose of the space is to display the power and authority of Their Majesties in the most intimidating manner.

Despite the large number of people present, the noise level is low, as everyone speaks in uneasy whispers like frightened children. Among them, the ambassador tries not to gawk at his surroundings while maintaining a look of implacable but respectful calm. When the people see him, they part to make way to the throne on the other side of the hall, gradually falling silent to watch his progress. With his dread mounting, he deliberately keeps an even pace as he proceeds, neither hurried in desperation nor slow in insolence.

The ambassador has encountered many unfamiliar and disquieting things in foreign lands in the course of his long career, and he was warned of the appearance of Their Majesties by diplomatic colleagues. But he cannot help being utterly appalled at what he beholds upon the wide throne, which is made of solid gold on the left and iron on the right. Their Majesties are young brothers conjoined at the lower torso, their bent spines coming together at the pelvis to share the same pair of legs. On the golden side of the throne is Solar Eye, the political mastermind, and on the iron side is Dark Fist, the military prodigy.

Despite their bodily connection and facial resemblance, they have arranged themselves to appear in stark contrast to each other. Their oversized coat is red on the side of Solar Eye and black on the side of Dark Fist, while their trousers are black and red on opposite sides. Solar Eye wears a golden crown, beneath which his flaxen hair is long, reaching down to his shoulders, and his face is clean shaven. Dark Fist, on the other hand, wears an iron crown on a head that is close-cropped in the military manner, but he sports a thick beard that is jet black. Solar Eye holds a long scepter of gold, topped with a ball with spikes on it, while Dark Fist wields a great broadsword.

As if the sight of them is not horrifying enough, there are further abominations on the sides of the throne. Next to Solar Eye, a dwarf fool sits on the floor with his head bowed mournfully, dressed in the same manner as Their Majesties, with a jacket and trousers that are red and black on opposite sides. In a grotesque imitation of the rulers, he shares the clothes with the upper body of another dwarf who is clearly dead, perhaps from his body having been cut in half to fit into the jacket. The gray, decaying face next to the living one is frozen in an open-mouthed expression of horror. The ambassador has a nauseating sense that the severed cadaver was sewn onto the living dwarf's body. At the side of the Dark Fist is a brass automaton in the shape of a large and fierce dog, its glimmering body crouched as if about to lunge at him, and its mouth full of blade-sharp teeth slowly opening and closing while it emits a screeching noise that is a mechanical imitation of a growl. As if the machine was not terrifying enough, the severed head of an actual dog has been fixed next to the brass one. The ambassador cannot bear to look upon either of these awful sights, so he faces Their Majesties while trying to suppress any sign of emotion.

Solar Eye looks down on him with a snide smile of amused contempt on his delicately featured face, while Dark Fist glares at him with stern hostility. Despite their contrasting expressions, the same sense of malevolent aggression emanates from both of them. "I can easily manipulate you, play with you, until you fall to pieces," Solar Eye seems to be saying. "I can dispatch you at any moment, cut you down with my sword," Dark Fist seems to threaten.

In the course of their bloody lives, they have made full and harmonious use of their disparate talents, political and military, to turn themselves into an irresistible force of absolute terror. When they were born, every member of the royal court wanted to get rid of the monstrosity right away, even their mother, who was a superstitious woman. But the half-mad king, with his macabre sense of humor, guffawed with delight at the sight of his attached offspring. He not only warned that he would punish any who caused them harm, but he also took personal interest in their upbringing. When they became old enough, they were taught to sing and dance for their father's pleasure as the king groomed them to become his most extraordinary fools. The two took to their training with gusto and apparent good cheer, entertaining their father and his court, but all the while watching, learning, and planning. In their youth, they gathered a group of followers, mostly disgruntled members of the lower nobility, and a retinue of ruthless thugs.

Their time came when the king fell seriously ill, which brought all members of the royal family and the most powerful aristocrats to the capital to discuss the realm's future. Following a plan that Solar Eye had meticulously put together, the princely fools unleashed their henchmen in a wave of bloody slaughter in which every single one of their numerous siblings and cousins were murdered. Their mother was put under arrest and was tormented in prison for months before she was finally executed. The twins then took the nobles hostage and forced them to swear their allegiance to them, killing all those who refused. Those who escaped the capital or were not present at the time were all eventually hunted down, their lands and wealth granted to participants of the coup. Once everyone standing in the way of total control of the kingdom was eliminated, the twins visited the ailing king. They playfully climbed onto the bed and sat on his chest to sing his favorite vulgar ditty. Then they slowly strangled their father to death.

So they ascended the throne, but that was not the end of their plan. They decided to solidify the legitimacy of their reign and bring glory to themselves by commencing a series of wars of conquest to turn the kingdom into an empire. Dark Fist masterminded the strategy and personally led his forces in many battles, proving himself to be a commander of unprecedented brilliance and ruthlessness. One land after another fell to their might as they utterly destroyed those who resisted them and subjugated those who surrendered, none prevailing against the terrible machine of their limitless ambition.

And now, they are coming for the ambassador's country.

As he stands before them, though not a single word is uttered, he can tell by their attitudes that he has already failed in his mission to negotiate a way out of war. Their Majesties have already decided to invade, and there is nothing that the ambassador can possibly say that will deter them from their course. The only thing to do now is to return to his country as quickly as possible and present two courses of action to the government, both of them dire. Either surrender to Their Majesties right away and hope for easy terms of subjugation, or begin preparations for defense. Given the might of Their Majesties' army as well as Dark Fist's martial genius, the only way the coming war could be conducted with any kind of hope for survival is to engage them in a war of attrition over a long period of time and at a great sacrifice to the people. Whichever course the government decides to take, the country will inevitably enter a time of blood and fire.

WAIT. I CAN'T *write this. Not like this, anyway.*

Reader, please indulge me for a few pages as I explain.

The inspiration for the beginning of this story came from a powerful dream I had in which I was the ambassador entering the audience hall. My late father was on my mind a lot at the time, so I must have taken his profession as a diplomat for the South Korean government and placed myself in the situation he had been in on a few occasions, negotiating with officials of a hostile country. When the horror of the conjoined ruler was revealed to me, I woke up in a fright. As I lay in bed, I had a sense that the dream was a gift from my subconscious for my creative work, so I began to work the images from it into a narrative. After I finally got up and began my day, I sat before my computer and wrote it down before trying to figure out how the story would proceed from that point on. But I soon had to leave my place to teach a class at the university where I work.

While I am a writer of fiction, my main occupation is that of a professor of history. One of the regular courses I teach is "The Historian's Craft," an introductory class on the methodology of academic history that all first-year graduate students are required to take. In response to a student's question about the cliché of history being stories written by the winners, I gave the following response.

"That may seem like a common-sensical thing to say, but it is at best a gross simplification. People who assert that do not know the difference between propaganda and proper history. Yes, historians throughout the ages have supported the status quo with narratives that glorify and legitimize the established powers. But they have also been speaking for the vanquished and the powerless since ancient times, as when Tacitus preserved the memory of people subjugated by the Roman Empire, and Sima Qian defended a maligned general of the Han dynasty at a great cost to himself. And we continue to tell stories of the lost and the forgotten, the exploited and the disenfranchised. In addition, we are expanding the circle of those whose past deserves to be told and understood. So now, historians are seeking to give voice even to animals, material objects, and environments."

On that day, I lectured about one such expansion, namely in the recently developed field of disability history. I discussed the historically determined nature of the very notion of disability, based on changing notions of the "normal" and the "ideal" body, and the ways in which people categorized as disabled have been treated.

Modernity, even with its astounding advancement in medicine, has often been unkind to them, as those who have been integral members of traditional societies suddenly found themselves identified as physically or mentally abnormal enough to require detention, isolation, and intrusive treatments. I also pointed to historical prejudices against the disabled, how outward physical difference was regarded in many contexts as an expression of inward abnormality, often of an evil nature, for instance in Shakespeare's representation of Richard III (as opposed to the actual historical figure, a ruler of no extraordinary cruelty or tyranny for the period, whose deformity from scoliosis was minor).

In our time, people may find it objectionable to regard a disability as a manifestation of a moral defect on the part of the afflicted, but the idea continues to be perpetuated in fictional depictions. How many movie villains have been represented with a blind eye, a missing limb, scarred skin, twitching or stuttering, limping or on a wheelchair, or fitted with terrifying prosthetics? The situation is the same for mental disability. Evil desires and acts are often depicted as the products of psychological abnormality (ignoring their banality as noted by Hannah Arendt), vilifying people with any form of nontypical mentality. Even without making an explicit connection between their disability and their villainy, the prejudice is reinforced through repetition.

At that point in the lecture, I stopped in mid-sentence as a realization dawned on me. After a pause that was long enough to make my student uncomfortable, I burst out, "Oh my God! I did that just this morning! I engaged in that prejudice against disabled people!" And I went on to explain about the story I had begun to write.

After the class was over and I returned home, I looked at my story again, wondering if I had to abandon it because of its offensive nature. But then it occurred to me that I could turn it into a learning moment for both myself and my future readers by making it precisely about the prejudice. So now I find myself constructing a new version of the tale, like a filmmaker doing a reshoot after a sudden inspiration. And I do so in a different cultural context, with a different gender as well, in a narrative that takes place under a new sun, if you will.

*　*　*

THIS TIME, I imagine not a lofty diplomat but a humble provincial scholar (學者), dressed in a well-worn cotton robe and a shabby horse-hair hat. As a young man, he chose not to go to the capital of the empire to take the civil examination and enter the officialdom of the government, opting to pursue pure scholarship instead. Many years later, however, he finds himself traveling to the great city as a solitary middle-aged man on a desperate mission.

A persistent drought resulting in bad harvests three years in a row has caused a famine in the district of his hometown. The local magistrate should have requested aid from the government right away, but he refrained from doing so, fearing that official scrutiny of his jurisdiction would reveal his corrupt dealings in accumulating wealth. He even sent out soldiers to guard the roads, preventing destitute peasants from moving to other areas, lest the news of the conditions there got out. With people falling ill and dying every day, the townspeople decided to secretly send a representative to the capital in the hope of appealing directly to Their Majesties. As the most educated man among them, the scholar was chosen for the task.

After he barely manages to evade the magistrate's soldiers at the border of the district, he embarks on a long and grueling journey of many *li* (里), finally arriving at the outskirts of the capital, where he rests for the night at a cheap inn before heading into the city at dawn. Despite the early hour, many people have already gathered at the great gates of the imperial palace that are opened by trident-bearing soldiers in red leather coats, who act more like welcoming guides than fierce guards as they usher the people in.

Since the ascendance of Their Majesties to the dragon throne (龍椅), it has been their practice to sit at the Serene Autumn Pavilion on the last day of each month and allow any subject, no matter how humble, to come before them to submit an appeal. The line that is formed before the pavilion is long, but the scholar is grateful to have the time to calm himself before facing Their Majesties. He is helped in the effort by the sight of vast gardens in the palace grounds that are filled with white, red, and purple peonies, their comely tranquility settling his nerves.

Yet he finds the beauty of the environment to be insignificant when he finally comes before Their Majesties, whose luminous presence fills him with wonder. Upon the wide throne of lacquered red wood sit the divine sisters, Heavenly Wisdom (天智) on the left and Radiant Benevolence (明仁) on the right. With their bodies conjoined at the hip, they share a single robe of luminous fabric, the left side yellow and the right side vermilion. On their heads are small ornamental coronets, the one on Heavenly Wisdom decorated with green jade, and the one on Radiant Benevolence with red jade. Despite the unusual nature of their bodies, there is nothing monstrous about their appearance, which overwhelms the scholar only with a sense of awe as if before a sacred vision. With them are their beloved animal companions, a white cat sitting on a thick mat next to Heavenly Wisdom, looking fat and content despite having only one eye on its fluffy face, and a small brown dog with three legs sleeping soundly next to Radiant Benevolence.

Before Their Majesties were conceived, their father, the emperor, committed a great sacrilege against the gods, murdering a holy man in a drunken rage for reprimanding him on his unrighteous rule, which had caused much suffering to his subjects. The act brought divine punishments upon the land with floods, earthquakes, and plagues that threatened to destroy the realm altogether. The emperor's primary consort, a woman of great virtue, could not persuade the proud ruler to repent his deeds, so she decided to take matters into her own hands. She traveled to the nearest port city and boarded a ship before ordering the sailors to take the vessel into a fierce storm. There, she offered herself as a sacrifice to the gods to atone for the emperor's transgression, and threw herself into the waves.

The gods were so impressed with her action that they not only sent a great turtle to carry her safely to land, but they also ended the calamities. When the emperor heard of what she had done, he was moved to repent at last, swearing never to touch liquor again. He also dedicated the rest of his life to rectifying the wrongs he had committed, enacting policies to enhance the lives of the common people, and supporting religious institutions.

A year later, the emperor's consort had a vision in which the Merciful One appeared and told her that because of all the positive outcomes of her willingness to sacrifice herself, she would soon be elevated to the Heavenly Realm. And on the occasion of her ascendance, a double blessing would be laid upon the land. In the days that followed, the emperor's consort displayed signs of pregnancy.

After the passage of ten months, she gave birth on a most auspicious day. She had the opportunity to gaze upon her offspring with a serene smile before her soul left her body to ascend to the Heavenly Realm. What she left behind was indeed a miraculous double blessing, a pair of beauteous girls conjoined at the hip. Given their sacred nature, the emperor thought they should be raised in a holy environment, so he sent them to be brought up in a monastery. As they grew, they were educated in the classics, displaying great intelligence as well as pleasure in learning. But what they enjoyed the most, even when they were children, was participating in the charitable activities of the monks and nuns for the benefit of the common people. With the passage of years, they became women of extraordinary intelligence, kindness, and virtue. When they ventured outside the monastery, they were frequently visited by animals and birds with unusual bodies, marked either from birth or injury, seeking to be blessed by the divine sisters.

Soon after they came of age, the emperor passed away. His

rapacious younger brother, in collusion with unscrupulous noblemen, set about taking power for himself, first by sending assassins to the monastery to kill the twins. Before the killers could get to them, however, an earless tiger, a one-eyed bear, and a three-legged wolf intercepted them and tore them to pieces. The twins then left the monastery and headed for the capital, accompanied by all the priests, monks, and nuns who sang holy hymns along the way. Their uncle mobilized his soldiers and went forth to slay them, but just the sight of his conjoined nieces, radiant with flawless beauty and the aura of holiness, brought him and his allies to their knees, weeping in shame and remorse. The conspirators begged for forgiveness, and Their Majesties graciously granted them pardon before proceeding to the imperial palace to begin their glorious reign.

Knowing their wondrous tale, the scholar dares not gaze upon Their Majesties, so he falls on his hands and knees to deliver the appeal that he has practiced countless times since his departure from his hometown, detailing the sufferings of the people there and the corruption of the officials, and finally begging most abjectly for intervention. He finishes making his appeal, but he hears no word from Their Majesties. Their silence makes him fear that he has done something wrong, that through some unintentional breach of protocol or insolent wording in his speech he has doomed the poor people who sent him there. Filled with great trepidation, he dares to raise his face to Their Majesties, ready to beg their pardon.

What he sees is a look of serene understanding on Heavenly Wisdom's face that shines like a full moon, and tears in Radiant Benevolence's eyes that are like the nourishing rain that the people have been praying most ardently for. As the scholar gazes upon their knowing and kind visages, he too begins to weep, not from the despair of failure, but from pure joy and gratitude, knowing that Their Majesties will grant his appeal for relief and justice. And he is filled with love as well, for the wise and benevolent Majesties who are the people's most sacred goddesses, their most gracious sovereigns, and their most caring mothers.

MY IMAGINATIVE IMPERATIVE *urges me to elaborate further on these stories.*

Perhaps they could become the basis of a grand epic in which the two realms come into conflict, leading to a confrontation between the two conjoined pairs of Their Majesties. Will the violent ruthlessness of Solar Eye and Dark Fist destroy the pacific realm of Heavenly Wisdom and Radiant Benevolence, or will the humanity of the latter prevail over the hubris of the former?

But I feel compelled to put my fantasizing in abeyance once more to further ponder the nature of the stories. In order to extricate myself from the persistent cultural prejudice against those with extraordinary bodies, I have re-visioned the story of the conjoined rulers from that of murderous conquerors to compassionate divinities. But that also follows established cultural patterns that render my depiction problematic.

In certain societies, the birth of a child with an unusual body was indeed regarded as an abomination, the result of a curse or divine punishment. And so it was quickly gotten rid of, sometimes with the unfortunate mother suffering the same fate as well. In other cultures, however, such a birth was regarded as a sacred or miraculous event, and the child was accorded special status as a godly being, and often given a religious position in adulthoodt, as a shaman or a priest. Between these two tropes of the monstrous and the divine, however, what may be the most challenging task is to represent such a being as neither inherently evil nor good, unholy nor sacred, but simply as human. In fact, the most essential thing may be to depict their lives as human beings.

So in my further exploration of these tales, I imagine moments of doubt on the part of Solar Eye and Dark Fist, how they whisper to each other when nobody is around, questioning why they toil so hard to obtain more and more power. They wonder if their physical state destined/condemned them to such a life of ceaseless aggression, or if they are driven by some compulsion born of how they were treated as freaks and fools since the beginning. Perhaps they can free themselves of their inner drive if they manage to fully comprehend their formative influences. "Can we stop?" they may ask, in a time of weariness with their ambition. "Can we freely choose to become different, and try to lead as normal lives as possible?"

And I imagine Heavenly Wisdom and Radiant Benevolence being fully aware of the performative nature of their divinity, which weighs on them as well. For all the good they have done for their realm and their subjects, they know that it is necessary for them to maintain the façade of holiness to continue their work. Perhaps if they reveal themselves to be ordinary women inside, the breaking of the sacred illusion will lead to terrible consequences. People may suddenly regard them as monsters, resulting in their ouster from power or worse, with the land falling into chaos. So they sigh and continue to play their roles before their worshipful subjects. But given the fact that their enormous responsibilities were forced upon them by the circumstance of their birth and their extraordinary body, they wonder if they have the right to be selfish, or even bad, every once in a while.

Those moments of melancholy introspection reveal the commonality of humanity between the monstrous tyrants and the virtuous divinities. The constant companionship of being conjoined twins provides some consolation (perhaps occasional or even constant annoyance as well?), but it is inevitable that they would also be beset by a great loneliness caused by their distance from everyone else around them. My imagination finally takes me to a meeting between the two pairs of rulers. The encounter would also disrupt another cliché of fictional narratives about the disabled, namely their isolation from the rest of humanity, like Frankenstein's creature skulking on the edge of society. In fiction, the disabled rarely get to meet others like them and to establish a relationship and a community.

In the face of a possible military conflict between their realms, the two pairs of rulers meet at an isolated place of neutrality where they agree to come with no guard or official to accompany them. They talk initially of war—Solar Eye and Dark Fist: "Surrender now or we will crush you," Heavenly Wisdom and Radiant Benevolence: "We will never surrender, and we will prevail against you." But then they speak of their bodies and how their lives have been determined by their extraordinary nature. In the ensuing conversation, they are surprised to recognize their common experiences and feelings as humans, not as monsters or goddesses. They also realize that their respective narratives of evil and good, of tyrannical and benevolent reigns, are conjoined like their bodies (as is this very story that I am writing in which fiction and meditation are conjoined—will its readers regard it as an unnatural freak?). And that makes them feel less alone in the world. Perhaps that intimate connection allows them to avoid war, perhaps not, but it is in that moment of shared understanding that I would like to conclude my meditative fantasy about them—at least for now.

HAUNTED BODIES OF WOMBMEN
Tlotlo Tsamaase

I'M BACK IN the womb. Prison. Except no escape this time.

I was born three times. And three times they tried to kill me while I was inside. But I came back. And then, when I got outside for ten years, they killed me anyway, mutilated my sex. Again. I was born first as a male, then born as a female, then born as other genders.

I kept returning. Decided to castrate myself of such genders. I traveled the spectrum of identities, eventually folded myself into x, an unknown value of the xeninity of my spirit. Within, I became the constant fluctuation of the masculine and feminine energies, their tides ebbing and waxing onto the landscape of the human confines of my body.

My attackers tried to refine me with the initiation rites of bogwera and bojale. Failed. So they extracted the elixir of my identities from the marrow of my spirits. Killed me. But I kept coming back until I grew to the age of an adult. Still they killed me.

I'm back. Again.

I can hear the chains singing in the distance, the feet sweeping through dust, the bleat of a goat before its last bleeding. I can taste the knife that will sever its neck, and the copper tang of the blood before it explodes into the air. I can hear the singing palm fronds, reeds, and grass as the breeze cries through the villages. The mother tongue of a lost language singes the air as it twists me into this curse, strokes my unborn eardrums. They've already taken parts of me, burned me into a mixture, given me to someone. Now parts of me remain in that someone, unable to be perspired, excreted, or purged. I am still inside them. A GPS tag. A disease. A disorder. Always knowing where they are. My fullness is focused into their sight and their skins, which are draped in gold and flames and flaring lights. Heavy cloaks whisper against the floors as they drink the syrup of my life.

Those words. I'll never forget those words:

"If you promise to behave, we'll give you back your arms and legs…"

X, AN UNKNOWN *value Anele's assigned xemself. Rare and noble as xenon. Uncolored by gender.*

Anele opens xer window, stares out into Kgale district's atmosphere, warm breeze peppered with soft rain. Xe climbs onto the sill and hurtles xemself into the night.

Xer knees, crushed.

Cartilage of xer face, dripping.

Elbows, no joints, xer body is biologically streamlined into a blunt shape for locomotive purposes. Xe roams, a bullet in the night, and the dogs howl like wolves at xer sight. Anele's skin is charred by the sins of xer previous attackers, giving xem the golden glint of mysticism and the preternatural ability to appear human when human eyes lock onto xem. Xer bones, splintered, interlock xem into a compact object. Xer air-prowling abilities are fueled by the lifespans xe has imbibed from the De Waal, Nair, and Morake families. Tonight, Anele heads for one of them.

It's a chalky night, dusty with dead flies; beaten crickets cry into the serenity of Phakalane's gated estate at the sudden, thunderous notice of xer appearance. Eyes, beady in the dark, streetlights faint. Anele's boy-hunting bird rests on a staff hostel's rafters, its beak sharpened by moonlight. Moon watches. The house, eyes sealed shut. The bedroom, half-lit. The black-out curtains stir as xe clings to the window, forming into a sticky condensation. Cold, cold, cold Anele is, transmitting xer vapor through the double glazing to the other side of the windowpane.

Anele's constellated form coagulates into the shape of a vague body. Xe stares at the married couple, asleep in bed, nightmares giving them furrowed foreheads. Anger fills xem as xe stares at Imka De Waal. All those years of being insulated in the riches of the De Waal family has earned her the privilege of life xe never got, has isolated her from the true reason of her being. And she sleeps in comfort and pleasure, ignorant of the corpses that built her wealth.

Xe crawls onto the bed, a creature thing. Climbs onto Imka's frowning face, wraps xer thighs around Imka's head: headlock, thighlock, perhaps. Imka jerks but is unable to wake as her husband is ligatured by the ropes of an unnatural deep sleep. The singing of grass, reeds, and palm fronds beckons xem. Anele almost folds into the memory, forgets xemself and what made xem. But xe can't, because xer purpose has become xer organs, xer spirit, calibrated into xer genes, the sadness so raw. Xe resuscitates xer wrath. Stares at that cliché sharp nose that's blipped through generations of the De Waal family. Xe feels the heat of hell toil in Imka's uterus. Xe caresses xer serpentine tongue along Imka's neck, the folds of her body, the nib of her sex—the places where xe was robbed, made palatable for them, their riches, their greed. In those very same places, Imka becomes potent with the violence of the past. A scream leaps through the open door and Anele catches it quick, smacks it back into Imka's face as her husband lies restless beside her.

Quickly, Anele steeps xer nails into Imka's bones and siphons the marrow from within. Strangles her with xer thighs. Crawls off the woman's face. Scuttles to the corner, and a shiny, hard exoskeleton unhinges from the seams of xer skin and in layers *begins to cocoon xer whole form. Xe nests in its dark-frothed folds, feasting on part of Imka's spirit, waiting for daybreak and for what xe's worked for for months. Xe's done the same to Imka's uncle, Piet, and twin brother, Theuns. Now Anele waits for the results...*

Within the husk of these hours leading up to two a.m., a De Waal man groans, screaming, blood burning his thighs. A baby cries from his ingrown womb, all the way down in the secret haven of the De Waal abode, its arrival tended to by a midwife sworn to secrecy. But this rumor's been spread for centuries; there's no hiding it. This is the three hundredth instance of virginal birth, a trait of the men in the De Waal family.

In the far-away Molepolole region, a webbed creature crawls from the outcroppings of Kobokwe Cave into the burning thoughts of the families Anele has been haunting. Xe sleeps by the married couple's dresser, listening to the chaos fill xer body as the animal creeps into the space beneath the married couple's bed. The animal waits for xem to wake. The night folds, dissipating the presence of the baloi as dawn lifts its mask. Morning. Rain-scent on moist earth. The fruit trees flowering in the garden perfume the air softly. Sunlight, dewy against the windows.

Anele wakes, pats the creature, which groans in pleasure at xer touch and purges something onto xer palm. The thoughts. Yes, the thoughts. It's their fault I am the way I am. Me I must be. Anele is thankful to the creature, which is born from the amassed amounts of the families' sins. Now it's xer loyal servant, torturing them in the late hours. Xe's been traveling through the genes of the De Waal, the Nair, and the Morake families for centuries—because their ancestors were the culprits of xer demise—and now xe haunts their progeny.

Imka and her husband, Danie, wake, unseeing of the creature huddled in the corner of their abode. Imka gets out of bed, stares at herself in their full-length mirror. Her cellphone rings as she traces the fear in her face. She answers. Gasps. Brings trembling hand to mouth. She hangs up, clueless. Drained. It was her twin brother, Theuns. Uncle Piet has given birth and he's deceased.

"We're next," Theuns said, breathless, before crumbling into tears. And she could hear the soft, husky voice of his wife consoling him as a cold draft filled her with fear. Her father gave birth to her and Theuns, then died immediately. This curse has been carried by the males of her family for centuries. They've hidden it by having the women play pregnant at all events, wearing silicone pregnancy bellies as the men hid in the shadows, waiting for birth, faking sabbatical leaves. Studious as ever, she tried to evade the curse. Now her twin brother carries the curse... but she can't lose him. Soon it'll be her turn.

THE SLIPPERY SLIDES of their X-rays show nothing but health and normality. The MRI, the blood tests, the neurology reports, the health checks—all's in order. No hints of cancer or predilections to cystic fibrosis, sickle cell anemia, Huntington's Disease—nix. So Imka doesn't understand why she and her twin brother have fallen sick with torturous purging of the gut, fevers, and crippling pain. A psychosomatic illness? Her uncle showed similar symptoms before collapsing on his thirtieth birthday. She was only a month old then. What followed were a series of uncanny events; through the centuries she'd hear whispers of identical happenings on their great farm, maintained by over a dozen servants. Her cousin three times removed showed similar symptoms. His brain was sucked dry by an illness similar to Alzheimer's. He died in his sleep, skinny as a twig, on his twenty-ninth birthday; the air in his room was a sickly-sweet taste of illness, sweat and death. She tries to erase it from her mind as she pours her fifth beverage from the coffee press. That's when she hears two colleagues talking in the room adjacent to the office kitchen. It's her husband, Danie, and his stupid bitch of a colleague, Hanli.

"Why'd you marry into that family?" Hanli asks. "No one in that family lives to see the age of thirty."

"She's done all the routine check-ups, disease screenings," Danie says. "Doctors found nothing. She runs four times a week, doesn't drink, doesn't smoke. Eats healthy, takes her supplements. She's reduced her workload. She's the healthiest woman in the world. Even does those religious retreat things. Even spiritually she's clean."

A thought flares in Imka's mind: *But weren't all my relatives healthy too?*

"You've married a dead woman," Hanli says. Sure, she's been after Danie for God knows how long. But she's never been this direct about him pursuing a wrong choice. "Save yourself the heartbreak and quit early. It's going to take you a while to pick yourself up when all this ends." A long spell of silence and Imka doubts their existence in the next room, until Hanli whispers, "Is it true?"

"What?"

"That they killed a young girl."

"Don't be cruel," Danie says.

"My grandmother was close friends with your wife's grandmother. She told her that the reason why the family keeps dying like this is because her grandfather had killed a young girl or something like that."

He gasps. "It's rumors, for God's sake. They were devout Catholics, true patriots of our country, and founders of NGOs. It's not in their blood to do something so horrid. And why the hell would they kill a young girl?"

Hanli scoffs. "Didn't the devil once reside in heaven?"

"I can't just unlove her."

"Well," Hanli says, shuffling some papers together, "if you must know, I've picked my funeral outfit."

"Fuck you."

"The pleasure is all yours."

And Imka walks away, feeling faint, thinking to herself: *I'm not going to die. I can't. I've so much ahead. Planned. Wanting. What if it's true? If I die, all that love, all that pain, why should my husband put himself through that?* She chucks her coffee into the sink, without so much as a sip, having lost her appetite for anything.

IT WAS THE *year 1721 when Mama had twelve children, and now I am ten generations evolved. Each relative lived to the age of thirty, gave birth, and died. But when I look in the mirror, my features are vague, non-descript. I have a forehead, a nose, and a chin in a landscape of brown. But the way they sit arranged together is like a person who doesn't exist. A person I hate, for those features look like my mother and father. I smash the mirror, shattering their image, but I can't dispel the anger they incite in me. It erupts in me: I am a disease to myself that I will never be free of. This vengeance does not satiate me. It only makes me worse. A delicious pain, sometimes it is.*

Outside, I stand on the Moruke's driveway, burning from last night. The memories that body held are still cold and dripping from my mouth, I sucked from his brain with my nails, tongue, and mouth, squeezed him of life until nothing was left, not even bones. His thirty-year-old body still held those vibrant, mordant memories of my father. He was supposed to be my father. My protector. My savior. Not my... not my...

An old woman stares at me, cataracts lapis blue, grabs my arm. "What are you doing to that man? The family will never accept you."

"Who said I'm after marriage?" I slap at her arthritic fingers. "I'm not like the women from your times: chasing men, rings, marriages—useless things." I hiss at her. "Do you want to be next? Because I go both ways."

The old woman stumbles back, grasps at the fear shivering on her lips. Feels her blood pressure worsen as sweat prickles her forehead. The dull tinnitus reverberates in her eardrums as I walk off thinking about my brother. The man I killed last night was my ninth great-grandnephew. My brother's ninth great-grandchild. Three hundred years separate us. Ten generations separate us. There are still more to kill. Those who cursed me, their children will suffer. I am a disease I wish to not be.

I have embodied the generational trauma that our parents started. I am the ivy growing woven into the structures of their chromosomes. I am an abscess of their sins. I will live through different bodies, different lives, and become someone...

AT SOME TEA function in a highbrow Johannesburg estate sit several tables of women on green lawns emitting the perfunctory notes of Chanel, Elle, Hermès... And her. Imka, the De Waal family's golden girl. Twenty-nine. Erudite. Posh. Sensitive. A glass-spun replica of her 8th great-grandmother, the woman who held my limbs as they hacked them off. And just like her ancestor, she is the benevolent receiver of my blood that she drinks annually at their private gatherings where the De Waal, the Nair, and the Morake families congregate. My blood, which remains in constant flux in their wine cellars, never runs dry due to the spells they imbibed from my screams. In their secret gatherings they drink it, never really airing the history of that ritual, the truth of where that blood comes from. Ignorance is a peaceful state; Imka feels that she does no wrong because she didn't kill anyone. It's just like with the meat she buys from the butcher, all neatly packaged and presentable—she never killed the cows. If she doesn't buy the meat, someone else will, or it'll rot and be discarded. Why let that go to waste?

Imka will never reveal to anyone that the spots of brown amidst the white of their gatherings bothers her. For some reason that she's not privy to, her family must interact with the Nair and Morake families. They are allies and she must abide by those rules. The Nair and Morake families feel the same;

they may be brown and black, but they sit above that crop, and they despise being associated with such ethnicities. They are Nair and Morake, an ethnicity of their own.

The blood, the drinking—it is why Imka was able to attend Ivy League universities, work for Fortune 500 companies, speak several languages, and come back to help the destitute black children, to feed the mouths her family dug from. She is the Mother Theresa of our century. Young, beautiful, and giving. She smiles, drinking in this standing ovation.

Of course she's young: her family stole our time.

She hopes now people will stop calling her selfish because she hasn't yet had a child. Stop saying that she needs to a bring a child in this world to receive and carry their estate forward. But she's having too much fun to really care. Giggles pour from Imka's mouth. Everyone watches with awe, fascination, lust, and envy. They ogle her hair, that slender, ballerina body. I remember every part of it in that boarding school, with the river that shivered across its borderlines, and the smack of chlorine in the air from their swimming pools. Nothing for miles, except the plains of pure farmland, where secrets clung to the rocky outcroppings like geckos. Clear, white skies giving the illusion of peace. The dorms, late at night, were abuzz with mosquitoes and hands slapping skin to kill them. In that school, there were only three black students, who'd migrated from the sparse villages of Botswana to the farmlands of South Africa, where it was all veld with sun-intoxicated crickets, a din in the heat. That's where I started growing in Imka's body.

Here, everyone sees her face and her body as the emblem of delicacy, not knowing the lava of evil that swarms beneath that "delicate" veneer. Socialites from the De Waal, Nair, and Morake families host this charity event to also celebrate their queen, Imka. Hypocrites. Playing charity for media, for reputation, yet still reaping rewards from the mutilation of our bodies. Hypocrites. I storm through their veins, through their mouths, wrecking them with a speech announcing their cruelties. Gibberish they are. Fatigue they feel. Apologies they proffer to their audiences as they flee in their expensive cars.

Imka flees at 200 km/h to the home of her aunt, Sonja, in Fourways, Sandton. She needs to do this quickly before catching her flight back to Gaborone. As usual, Aunt Sonja is her mecca when she needs answers. Wanting to know why this is happening to her. Why these symptoms torture her family. She demands answers. Hopes that Sonja is weak this time and succumbs to her interrogation, since Sonja has lost her husband. Without remorse, Imka decants the secret slowly from the caves of Aunt Sonja, and a disheveled cold brittles her chest. She almost can't breathe when she hears the truth.

ENTERING HOMES WHEN *it was dark, they drew our menstrual blood or my nephews' semen. That's how it started at first, until they needed to rip certain organs from us, while we were still alive. It was a necessary part of their rituals. As they hacked our hands, kidneys and hearts for supernatural benefits, the sheer pain was so cataclysmic that our screams poured all over the attacks, blessing them further. Whoever ordered this wasn't even there for the first round. It was during the fourth round that I saw who ordered this.*

A De Waal grandmother and son and his wife.

A Nair grandfather and brothers.

A Morake mother and father.

They killed me the many times I was born.

Parts of us were used for their desires: To conceive a male heir (my brothers and nephews). Then to beat their opponents in the industry, then for protection from their enemies. Then to acquire the lands they wanted. For political advancement…

For everything they desired, they took the lava of our screams as ointment for their heinous acts.

*　*　*

IMKA SHAKES HER head. "No, it's not true." Tears tremble down her face. "How could they do this to me?"

Sonja's shocked wide eyes stare at her niece. "To you? What about those poor children who suffered?"

Imka recovers, refines her expression. "Aunt Sonja! Of course I'm hurt about what happened to them. How could you think that I meant anything else?"

"Your eighth great-grandfather along with his son and his son's wife were some of the people who did that thing to the girl," Aunt Sonja says, face strained from mourning. "It seems that because of the taboo manner they went about it, she was born several times."

"The girl? What girl?" Imka asks, decapitated by the news.

"Your mother will kill me."

"We're dying!" Imka shouts. "We're already dying, Aunt Sonja. Oh, you have to tell me, please, so I can stop this. I don't want to die. I can't die!" Panicked, she realizes she needs to employ a different tactic. So she gathers herself and holds her aunt's hands. "Aunt Sonja, if you don't tell me, I won't be able to stop what happened to Uncle Piet happening to your son. I need to know so I can also try save your son."

Sonja's frayed, living on insomnia since her husband died. She never believed the curse would take him. But he was a De Waal after all, and history has repeated itself for three centuries. Why would it change for her? Just because she loves him? Love is not enough to save someone. She should know this by now: love didn't save her mother from her father. What does it matter if she spills it out to her niece? She can't suffer this pain of knowing, of mourning, of loneliness alone. Wants to punish someone for *this* pain. Even if it's her sweet niece. She needs to save her son.

"They took her entire life, tricked her father and mother," Sonja whispers. "Anele Morake. That was her name. She was the required ingredient to advance their businesses, their wealth, to fund you and what you've become today."

* * *

IMKA ARRIVES HOME, wan, depleted and devastated. Enters the house. Her thoughts form a beehive in her skull:

How is it possible that someone I revered and idolized could be capable of such acts? Is it even possible that they reared me without sullying me with their ungodly touch? What does that mean for me, since I carry their blood? Does that mean I carry their evil too? And if I don't carry it, what if down the line, my child, or their child, or their child's child gives birth to a person so like my ancestors? Someone who murders children or commits worse crimes. Isn't that what's common in families? Somewhere along their genealogy you find a crop of malefic doppelgangers amidst a field of innocent relatives, so alike in nature and behavior. I've seen it in true crime documentaries. The nephew, glorifying their serial killer great grandfather, becomes the worst serial killer humankind has seen.

You can't beat it out of your child.

You can't think that you will do all that you can to perfect your child so they don't end up evil.

Somewhere down the line, someone will give birth to my father. I can't, without a doubt, be a vessel of this disease. I can't be the mother of progeny with a genetic predisposition to murder. But I also have to be honest with myself, because this is an excuse masking the real truth: I don't want to have a child. Never fancied the idea like other women. I don't want to experience motherhood. To care for that child for my entire life. No. Pregnancy and childbirth terrify me. I don't want to change my life and my body for children I don't want. I don't want to lose that freedom. All mothers can try to convince me otherwise. Children deserve a whole lot more from parents, something I can't give, and I can't put them through that. I don't want the realities of this body. The female body, a kingdom of terror, its tributaries flowing with unwanted rivers of suffering. I don't want it anymore. This body. This me. I want to align my body to the true me. To who I feel I am to be. I don't have to force myself to be the woman the world defines. I'm not running away, I am making my home, finding me.

WITHIN THE NEXT few days, I'm amused that Imka's gotten opinions from several doctors and an appointment for a hysterectomy, the first step to separating herself from what this body is forced to do. By her family. Her city. This world.

"At least give your eggs to someone who can't have kids. Give them that opportunity," her husband says later, aggrieved at the news, aggrieved that he never signed on for this when he married her. But he has to be supportive or that short temper of hers will devour him. He feels trapped suddenly, unable to swallow, chokes on the air entering his mouth. "Don't let it all go to waste," he whispers.

"No. I don't want the thought that I have kids with my DNA out there," Imka says. "I wouldn't be able to live that way. I'm not sacrificing anything. Can you just be okay with that? Even if you don't understand my decision, can you put yourself aside and support me?"

His answer doesn't matter. Weeks later, she ends up on the front cover of reputable magazines, discussing feminism and the plight of women. Educates them on her real identity: bigender; they/them pronouns. And strives to help marginalized women with their struggles with gender and identity. Receives a Woman of the Year Award for being the voice of the silenced. She feels at home in a way I wish I could, but the home of my body and my life was stripped away from me, and her family's getting rewarded for it. Soon I will take back my home...

ANOTHER LATE NIGHT. *Anele cuddles Theuns' in-between with xer fingers. This sac of seeds. So fragile, bursting with wanton desire. The numinous flow of Theuns' soul, within this shell of a human, hanging in there like a ripe fruit. Xe flagellates it with xer spirit. Slides into him, impregnating him. They let Anele into them, now xe's free to roam. Xe does this to the twins. First, the brother. Second, the sister. It only takes moments. Moments that last a lifetime for them.*

Theuns is crippled in bed with pain, as he groans to his wife, "There's a bug inside me. Born with me. Grew with me. It's here now..."

In the morning, Anele hovers by his feet as xe listens to the couple's conversation.

"I had a weird dream," Theuns whispers to his wife. Voice hoarse. Clears it. Coughs, phlegm stuck. Hacks it out. He can still smell the thing that was here last night, like citrus with cinnamon and something burning. He opens the windows, and a breeze streams in with the sunlight and morning traffic.

His wife perfumes herself as she eyes his reflection in the mirror. "You're going to be late for work."

He pats himself; he's entirely there, bones, skin, sinew—but something's amiss. "I need to go see my sister..."

HER TWIN BROTHER came in early that morning, all the way from his Mokolodi estate, weeping. Poor Theuns.

"There's nothing terrible about carrying a child," Imka says, staring at the protrusion of his abdomen. "If you're that embarrassed, just tell people it's a beer belly."

His eyes widen, dripping with tears.

So months after her hysterectomy, she hires an old woman to come to the house to help them with their problem. The old woman with traditional paraphernalia and medicine talks in Shona and Setswana as she burns herbs that barely choke me throughout the rooms. I follow the old woman around, floating about her afro as she "heals" every room. I find it amusing, because as she's healing every room she's healing me further into a potent essence, empowering me. I do hope she comes again. Imka follows her around, frail with anxiety at having to resort to this. The strawberry blonde hue of Imka's hair glints around the fragile bulb of her scalp. I trace along the papery skin of Imka's spotted arms, veins a visible shade of green. The smoke pillows around her face, she coughs and waves it away. Her fragile-presenting nature has been my chloroform for decades. Within her is a robust flow that has drowned my existence, and continues to drown those like me. And she thinks she can get rid of me? Just like that? Using people like me against me? No.

"How long is this going to take?" Imka asks, coughing. The old woman ignores her. I hover above the branch of herbs she waves about, inhaling its smoky breath, intoxicating myself with it to a cataclysmic climax in which every light bulb explodes, raining the marble floors with shattered glass. Imka takes cover under the shield of her arms as an earthquake attacks the foundation of her house, rambling through the walls and ceilings, shaking fury into the head of the chandelier as its strings of diamond-décor dance feverishly.

But this is not an earthquake. This is me.

And I transport them to the memory of the past. The Morake family gave me up for them. Them. The De Waal and Nair families sacrificed none of their own, tricked the Morake head, who sacrificed me over and over, and had to, to replenish himself, to protect himself as he was cursed. That justifies not what he did to me, his daughter.

THEIR FIRST SON *was useless. Had no proclivities for any form of art or sport, nor any cerebral tendencies. He did so poorly in school as well as at home, managing "men" stuff, that I was reared to tend to him, the cooking, the cleaning. It was due to my father's relationship with the founder of the university that my brother was enrolled into the school of medicine despite a below-par GPA. I had to go behind my father's back, apply to a different school so he wouldn't influence them to reject me. The only thing that made my brother important was that he was the firstborn and a son, heir to my father's business and estate. And that because men carry names, he could immortalize our name. But I didn't care about it; I thought I'd make my own name. Although sometimes I do wonder that if I was in invested in as much as my brothers, nephews, and uncles, how far would I have gone? I was a loss to my father, except for the lobola he wanted to cash in on. But I was taking too long to get married. "You're so far behind, it's a disgrace," he grumbled one evening, over the newspaper he was reading. "You embarrass me."*

"My brother's not married, yet you're not harassing him."

"He's focusing on the business."

"Me too."

He side-eyed me, ignored my response. "Women marrying women. So who receives the lobola? I'm not going to give you away. Away, for nothing."

"I didn't say I'm marrying a woman, I said I don't identify as one." I sighed. "Even so, I am attracted to anyone who's a person. I don't think my attraction to someone should be limited by gender standards."

"Same difference," he spat. "I don't understand you people of these days. What's wrong with you?"

"The past was so good at burying us you thought we didn't exist. We've always existed."

He narrowed his eyes at me. "You should learn to shut up more and listen. It'll do you great justice."

"That's the worst advice you could give your daughter."

"Keep disobeying me and you won't be one for long."

Something curdled my soul, a bitter chill that wove into my spine. But I ignored it. If I hadn't, maybe things today would be different.

Even when my brother "interned" at my father's firm as a CEO, he brought losses. I assisted the creative director with concepts and campaigns to new markets based on the networks I created outside our country, to shield against the losses my brother brought to the firm. But my father couldn't stoop that low, to go against all that tradition within himself to see value in me, a woman. It was beneath him, that idea or the need to equalize the system. It was the system he grew up in, that his parents, great-grandparents and forbears grew up in. Who was I to change that? To insult that? Who the fuck was I to disrupt an institution of patriarchy in existence since time immemorial? Me, who'd only been alive for thirty meagre years.

Men want men so strongly but they won't have each other...

After several of my deaths and hauntings, I got to see how my father ordered hits on me by drinking the memories trapped in the De Waal, Nair, and Morake families' bodies. It's where I saw the truth.

The truth took me to the memory of my father arguing with his witch doctor. In the dark of the hut, my father thrust a couple of items toward the man. "You didn't give us what we wanted. A son. Send it back." My father pointed to a photo of me he'd brought along. He didn't want me anymore.

"It?" The man looked at my pubic hair and the photo of me. I don't know how he'd collected the hair. "I don't presume you mean the girl." The small room smelled of old, wet shoes, and body odor that had infested the surfaces and air for decades.

"Yes," my father said, face swelled with wrinkles.

"B-b-ut... she's thirty years old—you—can't refund a person—with those years—"

"If you divide a land, you get more value out of it than if you sell it whole," my father continued unperturbed. "So, fine, what can we get in exchange for her parts?"

"H-h-her parts?"

"You know exactly what I mean. I've come to you many times."

"But for a woman at this age—" My father stood up to leave, so the man stopped him, afraid to lose a paycheck. "I can do it." He wrote something down, an invoice of sorts. Handed it to my father.

Papa scrummaged for his spectacles, narrowed his eyes with concentration at the slip. Shook his head. "Separate these." He stabbed at a section on the slip. "I think her vulva, uterus, and so on are worth more separated than if sold together. They've never been used before."

"Depends if the girl's menstruating. Girls who haven't started puberty yet are of higher value. The body is still pure."

Papa nodded. "My wife's pregnant again. We already have five children. I don't know why the woman can't control herself. She only has one job. One job. To not get pregnant. She refuses to take medication to avoid this and can't even tell proper when she's ovulating. Anyway, the baby's a girl. We'll hold onto it for five years and I'll bring her to you."

"I'll always be at your service." The man swallowed. "In the meantime, please, sir, if you could discreetly recommend my services to your fellow mates, I would do you the honor of offering a free session."

"Of course, once you fulfill this job."

The man coughed. "If I may, sir?"

"Go on."

"Pregnancy is potent and vibrant with goodwill. The old times were our fortune. But we don't live there anymore. The small house you have, I could make that permanent, without incurring the loss of the main house because of current regulations."

"All my houses are high-end real estate. There is no 'small' or 'main.'"

The man's eyes grew wide with shock at my father's lack of understanding of the terminologies. He coughed again. "I was referring to your mistress and wife." Lowered his eyes quickly so Papa could be colored in shame privately. "How far along is your wife? If she's in the third trimester, I can prepare my team to bring her in. Efficiently. In such a way that doesn't point to you."

"She's three months pregnant."

"Good. We have time, then. And this is very critical: I strongly advise that in the next three months you maintain good relations

with your wife. That way, if the police conduct an investigation, they won't come across anything suspicious. Make certain that your social circle sees your good graces, but don't be too obsessively good—otherwise that's also suspicious."

Papa nodded, pleased with the instructions...

THE NEXT DAY, poor Imka calls in sick at work and stays in bed, watching the rain pit-patter across her window as she gazes at the grey skies in deep thought. *What am I going to do?* She pinches her lip with her teeth until blood comes. "What am I going to do?" She rakes her hands through her hair, and strands of the cinnamon-tinged hair flake onto her hands. She crumbles into tears. Within three months, she's turning thirty or turning dead. *I can't die. Please.*

Desperate now, Imka has brought in a priest. My cackles shake the house. She screams as the priest carries his cross to and fro as if searching for a signal; the signal of evil, perhaps. He splashes holy water on the walls, the furniture, the chandeliers which chime in wonderment. First the traditional doctor and now a priest. Doesn't she realize how untouchable I am? The disorder runs through the house's foundation and the family's foundation too, exporting culture from the breadth of their skins, the etymology of their minds, the language of their sins and exhaling it back into their bodies.

"Who are you? What is your name?" the priest asks in gibberish, in tones of fear. "Name yourself, beast!"

I stare at the woman and drag them into the pain of the past...

THROUGH THE DARK, I stumbled, fingers clasping for mercy. I stared at Mama. She hesitated. Looked away. Face masked in shame. Hands trembling. And that's when I knew it was over for me. She wasn't going to save me. She was too weak. Compared to him. To the world. To this system. How... could she do this to me? She, wearing the same gender, the same curse, joined together—shouldn't we be allies? Do I mean nothing to her because I exist outside of her now, no longer co-dependent? Or do I mean less because one of us has to live, and she picks herself. How is that life: existing beneath the suffocating thumb of your husband? She's not living, she's dying every day. And now she's killing me.

She was just my vessel into this world. Nothing else.

How could a parent proudly bury their own child before their time? Stick a knife in me and cut through the cartilage of my screams without hesitation? Have my blood wail across their faces and still see no reason to stop killing me—their own child? Hold down my small body and reap from me my organs while I cry to them, cling to them, asking them, "Papa, Mama, why?"

How could they do this staring into my eyes, and still make me feel guilty for wanting to live? Feel no remorse. See nothing. Hear nothing.

How are such people allowed to be parents? Why, if there's a God, would He allow this? Allow me to come into a family, into a world, where this is normal? And this continues around the world. We're everywhere. How could anyone expect any joy or love from me when they killed any hope I had? They killed me. And now all I know is killing. And I will be a better killer.

From birth, my womanhood determined my fate. And now in death it determines my existence. Where do I find control? Freedom? Peace? Love? Not in this earth, not in this heaven or hell. Where is my universe when this world continues to dominate me? Then: I must dominate it. Those that destroy others, I will destroy them. Destroy them before they progenerate and replicate their kind.

IMKA FALLS TO her knees. "I know her."

"Her?" the priest asks, weary. His interruption stirs me, and I smack a concrete vase at him. *This* is between me and her. He collapses to the floor, still gripping his cross, a trickle of blood trailing from his head. The current of the air rises into a storm: curtains remain adhesive to the windows, but every particle in the room spins in the tornado of my fury—vases, cutlery, chairs sweep around the room in circles, as Imka remains trapped in the center, shielding herself with bare arms. She begs, pleads for me to stop. Pisses herself. Hot tears stream down her pink face.

"Who am I?" my hoarse voice ensnares her.

"The boarding school I went to. You possessed me," she says, voice quivering. "They said I was having a psychological breakdown. But it was you. *This*. All of this reminds me of my time at the boarding school. Then you disappeared." She stares about, unsure how to pinpoint me. "I heard whispers. Of what they did. To the girl, Anele. That's you, isn't it?"

"Anele was my twin sister," I whisper.

"I didn't know there were two of you."

"We were born together once. Your eighth great-grandparents killed her. They extinguished her as a ghost every time she returned as one, but sometimes she lives through me, and I see the haunting that she does."

She pleads, "I'm sorry. Please, what can I do to stop this?" she asks, with watery eyes. "I'll do anything."

"I want to live the life that was stolen from me," I say, through the hot glare of the air, crackling, snapping in the heat of my presence.

"I will carry you, then." She motions to her knees, drops onto them. "I will carry you to life. Just please... please stop this. I don't want to die." She's trembling, so insanely afraid, that I pity her for what her parents did. For what she suffers because she's their child. For what I suffer because of my parents.

I eye her. That's all you need for some of these rituals: permission from the sacrificial lamb. Whereas in other rituals, they abducted, stole, took without the victim's acquiescence, the most powerful ceremonies are those of the sacrificial lamb decanting its life onto the flames of desires.

"You declared you're not interested in pregnancy," my voice splinters through the shards of air.

"I'll do anything to save my family. If you'll stop killing us, I'll do it."

"Women, always being sacrificed, and always sacrificing themselves."

Imka looks around bleary-eyed, at the ceiling at the floor. "B-b-b-but... I got a hysterectomy."

"I made men pregnant," I whisper, "this is hardly a problem. But childbirth will be an atypical pain."

She lowers her head, weightless in the tangle of her thoughts, like reeds swallowed in the current of blood. "Then I will do it. *Only* if you promise to stop killing my family. I surrender my body to you, for your possession."

The statement is an instant tranquilizer; the room calms, and the hurricane of my fury settles into a serene quiet that reverberates with a startling silence. She folds her arms around her body, protecting herself from the cold whisper of the air.

I can't but feel sorry for her. For the past, for what got us here. The people who should be receiving the severe punishment are long gone, buried in the peace of their graves.

"Don't worry," I whisper. "I'll make sure not to hurt you."

I throw myself into Imka.

I'm back in the flesh. Prison. Except no escape this time. This time I will be born. No longer immortal and hunting through the generations of families. I'll be imprisoned within the typical running length of human lifespans. But that prison offers me freedom. I will no longer be a disease.

Time speeds, as I travel through her system, weighed down by the gravity of her emotions, intermixing with genes of the past, present and future. None more distinct than the other, existing all in one body, occurring all in one space, in one time.

For months I live in a house, in a gated estate. In a house I live. A house, a machine for living. I live in her body. Her body, a house for living, a machine for living. I travel the labyrinthine network of the veins, the pipework, and fold into the eggs, into the fallopian tubes of this white house rooted in the privilege of all my deaths.

Out of this white house I travel its body, its length, as it is enceinte with child: the white woman gives birth to a black child. To me. I am free. I am born... free from the restraints of the singing chains. My life sweeps through the dust of time at the cry of the haunted bodies of WombMen and their last bleeding.

DRAGONS OF YUTA
Rochita Loenen-Ruiz

TWENTY-NINE DAYS AFTER the harvest month, the dragons came for me in Resha. I was threshing rice when the portal opened, and from where we stood I could see the doglike shapes of their faces and the stiff ruby-red comb that graced each dragon head.

More than twenty years had passed since I'd said farewell to my beloved dragons. After Cordero's death, they who were called Bangkawi established a puppet council, which sentenced me to exile on Resha.

I was too dangerous, they said. And life among the Resha would teach me peace and gratitude.

When the sentence came down, I was only glad that I had thought to send the dragons away to the forests beyond Payay, where the Bangkawi could not touch them.

We had lost the war, I had lost my mother, and only the gods knew if I would see Yuta or my beloved dragons again.

I WATCHED THEM now as they flowed out into Resha's sky. The sun reflected off the plates that lined their sinuous bodies. Hewn by the dragon makers from the heart of the iron tree, those scales had deflected numerous arrows and spears in battle.

I was struck yet again by the beauty of their form. It had been the same when I saw them come to life for the first time.

My tongue clove to the roof of my mouth and my heart pounded like the gongs during the harvest dance. They were my dragons—born of my mind, shaped by the hands of Yuta's master carvers, and brought to life by the breath of Cordero.

For a moment the sky above Resha was awash with emeralds, purples, and magentas. Then they flew onwards to the central hall where Resha's high elders dwelt. Their tail feathers flowed behind them like brilliant banners spread out for show.

I felt a sting in my heart as I watched them go. I knew of only one other who had the power to wake my dragons, and I could not conceive of her yielding that power into the hands of the puppet council who now ruled our home.

I shrugged and bent to pick up another bundle of rice. Yuta was no longer my concern. The council had made that clear when they exiled me. Cordero was gone. The cause was lost. There was no way of going home.

My earpiece crackled as High Elder Hinabi's voice came through.

"Come."

One word was enough.

THE BANGKAWI MEN *were encased in metal and there was no compassion in their eyes. They had carved a way through the mountains with their fists and tramped down the earth with their feet. Behind them a cavalcade of soldiers followed, and their leader sat on a horse that was taller than any we had ever seen.*

"We are your elder brothers," their leader said. "The gods of the Skyworld sent us to teach you. If you are worthy, you will ascend and be allowed a place among us."

Cordero was the first of the Aunties to speak up. She was eldest of us all, and strong in power. Long before I was born, she had communed with those who walked the veils. She had been gifted with foresight and she was the one to whom we all turned for guidance and leadership. She stood before the leader of the

Bangkawi, her eyes never flinching from his and her voice never wavering in its tenor.

"What proof do you bring us?" Cordero said. "Prove to us that you are kin to us and to the gods we adore."

"We have hewn a path through the mountains," the Bangkawi leader said. "We come with the might of men, a cavalcade of soldiers, and the strength of fire in our hands. Is that not enough proof of who we are?"

He leaned down and sneered into the eldest's face.

Cordero met his gaze. She held her chin high and did not flinch. Then she turned her eyes to the side and spat on the ground before him.

"If you are not of the earth, you are not my kin," she said. "And if there are any who are wise among us, they will refute your claim."

Her eyes met mine and I tightened my grip on the weapon in my hand.

Cordero's refusal was our refusal. She was our eldest, and the one to whom I had pledged my undying allegiance. Yuta would rise to arms if needed, and if she asked for it I would lay down my life for her.

"There is no need for bloodshed," the Bangkawi leader said.

He lifted his eyes from Cordero and his gaze trawled over us all.

"Little people," he said. "Understand that what I say is not a proposal. It is a demand. I am eldest born of the Bangkawi and I have come to liberate you from an excess of superstition. If you resist, I will crush you without remorse."

WE ALL HAD our ghosts. Even Resha's high elders had ghosts of their own. Sometimes, I thought I could see the ghosts of their past walking in their footsteps. Resha had been contained for a reason, but what those reasons were, I never found out. I did know that they were not warlike by nature and that they had accepted the constraints laid upon them by the dominant Bangkawi. But the ghosts of past suffering and violence had marked Resha's dwellers just as the ghosts of my past marked me.

Still, Resha was a haven that allowed us to live without having to address the past. I asked no questions of its inhabitants, just as they asked no questions of me.

Here, I had buried my memories of Yuta, thinking I would never see it again. I was forty-six years old. I had stood beside Cordero when she resisted the onslaught of the Bangkawi. I had seen her beheaded, I had wept when they fed her body to the alligators, and when they brought me before the puppet council I declared my intention to remain insurgent.

"I will fight to the end," I declared. "If the Bangkawi truly loved us, they would have given Cordero a place of honor and respected our wish to continue in the ways of the foremothers."

I pleaded guilty to the charges laid at my feet and I did not deny that I was a dissident and an insurgent. When they pressed me to keep from stirring the people of Yuta to protest and to trouble, I refused.

"Cordero spoke with the wisdom of the foremothers," I said. "I will not bow my head to these Bangkawi Manongs, and I will not promise to live with them in peace. If I bow and if I yield, I will bring dishonor to my mother's blood. You cannot ask this of me."

It was one of the few moments when I could acknowledge Cordero as the woman who had given life to me. Fighting was the only way I knew how to honor her memory.

For my words, they should have sentenced me to death. Instead, they sent me to exile in Resha. The distance and the containment were the same as tearing out my heart and feeding it to the crocodiles.

"DO YOU WISH *I would relent?" Cordero asked me.*

We had been fighting all day, and the ground beneath our feet was soaked with blood and gore. In the distance, I could hear the clamor of the dragons as the Mama-oh tended to their wounds.

"You lead us," I said. "Your vision is our vision, Cordero."

She looked at me then, and there was sadness in her gaze.

"We can retreat," she said. "We could send the dragons to sleep in the woods. We could disperse the garda and disappear from memory. We could be swallowed up in the mass of those who yield to the Manongs and their intentions. I would be nothing more than a woman bowing to the dictates of a man."

"You are my mother and my leader," I said. "You have taught me the histories of our tribes and the ways of our foremothers. Should we yield those things to the hands of a stranger?"

"If we yield, those things will fade from the memory of Yuta," Cordero said. "Even now, everywhere the Manongs have been, memory turns to dross. Even in our midst there are those who begin to believe our cause is a false one. They whisper among themselves and say that a man who commands such a cavalry must truly be of the gods, and we are little people who cannot win this war."

"We have the dragons still," I said. "And as long as I live I will stand by your side."

WE NEVER STOOD on ceremony in Resha. It was one of the perks of living in a place banished to the periphery—sundered from the world beyond by shields that they themselves could not penetrate, the high elders saw no reason to demand ceremony but let us come and go as we were, just as we let them be in their selves.

I came into the presence of Yuta's garda and Resha's high elders in the same clothes that I had on when I went out to help in the fields.

If the garda had been sent to end my life, pomp and circumstance would not save me. If they had come to drag me back into the presence of the council, if they had come expecting me to kowtow to the Bangkawi Manongs who had demanded my exile, they would have to return and say that I remained unrepentant.

Of the garda who had come on their dragons, I only knew one face. It was a face I had not forgotten in all my years of exile. I stared and stared, wondering if it was good or bad that I should see that face in this place that had taught me peace and acceptance.

"Kyri," she said.

Do you blame me that I wept when I heard that beloved voice? It had been twenty-one years since I'd been exiled from Yuta, and now they had sent her to me. Whether it was to end my life or to save it, I did not care.

I felt her cheek on my cheek as the storm of my weeping passed. Looking up at her, I saw myself mirrored in her gentle gaze. When we parted ways, I still wore the garb of a warrior. I had been a woman in my prime. Strong and sure of myself, even on the eve of our final battle.

I wished then that I had donned festive raiment for this meeting. How drab I must have looked in the earth-stained brown of my harvest clothes. Did she see the havoc time had wreaked on me? Did she notice the slivers of silver among the black strands of my hair?

"It's good to see you again," she said.

Her voice resonated with truth, and the eyes that looked on me held the same look as when we had parted twenty-one years ago.

"Mitos," I said. "You have not changed at all."

And it was true. For where my skin had grown tough and lined from exposure to the sun, her cheeks were smooth, her brow unlined.

"Of course I have changed," Mitos said. "It has been twenty-one years, Kyri."

She stepped away, and looking at her in the red and black of Yuta, I could see that she had indeed changed. Now she exuded strength and authority, and I could see her leading the garda into battle and commanding without fail.

"Have you come for me?" I asked. "Have you given yourself over to the Manongs then? Is this why they sent you, Mitos? Do they send love as consolation for the end of my days?"

"It is not the end of your days," Mitos said. "And I am not a consolation. I have come to take you back, Kyri. Back to Yuta, back to where you belong."

MITOS HAD COME to us in Lagwe, for we had been pushed far down into the curve of Yuta's belly.

"Our chief has surrendered," Mitos said. "And the Bangkawi Manongs have declared Cordero an enemy of the people."

"We cannot give up the fight," I said. "If you have come to convince me to go into hiding, Mitos, then you do not know me."

"I know you will not hide," Mitos said. "Not even if I should wish it. But I am watched now. They hold me responsible for the lives of my clansisters, Kyri. If I rebel, it is not I who will suffer their rage."

I wanted to tell Mitos to come to me, to stand by my side. I wanted to tell her that we would rescue the clansisters from the clutches of the Manongs. But Cordero had already predicted her own death. Too many had perished on our side, and the dragons fell under the onslaught of the enemy's fire. We did not have enough sisters, and for all their valor, the number of our garda was not enough to fight off a never-ending stream of metal men.

"This fight may be drawing to a close," I said. "But it doesn't mean it is over. A time will come when we triumph over the Manongs."

"I wish I could do more," Mitos said.

She was still so very young, this woman I loved. Eight summers stood between us, and I sometimes wondered why she loved me when we could not live together in peace as other lovers did.

"I may dwell in the house of the Bangkawi Manongs," Mitos said, "but that doesn't mean I have surrendered all power. If you could persuade Cordero to surrender, too, the sisters in Payay have offered refuge for you and for her and for the garda who remain."

"Even there, they will follow us," I said. "Cordero has seen it all, and she has no wish to visit more sorrow on the weavers who have shown us their unending support."

"They have burned everything in Hirac," Mitos said.

There was sadness in her voice, and I understood it, for Hirac was her mother's home, and we had hiked those mountains in the days before we discovered our mutual love.

"My mother's clan chose to burn the fields rather than surrender them to the Bangkawi," Mitos continued. "My mother is gone, Kyri."

I opened my arms to her, and she came to me. Her tears trickled down the side of my neck, her breath came in short sobs.

"They called her a daughter of the dogs," she said. "Then they made her an example for all of us."

I could not speak for my rage. A vision of Mitos's mother rose before me. She had been small and sturdy, but her soft-spoken ways hid the hardness of her resolve. The spy who had told us of her death had run the long distance from Hirac to Lagwe. He had no more tears when he reached us, but his voice was filled with the rawness of horror and grief.

"We are returning to Yuta tomorrow," I said to Mitos. "Cordero has decreed it. If her death will bring an end to the suffering of the people, she is willing to perish."

"No," Mitos said. "No, Kyri. You do not understand the half of their ways."

"Keep faith for me, Mitos," I said. "Whatever befalls me, promise that you will find a way to shield the garda. Promise me that you will do all in your power to keep the dragons from the hands of the Manongs."

It was the last time we would be alone together, and perhaps it was premonition that made me give her the words that would wake the dragons in time of need.

I THOUGHT OF the years as I prepared to leave Resha. I said my farewell to Hinabi, who received it with a considerable absence of surprise.

"It was foretold that you would leave us," they said with a smile.

When I stared at them in surprise, they laughed softly.

"Don't look so surprised, Kyri of Cordero. Resha has been kept separate from the world, but the shields can only keep the body here."

Hinabi's revelation was a confirmation of what I had suspected—that the Resha self had that power to traverse the gaps.

"If the council had wished the revolution dead," Hinabi continued, "they would have sentenced you to death. Cordero's will was stronger than the will of any council the Bangkawi would elect. Cordero's was the ultimate sacrifice. But in making it, she made sure that the war would be won when the right time came. Remember this, Kyri: even the strongest man cannot keep a country in subjugation for very long. And not all freedoms are won on the battlefield."

I stared at them in wonder, for this was the longest speech they had made to me in the years that I had dwelt in Resha.

"We don't ask questions in Resha," Hinabi continued. "Even I have my secrets. Resha won't be sundered from the world for long, and we may meet again beyond the confines that hold us here for now."

"I shall look forward to it," I said. "And I hope we meet as allies."

Hinabi smiled.

"I don't think we will be enemies," they said.

* * *

MY EXILE IN Resha was over.

It had been years since I'd donned the red and black of Yuta's garda. Years since I'd put it off and hidden it away, with the soft boots and the jingling spurs of a dragon rider. As I took each item from its hiding place, I felt as if I was unearthing bits of the spirit that I had buried when I accepted my exile.

I was going home. I was no longer the young woman who led the garda into battle, but I was still a warrior. I carried my mother's spirit inside me, and if Yuta was in need, I would not falter. I would rise to meet destiny.

"Ready?" Mitos asked.

I turned when I heard the quick intake of her breath, and I stopped at the image that confronted me.

There was a stranger staring at me in the mirror. Her hair was swept back and wrapped in a braid around her head. Battle spikes adorned her hair, and a brass headband encircled her brow. There was fire in the stranger's eyes, there was passion, and there was fierce delight in what was yet to come.

I threw my shoulders back and stared. It was still me. Kyri, eldest daughter of Cordero, grandchild of the great Matriarch Sinukuan. The blood of my foremothers flowed in my veins. I would not shame my ancestors by appearing before Yuta as a trodden down warrior.

I tilted my chin at my reflection. How long had it been since I'd last looked, really looked at myself? I was looking now. Whatever was to come, I would not turn away from the challenge that faced me.

"YOU MAY FIND Yuta changed," Mitos said. "It was hardest in the beginning, but now the groundwork has been laid. The Bangkawi still occupy the ancestral places of power, but time changes even they who seem immovable."

"What do you mean?" I asked.

Mitos shrugged.

"I don't know what will happen, but I know that we now have allies among those who sit in power. A new generation of Bangkawi have sprung up, and they believe their elders were wrong to take Yuta from the hands of the Aunties."

I couldn't believe what I was hearing.

"Are you making a plea on their behalf?" I said. "I have lived in exile long enough, Mitos. If war is what the Bangkawi want, war is what I will give them."

I clenched my fist and tried to keep from lashing out at her.

"Don't be mistaken," Mitos said. "All these years, I have worked and waited patiently for the right time. If you demand it of me, I will fly and fight for you. My life and my loyalty belong to Yuta and to the foremothers of our land. If you fly into battle, I and my clansisters will fly by your side. But I want to caution you, as I know Cordero would caution you. Not all battles are won with the shedding of blood and the taking up of arms."

"Kyri," Cordero said. "All our lives you have called me Cordero. You have given me honor and respect as is due to an elder, and I have not been a mother as other mothers are. But that doesn't mean that I have loved you less."

Even though it was the first time she showed it to me, it was not the first time that I had known of my mother's vulnerable heart. I understood more than she said, and I understood her terror should an enemy discover that her greatest vulnerability was me.

"You are the child of my flesh," she continued. "But even more than that, you are the child of my spirit. Tomorrow, we return to Yuta and I will pass on to certain death. But my fate will not be your fate. I have seen to it, Kyri. In time you will rise as you were meant to, and when that time comes, you will remember the things that pass between us tonight. I want you to remember

that even though it may not seem that way now, we are all of the earth. We are all of Yuta."

I watched as she unwound her hair and as it fell around her in loose strands, it seemed as if she let go of Cordero and became again the mother who had crooned to me when I was a child.

WE LEFT RESHA without fanfare. I was riding again on the back of a dragon, and I could feel power rising and falling beneath its skin. When I was younger, I had gloried in that power. It had filled me with pride and a feeling of invincibility.

When we were outnumbered by the Bangkawi and their metal men, when the dragons fell wounded from the skies, my frustration and my fury knew no bounds. How could we fall? How could we lose?

In my heart, I had raged against the gods and questioned how they could turn a blind eye to our need.

Now, I understood that we had lost because our enemy bore weapons we did not understand. They were ready for our dragons, but we were not ready for them. This time would be different.

"Where do we go?" I asked Mitos.

"To Payay," Mitos replied. "The garda have assembled there. But most importantly, there is a delegation waiting for your arrival."

"What delegation?" My voice was sharp. Sharp as the suspicion that grew in my chest.

"Listen to me," Mitos said. "There are none who will betray you there. Not in Payay, not in Lagwe, not in Hirac, not in Yuta. Promise me you will listen. Before you decide anything, before you raise a call to arms, before you signal a decision, promise me you will listen first."

This was a Mitos I did not recognize. She was fierce in her pleading, her voice filled with determination.

"Did they listen to us?" I retorted. "How certain are you that this delegation are true-hearted? How do you know they don't mean to trick us?"

"KYRI," MY MOTHER said. "Don't cry. I will leave the flesh behind, but I will not leave you. All that I am goes with you."

I held onto her words the next day. I held onto the memory of her arms holding me close as mothers hold their cherished children. I closed my eyes when they took her life. And when they parted her flesh and fed her to the alligators, I envisioned her eyes shining with pride as she looked down at me.

I heard her voice whispering my name and telling me of what the future would hold.

"Take heart," she said. "Remember your foremothers and the wisdoms that are passed on through the blood. Hold fast to these mysteries that connect you and me to the world of the beyond. Because we have lived so close to the earth, we haven't forgotten what binds us to one another. This wisdom you mustn't forget."

IT WAS CLOSE to sunset when we broke through the skies over Payay. The sweet scent of roasting rice rose through the air and tickled my nostrils. Tears pricked at the corners of my eyes, and I blinked them away. I could see the smoke rising from the thatched roofs and I could imagine the women sitting around their fires, tending to the rice and to whatever fare they had found or won from the hunt.

A shout arose from the village. And I stiffened in the saddle.

What did the weavers expect of me? Would they accept my return, or would they turn away in disappointment?

As if she could read my thoughts, Mitos clasped her arms around me.

"They have waited for you, Kyri," she said. "We have waited. We wish for no other to lead us but you."

*　*　*

THERE WERE MORE strangers in Payay than I had expected, but there was no animosity here. From the welcome they accorded her, I could tell that Mitos was loved and honored. Even if they greeted me with respect, it was Mitos to whom they looked for guidance, Mitos whose opinion they asked.

Was it any wonder? I thought. After all, she had lived here among them, while I had been away in exile.

I felt ashamed of my suspicion. Ashamed, too, that I had thought to return like a conquering hero. What right did I have to demand that the people of Yuta follow me into war? What right did I have to leadership when I had pushed the memory of them to the back of my mind while I was in exile?

"Kyri," Mitos's gentle voice intruded on my thoughts. "The Aunties and the delegation are waiting. We can share a repast together with them, if you wish."

I could see the question in her eyes, and I thought of the plea she'd made during our journey back from Resha.

What hardships had she suffered in the years of our separation? What resilience she must have had to keep the flame of resistance alive during the years of oppression. If there were any in Yuta who remembered me, it was because of her.

"Mitos," I said. "I promise, I will listen. Whatever happens, I will listen first."

ON OUR BANNERS, Yuta's dragon flies rampant across a field of red and black. Around us, the air is redolent with the scent of ripening rice. Soon, the fields will be golden. The harvesters will go out and gather the rice, there will be singing, there will be feasting, and there will be the tasting of the first rice wine.

On harvest nights, there are songs and stories told around the evening fires. We dance and we remember those who fell in that first battle, but we also dance and link hands and remember that even the Bangkawi belong to the earth, just as we belong to the earth.

In the long years of my exile, the weavers had studied the ways of the Bangkawi. They had penetrated the folds of the Bangkawi political systems and opened their knowledge to the young ones at their centers of learning.

By the time of my return, coalitions had been forged with Bangkawi who believed Yuta must be returned to those who were born to lead it. To the aunties, to the clan elders, to the healers and the teachers, to the garda and the shapers, to those who could speak life into the weave of made creatures.

Together, we went with the delegation to the capital, to where the eldest of the Bangkawi still sat on the first seat of power. There was no skirmish. There was no bloodshed.

When he saw me, the eldest of them descended from what he called a throne.

As in a dream, I saw him kneel before me. I saw him bend his neck and offer his head in return for the wrong his people had done.

THE MOUNTAINS ARE an aching green. We have buried our dead and mourned the loss of our comrades. Their names are inscribed in our hearts and in our minds.

We lost many to the war that took my mother's life, but in the end, we prevailed.

"At peace, Kyri?" Mitos says from behind me.

I turn to meet her gaze.

This too is part of my heritage. To know that there are wounds that still need to be healed.

"We must meet with the council soon," I say to Mitos.

She nods.

There is no returning to that idyllic time before war touched us, but we can move forward. A peace has been made between us and the Bangkawi who wish to live among us.

I think of all my mother's final words to me. Words that stayed my hand in that moment when I was tempted to take a life for a life.

"Remember that we are all of the earth," she said. "Remember that we are bound and connected to one another in ways that go deeper than blood. If our enemies have forgotten mercy, we must never forget it."

In the skies above us, the dragons circle and dive. A garda waves his pennant, while another sets up an ululating cry. The dragons wheel about, giving chase after each other. Free and wild, they whirl about like colored pinwheels in the sky.

THE PLANT AND THE PURIST
Malka Older

WE FOUND THE volcano by the tremor in my right hand.

An ancient map, ravaged by wear and rot, had gotten us to the general vicinity, but it was imprecise and massively outdated. I had never before used my seismic implant to locate an active lava conduit, or I might have realized earlier that something was wrong.

Perhaps it was also that I was enjoying the voyage too much. I had avoided airships from a superstitious concern that the speed and distance from the Earth would disorient me to the point of nausea, or maybe actual illness. Then, at a fair, I had agreed to go up with some friends in an airship that was offering simple vertical elevation, for the view. It was spectacular: the currents in the air were so untethered, and the perspective allowed me to connect moisture content with the shapes of clouds in new ways. I could almost feel the synapses forming, adjusting the intimate interpretation between input and meaning.

After that I experimented with a few short journeys, and was delighted to discover that the sensations were not distressing at all; rather the opposite. I added and calibrated an altimeter implant, and a method for calculating velocity at rates I had never before experienced, and began to learn about air currents.

It did not occur to me that I could apply my abilities to fossicking until Org. Zepla Pindarband approached me with the idea. We had several consultations to consider if and how I could be of assistance, and while Org. Zepla did manage to intrigue me with her passion for understanding history, as well as the descriptions of (mostly) comradely competition among fossicking teams and thrilling races to discovery, I must admit that the idea of long journeys by airship was an important attraction.

It was as marvelous as I had expected. The airship was designed and appointed for lengthy voyages; some of the crew shared rooms, but I had my own cabin and recycler, with pleasantly large windows and awnings to attract or fend off the sun's warmth. Still, I spent most of my time on deck, both to contribute to the search in whatever way I could, and for the sheer pleasure of being surrounded by atmosphere, hearing the heartbeats of passing birds and tracing wind patterns. I had a retractable nerve extension in my big toe, and when we were not moving swiftly—usually at night—I sometimes requested that we descend to where I could dip it into the ocean below us and feel the quivers of currents and the displacements caused by behemoths of the deep.

IT WAS NOT until we had been at sea for some days that, one evening after dinner with the windows open and the night breeze wafting salt and whale saliva, Org. Zepla unrolled the tattered document upon the table.

We all caught our breaths, I think. Organizational Zepla has in full the requisite panache of her class, and even those of us without expertise in ancient objects were alerted, by the care and deliberation she used, that this artifact was rare and impressive. Only Cassar—I noted when I looked over at the ancient history scholar—appeared unmoved, leaning back in his seat and watching us. But perhaps he had seen it already. Perhaps he had found it. While I looked he winked at me. I let my infrared filter flicker down semi-transparently over my eye—it would either provoke or disturb him, I was fine with either—and turned my attention back to the table.

"This is incredible," oozed Rinkton, the fossicker apprentice, his fingers hovering over it, their sensors doubtless tingling with spectrographic information. I would have liked to scan it myself. "Late Extravagant period, no? Most ephemera from that long ago have disintegrated."

"Indeed," Org. Zepla agreed. "Our Cassar has dated it precisely to that time. He found it—but, it is his story to tell."

"Not much to tell," Cassar said. "It was part of the cache I discovered in Antarctica, in a container that had been vacuum packed."

"This," Org. Zepla reprised, "is an advertisement: an announcement designed to encourage purchases or other outlays of money. In this case, as you can see, it is for a burial site—that is what they mean by 'post-mortem corporeal preservation'—in a volcano."

There was a collective gasp. Even Eora, the general factotum of the expedition, who was on kitchen duty that night, looked up from the pots they were scrubbing.

"How does that make any sense?" Mibelle was just a deckhand, young and new to fossicking and airships alike, but the more experienced ones looked pleased she had asked.

"Not sure it does," Org. Zepla answered, "although whether that is our lack of understanding or their ancient lack of sense..." She trailed off under the general laugh. I looked back at Cassar, as the person with the most expert opinion on whether those far away ancestors of ours were irrational or merely stupid; his eyebrows were frunced, as though he were wondering the same.

"It's not enough data," he said. "Obviously this is only an attention-grabber; it doesn't give any information about the technology used, or the pricing—that's how much people would pay—which would suggest the level of technology, or—or anything. It could be a ridiculous proposition that no one agreed to, or a scam that people paid for and received nothing in return." He smiled ruefully at us. "It's very possible we may arrive and find that no one was buried there at all."

"Indeed, indeed," Org. Zepla said, "but the first thing is to find the place. As you can see—" She pointed her small finger at the square of cartography that occupied about a quarter of the artifact. "—the map gives only the vaguest suggestion for where this volcano might be found."

We all leaned forward again. The landmarks on the map were long-ago shapes that, if they still existed above the waves, certainly looked very different; still, they could surely be identified by historical geographers. The more significant problem was that the map was cartoonish, not to scale; the directions and distances from those landmarks could only be approximate.

"According to the conventions of fossicking, we had of course to share copies of this map into the collective library. It's created some interest, so we must consider the possibility of competition. I must say I suspect Org. Cranson of holding back some cross-referential information. I know her *Spun Sugar* has been on the trail of this site, and I suspect the *Mad Alacrity* is not far off either. But I'll wager neither of them has a 'plant like ours!"

The crew enjoyed that. I had more mixed feelings. It was true, I knew of no one in the inhabited world with as many implants as I had, but I was unsure how useful my sensitivities would be.

"So Velan's role is to help us find it? I had assumed you wanted her to analyze the construction of the tombs and any artifacts." That was Miraina, the senior fossicker, who nodded at me in apology for the indirect reference.

"That too, naturally. But volcanos are crucial nodes of the planet, are they not? Pores, liminal portals, connecting the surface to the depths, channels for molten matter from a primeval space to our own environs, a change so significant that the material they transport fundamentally changes its nature once exposed to our atmosphere. In short—" *Too late*, I thought automatically. "—who better to find one than someone intrinsically connected to the planet in as many ways as possible?" She beamed at the crew; as their gazes shifted one by one towards me, I smiled as well, but it felt brittle. If the volcano had gone extinct, I wasn't sure I could find it; even if it was still active it might not be rumbling, or we might not get close enough in these vast seas.

And so I was relieved, a few nights later, when I felt the seismometer in my rightmost metacarpal begin to quiver.

I had explained to Org. Zepla about the uncertainty involved in assuming that a given movement of the tectonic plates was attributable to a single volcano, and indeed, we had already had one false alarm. Org. Zepla, when not in front of a crowd, was not a bad listener, and she nodded and patted my arm (my left arm, so as not to disrupt my seismography even for a moment). But this instance did not fade, and as we moved I was able to triangulate it to a rough point rather than a stretch of plate interaction. And so we followed the tenuous tremble in my bones over the featureless ocean for three days.

IN THE EVENINGS I often sat by the small patch of carrots and bulgar being grown on the airship's roof. There were sloping seats around the garden, and I could sit there and watch the sky, tidal patterns ticking in my consciousness, tasting the moisture content of the air and sometimes letting my hand drift down to touch the soil. Isolated soil like that always felt different than ground soil: the composition was artificially balanced, less dynamic, but still interesting as a constructed puzzle.

One evening Cassar joined me there. We sat in silence for some time before he ventured his question.

"What does it feel like?"

"Which—?"

"Any of it. But I guess I mean, having so many at the same time. It seems that it would be... loud. Confusing. Complicated."

I let out a chuckle. "To me it feels... complete. No, not exactly complete, there are too many things I don't know, but... connected." I could have, without looking, pointed towards exactly where the moon hid behind her sheaf of clouds, her position indicated by a cool spot on my skull; I could feel the distant tug of the magnetic pole and the curvature of the planet. "I take it you don't have many?"

Cassar grimaced a little. "None."

"None?" It was unusual, if not unheard of; most people at least corrected their vision, or added a more precise sense of time, or set an internal barometer. "Are you Virgin?" My friend Blin was Virgin, and so I knew that arcane religion discouraged implants, although usually not with such complete success.

"No. It's not religious, just preference."

"You prefer to be so... so disconnected?"

He was tugging at a loose thread on his sleeve. "I... I don't think of it that way. More like... being more connected to myself?" He shrugged helplessly. "I don't mean any criticism... I have nothing against 'plants..."

"No, no," I agreed. "I don't take it that way, and I didn't mean to criticize you, either." I listened to my voice speaking the previous question and grimaced myself. "Even if it sounded that way."

"I—my mother's brain did not assimilate implants well; she had difficulty syncretizing the new inputs—"

"It's not uncommon," I said, trying to be encouraging, and he nodded.

"Yes, they eventually found a modified interface and she ended up getting a few, but it meant that she didn't approve any for me when I was a child, and when I got older I decided I'd rather stay this way. Out of a kind of perverse stubbornness as much as anything, I think."

I laughed with him, not because it was funny, but because that was how he wanted to guard his uncertainty. I almost let the subject drop, for the same reason, but I was curious. "Is it not difficult for you, as a historian?"

He waggled his head. He did have a gloriously full mane of hair, his marker beads woven through different locks; I had shaved most of mine at various times for various implants, retaining only a few braids from birth. "In some ways, yes. But it also makes it easier for me, I believe, to imagine the experiences of people who lived in a time when implants were much less common."

"That makes sense," I agreed, rather surprised by the perspective. It also reminded me of something I had wondered about. "May I ask you something?"

He inclined his head, without looking away from the horizon.

"I don't know much about the late Extravagants but... is it usual of them to seek burial in a volcano? I would have thought they would seek preservation above all."

Cassar was silent for a moment. "It is unusual. Perhaps... perhaps they believed the volcano to be extinct."

I didn't know what his fully organic memory capacity or experience might be like, but I could pull up the image of the map that I had snapped earlier and filed along a short and well-marked mental pathway, and see again the stylized flames leaping from the drawn volcano.

As we approached the tremor, I became aware of a deep discomfort, a sense of wrongness. I found myself turning my head from side to side, as though searching for an elusive scent or other chemical signature, and tapping my fingers uneasily on the rail, as though the arboreal history of its wood would resolve my malaise.

It was not until we saw the cone of the volcano—gracefully curved, nearly symmetrical, exuding a gaseous plume—on the horizon that I understood the dissonance.

"The smell—the gas—the smoke is wrong!"

"Are you sure?" Mibelle asked, peering at the darkening sky—for it was nearly sunset—from her haunt in the rigging. "Looks to be smoking all right."

There was no hint of ash in the air, no sulfur that I could identify, no carbon dioxide above expected levels at that location. "I can feel the rumbling," I said, the understanding of my unease breaking over me all at once, "I can *see* that smoke, just as you can—but it's only vapor, there's no release of gases or magma, nothing to show it is emitting at all."

The crew and fossickers around me shared a ripple of disquiet.

"It *could* be extinct," Rinkton suggested, without much confidence. "Perhaps there is localized seismic activity..."

"It might not be the volcano we're looking for at all," Eora reminded us (as the quartermaster, she always seemed to be expecting that our trip would be longer than planned).

I said nothing, but my gaze met Cassar's, and I could see he was also thinking about the Extravagants and the barbarities they had so often wrought.

MY CONCERN INFECTED even Org. Zepla, or perhaps she was simply more cautious than her style of rhetoric would lead one to believe, for she had the *Blooming Vibrance* tether to the most outstretched spur of the island. Our small landing party descended by rope ladder, my finger pads telling me the thread count and composition of its rungs, and began a scramble up the slope.

I brushed my fingertips along the rocks. The atom-bouncers in my left third finger let me feel its hardness, the way it would break; when I added the forefinger, I could taste its components. Looking over, I saw that Cassar and Rinkton were scratching at the hardened ripples of the slope. My heart accelerated. Without tools, they couldn't be doing much damage to the volcano, to these hallucinatory, irreplicable flows, but it still felt deeply wrong to see them attacking it. I hurried over as quickly as I could across the fragile rock.

"We're not digging," Cassar said as I approached, immediately understanding my concern. "It was broken here already—must have been hit by something, maybe a rock dislodged from above?" We all glanced involuntarily upslope, then Cassar went on. "Do you think you could date these layers? I'm wondering what the cone looked like at the time the burials were advertised, how many layers have increased its size since then."

I had to consider, having never tried to use my senses to estimate geologic age. I squatted and touched the surface, pondering the different sensations I received from different layers of solidified lava. It took me only a few seconds to sort out the way some signals had faded more than others but—

"This is old," I said, looking up in shock. "This tuff is from around the time of the map! I can't be exact, you understand, but unless I'm very confused, there hasn't been any new lava flow since approximately the Extravagant period."

"Maybe it *is* extinct," Rinkton said, unconcerned, but Cassar's grey face mirrored my own shock, and I started for the summit with renewed energy, the wrongness of the microenvironment clacking now like a broken branch swinging against a tree trunk.

It was nearly sunset when we reached the crest. Cassar was straggling some meters below as I leapt onto the ridge to look into the caldera, and Rinkton was a few seconds behind me. I stared down in horror.

"What is it?"

I looked over, wondering why Cassar was asking when he stood beside us, then remembered: he couldn't see in the dark. "It's not there." No wonder he had been falling behind, if he couldn't see the rocks.

"What's not there?"

"The conduit! The lava!" I gestured, even though I knew he couldn't see. "They blocked it off somehow!" The flat featureless surface of the caldera, some way below us, *felt* painfully wrong, like coming across one of those ancient gaps in the land with the veins hacked out of it, or one of the places where hectares of human detritus blanketed out any growth, or a mountain that flattened ungracefully where it had been disfigured by some unknown destruction of antiquity.

"Was this some kind of attack on the graves?" Rinkton speculated. "Or perhaps a superstitious attempt to prevent any kind of resurrection?"

"I doubt it." Cassar must have been almost blind, but I could see his grim expression clearly. "I suspect this was part of the original plan, a way of protecting the sepulchers from eruptions."

Bile soured my saliva. "But then why bury people in a volcano at all?"

"They knew the seas were rising," Cassar answered, "if not quite how much. There is much evidence of higher ground being appropriated by the rich even for post-vitality usages."

"But why a *volcano?*"

Grimmer still: "Imagery and symbolism were very important to them."

"You mean they did *this*—" I could feel the lava pounding below me, the venerable ache of the frustrated conduit vibrating through my bones. "—because they thought it would seem *cool?*"

"There's the Organizational," Rinkton said. Indeed, Org. Zepla and Miraina were cresting the summit, a few arms' lengths west of us.

I was too nauseated to listen closely to the latecomer's expressions of horror; I sat on the ridge, facing away from the eerily closed-off caldera, a hand over my eyes, and inhaled the sea air with every sense I had.

"Do we think the sarcophagi are below that?" Org. Zepla was asking, when I started paying attention again.

"It doesn't seem likely..."

"Could we have missed them along the outer slope? Or perhaps they're on the other side?"

"I'd say there." Miraina was pointing into the caldera Looking over, I could see the darker spaces of caves drilled into the rock. I tried to imagine what Cassar saw: just dimness, the barest grey scribbles limning the outcroppings.

And then the view lit with a sudden flash, like lightning, but without any of the pressure differential. I scanned the sky. "Pirates?"

"Grave robbers!" shouted Org. Zepla. "They followed us!"

"Or happened on our trail," Miraina suggested.

Org. Zepla waved her arm. "Quick, everyone!" she yelled. "To the tombs!"

There was some disagreement; Rinkton wanted to return to the ship, but Org. Zepla reminded them that the *Blooming Vibrance* would attempt to draw the assailants away from the tombs.

"They are still distant," she said, as we picked our way down the steep slope into the crater of the volcanic sarcophagus. "They likely may not have scanned us here. Better we hide for the moment."

Cassar said little, but his face had taken on an entirely different animation at the suggestion of entering the caves. He attached himself to Rinkton (why not me? My night vision was surely superior), and the two of them led us, descending with a perilous speed towards the caverns. I could see the terrain clearly, but I was distracted by the inside of the volcano, thinking about the extreme heat that should have coursed through it and, for so long, had been missing. "We have to open it up," I said, but I was speaking to no one in particular: the historian and fossickers were too far ahead, the Org. struggling with the slope behind me. A rock skittered off the slope somewhere ahead, pocking off the surface of the concrete cap with a false note.

"Careful ahead there!" I called, wishing again Cassar had grabbed my arm so I could guide him down safely. Org. Zepla hissed at me to be quiet, and instead of telling her that the faint hum of the intruders' airship was moving away from us, I concentrated on my feet and eventually gained the nearest cave.

Cassar and Rinkton were sitting within the mouth of it, side by side with their backs against the wall, breathing hard. "All right?" I asked, as I scanned the walls of the cavern. It had been enlarged, no doubt about it, and my neck prickled as I peered ahead into the darkness and caught the blink of lights. "What is that?"

"Some kind of barrier," Rinkton said.

"They wouldn't have left the volcano as their only defense," Cassar agreed.

"But..." Before I could ask about the lights, Org. Zepla and Miraina arrived.

"Well, then," the Organizational said, sounding pleased. "Shall we take a look?"

Cassar produced a lantern—tallow, by the smell of it—so he wasn't completely dependent on our augmented eyes. The glow softened the pinpoint pain of the beadlike, winking illumination that studded the metal door blocking the tunnel.

"This is incredible!" To hear Rinkton, you would think the door itself was enough of a find to justify our entire trip, and perhaps it was. I certainly had never seen anything like it in the illustrated fossicking accounts I had accessed after Org. Zepla originally contacted me. Rinkton was doubtless assaying the composition himself—I caught something that sounded like percentages in his muttering—but since I couldn't see his results, I leaned my fingertips against it. "Why would they include platinum in a door like this?" I wondered aloud.

"Prestige," Cassar said. He had a notebook out and was scratching frantically into the wax. "It was probably in the agreement they signed. I wonder if they might have a copy somewhere inside... the Extravagants were very legalistic in many ways... the knowledge we could extract from such a document..."

I gave up on him and turned my attention again to the door itself. I was still wondering how the glowing lights were powered. Or could they be of some kind of phosphorescent material? I ran my fingers over them, but the surface was glass—ancient, factory glass—slightly warmed by the power behind it. Could that explain the vapor rising from the capped volcano? I followed the line of lights to a pattern of shallow holes backed by waffled wires. My fingertips found an indentation.

Click.

I skidded back as light and sound erupted from the door simultaneously. The sound was a boom, a cross between thunder and the popping of ears clogged by congestion, and the light was a glow that spilled into the middle of the cave and then resolved itself into the image of a man, wrapped in ancient clothing, hair as short as a toddler's, smiling into the dark. His left side painted over Rinkton, who had fallen back onto his heels, distorting the shape of the image.

"Grievings," the man said, with a confident mien; then my brain caught up with the word that unfurled, written, above his head, and I realized he had said *Greetings*, but with a strange ancient accent. Rinkton stopped gaping and scuttled to the wall, restoring the man's body to plumb-line straightness. "Welcome to the tomb of Joshua Nestor Winserton and family." The light flickered and a woman appeared next to him, two improbably clean children crowding at their legs.

"They buried *children* here?" I was too horrified to modulate my tone, and the two fossickers and the historian responded with a hiss as the man continued talking.

"Probably not," Org. Zepla murmured, stepping closer to me. "As you see, none of them were dead when this image was created. He probably reserved their spots, but whether they chose to be packed in there—assuming they outlived their father—or whether the burial company was even still running when they died... well, we'll know more once we get inside."

The man, or ghost, or recording, was still talking. "—intent is not as a place for mourning, but an inspiring monument to what I accomplished in my time on Earth." The woman and the disturbing children had disappeared. "Inside, you'll find a celebration of my life and work. Naturally, security measures have been put in place to prevent desecration, but those with proper credentials should have no difficulties, so—" The phantom smirked. "—'Speak, friend, and enter.' As they say." The image winked out.

We stood silent in the after-echo.

"Is that... normal?" I asked at last.

"I've never seen one," Cassar said at last, "but then, of the several dozen tombs I've assessed I don't think I've ever seen one this opulent. Rinkton?"

"I've never seen a functioning one," Rinkton responded, "but I have heard of them from other fossickers, and we found a mechanism last year that we thought was intended for such use."

"It's utterly marvelous." Org. Zepla rubbed her hands together. "If that's what's on the outside, *imagine* what gems from the past we might access within! Metaphorical gems, naturally. And as for this... can we run it again? Record it somehow?"

"It's recorded in my sensors." I said it quickly, finding myself reluctant to see that strangely immature face again, hear that smooth voice. "How do we get in? Do we have the 'proper credentials,' whatever that means?"

Both the fossickers were shaking their heads before I even finished. "They often had intricate locks and protection on their tombs," Miraina explained. "There were systems for people—family members, colleagues—to bypass them, but it was all dependent on ancient technologies, long obsolete."

"What kind of technologies?"

Rinkton shrugged. "Sometimes biometric, sometimes tied to some kind of implanted identification. DNA was popular, allowing descendants to enter—there's a story that goes around about a fossicking crew accessing a tomb because one of their apprentices was, all unknowing, an incredibly distant descendent of the interred, but I don't know if it's true."

"Worth a try," said Org. Zepla, eagerly rolling up her sleeve.

"Easy, Organizational," Miraina said. "We don't even know whether this one has a DNA reader."

"How would grave robbers get in?" I asked.

"They'd blow it up," Rinkton said, and I was so desperate to get the cap off the volcano that, even in the fascination of the fossicking developments, his words inspired an immediate and pleasing image of concrete exploding into dust.

"Or drill through, possibly," Cassar interjected. "Either way, they would do terrific damage to the historical record..."

"The door itself, of course," Rinkton agreed, "But there are usually things just behind it—"

"Sometimes snares," Org. Zepla put in with a combination of relish and warning.

"So how do fossickers do it properly?" I asked, hoping to forestall an intensive discussion of all the ways we could muck it up.

"Slowly," Cassar said.

"There have been some cases when they managed to unlock the door by tricking or undoing the mechanism. Quite often the clever technology of the lock has already degraded. Or, usually, we dig the door itself out. Slowly, yes. Very carefully." Rinkton eyed the rock around the door as he spoke.

I hated the idea of doing any more damage to this volcanic cone. "Perhaps I can trick the lock." I had no idea if I could, but it seemed more likely than anything they had suggested.

The cave lit up for a moment with a flash: lightning, or some kind of attack from the grave robbers? I felt for my internal barometers, but they felt inconclusive: if it was a storm it was at some distance.

"Right." Org. Zepla shifted into action. "Which of you think you can assist with the lock mechanism here? Cassar, you've seen this kind of thing before?"

He nodded. "I can't rewire it, but if you want guesses about what the triggers are, yes, I can provide some ideas."

I didn't look at him during this. He couldn't see my face clearly, and I thought I might return the favor.

"Very well. You stay. We'll go take a look at the next cave, and possibly the rest. In case we lose this site—" Was she worried about the grave robbers? Or the volcano? "—the least we can do is record any other messages from the past." She whirled on the two of us. "If you're able to unlock it, you fetch us at once, understood? Before you even open the door. One comes for us, the other stays here." A final glare, and she left, carrying the two fossickers in her wake.

I felt myself relax into the darkness, which was odd considering that I still wasn't sure whether Cassar admired me in the way I admired him. Oh, I could smell his pheromones, but experience had taught me there was a vast gap between sexual urgency and sexual willingness, much less compatibility. But while being alone with him carried a charge of jitter and static, the absence of Org. Zepla's aggressive certainty and the obsessive expertise of Rinkton and Miraina was a relief.

Not that Cassar didn't have his own expertise, his own obsession. I was aware of his awareness of me—I could see the heat on the back of his neck—but he was leaning close to the door with his lamp, following the tracery.

I wondered suddenly if he, absent so many senses, was unsure of *my* attraction. I tried to sieve through my inputs, wondering what he might feel, but most of my implants had been with me long enough that my brain interpreted them directly. I *knew* where in the sky the moon was at that moment; I had to think about it carefully to remember that it was a slight coolness on my scalp that informed me. But pheromones were evolved for unaugmented human signaling; surely he could feel my interest?

Instead of asking him, as I should have, I found myself voicing a different question entirely. "What did it mean, that last part? About friends?"

In the weird partial light of the lamp, Cassar grimaced. "It's a reference to a book, one old enough to already be considered a classic at the time this was happening, a sort of inside joke among a group of people. Unfortunately, we have not found any extant copies, but the phrase is used enough that we understand the gist of the point: it was a riddle or password that required the person to say 'friend' in a certain language."

I said it automatically. Nothing happened, but Cassar grinned at me over his shoulder. "It seems a bit simplistic at face value for someone with this degree of security. I suspect it had some additional meaning... perhaps indicating voice recognition, although that seems extremely time-limited... It may also," he added after a pause, "simply be a way of signaling membership in the particular tribe that put value on literature, and have no relevance to the lock."

"Still, he seemed to think it would be easy for those in the know..."

"It's not voice-activated," Cassar said, suddenly more sure. "Look, this... alcove? It's designed to scan a three-dimensional object."

"A key?"

"Perhaps an item—they did have the possibility of mass production, or even personal production. Something could have been given away at memorial services, or the specifications could be included in the will. But I wonder if instead it was hand-speech."

I reached towards the space and Cassar leapt towards me. "It could be booby-trapped!"

His hand was on my arm, and I held his eyes as I extended a sensor from my little finger towards the space.

"It won't hurt you? If it gets cut off, I mean?" He barely whispered it, and I could feel his breath on my neck.

"There are no pain sensors in there. I will have to replace it, but..." I leaned towards him, just a little. "I'm starting to understand the allure of the lost past. I'm willing to risk it."

His inhalation stuttered.

"Ah." I felt the tickle of lasers along my sensor. "See? No guillotine-razors slamming down to amputate." I turned towards the door and introduced my hand. "Do you think you can register any reactions from the lock system?"

It took some time, but the sense of working in careful connection with him was almost as satisfying as the moment when I honed the possibilities down to the required gesture and the lock finally clicked open.

I sat back on my heels, not sure until I reached for my internal clock how many hours had passed, looking up at Cassar with a smile, but his focus had shifted entirely to the door, staring at it like a forbidden portal—which, I realized, it was.

"Should I go for the Organizational?" My voice faded even as I asked.

Cassar looked down at me, his palm on the door. I imagined what he felt: cold and smoothness, but with no hint of the taste of the metal, its molecules, the dense sheen to the platinum, the tense quiver of steel. "Or," he said, "we could look ourselves."

I never would have thought of disobeying Org. Zepla—it was her expedition, she had encouraged me to join, she understood the rules of fossicking—but the moment he said it I was ready. We had discovered the key, through our determination and insight and our different sensitivities—mine implanted, his learned; why should she claim the privilege of the first look? Wasn't that thrill of revelation due to us? It wasn't as if we were going to steal anything.

Or were we?

"It would," I said at last, a bit breathlessly, "be a good idea to check for snares."

He held my gaze for another moment, confirming that I meant it, that I agreed, and then he dug his naked, unaugmented fingertips into the gap and pulled open the door.

It swung open into a bare corridor that curved widdershins along the interior of the cone. As Cassar raised his lantern, the light glimmered off astonishingly detailed filigree in the walls. "That's circuitry," he whispered. "That's... this is unbelievable, the sophistication—"

I put out an arm to stop him as he stepped forward. "Snares, remember?" I edged my toe sensor out, tapping softly to read the echoes—

The whole chamber, the whole volcano shook.

"Was that us?" Cassar was clinging to the arm I had blocked him with. I had fallen shoulder-first against the wall and was still leaning there.

"I didn't *feel* any kind of trigger, but..." But even my sensory inputs were not exhaustive. The cavern was spinning around me, and I closed my eyes and concentrated on the pull of magnetic North until I felt stilled and stable. Before I could open them, I heard Org. Zepla's voice in my ear, reverberating along the channel we—those of us with hearing and vocal implants—were keyed to.

"They're not grave robbers!" She sounded ragged, and so did my voice as I repeated the words out loud for Cassar. "They're reclaimers. They're trying to open up the volcano."

"They're trying to open up the volcano!" I felt a swoop of elation, so strong that I was grinning as I met Cassar's eyes. He looked horrified.

"Come on!" He grabbed my hand and pulled me into the tunnel.

"Shouldn't we be—" I waved in the direction of the exit. "Wait—Snares!" I yanked him back as the floor fell out from under his front foot.

"I can jump it! Look, the burial chamber is right there!" It was true: the space ahead of us glowed with flickering lights, each small—sensors? Indicators?—but so many that he must have been able to make out what I could see clearly: the shape of an Extravagant-era coffin, fitted for a person stretched out instead of curled.

"We don't have time! They're going to release the volcano!"

"Not yet," Cassar argued, yearning towards the lights in front of us. "I'm sure the *Vibrance* will have alerted them to our presence. They *must* allow us a reasonable time to evacuate!"

"Then maybe we should use that time to, you know, *evacuate?*" My fossicking fever had evaporated in the elation of imagining the unleashing of the volcano, and now I wanted only to leave so that it could be set free as soon as possible—not to mention that I had no desire to perish in the event.

"We're so close! The least we can do is record whatever we can see before it's incinerated—all that data about the past gone forever!"

I hesitated, the lava pulsing below us under its cruel shell of concrete, the lights with their unnatural brilliance winking incessantly. "Five minutes." I set a timer, each second another sand grain's worth of weight hallucinated on my left shoulder. "Wait!" I hissed, because Cassar was about to jump. I uncoiled my fingertip sensor to its maximum length, magnetized the end, and tossed it at the ceiling, as far ahead as I could reach.

"That's really going to hold two people's weight?" Cassar asked, skeptical.

"If you don't trust me I'll go ahead and tell you all about it," I said with as much nonchalance as I could manage, given that we were in the depths of a snare-ridden tunnel in a volcanic mausoleum under attack by explosives intended to trigger catastrophic lava flow. In truth, I wasn't completely confident that the cable would hold: the material itself certainly had the tensile strength to support both of us, but the place where it snagged into my nervous system might not be as robust. "Anyway, it's just a back-up; as you said, we can jump it." I raised my eyebrows at him and Cassar sighed and wrapped his arm around my neck; I reciprocated at his waist. "On three, then. One, two—"

As it turned out, it was a good thing that we used the cable, and that it held (though I felt at least one nerve uproot; that would need to be repaired if and when etc.), since the temptingly close opposite edge of the pit crumbled under our feet and we had to leap and scrabble our way to ground that seemed, at least, solid.

It was also no longer rock, or at least, metal had been laid over it, a good centimeter thick. "Silly of them," I said, when I had caught my breath. "Look at how it's rusted and warped. The rock would have been more durable."

"They were great believers in technology," Cassar said absently. "Come on!"

We took a step forward, then another, and with the third—I felt the metal flex beneath my feet, the charge as the circuit closed—the remaining cul de sac of cavern was full of light and movement.

"Look at this. *Look* at it," Cassar breathed; I was, in all conscience, trying not to. The not-large space was full of moving, projected images like the one that had greeted us, all of the same man at different ages: swinging things, gesturing while talking, wearing various antiquated garments clearly associated with various values or virtues. It was a visual and aural cacophony, and especially with the difficult dialect I couldn't follow any of it.

"Why is it all playing at once?"

Cassar shrugged. "A malfunction, perhaps."

"I don't see much about his family. Maybe they decided not to go along with his collective burial plan."

"Or maybe he didn't buy the full hagiographic package for them," Cassar responded, and went on before I could react. "Look at all of this!" He pulled me through the images—not really all the way through, since they crowded the room nearly to the edges, but close to the walls there was enough space to see without that smug face getting in the way.

The walls were lined with shallow shelves, each filled with items that required no expertise in history or fossicking to be identified as valuable, or at least valued in the time when they were made. Many contained the (already unpleasant to my eye) physiognomy or name of the deceased, doubtless lauding him for some accomplishment; others seemed to be displayed for their own sake rather than for what they said about him. Cassar ran his fingertips along a shelf in such thrall that he did not even feel the floor shake below us—or perhaps the seismometers in my hand made me aware of a tremor he couldn't register.

"We have to go," I said, shaking his shoulder. "Maybe we'll be able to negotiate with the reclaimers for a bit more time..." I didn't believe it; honestly, I didn't even want to. The flow of magma according to the physics and divinity of the planet was far more valuable than this inflated pageantry. I didn't want this man's name to survive, the selfish details of his life; what was the point? But when Cassar turned to me his expression was agonized: he didn't believe it either.

"They won't give us anything. Everything we could learn about the past, about how they lived and why, maybe what went wrong—Don't you understand? It's where we came from!"

I couldn't bring myself to agree. "The volcano is important, not one person who paid for his own shrine."

Cassar groaned, or maybe it was a grunt in reaction to the floor moving. "If that's what you believe," he said at last, wildly, "we may as well desecrate it! Grab what you can."

I hesitated; I didn't believe in curses other than as a story to deter grave robbers, but I couldn't help feel that the shine of these objects was unhealthy somehow, their value dangerously out of proportion; that, in short, the Extravagants might still contaminate us from afar, as tenacious and sapping as any ghost. But Cassar was already filling his pockets, and I noticed that even in his hurry he was not reaching for the most valuable materials, and he seemed to be avoiding anything with the dead man's face or name on it. Still moving with some reluctance, I caught up an intricately designed miniature scene, a building with many rooms and small people dotted throughout it, and though some of it crumbled in my grip I managed to catch most of the pieces and add them to my pack. That freed me from my indecision; I grabbed and stowed as discriminately as I could, even after the weight of five full minutes had settled on my shoulder with its dully repeating alarm. It took another tremor strong enough to make us stagger before I started urging Cassar towards the exit, and even then it wasn't until we heard Org. Zepla's voice calling from the passage that, with the sudden shame of miscreancy, we ran.

The Organizational was waiting to catch us in her arms when we leaped the pit. I remember babbling something to her, some apology for going in without her. She ignored me comprehensively, as did Cassar, both of them charging towards the exit. Rinkton waited at the cave's mouth, urging us on with gestures and yelling. I remembered, as the scree of the inner slope slipped beneath my feet, that Cassar wouldn't be able to see, and I slid back down to grab his arm and help him upwards. Above us, the reclaimers' airship loomed, and Miraina screamed at us at the edge of the cone. We had nearly crested the ridge when I felt, or smelled, or knew that the magma was convulsing below us. "We don't have time," I gasped, reaching for Miraina's hand, looking up over my shoulder at the reclaimers, so it wasn't until I turned back that I saw the *Vibrancy* hovering just below us.

We had just enough time to get away, whether by chance or blessing or by grace of the retainers. I sat with Cassar on the top deck by the garden, holding his hand as we watched the eruption, myself with joy and him with a loss deep enough for sorrow.

THE FAST-ENOUGH HUMAN
Kathleen Alcalá

SORREL LIFTED HER mallet and gave the stake a final, mighty blow. Ana and Chia stepped forward to wrap and pull the barbed wire and finished this section of fence just as the sun began to rise. First the false dawn, then the increasing light becoming less and less diffuse until the sun showed her face and claimed the yellow sky. Soon Sorrel would sleep hard.

Sorrel woke to pounding rain on the salvaged metal roof. The day was dark, but it sometimes cleared before nightfall. The Day Workers were long gone to their assigned or chosen tasks. She stood and stretched, easily touching the low ceiling with her fingertips, before rummaging in her hanging basket for clean clothes. Sorrel's dreams had been brief, but included a reminder to excavate her pockets for the herb she had discovered the night before, growing in a natural basin formed by the roots of a hemlock.

The plants were wilted and a little crushed, giving off a slightly medicinal odor as she held the leaves to her face. Sorrel held the leaves lightly, balanced on her fingertips, sniffing, before crushing them in her strong grip. A bitter lemon smell rose from the green pulp when she opened her hand.

The smell, regrettably, made Sorrel remember the night her mother died. The night she and her siblings were thrown out of the shelter they had lived in for several years, the only place

Sorrel's young brothers and one sister remembered. As the oldest, she recalled a farm with animals—real, domesticated animals—and a bed to herself.

Then the men had come bringing guns and a piece of paper and thrown them out with what they could carry in their arms. The men had come at dawn, stealthily, so that the family could not defend themselves. They came to steal land. Again. The first thing they did was shoot her father.

When Bear decides to run, she is very fast, faster than any human. Sorrel thought about this a lot while growing up. The joke was always, I don't have to run faster than Bear, I just have to run faster than the slowest human with me. The trick is not to be the fastest human, but the fast-enough human.

This was a story Sorrel's father used to tell. She grew up thinking, if only I had been stronger, bigger, I could have saved my family. If only I had been faster.

Pushed out onto the street, Sorrel took her younger brothers and sister to the border, then across the border with the United States on the trains that ran north. They dodged the ticket-taker, whose hopeless task was to try and make every passenger pay. Mostly, he looked for people who might have money, and that did not include Sorrel and her siblings. At the border, before letting them pass, a man in a uniform took Sorrel and her sister into a room and did things her mind flinched away from, trying to not-remember while remembering enough to seek revenge someday.

When they crossed, the Chirachua Apache took them in, recognizing her face as an Ópata relative, and recognizing her power. When the time came for her introduction to Changing Woman, she fasted with the other girls, and on the fourth day there was an earthquake, a terremoto that shook the ground for miles. Sorrel, in her first menstrual agony, cried out with the earthquake, and they said she spoke with the voice of the earth.

So she grew, and she worked, and she grew some more, until she was almost as big as a small bear. The Chiracahua did not use that word. They called the being "Mother's Sibling," and tried to not call attention to themselves when they said it. Her sister found a man, and her brothers found companions among the Apache. No one claimed Sorrel, maybe because of her nickname of Mother's Sibling, and she claimed no one. It was unlucky to touch anything Mother's Sibling had touched, or to sleep where Mother's Sibling had slept. When there was not enough water for three years in a row, Sorrel joined those going further north. With a Chiracahua blessing, Sorrel took with her some knowledge of medicinal herbs.

Sorrel walked. She traveled with others fleeing north, away from the fires that choked the land and the air with ash. There were days when she did not see the sun at all, the air filled with a yellow haze of grit and smoke. Her already husky voice turned deep and textured, reflecting the smoke particles that she breathed and absorbed every day. In her head she recited her knowledge of eucalipto. Ibahaca. Mejorana. Menta. Oregano. Romero. Salvia. Ajo. Zagosti y osha. This was when she acquired her lifelong habit of picking unfamiliar plants to see what they could do.

As she traveled north and west, Sorrel's knowledge of herbs grew to include alum, yarrow, yierba mansa, wild ginger, and yierba santa. She learned the berries, the stinging nettles, and when to dig for camas.

Sorrel earned her keep mostly with her powerful size and looks. She often walked at a back corner of a caravan, watching for marauders, for Border Patrol gone rogue who preyed on travelers, even far from the border. The Texas Rangers had been revived, and again attracted the violent and the twisted in spirit. Any time she caught one of them, Sorrel's rage made her violent. Her traveling companions had to restrain her from beating the predators to a pulp with the long, weighted staff she carried, which would draw unwanted attention to the wagon train. Outlaws soon learned to avoid the caravans with which she traveled, her reputation preceding her as a powerful antidote to violence.

Sorrel began to think of herself as the fast-enough human, fast enough to get it done, fast enough to survive.

Much of the terrain they crossed was scorched bare, the great forests of the Sierra Madres burned off in the last great wildfires of the twenty-first century. The weather had changed from the mild winters and glorious summers of the past to treacherous winds and driving rains, followed by months of drought that only the hardiest crops could survive. Humans huddled in rammed earth dwellings built close to the ground, protecting their water sources with their lives. Only the hardiest of herbs still grew wild in California, and Sorrel acquired much of her knowledge from the last herbalists around, rather than from direct interaction with the plants.

In spite of the terrible air, there were a few hearty species of bees that continued to fly and seek nectar, that still knew the ancient dances of bee and flower, flower and bee. Sorrel was drawn to the beekeepers, and spent two or three years on the mid-California Coast with a colony of keepers who taught her their secrets. The main one: don't be afraid. This was a lesson Sorrel learned over and over again, to take the sting in exchange for the honey, to offer peace to the bees no matter what was going on around her, and more importantly, in spite of what was going on in her head and her heart. Sorrel knew she was not the only one—she saw the pain, shock and suspicion reflected back from the eyes around her, especially if certain events or places were mentioned.

WHEN SORREL REACHED the Northwest, where water was not as scarce, she found society slightly better organized. There were places, towns even, where people came together to find new families, new jobs and occupations. There were women skilled as midwives, and those who knew how to raise children in a kind and loving environment. There were people who knew how to make the ash-filled soil productive again, and there were seed-keepers who knew their precious collections needed to go into the soil in a timely manner to pass on their food-making magic.

All of this time, Sorrel slept alone. She knew most people were afraid of her, of her size and the smoldering anger in her eyes. She realized it was more than her resemblance to Mother's Sibling. She slept in the bunks offered by beekeepers' collectives, or on the floors of strangers. She learned to ball up her jacket and use it as a pillow, her staff at her side, and to imagine her mother's soft voice putting her to sleep at night. "Duermete, dueremete," she heard, sleep, sleep, as the world faded and she was sometimes transported back to what had become a golden time for her, when her parents were alive, and smiled at their children. She could feel an arm around her shoulders and a "Buen hecho," well done, murmured in her father's deep voice into her hair.

Then she found Earthswell. Hunting was not Sorrel's favorite activity, but she was good at it, and it earned her a place in the small collective. The house, her sister homesteaders, needed the meat, the fat, the sinew, the skin, the bone marrow for the coming months.

Sorrel cut her hair with the waning moon, letting the dark, rough curls fall between her fingers until the ground around her seemed covered in small, dark leaves. This was her ofrenda, a sign of her willingness to be the hunter.

Tater held out the ceremonial shirt, tanned and stitched from soft deerskin, and Sorrel slipped her arms into it. Tater had beaded the shoulders in red and blue. With the shirt wrapped and tied snugly around her torso, Sorrel felt good, as though the loving arms of her clan held her tight. On other nights, Tater performed the deer dance she'd inherited, which helped them gain and establish territory against the exterior forces they did not entirely understand. They only knew that there was a precarious balance that needed to be maintained, and this little house stood on the brink of it.

Leaves were turning and falling, and Rosa, their woodskeeper, was distracted from the preparations for the ceremony by a rusty brown Doug fir. It had died over the summer, failing to renew its needles. Sorrel could tell that Rosa was measuring how many cords of wood the tree would supply if she cut it down. Or rather, when, because such a dry store of wood could not be allowed to stand so close to the house, unprotected from the elements. Rather than their guardian, it had become a liability that forced them to let go of the past, to move forward in all things. This was Earthswell's motto: "Forward in all things." It meant change, it meant growth, it meant spiritual bloom and exploration. It also meant leaving behind those who could not keep up.

This had happened once since Sorrel joined the group, but they had gently placed Jocassa with another group that was not as demanding of its members. She was a natural fit with the Weavers Guild producing cloth needed by all the homesteaders, where she could be both productive and supported. Jocassa's keen sense of perfection was an asset to a weaver, who could work at a different pace than those on the front lines of homesteading. Decision-making on the edge needed to be quicker and often less perfect than in the Protected Arts, such as music and cloth-making. A deliberation that took too long could mean death.

The Doug Fir had been their ceremonial tree, one of the reasons they had chosen this house to rehab. Its death forced them to go a little farther from the house to perform ceremony, which was not always safe. Rosa, the woodskeeper, had conferred long and hard with the dying tree before coming to this decision. Earthswell decided to give Sorrel companions during her fast, two at a time assigned to stay with her through the lengthening nights.

The first night was easy. In her wanderings, Sorrel had gone much longer without eating or drinking, and the perimeters were quiet for once, even in the dark of the moon. She could hear Rosa snoring lightly, although she was supposed to stay awake. Sorrel rested in a crouch, her staff across her knees and supporting her forehead. She had taught herself to stay many hours at a time in this position, muscles already contracted, after hearing that Maori warriors slept in constant readiness to spring up and attack the enemy with their cudgels. Tater, in particular, doubted this story, pointing out that the constant crouch would restrict the flow of blood to her legs, and was more likely to temporarily cripple her should the enemy indeed attack. Sorrel admitted that this method was very painful, but liked the discipline it implied, the self-sacrifice of the single warrior for the whole.

As dusk fell, or rather, accumulated around them until it was too dense to see through, Sorrel stood and walked a few paces forward, searching the ground for prints or other signs. That's when she discovered the steps.

As she stepped into a soft accumulation of leaves, Sorrel felt a straight edge under her moccasin. Backing up, she used her stick to clear the duff from a line of cement. As she kicked aside the dirt and leaves, Sorrel realized there was a set of cement stairs following the steep incline of the hill. If she looked carefully, she could see the way down into a deep ravine. She began to descend, cutting aside tangles of blackberry and ivy, both invasive weeds that had taken hold in the Before Times, choking out the salal and its huckleberries.

When she reached the bottom, Sorrel stopped and looked around. She could hear running water, and see that there had once been a bridge across the ravine that ended at the base of another set of steps leading up the opposite side. The bridge had collapsed long ago, its rubble choking the stream bed that had probably once hosted salmon fry.

Then she saw the fresh print, its edges just beginning to dry. It was the size of a dinner plate.

"Sorrel, Sorrel!" She could hear Rosa calling her, bringing her back to her other senses.

"Shh!" came Tater's voice in a stage whisper. "We're supposed to be silent!"

Sorrel walked back up the steps, her staff over her shoulder. She had not realized how far she had wandered.

"Here I am!"

Both jumped when she spoke. "Where have you been?" Tater scolded.

"You just—vanished!"

"Sorry, I was just exploring."

In her agitation, Tater finally threw her arms around Sorrel, then Rosa piled on. Sorrel held her club above their heads so as not to hurt anyone. Usually Sorrel did not stand for this kind of nonsense. But tonight, for the first time, it felt okay. She realized that the two, hardly warriors, had come looking for her in spite of the wolf-sighting the night before. They didn't even know what she had just seen.

"I think I found something."

"A vision?" asked Tater.

"Does this mean we can go in and eat now?" asked Rosa, who was always hungry.

They laughed, then walked carefully back to the homestead while Sorrel described what she had come across, saving the most disturbing bit of information for when they were within sight of the house.

THE SECOND NIGHT was less comfortable. Sorrel was in pain during the following day from sitting on her heels most of the night, although she would not admit it, and now sat up against a tree trunk. Listening to the silence of a forest, she thought, shows how noisy it is at night.

This time, Tater dozed off, and began to cry out in her sleep. This was not uncommon in the house, even among the non-Dreamers. Almost all were traumatized before finding relative peace in the Earthswell household, but Tater's cries sounded loud and piteous outdoors, and Sorrel wondered if she should leave her station to shake her out of the dream.

Finally, Sorrel felt her blood sugar drop and she began to have a night-vision of, she thought, the animal she would slay in order to nourish the household.

It was dark all around, but in the near distance she could see eyes glowing like moons around Jupiter. Sorrel tried to open her eyes as wide as possible, her pupils fully dilated to let in all the light.

The air filled with a crackling sound, like cornhusks burning, then a keening that did not sound like any animal Sorrel had ever heard before. It reminded her of the Grey Ones the Apache spoke about, the beings that did not consider themselves good or bad the way humans did, but rather acted out of sheer self-interest. Sorrel's hackles rose up, the back of her neck both cold and sweaty. She felt a growl begin to form at the base of her throat. Sorrel moved to protect her companions, knowing they were oblivious to this danger.

As soon as Sorrel cautiously lifted one foot, disturbing the duff on the forest floor, the eyes came to alert and focused on her. They might not have known Sorrel was there before. They regarded her curiously, as though assessing her danger level, or perhaps trying to decide if she was good to eat. She tried to determine how many creatures there were.

Sorrel stepped to place herself between the creatures and the other two women. As she moved towards them, Rosa, who was awake but drifting, cleared her throat and then froze. She slowly turned to face Sorrel and whatever stood beyond her.

"Holy Mother..." she whispered, shifting her bow to aim above Sorrel.

"Wait," said Sorrel in a tight voice.

Sorrel kicked Tater lightly, but Tater lost her balance as she came awake and stumbled before righting herself.

"Get back. Get behind me." Sorrel assumed a stance she had often taken, lining up her family behind her, counting on her bulk to both hide them and give her courage to defend them.

Then the howl.

It was the sound of anger. Sorrel recognized it as she would recognize her own rage. It howled again, angry at the loss of prey, prey that had bigger teeth than anticipated.

The creature gave out with one last horrible noise. Between a series of barks ending in another howl, a whiff of carrion-laden breath reaching Sorrel before it turned to lope away. With one last frustrated snarl, the creature disappeared into the early morning mist to seek other prey.

"That was too close," said Tater when she could speak.

Sorrel allowed the tip of her staff to rest on the ground as she released the breath she had been holding.

"All they would have found of us," said Rosa, looking around, "is our hair ribbons."

But Sorrel was confused. She could not determine how many creatures there had been.

None of them fell asleep again that night.

The next evening over dinner with the others, Sorrel, Rosa and Tater discussed whether or not the giant animal was Sorrel's vision.

"We all saw it," said Tater. "How can we all have the same vision?"

"Stranger has happened," said Sorrel. "You are all in this with me."

"Yeah," said Rosa. "But we can't eat it, can we? I mean, I don't want to eat it. I mean, if the Creator wants it, maybe?"

Rosa often talked herself into a corner.

The Earthswell collective finally agreed that the creature had not been a hunting vision, and that they would stay out one more night in hopes that Sorrel would receive direction for hunting and provisioning their household for the coming winter. One deer would suffice, if they were thrifty.

FOR THE THIRD time, Sorrel donned her ceremonial garb with the assistance of her two helpmates. For the third time, they burned sage in a small pot and smudged each other's foreheads with the smoke. For the third time, they invoked an all-seeing Creator and respectfully asked permission to harvest game from this ravaged land.

The final night for Sorrel's vision to unfold brought the same weather, cool and dense with the smoky tinge that had come to be normal all year round. Only one member of their household had the hollow cough that presaged a permanent, eventually deadly condition called "the Hack." They tried to assign her mostly indoor work, but even she wanted to be outside sometimes. They discussed whether or not to send her north to New Victoria, the current capital of the region, but even there the air had grown dense with the funereal smoke of a dead civilization.

There was no moon that night. Sorrel, Tater, and Rosa regrouped and walked out past the perimeter, Sorrel in her regalia, hoping for the vision that would lead her to food for the household, food that could be cooked, dried, jerked, pickled or otherwise preserved for the long dark season ahead.

Autumn was when the animals were fat, their fur growing in sleek and thick. After growing up wearing men's castoff boots, Sorrel reveled in the flexibility of her double-soled moccasins, cut only for her. She felt the dance of the drum in her legs, and knew she would receive an answer tonight.

A song came to her, just humming at first, then the short syllables that started a hunting song. Rosa joined in, and Tater threw back her head and added a screechy, jubilant descant as they called out the long notes of the chorus. They were not trying to hide tonight. They were calling their brother and sister animals to give of themselves for the good of all, to come gently and gladly, slowly, then quickly, slowly, then quickly, yip yip yip.

A series of yips answered them out of the forest, and they piled against each other in a sudden stop like quail crossing a road.

But this time they were better prepared for the creature,

forming a triangle, facing out, to watch the shadows as night closed in. When Tater sucked in her breath, Sorrel positioned herself towards the deep woods, and waited.

The three were somehow close to the bottom of the ravine that Sorrel had discovered earlier, that channeled a stream near their home. Sorrel realized this was related to their water source, and they should come back during the day to keep it clean—not just for fish that might return, but for their own health.

It is time to bring yourselves
Yip yip yip
Fish can flip and otters dive
Yip yip yip

Sorrel subvocalized the song as she watched the tree line for any shadows that did not belong. The forest seemed devoid of most sounds, even the birds silent at this hour when most were just settling.

Sorrel had a flash of memory of a woman's hand at her throat and she raised her own hand to either grab it or push it away when she heard the tiniest of noises, a little whine of hunger.

"Back up, back up," she whispered, not daring to turn around as she crept back up the slope, heels first. She could just make out a hollow at the base of a tree.

Suddenly, the creature was on them, snapping and snarling. Sorrel whirled her cudgel and connected squarely with a body. Tater screamed and Rosa fell to the ground. What looked like a huge wolf clamped her jaws on the back of Rosa's neck before Tater pulled the animal's head back by the ears and stabbed her in the eye. With a cry of pain the wolf released Rosa and lunged at Tater, catching Sorrel instead as she thrust her arm and staff between them. The wolf bit hard but Sorrel did not scream. She and the wolf lay for a moment eye to bloody eye. Many eyes, Sorrel thought. Sorrel summoned up all her teachings, all her protocol, and opened her lips to say, "I am not afraid." With that, the wolf abruptly released her and scrambled away.

Sorrel and Tater pulled Rosa upright, blood running down

her back. She'd never had the chance to wield her hunting bow—the wolf had been upon them in a flash.

"You're hurt, too," said Tater to Sorrel. The teeth marks were deep and would need cleaning and stitches. Sorrel licked her bloody arm and pulled out the herb she had encountered a few days ago, applying it to her wounds. They wrapped her arm in a piece of Sorrel's buckskin shirt that Tater cut off with her knife.

"What does this mean?" asked Tater as they limped up the steps towards home. "Why did she leave when she could have just as easily killed us?"

"There were three of us," said Sorrel. "She has pups to keep alive."

"I thought you said it was a pack."

"I thought so too," said Sorrel. "I saw many eyes in the dark that night. Now I see that they all belong to her."

"What? I don't understand."

"She has a circle of eyes around her head."

They considered this.

"A mutation from the chemical badlands?"

"Maybe, or from Eastern Washington, where the nuclear waste is buried."

Sorrel's arm began to ache as the adrenaline wore off. Soon the lights of home would welcome them. "When the pups are older, they will hunt us."

Yip yip yip.

A FEW DAYS later, Sorrel woke in the late afternoon and dressed. It was beginning to get chilly, and she threw on an extra shirt before walking out to the tenacious woods that had survived being around humans this long. Her ceremonial shirt had been trashed in the struggle with the she-wolf, but Tater had cut out the beaded patches to sew onto a new shirt—when they had some deerskin. Sorrel passed Rosa and another discussing what to do with the ceremonial tree that had died, how to take it down with respect, what to plant in its place. It would be mourned as a fellow forest dweller, one who had shared much of their joy and sorrow.

Sorrel's feet led her to the ravine, then downhill along the water course where the plants were still green. Again, this time in daylight, she heard the smallest sound of a whimper. Kneeling by the hollow base of a venerable cedar, Sorrel could smell the strong animal odor of a den. But she could see nothing inside.

"I might regret this," she thought. Sorrel took off her overshirt and wrapped her hand in it, her less damaged hand.

"I am not afraid," she said again, her inheritance not from Mother's Sibling, she realized, but from the bees.

Then she reached all the way in until a furious snarling and whining revealed one last pup.

"What happened?" Sorrel asked the squirming form as she pulled it out of the dark. "Did she leave her runt behind?"

Then Sorrel saw that the wolf pup had not two, not three, but four eyes, two on the front of its head, and two on the sides. When she looked closely, there appeared to be two more vestigial eyes behind its ears, forming a crown of eyes around its head.

"Oh, how could she leave you?" Sorrel whispered, as she wrapped the pup in her overshirt and stood, cradling it against her chest. A deeply protective feeling stirred her. She had not felt like this since leaving her brothers and sister behind in Arizona. Sorrel had waited all these years for Bear to claim her, and it had never happened. Rather, it had been up to Sorrel to do the claiming.

Almost in a daze, Sorrel walked back to the house. She had meant to check the stream for a possible fish weir location in case there proved to be fish. The house stirred with dinner preparations, and Chia was outside pulling chicken eggs from the straw in the coop.

She turned and smiled at Sorrel's return, then looked horrified when she saw what was in her arms. "Oh, well," she finally said. "I've been meaning to reinforce the chicken coop anyway."

"She might not live," Sorrel answered.

"Mm-hmm," Chia said, as she passed her hand over the many half-closed eyes, the velvet ears, noting how gently Sorrel held the pup, now settled against her vast warmth. "She'll live."

That night, Sorrel placed the pup on the dinner table, where she peed a little, and drew considerable attention.

"I choose her," said Sorrel. "I choose Wolf as my companion." Her arm burned where she had applied the wolf's bane. There is no known antidote to the herb, which can be fatal if swallowed.

The others realized a formal alliance had been declared, and although it would complicate their lives, they would all benefit from this new companion.

COUNTING HER PETALS
Christopher Caldwell

Now

ON A WARM, clear day that smells like pink jasmine, Cleo stands on the front porch of her girlfriend's craftsman bungalow, opens the screen door and knocks three times. She holds the key to the house in her right hand. The jagged edges dig into her palm. Starlings in the big ficus shading the front yard startle upwards, but nothing comes from within. She tries the doorbell again, hears the three tinny electronic bongs one after another, but nothing stirs. She sighs. Aster had given her this key. For emergencies, Cleo had said. Or if you just want to surprise me in the bath, Aster replied. Cleo unlocks the door and turns the handle. Daylight pours into the front room, casting a long Cleo-shadow across the hardwood floor. Motes of dust dance in the light dappled through the leaves of the ficus. "A-babe?" Cleo calls.

Cleo steps inside. The front room is neat. She can smell the lemony scent of furniture polish just underneath the heady fragrance of pink jasmine that wafts in behind her. She smells no onions or garlic or fried peppers from the kitchen; Aster loves to cook, and never uses a light hand with aromatics or spices. Cleo sometimes teases her about her hands smelling good enough to eat; Aster uses lemon juice and soap to tame down the allium scents, but they cling to her fingers after chopping. Cleo walks into the kitchen. "Aster?" she yells, not expecting an answer. Everything stored properly, nothing in the sink. She opens the fridge. No leftovers. No fresh fruit. Aster always, always makes too much food for one or even two people to eat. Cleo bites her lower lip.

She makes her way to Aster's office, past the master bedroom. Its door is open, the bed made and no clothes laid out for the next day. The office door is closed. Cleo feels apprehensive as she places a hand on the door. "Aster?" she calls. This space is the most private place in the house. She opens the door. Cleo is not a screamer. There is a willfulness to her practiced calm. Nonetheless, she finds herself biting back a shriek at the scene. What comes out is half-swallowed, "No."

Aster lies naked on the floor, tangled up in cables and tubes. Cleo kneels next to her, feels warm breath on her cheek, and reaches for Aster's wrists. She pauses, sees an arterial line snaking out from Aster's right wrist. Above them, monitors display heartrate, blood pressure, and other numbers that Cleo doesn't recognize. An empty IV bag is on its stand, a tube set up for a fluid drip inserted neatly into Aster's left arm; a machine attached to it beeps softly. Aster's skin is dry and cool, slightly ashy. Her lips are chapped. Eyes shut, but Cleo can see Aster's eyeballs dart beneath her eyelids. Tangled in her hair are LED lights and cables glued to her scalp at irregular intervals. The lights display numbers and sigils that Cleo doesn't recognize. Server lights blink. Cleo brushes her hand gently across Aster's cheek. "A-Babe?"

Cleo draws back her hand and slaps Aster sharply across that cheek. An HDMI cable connected somewhere just below Aster's ear jiggles. Eyelids flutter, but no answer. Cleo follows the cable along its path, one of a bank connected to a server near three monitors on a desk with a keyboard.

She places a hand on the server, closes her eyes, and reaches for Aster, holding in her mind Aster's smell, the sound of her laugh, and the tender places at the back of her knee, as a bright minty color. After a moment, Cleo feels the color bloom faintly from the server in response. *There*.

Cleo sighs. She sits on her haunches and listens to Aster's breathing. It is steady. She leaves the room to gather her supplies.

Long Ago

SHE NEVER START a story with once upon a time. No, she say, "Long ago..."

Well then, long ago there was a little gal with little gal black patent leather shoes. She had dust-brown hair tied in tight pigtails capped by plastic barrettes in the shape of a ribbon. She was best-loved by her mama, her Gramma Augusta, and her Great-Gramma, Dear. Dear lived in a little yellow house with a big garden and it was the place that the little gal with pigtails and a hard head loved best in all the world.

One day Dear give her five dollars to bring back some butter. Now, Dear tell that gal to walk straight to the store and straight back, and tell her she can buy something for herself. The gal walk straight to the corner store and she use her "Yes, please," and "No, thank you, ma'am," in the shop, and the shopkeeper give her an extra pack of Now and Laters for free because the gal has such nice manners. Skipping over the cracks in the sidewalk, the girl sing an old, sweet song. That song tickle her throat, and the sweet red Now and Later tingle her tongue. She had good manners, like a big girl, she think, and just like that, she grow hard-headed. "Come straight home," Great-Gramma Dear told her, but the girl saw an open gate into a yard full of flowers. They smell so sweet, she think she could stop and look for a moment—looking ain't hurt nobody—and she walk right into that garden without a care for what she been told.

* * *

Then

THE SECOND TIME I met you I was working. Sustainability was a buzzword, and the nursery had been contacted by a big nonprofit who wanted the decorations for their benefit gala to be repurposed after the champagne stopped flowing to enrich some underprivileged school's parched asphalt playground. Thing is, the kind of showy florals that look good in a glossy press release ain't always the same kind of plant that survives a dusty shade-starved schoolyard and the curious hands of children. The hibiscus, strelitzia, petunia, and chaparral clematis planted in boxes or carefully draped over trellises wouldn't survive a night of drinking and dancing, much less enrich the lives of inner city kids and their tetherball courts without some personal attention. That attention was me, the "miracle worker."

You were also working. Setting up some kind of complicated digital displays, hiding the wires and electrical tape, and making it look easy. I had seen you a week before on the balcony of Lita's Miracle Mile apartment looking out towards the Hollywood Hills. I'd had three beers, and asked Lita about you. She scoffed and called you "Little Miss Perfect," and I thought you *were*, with your long legs and smooth dark skin—what Mama called "blue-black"—and the hollow at the base of your throat. You were wearing a backless blouse that looked expensive, and even though I was a little tipsy and very *thirsty,* I was too shy to try my game on Little Miss Perfect.

I trundled in a flower box full of purple petunias, and you talked to me. Your voice was low and every word perfectly enunciated. "Such a lovely color," you said.

"They're a kind of nightshade! Relatives of deadly nightshade, but also potatoes, tomatoes, chili peppers..." I trailed off. I was being boring about plants again.

But you smiled at me, and your interest seemed genuine. "Fascinating. You must tell me more—" A question hovered in the air.

"I'm Cleo." I held out a hand. You shook it. Your skin was cool and soft.

"Aster," you said.

"Pretty name! It's also the name of the genus of flowering—"

You laughed. It was like the thrum of a guitar. "I know, I chose it."

Now

CLEO WATCHES THE rise and fall of Aster's chest for a moment before she begins. No cornmeal in the kitchen, so she has chosen to improvise instead of leave the house. She opens a box of instant grits—the Quaker smiling beatifically from its side—and crouches down to carefully trace out a complicated sigil on the hardwood floor. With her fingers she deftly defines straight lines and sweeps dry grits into circles with the same care she pinches back marigolds. She fights her impatience and sense of urgency and throws herself into the work with care and precision, and the vèvè takes shape. She looks down at the central cross, the curls that radiate out from it, and the four small circles with their own crosses. It is a respectful rendering. She stands, and pours rum into a pair of mugs; one with a cartoon figure smirking, a chipped rim and dark rings where it has been stained by tea, the other a deep-blue with gold specks, handmade by Aster and fired in a kiln just north of Santa Barbara.

She takes a swig from the tea-stained mug. The rum is caramel against her tongue, then licorice, then fire at the back of the throat. Warmth spreads through her chest. She holds up the blue mug and offers it up to the air. Her voice is hoarse and husky. "Papa Legba, open the barrier so that I may pass. Open the barrier to the spirit world so I may pass. Legba, Open the barrier."

Nothing happens. Cleo takes another swig and continues to chant. "Open the barrier so that I may pass to the spirit world.

Papa Legba, open the barrier." She feels a prickling at the back of her neck. An itch in her scalp. "Open the barrier so that I may pass. Legba, open the barrier to the spirit world."

The curlicues and lines of the grits-vèvè glow a soft green—the glow-in-the-dark color of children's toys—and the rum in the blue mug begins to roil and froth. There is thunder in Cleo's voice now. "Papa Legba at the crossroads, Papa Legba behind the mirror. Open the barrier to the spirit world so that I may pass!"

Aster keeps the windows in her office closed, but a hot wind heavy with the scent of sumac and cumin whips through them, scattering loose papers and rattling the venetian blinds. Cleo downs the last of the rum in her mug. Streams of vapor from the blue mug waft into the wind. Grits are caught up in a dust devil, but the vèvè keeps its shape and glows a darker green. "Royal Legba, guardian of the gates! I cry out to you, open the barrier, unbar the gates so that I may pass."

An electric hum permeates the room. Cleo can feel its resonance in her bones. The wires and the monitors are limned in a pale blue. *Saint Elmo's fire,* she thinks. She looks down at Aster, recumbent and peaceful in the localized tempest. Cleo clenches her fists. She roars. "Open the barrier!"

The wind howls. The screensaver on the central monitor—a slideshow of Aster's favorite places—is dispelled and Cleo sees an old-fashioned dialogue box with a yellow border appear on the monitor. It has buttons marked *yes* and *no,* and a single sentence written in all caps: *ARE YOU SURE?*

Buffeted by the spicy wind, Cleo crosses over to the keyboard, which glows with that unearthly cold fire. She presses "tab" and then hits enter to mark *yes.*

The wind's whine becomes a howl and the monitor wrinkles and warps, splitting in the middle. The air smells of ozone and burning plastic. Fractal lines radiate outwards from the tear. Auroral reds and oranges dance from in the darkness beyond the gap, which seems to open onto a chasm much deeper than a flatscreen monitor could hide. Cleo reaches one hand towards the widening hole and vanishes.

Then

YOU COOKED FOR me on our first date. Rice and peas with ackee and saltfish. It was delicious, and I said so. I said I would have to make you my special gumbo.

You said, "That presumes we're going to see each other again."

Ain't gonna lie, I was cocky. I saw the way you looked at my biceps, and I was dressed sharp. "Oh, I bored you already? Girl, you ain't even seen my good tattoos."

"I'll admit, I am curious." Your voice was a purr. "But you've put me all out of ackee."

I smirked. "I got you. With the gumbo. The next time."

You said, "I do like a woman with healthy appetites."

I stood up and stretched. "You can see I ain't been missing too many meals."

We kissed. I put my hand on the back of your neck. Your skin was so soft.

"I ain't got nowhere to be tomorrow," I said.

"I do," you said, "but I think I can live with being late."

Your body was tight and lithe against me, and I wanted to lick that hollow in your throat.

You placed your hands on my hips and gently pushed me away. I was surprised, but figured if you had changed your mind, wasn't nothing I could do.

"You should know that I'm trans," you said.

You were all confidence and coolness before, but there was something fragile in your eyes. I said, "I'm Cleo."

You laughed and told me to shut it and took me to bed.

* * *

Long Ago

THAT GARDEN OWNED by a woman call herself Mother Bea. Say Mother Bea knew magic. From the window she look at that hard-headed brown girl with the pink barrettes and skinned knees play in her garden's forked paths among the hydrangea and the frangipani. She think to herself this little girl could be her own sweet Sarah. She knew a conjure that command the bees. She say a word and they close the garden gate behind them. She say another word and they fly to the four o'clock flowers. They bees tease them open and the smell drift out heavy, like perfume. That nobbin-hearted gal feel dizzy like she been drinking wine. Ol' Mother Bea creep out and say in her goodest, sweetest voice, "You look unwell, my child. Can I get you a cool drink? Maybe a piece of toast and jam?"

Now this gal's gramma Augusta, and her mama, and her great-gramma Dear all been told her not to trust no stranger. But Mother Bea had a kind face and a soft voice, and the gal figure nothing bad could happen so long as she could see the garden gate, so she went and sat down at that woman's table.

And she get a cold drink, and some toast with plenty jam besides. The woman talk to her sweetly, and the gal tell her all about Dear's garden; not as big as Mother Bea's, ain't as many kinds of flowers, but it had the prettiest flowers that looked like birds made of fire. And Mother laughed, and poured her another cold drink. But when the gal went to get up, she heard the woman cluck, "Oh, my dear. Your hair is so tangled. Let me fix it for you."

Her barrettes fall to the floor, and her pigtails come undone. That gal hear the gas on the woman's stove, and see a straightening comb burn red hot, but she don't get up. Mother Bea sing an old, old song and comb through the gal's hair. Burnt hair smell coiled in her nose, washing away toast and sweet blackberry jam. When she done, the gal's hair is bone straight, but she can't remember the name her Mama give her.

Mother Bea smile at her, blackberry jam sweet, and call her Sarah. She show her to a bedroom where everything is just her size, and the gal lie on the bed with its yellow bedspread and fall asleep.

Then the old woman go out into her garden and find the flower they call bird-of-paradise. She point at that flower and it sink deep into the dark earth.

Now

CLEO FINDS HERSELF in what seems to be an endless field of flowers—Michaelmas daisies, Aster's favorite—under a sky the metallic dark pink of expensive lip gloss. No visible light sources. No sun. No moon or stars. No softly glowing streetlamps. But Cleo can see as clearly as if it were noon in summer. There is no wind. In the distance black mountains loom, their peaks snowcapped and glistening in the light from nowhere.

Cleo kneels down to get a closer look at the asters. The ground beneath her knees feels wrong, like soft matting on the floors of fast-food restaurant playgrounds. It doesn't move like soil. The asters feel right. There are variations in the purples, from lilac to indigo. A big, deep plum blossom near Cleo has a thin striation of white on its top petal. But as Cleo looks closer she sees that the variations begin to repeat. A few feet away is another deep plum flower with a white striation; at an irregular place beyond that is another. There has been effort put into disguising the perfection of this field, but it is clear to Cleo that this is a place that has been made, not cultivated, much less one that is wild.

In the chest pocket of her overalls, Cleo keeps a little pouch with important botanicals. She pulls out a little oxblood leather pouch. It contains the powdered root of an *Ipomoea purga* vine. High John de Conquer root. She licks a finger, dips it into the pouch and dabs the root on her tongue. The taste is bitter. She inhales deeply and sings a little song her Gramma-Dear taught her as a little girl. *Rise,* she thinks. She remains solid, on the ground. In the world she has already begun to think of as the wild one rather than the real one, she would have floated upwards like one of Peter Pan's joyous Lost Boys. But whatever was pretending to be gravity in this made world was weighing her down.

The taste of the John de Conquer root still sharp on her tongue, Cleo plucks the big daisy with the white striation. Michaelmas Daisies have the binomial name *Aster amellus*. She plucks the petal with the thin white streak and thinks of her Aster. A memory of being a small girl with tightly braided pigtails, wearing Mary Janes and a hated plaid pinafore, crouching over the sunbaked asphalt at the edge of a church playground, plucking geraniums and letting the petals fly. Like the memory, she says, "She loves me." She blows. The petal is born aloft on her breath and glitters like light on a river. It flies in a straight line towards the black mountains. Cleo follows.

Long Ago

EVERY DAY THAT woman comb the gal's hair. Every day it combed the gal forget something. But her head stay hard, and her heart still best-loved the garden behind the little yellow house. The woman say call her Mother Bea, but the gal see how she conjure the bees in her big garden with its shut gate, and she call her Other Bee. And she never call herself Sarah in her own head, no matter what the Other Bee call her. She know there are places in her heart where go the people who best-love her, even if they names and faces is combed away. She decide to run away from Other Bee before she combed down to nothing.

She see how the bees bring the old woman they honey, and how every morning she put a spoon of that honey in her tea and drink it. One day, the girl sneak into the pantry and take some honey for herself. It taste like sunlight. It taste like rain. It taste like *conjure*. She smile sweet and fake at Other Bee and ask to play in the garden. Other Bee pat her head and call her Sarah and watch her skip away.

But this time the gal could hear the flowers talk, and she ast them they stories. Hyacinth ain't had nothing but nonsense, and Primrose told lies, but Sister Magnolia told her truths even if she ain't know who the people who best-loved her were. Sister Magnolia come down from her place on the highest tree, and set behind the gal's ear, whispering kindness.

The girl walk among all the flowers, but she never find one that look like a bird on fire and she start to cry. Sister Magnolia ast why she so brokenhearted. And that gal say she looking for a flower that is a bird but also a fire to tell her its story, but she never find it. And the Magnolia whisper she has seen a flower like a firebird from atop the tallest tree.

Then

I TOLD YOU about magic. We were walking back from a bar downtown and tipsy on the craft cocktails you had ordered for us—last words, sidecars, more than a few french 75s—and I started to talk about how I came from a long line of root workers, and hoodoo priestesses. You turned to me and arched one perfect eyebrow. "You don't believe in all that junk? You don't even read your horoscope."

"Fuck if I sound anything like a Libra," I said. "But magic? It ain't fake."

You laughed again and punched my shoulder. "Come on, Cleo! Magic. I've never even seen an illusionist that convinced me."

Now here was my deepest, darkest places open to you. I think what could have happened if I laughed along with you and changed the subject. If we had ended up on the beach and watched the grunion come in all silvery and slippery. There's a kind of magic in that too.

Instead, I pulled out my John de Conquer root, and I sang my little song, and I showed you I could fly.

And you took my hand, and we danced on air on that dark shore.

Now

TIME FEELS DIFFERENT here. The light is constant and the shadows do not lengthen as the day passes. The daisies are always at full bloom. In the wild world, Cleo can tell how long she has walked by the ache in her calves, and the pace of her stride, but here movement feels effortless, and except for the ever-nearer black mountains, her path through the field of daisies following the glowing petal might have been a few steps. She wears a watch on her left wrist, a big mechanical brass thing with a scuffed crystal, but it stopped at the time she entered the made world as if she had never wound it at all.

At the base of the black mountains, Cleo can make out a slender spire, silvery in the light. A cascade of water tumbles down from the height behind it. Cleo begins to run, and as if in anticipation of her movement, the guiding petal speeds up. Cleo pushes herself and the field falls into a blur. She feels no fatigue. Her heartbeat is even. Her lungs do not burn in her chest. She rushes along, her feet only touching the ground because the made-gravity insists they must, first antelope fast, then freight train fast. The made world ripples around her like she has cast a stone in a pond. And then she is there.

The spire is the color of alabaster, but with a metallic sheen. It is crowned with an enormous magnolia blossom of what seems to be the same material, all in one piece. *Like The Neverending Story*, thinks Cleo. Leading up to the city is a spiraling, terraced street lined with cypresses and blocky buildings painted blue, gold, cinnabar. Vines snake down from the flat roofs, and orchids of uncommon size and color festoon the building walls, and bromeliads quiver with dew. Cleo smells the air. There is nothing, not the fragrance of vanilla nor the stink of crown-rot. The glowing petal zips up the spiral street, and she makes her way to the spire.

The terraced street opens out into a broad garden. Cleo sees tulips, daffodils, glory of the snow, birds of paradise, sea holly, and lavender, shaded by 'ōhi'a trees heavy with bright red blossoms. Plants that favor different climes and different seasons all in blossom, all textbook beautiful. She tastes bile as she remembers the Other Bee's impossibly perfect garden; like a sundew it sparkled and drew her in, waiting to devour her.

Cleo looks up at the enormous magnolia atop the spire. The flower had been a comfort and a balm to her. She had a magnolia blossom tattooed across her back on her twenty-first birthday. When they first made love, Aster kissed that place between her shoulder blades again and again. When Cleo asked why that tattoo and not the clematis on her hip, or the columbine on her thigh, Aster said, "The magnolia's like the pavilion in *The Neverending Story*. You can be my golden-eyed commander of wishes."

Cleo said, "I hope our story doesn't end."

Cleo stands at the base of the spire and puts a hand on its surface. It feels *soft*. Like silk or satin, not a hard, metallic thing. It pulses softly at her touch. Cleo calls lightly, "A-babe?"

Nothing. She presses closer to the spire. It feels warm. She cranes her neck up at the magnolia high above her and shouts. "A-babe! It's me! It's Cleo! Golden-eyed commander!"

The world shudders. The lip gloss sky turns poison apple green and the spire blinks out of existence. The black mountains are now white and textureless. Cleo feels her body under enormous pressure, as if she has been dropped into the deepest part of the sea. An agonizing heartbeat. Cleo feels that she will be crushed. Then everything rights itself.

Almost. She looks behind her and notices all the sea holly has vanished, leaving gaps in the lush garden. The daffodils look flat, like glossy photographs. The world shudders again and the colors shift, but this time there is no crush and the spire remains solid beneath Cleo's hand. Above her the magnolia blossom opens its petals. Golden light spills out between them. Again, Cleo thinks, *Rise*. This time, she soars.

Long Ago

THE GAL COME to a place in the garden where the soil is black and the flowers ain't grow. "That be where the birds were," the Magnolia say. "Maybe they fly away over the wall."

But the gal dig in the soil, and she call out to them. And the bees, them old spies, make they way to the Mother. Before they get there, the birds-of-paradise spring forth from the earth, and like the gal say, they look like they made of fire. And the gal ask they story. The birds say they ain't just no flower, but they were in a dance when the world began and so beautiful the hateful moon got jealous. And when they sang about they fall from heaven Cleo remembered Gramma Augusta playing organ in the church. When they told of they beauty, she remember her sweet mama's eyes, brown but specked through with gold. And she remembered how orange and blue and green the birds in her own great-gramma's garden was, and how that great-gramma call herself Dear.

The Other Bee come with her swarm to stop her, and she call her Sarah, and she beg with sweetness, and she threaten with punishment. But the gal remember her own name, Cleo. And when she spit it at the Other Bee, they both knew ain't nothing could keep her from going back to the yellow house with the garden she best-loved and the people who best-loved her.

Cleo stay hard-headed, but maybe she happy if she ain't find her ending yet.

* * *

Then

YOU CAN LOVE someone so much they are your light and your joy, but the world ain't going to let you just rest with that. The news had been bad; black boys getting shot, queers getting bashed, trans women killed. Some nights we ain't even enjoyed each other's company because something terrible happened. I used to keep track of the names and say them before bed like a litany, but one day it got too many. The world was supposed to be better than this.

You had been out at work since before I knew you, but the last six months someone had sent emails about you. There had been meetings. You told me about a teacher back in England who had committed suicide because they hounded her. There was a night out in West Hollywood when a woman screamed that I didn't belong in the woman's bathroom. Shit, I'm cis.

I don't go online at work. I try to pay attention to the plants and listen to their needs. I didn't know how bad it was until I got home. Splashed all over the internet was a hateful, bullshit article. Trans women are preying on lesbians, the headline screamed. Like you couldn't be both. The article quoted Lita who said nasty shit about "genital mutilation" and how tomboys are made to feel like they're men. It wasn't about you, but it could have been; we both knew Lita, even if I was a tomboy who ain't never once wanted to be a man. I called you right away.

"A-babe? You okay?"

Your voice was brittle. "Guess you logged on."

"Fuck that no 'count Lita. She just mad 'cause no one wants her Opie-lookin' ass."

You sighed. "Every day there's just another pile of shit. You hear they're introducing a bill in Wyoming to label gender-affirming care as conversion therapy?"

"No. Do they ban conversion therapy there?" I asked.

Another sigh. "Doesn't matter. They don't want us to fucking breathe."

"Do you want me to come over?"

Your voice cracked. "No. Don't you have that big shipment of orchids early tomorrow? Petey will shit the bed without you. And I have a project I'm working on that needs extra attention, so I won't be good company."

"Fuck those orchids. They can survive without me, and if they can't, Petey needs another business. And you don't gotta worry about entertaining me. I'm a big girl. I got books. But I want to be around if you need me." I meant it, and I hope you heard.

"No. I'll be fine. You don't need to come over tonight," you said.

Now

CLEO CRESTS ABOVE the spire. There, in the center of the magnolia blossom, sitting cross-legged among carpels as tall as birch trees, is Aster, clothed in white and holding a crystalline orb the size of a beach ball that she sculpts like clay. Cleo alights next to her. Aster stands. The orb hovers in the air. Already tall in the wild world, she stands a few inches taller here. Her lovely dark skin without blemish or freckle. The mole at the base of her ear is gone. Her waist is thinner and hands smaller. She smiles at Cleo. "You came! But you're early—I still haven't finished everything." She frowns. "I'm having trouble getting scents right. And tastes. It's the difference between grocery store orange juice and freshly squeezed."

"A-babe, I'mma always come for you. But how come you did all this without me?" Cleo feels tears sting her eyes.

"I wanted it all to be a surprise. How did you even get here? I haven't finished the documentation with the instructions."

"I made my own way."

Aster holds out a hand. Cleo takes it. It feels achingly familiar, but there are no scents of onion or pepper. This is the woman she loves, but the woman she loves remains out in the wild world, weakening every moment.

The world shudders again. Colors ripple and warp. Aster touches the orb and stability returns. "There are some glitches I'm working on."

"How long you think you been in here for?" Cleo asks.

Aster blinks. "I don't know. A few hours maybe. As long as twelve?"

"A-babe, it's been three days since you told me not to come over. I used the emergency keys."

Aster's brow furrows. "I guess I could put in some sort of internal clock to better track the time." She touches the orb. Numbers glow briefly in the pink sky, then disappear.

Cleo's voice is soft. She squeezes Aster's hand. "In here, you're radiant. Like you used both the butters to moisturize. Your bantu knots is flawless. But out there..." Cleo closes her eyes. "Out there, I think you're dying, A-babe, and I ain't know what I'm supposed to do without you."

Aster sighs and pulls her hand away from Cleo. "In here is a paradise where I—where you and me—can just *be*. Ain't no one to call me a trap. Ain't no dyke this and bulldagger that. Ain't no *niggers*."

"I know. But it ain't real, baby, it ain't *real*. What happens if the power goes out or one of your hard drives fails?"

"The spell should be self-sustaining. And once I'm integrated completely—"

"Spells ain't computer programs. They snakes; they slither away from you and bite when you ain't expect it."

The world shudders again. Cleo feels the crushing pressure. Aster grabs onto the orb and the pressure releases. She looks at Cleo with concern. "I don't know what you want me to do."

Cleo says, "I want you to come home with me."

Aster says, "Home? This is the home I built for us. A home

with peaceful gardens for you to work in and anything else we can dream up."

"A garden with flowers that don't smell of nothing."

"I'm working on it." Aster stares at her orb.

"I would do anything for you, you know that. But I can't stay here, and I don't think you can, neither.

"Your world keep tryna shove me out, or maybe it's breaking down 'cause you're breaking down. All of me is here right now, and every time this shit glitch it feel like it's going to crush me out."

Aster looks horrified. "The instabilities have been increasing. But I didn't know they were hurting you."

"Come home with me."

Tears streak down Aster's perfect face. They are pearls with a luster and roundness no oyster could produce. They float up into the sky of the made world. "You said you would do anything for me, and God knows I believe you. And God knows I love you. But you don't know how hard it is Cleo, you just don't."

Cleo shakes her head. "I don't, Aster. But I'm asking you to come anyway." She reaches out a hand.

Aster stares at it for a moment, weeping pearls, and now brilliant-cut canary-yellow diamonds the size of watermelon seeds. As a gemmed cloud forms above their heads, the world shakes. This time the poison apple sky is divided up into cyclopean triangles like a giant geodesic dome. The carpels of the enormous magnolia splinter and fly off in all directions. Cleo feels herself twist and flatten. A grey chasm opens in the world between her and Aster, who remains perfect and untouched by the tremors. Cleo reaches out towards her, leaning as the chasm pushes them apart.

The grey washes over them. Cleo feels nothing, not warmth, or cold, or pressure. She sees nothing but endless grey. There are no sounds.

Then she feels the warmth of a hand finding hers.

*   *   *

Now

CLEO FINDS HERSELF on her ass on the hardwood floor in Aster's office. Plaster from the ceiling rains down on her. The window has shattered inwards and broken glass glitters dangerously in the plaster-hazy murk. The server towers are an untidy heap of junk. "Aster?" she croaks.

Aster opens her eyes. She coughs. Cleo crawls across the floor, and over the debris, slicing her knee open on a long shard of glass. She takes Aster in her arms. Aster coughs and breathes in gasps, but her heartbeat is strong. They both weep, collapsing against each other covered in sweat and dust.

Aster sobs. "This is shit. This world is shit. It's shit."

Cleo presses herself against Aster. "I know it is, A-babe. I know. But your woman a gardener, and we gonna grow something from it."

FEVER DREAMS
Jaymee Goh

RATU JINGGA LOOKS over the storyengines, pulsating layers that spin, powering up through the retelling of the stories contained within. Down the river, a thousand different shapes with ten thousand more colors, with all the variation of flowers: storyengines with frills, and storyengines speckled and glowing, storyengines with flared manes and curious tentacles. The one he looks at is a deep blue, and it glows hot orange and yellow at its frilled edges. As its layers spin, each layer counter to the one above, it seems to hiccup, or sigh, Ratu Jingga is not sure which.

Legend tells of the time when the very seas churned with storyengines, carrying on their backs whole civilizations. They were foundations of the great palaces of yore; their legs were links between cities as they clung to each other.

Ratu Jingga cannot imagine it: he only sees floppy layers, circular communal blankets under which people seek cures for their illnesses. Like jellyfish out of water, they are flat and soggy, floating in the swamps and ponds where the storytellers still live. Between their gelatinous folds are stubs, remnant studs that were once narrative arcs, sharp as incisors.

The storyengines work quite simply: one rests under layers of them, comparable to one's height of illness. They spin, and tell an entire story-cycle. As they spin, they generate heat that burns away the illness. By the end of the story-cycle the illness will be gone, and the applicant healthy once more.

A far cry from what they once powered.

But Ratu Jingga is not here to contemplate history. He is here for a rest cure: physician's orders for his fever that seems mild, but has not released its hold after two full moons. It occasionally flares up, and Ratu Jingga cannot focus on his work as a result, feeling removed from the world and not quite in control. It is not comfortable, even for a petty aristocrat. So he has hiked into the forest, along the river to the estuary where the local storytellers live, tending to their marine machines.

He is perfunctory as he pays for the first available storyengine, resting in a pool by a short waterfall. Banyan trees grow around, hoary visages resting their branches on well-established roots, as if taking an interest in the patients who stop by. Ratu Jingga ignores them as he strips off his accouterments to bare tunic and trousers. He sets aside his songket in a nearby tree hollow.

When he slips in between the layers of the storyengine, he feels a warmth wash over him. It puts him into a comfortable haze.

Ratu Jingga dreams.

TIONG MERPATI WAS *a selfish man who lived during the Second Great Age. A small prince, he would never inherit, and vowed someday that he would escape the bounds of his duty since he saw no point carrying it out for a realm that would not give him what he perceived to be his due.*

So one day, during a great festival, he took to the waters, and jumped into the whirring of a small storyengine that lay at the very edge of the kingdom. He meant to take control of its narrative, but instead he was caught within it, and was thus folded into it. He became a king, doomed to retell the story of his bitter battle with the neighboring kingdom, over and over, until the end of storytime.

That is too bad, Ratu Jingga thinks. Everybody deserves a chance at freedom.

The storyteller drones on, telling the tale of the storyengine that Ratu Jingga lies under. At the edge of his consciousness, Ratu Jingga hears the storyteller's voice, the easy rhythms of the lyrics soothing his ears.

Ratu Jingga dreams.

THERE WAS ONCE *a giant whale that swam in the deeps of the ocean, under the great storyengines. It was old and ancient and sang with the other whales. Yet though it was ancient, it had the kind heart of a child.*

Into its path crashed an old storyengine, its characters struggling within as they sunk to oblivion. This was a tale of great kings at war, their princesses with hearts to match who sought to end their fathers' enmity. The storyengine came to rest on the back of the whale, the spikes of its arcs drumming into its flesh.

It could have chosen to throw off the storyengine, let it sink to the bottom of the sea where it would lie, forgotten, as storyengines eventually end. But as the storyengine spun its tale, the whale was fascinated by its narrative.

Great kings, *it cried to the storyengine,* how does your story end? Will you come to peace?

One king within it cried back, we do not know, and will not know unless we are allowed to unfold and tell the tale. Oh, give us strength that we might rise once more to join our brethren.

The other king within it cried back, we end in tragedy. Our daughters' friendship was all for naught and we are a narrative of unkindness and vanity. Let us sink to the bottom of the ocean. Let our story die.

Ratu Jingga sees one of the princesses then, Puteri Kuning, her arms wide in supplication, always wide in an embrace to her cruel father. She dies at the end of each cycle, by poison, by knives, by neglect, by gallows' songs, because her father cannot see the error of his ways.

Ratu Jingga sees one of the princesses then, Puteri Hijau, her fists ever clenched in rage, watching the downfall of her father's kingdom. She is doomed to watch the consequences of a decision her father makes, his regret too late in coming.

But might you not be saved? *the whale asked*. Might the next story-cycle see you make different decisions, that will enable the salvation of your kingdoms?

Yes!

No!

The whale believed in the goodness of others. It knew it could either shake off the storyengine, or spend its last energy giving it fresh life by spinning it back up to the surface, where it would rejoin the other storyengines.

So it chose to give up its ancient life, swimming in an ever-quickening spiral until its body was curled into itself, and it whirred the storyengine on its back until it launched up against the water currents of the ocean depths.

Ratu Jingga feels the revival of Puteri Kuning's hope and the teeth-gnashing of Puteri Hijau's despair. He does not admit that he wishes to be part of that narrative, to insert himself into the story, take Puteri Kuning away. In his dreams he enters the palace where she lives through the gardens where he finds her weeping alone, and asks if she would like to come away with him. He takes her hand and begins leading her away. She does not say no; that is part of her charm, and that is part of her tragedy.

Ratu Jingga awakens, triumphant at his intercession. "I'm cured," he announces to the storyteller, who watches the storyengine, perturbed. He throws off the layers of the storyengine, as one might throw off blankets.

"You're not cured yet. The story-cycle has yet to carry itself out," the storyteller says, suspicious, but not of Ratu Jingga.

"I saved the princess and interrupted the story," he replies, feeling proud of his actions.

A layer of the storyengine suddenly sputters into life. It sploshes and flails, then in a combination of whirring and lumbering, heaves itself up the edge of its pool. There, it falls into pieces, and a little figure speeds off into the woods.

Tiong Merpati! The man who so long ago tried to escape his place in life, and was caught in a neverending narrative instead, in a role that was admittedly suited to his personality. And now, because of Ratu Jingga's interruption, Tiong Merpati has found a way to finally be free of his prison.

The storyteller shouts as the mangled remains of the storyengine, having now discharged its interruptive occupant, creak and shriek as it sinks back into the water. "You see!" he yells over the racket, "you should have simply waited to see the story unfold. Then we might have seen the flaw in this engine and fixed it."

"But I'm well," Ratu Jingga insists.

"No, you're not," the storyteller says, placing his hand on Ratu Jingga's forehead.

"I saved the princess!"

"Sir, please be calm."

And Ratu Jingga is suddenly very embarrassed. He lets the storyteller take him to another pool, another storyengine, and sinks back down into the water, warm and cozy. "You cannot change the narrative, sir," says the storyteller. "You cannot change history."

Of course he knew that, he thinks as he lies back down. What a silly notion of his. His own selfishness, taken advantage of by another selfish man.

Ratu Jingga closes his eyes. This time, he does not dream.

INAWENDIN-GEE-WITAU-KUMMICK-BINESIWI-MIIKANA: EVERYTHING IN LIFE IS INTERCONNECTED-ALL AROUND THE EARTH AND THE MILKY WAY

Dr Grace Dillon

OUR CEREMONIES AND our stories, and especially our star stories, can consistently mirror our *bodymindspirit* selves in an ecology of intimacy: one of relationships in the absence of coercion, hierarchy, or authoritarian power. The Anthropocene is too often reduced by mainstream scientists, journalists, and writers worldwide to the *unintentional* impacts of humanity, and to general abstractions of climate change as the reason for numerous collapses and mass extinctions provides. But this provides too low a context, one which this anthology at the nexus of horror, the fantastic, and speculative fiction overcomes wonderfully with high-context BIPOC/Co-Futurisms and Indigenous/anticolonial, anti-imperialistic, anticapitalistic, and anti-racist sciences. (These sciences include visual art, ceremony, dancing, singing, and remixed and renewed language, along with intergenerational observations, experiments, and honorable traditions that respect all nations: human, animal, bird, fish, and so on, in a web that sometimes entangles us, sometimes enmeshes us, but always, consistently repels any discriminatory actions against *bodymind* diversities.)

Within these pages, we have been introduced to many distinctive forms of belief or worldview, enhanced by the imagination of a plurality of spacetime. Stories such as these often foster an awakening power, while simultaneously bringing to the fore the necessary trauma of awakening knowledges and histories more globally. Many readers have already experienced these traumas to a degree in real life; this may perpetuate our still open, leaking, unhealed wounds. But alongside the perpetuation of these wounds come the (sometimes necessarily slow) processes of healing through the stories themselves. The vibrancy of change permeates the air around all of our nations, human and more-than-human. These Awakening to Healing stories merge continuously, shifting the forms of self-determination and the natural right of motion migrations with the necessity to renew them seasonally. They not only encourage the decolonizing of our Anthropocene times but also celebrate the resurgence of imagined, or sometimes actual, veiled multi-histories; they provide us with appearances and disappearances of mutancy, active witnessing, and participatory observing of numerous fluctuations and fluidity of gender, sexual orientation, race, and nations interacting with the permanence of changes in full cyclic iterations.

These stories, true in their giving, provide generosity, mercy, and compassion for all in Mother Earth, and cheer, gladden, hearten, and delight us so that we can prosper. Whether they're set a long time ago, or today, or even in the time of my arms embracing my grandchildren and their arms embracing their grandchildren, they demonstrate a link between generations, between states of being, and even between individuals. This lifeline (literally, in Anishinaabe, "moving life"), is a human and more-than-human Milky Way, while Nisi Shawl, editor of these out-of-this-world, fantastic, wonders of wonders, becomes in my *bodymindspirit* "Kitchi Gabwik," "Standing Up Womxn," standing firm with a second volume that protects our communities via acts of resistance. May we treasure our kinship system, which connects us not always via direct blood relations but through our social relations and roles, filling each of us with star wisdom, circling in this way back to our own Returning Home Star. I say this wish with unconditional love.

CONTRIBUTOR BIOS

Kathleen Alcalá is the author of six books exploring forced migrations, identity, and our relationships with the land and each other. A graduate of Stanford University (BA), the University of Washington (MA), and the University of New Orleans (MFA), Kathleen makes her home in the Northwest on Suquamish territory. Kathleen has recent work in *El Porvenir Ya!*, *Zócalo*, *New Suns*, and *The Madrona Project*. Kathleen and Norma Cantú are co-editors of the forthcoming anthology, *Weeping Women: La Llorona's Presence in Modern Latinx and Chicanx Lore*, from Trinity University Press.

K. Tempest Bradford is a teacher, media critic, and author of speculative fiction steeped in Black Girl Magic. Her first novel, a Middle Grade mystery-adventure titled *Ruby Finley vs. the Interstellar Invasion*, was published in 2022. Her short fiction has been published in several anthologies and magazines, and her media criticism and essays have appeared on NPR, io9, and more. Tempest gives talks and teaches classes on representation and diversity though Writing the Other.com. Connect with her at KTempestBradford.com.

Christopher Caldwell is a queer Black American who lives in Glasgow, Scotland with his partner Alice. He received the Octavia

E. Butler Memorial Scholarship to Clarion West and was nominated for the Ignyte Award for Best Short Story. His work has appeared in *FIYAH*, *Uncanny Magazine*, and *Strange Horizons*, among other venues. He is @seraph76 on Twitter.

Hugo Award Winner **John Chu** is a microprocessor architect by day, a writer, translator, and podcast narrator by night. His fiction has been published at *Boston Review*, *Uncanny*, *Asimov's Science Fiction*, *Clarkesworld*, and Tor.com among other venues. His translations have been published at *Clarkesworld*, *The Big Book of SF* and elsewhere.

Grace L. Dillon (Anishinaabe), Professor of Indigenous Nations Studies in the School for Gender, Race, and Nations at Portland State University, has edited *Hive of Dreams: Science Fiction in the Northwest* (2003) and *Walking the Clouds: Indigenous Science Fiction* (2012). With John Rieder and Michael Levy, she edited a special double-edition of Indigenous Futurisms scholarship in the journal *Extrapolation*, and among many other scholactivist publications she's editing, along with Isiah Lavender III, Taryne Taylor, and Bodhisattva Chattopadhyay, *The Routledge Handbook of CoFuturisms*, forthcoming in 2022.

Tananarive Due (tah-nah-nah-REEVE doo) is an award-winning author who teaches Black Horror and Afrofuturism at UCLA. She is an executive producer on Shudder's groundbreaking documentary *Horror Noire: A History of Black Horror*. She and her husband/collaborator, Steven Barnes, wrote "A Small Town" for Season 2 of Jordan Peele's *The Twilight Zone* on Paramount Plus, and two segments of Shudder's anthology film *Horror Noire*. A leading voice in Black speculative fiction for more than 20 years, Due has won an American Book Award, an NAACP Image Award, and a British Fantasy Award, and her writing has been included in several best-of-the-year anthologies.

Jaymee Goh is a Malaysian-Chinese writer, reviewer, editor, and essayist of speculative fiction. Her work has been published in a number of magazines and anthologies, such as *Lightspeed Magazine*, *Beneath Ceaseless Skies*, and *New Suns: Original Speculative Fiction by People of Color*, and reprinted in *LeVar Burton Reads* and *Best American Science Fiction & Fantasy*. Her reviews and nonfiction have appeared on Tor.com, *The Los Angeles Review of Books*, and *Strange Horizons*. Find out more at jaymeegoh.com

Hiromi Goto is an emigrant from Japan who gratefully resides in Lekwungen and WSÁNEĆ Territory. Her first novel, *Chorus of Mushrooms*, won the Commonwealth Writers' Prize Best First Book, Canada and Caribbean Region, and was co-winner of the Canada-Japan Book Award. Her second book, *The Kappa Child*, received the Otherwise Award for gender-bending speculative fiction. She's published many books, and other honors include The Sunburst Award and the Carl Brandon Parallax Award. *Shadow Life* (First Second, 2021) is her first graphic novel with artist Ann Xu.

Saad Z. Hossain is a Bangladeshi author writing in English. He lives in Dhaka. He writes about djinns and the future in some combination of science fiction and mythology which should probably not be a thing. His books include *Escape from Baghdad!*, *Djinn City*, *The Gurkha and the Lord of Tuesday*, *Cyber Mage*, and *Kundo Wakes Up*.

Alex Jennings was born in Germany and raised in Botswana, Paramaribo, Tunis, and Columbia, MD. His writing has appeared in *Strange Horizons, PodCastle*, and *Uncanny Magazine*—among other venues—and he is a regular contributor to *The Magazine of Fantasy and Science Fiction*. He received the inaugural Imagination Unbound Fellowship at Under the Volcano 2022 in Tepoztlan, Mexico. His debut novel,

The Ballad of Perilous Graves, was published in June, 2022. He lives and writes in New Orleans with his dog, Karate Valentino.

Minsoo Kang is the author of the short story collection *Of Tales and Enigmas* and the history books *Sublime Dreams of Living Machines: The Automaton in the European Imagination* and *Invincible and Righteous Outlaw: The Korean Hero Hong Gildong in Literature, History, and Culture*, and the translator of the Penguin Classics edition of the classic Korean novel *The Story of Hong Gildong*. He earned his PhD in European history from UCLA and is currently a professor of history at the University of Missouri–St. Louis.

Darcie Little Badger is a Lipan Apache writer with a PhD in oceanography. Her critically acclaimed debut novel, *Elatsoe*, was featured in *Time Magazine* as one of the best 100 fantasy books of all time. *Elatsoe* also won the Locus Award for Best First Novel and is a Nebula, Ignyte, and Lodestar finalist. Her second fantasy novel, *A Snake Falls to Earth*, received the Newbery Honor and is on the National Book Awards longlist. Darcie is married to a veterinarian named Taran.

Rochita Loenen-Ruiz is a Filipino creative artist based in the Netherlands where she has a practice in community activism, writing, and story creation. She is the author of two chapbooks: *Decolonial Dreaming* and *Small Assemblage*, which were released by Alternate Munabol Productions in 2021. She is an Octavia E. Butler scholar (2009) and in 2018, she was one of the recipients of the Milford Writers BAME bursary. She has an online presence at rcloenenruiz.com.

Karin Lowachee was born in South America, grew up in Canada, and worked in the Arctic. She has been a creative writing instructor, adult education teacher, and volunteer in a maximum security prison. Her novels have been translated into French,

Hebrew, and Japanese, and her short stories have been published in numerous anthologies, best-of collections, and magazines. When she isn't writing, she serves at the whim of a black cat.

Walter Mosley is one of the most versatile and admired writers in America today. He has written over sixty critically acclaimed books, including the bestselling mystery series featuring Easy Rawlins. He has won numerous awards, including an O. Henry Award, a Grammy and PEN America's Lifetime Achievement Award.

Malka Older is a writer, aid worker, and sociologist. Her science-fiction political thriller *Infomocracy* was named one of the best books of 2016 by Kirkus, Book Riot, and the Washington Post. She is the creator of the serial *Ninth Step Station*, currently running on Serial Box, and her acclaimed short story collection *And Other Disasters* came out in November 2019. She is a Faculty Associate at Arizona State University's School for the Future of Innovation in Society and her opinions can be found in *The New York Times*, *The Nation*, *Foreign Policy*, and *NBC THINK*, among other places.

Nisi Shawl edited the original *New Suns* anthology. They also edited *Bloodchildren: Stories by the Octavia E. Butler Scholars* and *WisCon Chronicles 5: Writing and Racial Identity*. They co-edited the anthologies *Stories for Chip: A Tribute to Samuel R. Delany*; and *Strange Matings: Science Fiction, Feminism, African American Voices, and Octavia E. Butler*. They wrote the 2016 Nebula finalist *Everfair*, and the 2008 Otherwise Award-winning collection *Filter House*. In 2005 they co-wrote *Writing the Other: A Practical Approach*, the standard text on inclusive representation in the imaginative genres.

Tlotlo Tsamaase is a Motswana writer (xe/xem/xer or she/her pronouns). Xer novella, *The Silence of the Wilting Skin*, is a 2021 Lambda Literary Award finalist. Xer short story "Dreamports" was longlisted for a 2021 BSFA Award. Xer story "Behind Our Irises" won the Nommo Award for Best Short Story (2021), the first Motswana to win the award. Xer fiction has appeared in *The Best of World SF Volume 1, Clarkesworld, Apex Magazine, Africanfuturism Anthology,* and *Africa Risen.* You can find more of xer work at tlotlotsamaase.com.

Geetanjali Vandemark was born and raised in India and now lives on Bainbridge Island, Washington, where she is working on her debut novel. She is an Octavia E. Butler Scholar and a graduate of the Clarion West Writers Workshop. Her story "Voice of Gravaar" was a winner of the Butler-inspired Door to a Pink Universe contest held by the Seattle Public Library. Her story "The Last Standing Man" was published in the anthology *Stories for Chip,* and her "Violet in Love" was featured in *Nature.*

Nghi Vo became a writer because while there were alternatives, none of them suited her as well as a lifetime of endless research combined with simply making it up as she went along.

She is the author of *Siren Queen, The Chosen and the Beautiful,* and The Singing Hills Cycle, including *The Empress of Salt and Fortune* and *When the Tiger Came Down the Mountain.*

Daniel H. Wilson is a Cherokee citizen and author of the *New York Times* best selling *Robopocalypse* and its sequel *Robogenesis,* as well as *Guardian Angels & Other Monsters, The Clockwork Dynasty,* and *Amped.* He earned a PhD in Robotics from Carnegie Mellon University, as well as Masters degrees in Machine Learning and Robotics. His latest novel is an authorized stand-alone sequel to Michael Crichton's classic *The Andromeda Strain,* called *The Andromeda Evolution.* Wilson lives in Portland, Oregon.

FIND US ONLINE!

www.rebellionpublishing.com

/solarisbooks   /solarisbks   /solarisbooks

SIGN UP TO OUR NEWSLETTER!

rebellionpublishing.com/newsletter

YOUR REVIEWS MATTER!

Enjoy this book? Got something to say?

Leave a review on Amazon, GoodReads or with your
favourite bookseller and let the world know!

SINOPTICON

A CELEBRATION OF CHINESE SCIENCE FICTION

Featuring Stories by Jiang Bo, Bao Shu,
Regina Kanyu Wang, Anna Wu and more

TRANSLATED AND EDITED
BY XUETING CHRISTINE NI

FOREWORD BY XIA JIA

⊙ SOLARISBOOKS.COM

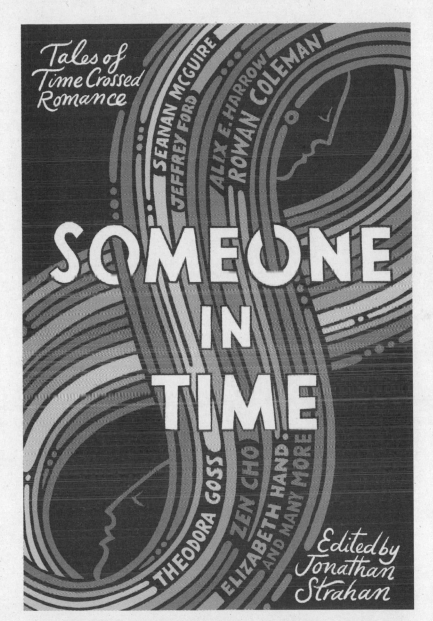

Tales of
Time Crossed
Romance

SEANAN McGUIRE
JEFFREY FORD
ALIX E. HARROW
ROWAN COLEMAN

SOMEONE
IN
TIME

THEODORA GOSS
ZEN CHO
ELIZABETH HAND
AND MANY MORE

Edited by
Jonathan
Strahan

SOLARISBOOKS.COM